CONSPIRACY IGNITED

AN ERIC RIDGE THRILLER

CONSPIRACY IGNITED

AN ERIC RIDGE THRILLER

RAYMOND PAUL
JOHNSON

Blank Slate Press | St. Louis, MO

Publisher's Note: This book is a work of the imagination. Names, characters, places and incidents either are products of the author's imagination or are used fictitiously. While some of the characters and incidents portrayed here can be found in historical or contemporary accounts, they have been altered and rearranged by the author to suit the strict purposes of storytelling. The book should be read solely as a work of fiction.

For more information, contact:
info@amphoraepublishing.com

Blank Slate Press is an imprint of
Amphorae Publishing Group, LLC
www.amphoraepublishing.com

Manufactured in the United States of America
Cover Design by Kristina Blank Makansi
Cover art: Adobe Stock
Set in Adobe Caslon Pro, Big Caslon, Gill Sans Nova

Library of Congress Control Number: 2023949478
ISBN: 9781943075836

To my wife June—my partner, my love, my muse
and truly the wind beneath my wings.

With liberty and justice for all.

CHAPTER ONE

Southern California, 2005

Gasping for air, Eric Ridge's body slapped the dark, cold water in the marina. Saltwater exploded everywhere as the whacking sound turned muffled, then quiet, like a closing coffin. Above surface, life at the marina went on. Below, Ridge knew he had to pull himself together. Move his arms, go deeper. Escape the huge, screaming sonofabitch in a black wetsuit who for no reason had bashed him in the head and tossed his 210-pound frame from the boat like a fisherman throwing back unwanted catch.

As Lieutenant Eric Ridge training as a combat pilot in Southeast Asia, he'd taken plenty of water survival courses. But none of them, *nada*, mentioned submerging at night with your head split open and no time to suck in air. In the pitch-black water, his eyes darted back and forth. His heart thudded against his ribs. It pulsated. What about the new stent? Left anterior descending artery. The widow maker. No time to dwell on that. Had to push past it. He had one chance. He flipped around, swam deeper and headed back toward the sonofabitch.

Ridge's arms stretched out and pulled water, like oars. His mind swirled. Decades, in courtrooms. Fighting for justice. Against the powerful. For those less so. Sometimes thankless, soul-crushing, even dangerous. But this? What was this? Payback? Intimidation? Madman on the loose?

Beneath the boat, Ridge grabbed one of two rear propellers. Pulled up. Craning his neck left, he pushed his right ear into the flat bottom, and forced his mouth and nose into a small air pocket created by the slightly elevated swim step. He hoped to God he hadn't left the boat keys where the psycho could switch on the props. Rip him to shreds. Ridge used short, measured breaths to control his heartbeat. But the real problem—was the blood. The asshole had sliced open his forehead. Ridge pressed his left hand above his eyes to slow the bleeding. Cold saltwater might help, but still. It hurt like hell. His mind raced. Who the hell was that guy and what new case was he screaming about?

He caught himself. Wasting time he didn't have. Any minute the maniac would figure out where he was hiding. Stay here? A sitting duck. Swim out? Be seen. Helluva choice.

Releasing his forehead enough to read fluorescent numbers on his dive watch, Ridge let two minutes tick by. His thoughts flashed to his son, Sean. Drowned during amphibious ops. Port city of Umm Qasr, invading Iraq. Ridge stopped breathing. Pictured Sean. Then he switched back on and drew in deeper breaths. He had to *do* something. But what?

Seconds later, sucking in a long pull of air, he released the prop, and started to sink. He reached into the right pocket of his jeans for his pocketknife. Hoping the cold water had slowed the bleeding, he dropped his left hand from his head and snapped open the knife. He quickly cut off both sleeves of his flannel shirt, tied the cuffs together and wrapped it tightly around his head. He pushed water down with both arms and kicked to propel himself back to the air pocket. Grabbing the prop, he pulled up, pushed his left ear into the fiberglass bottom, and took in a long, slow breath.

In through the nose, out through the mouth. Then another. He whiffed a strange blend of fish and fumes. Not good.

Another long, long breath and Ridge dove down. He was six-feet two-inches and estimated the bottom at twenty feet. He pivoted left and swam across the sand, like a manta ray, another fifteen feet north. Figuring he'd passed the finger dock and the sailboat in the next slip, he pivoted up and pushed water down with both hands, twisting in place to face south toward his boat. As his wrapped head slowly broke water, he sucked in a deep breath. The neighboring 30-foot sailboat was between him and the maniac. Ridge pulled himself along the side of the sailboat, peered out beyond the back toward his boat, and witnessed all Hell break loose.

Fire erupted from the rear of his boat like a flamethrower aimed at the heavens. He choked on burning rubber and smoke. Grit in the air. Heat braised his face. The water's surface had turned colors—eerie orange, blue, and red hues—against the night sky, broken only by sheets of reflected flames. Just south of his slip, a Los Angeles County patrol boat, red and blue lights gleaming, began spraying a torrent of high-pressure water into the blaze. His heart and stomach sank.

A moment later, a flood of light engulfed him followed by a familiar voice calling out, "Eric? Eric Ridge? That you?"

He pivoted toward the sound and managed to call out an acknowledgement.

"Thought it was your boat. It's Patty Barnes. Hang on, we'll get you out."

Ridge had met Patrisse Barnes, the first African American woman in the Redondo Beach Harbor Patrol, fifteen years ago. She'd testified for him at trial, and they'd kept in touch. Now she held senior rank. "Jones," she said to another patrol officer, "jump in there. Help him mount that swim ladder. Then cross the sailboat to the pier. Meet you there."

By the time Ridge flopped exhausted on the wooden dock, Patty was down on one knee with her medical kit open. Ridge's hand went to his makeshift headband and throbbing head as she started unwrapping the sleeves. "That's a hell of a slice. Here, stay down. Put pressure on it with this." She placed a compress on his forehead. "Paramedic's on the way. You're gonna need stitches. I'm guessing at least a dozen."

Ridge, pressing harder on the compress, stared up at her. "With this hard head, it'll take a riveting gun. The boat's gone?"

"No. Fire's under control. We'll have it out in a bit. But *you* need to lay back. Keep that compress tight to your head. Don't shut your eyes. No snoozing! Why did this happen? Talk to me."

Laying back, woozy, fading in and out, he turned toward Patty. "No idea why...why these things happen to me. Lucky, I guess."

"I meant, how'd this happen?"

"No moon. Gonna watch a movie with my laptop. On deck. But the rear lights—too bright. Shit. I lit a candle."

"*This* wasn't caused by a candle."

"I'd just lit the thing, and someone showed up on the finger dock, headed my way."

Patty moved in closer. Her face twisted into a question mark. "Looking like what?"

Ridge's eyes opened fully. His heart thumped. "That's the thing...hulk of a guy, huge shoulders, in a black wetsuit and diving mask. At first, figured it's the diver who cleaned boat bottoms in the marina. But he never works at night. And anyway, this guy... huge...carrying one of those four-foot bodyboards. Like the ones near my dock box."

"What'd he say?"

"Nothing. Just hauled off and smashed the board in my face. Like a firecracker flashing in my head. Must have blacked out. Next thing, I'm sprawled on the boat deck, near the rear door. He jumped on me. Shined a flashlight in my eyes."

For the first time, Patty smiled. "No damn manners these days."

Ridge grimaced. Damn, it hurt. "Remind me to sue his butt."

Nodding, Patty said, "Did you see his face?"

"Couldn't see. Wiped my eyes, and my hand came back bloody. Then the son of a bitch lowered his head into my face and yelled, 'We're watching you. Drop the fuckin' new case. Now.'"

"That's it?"

"Yeah."

"Did he say anything else?"

"No. Just flipped me over, yanked me up and flung me from the boat. Shoot—he could have just asked to use the board."

"Right. What did you do next?"

"I swam back...underwater...came up beneath the stern near the props. The only flat area under the boat. Used the swim step as an air pocket. Then, worked my way underwater to where you found me. See anyone?"

"We were on night patrol, in the outlet, passing your dock. Saw the fire erupt, and got on it right away. But didn't see a soul, not a soul, til you."

"Anything left of the boat?"

Patty's straightened up to look over at his boat. "Looks like the fire's out, stern's a mess."

"Anyone else hurt?"

"Eric—there you go, frettin' about other people. Let's worry about you."

Ridge tried to sit up. Patty's face filled his vision. "*Was* anyone else hurt?"

Patty rolled her eyes and shook her head. "No."

Ridge lowered himself. Head back on the dock. "Got people counting on me. Gotta get back."

"We'll get you back. Just keep talking."

He turned his head and looked directly in her eyes. "How the hell did my head get torn apart by a lousy plastic bodyboard?"

"That one I can answer. Found the front part of the board in the water. Looks like it was the see-through bubble; the one you look through to see under water. Brittle. Curved outward. Must have shattered and sliced your skin where the board hit. It's nasty Eric. Lotta blood. Stay awake. Keep pressure on it."

Ridge pushed harder on the compress and shut his eyes. His mind slipped to never seeing his wife again. Or his daughter.

"You alright?" Patty's voice sounded far away, pulling him back from his thoughts.

"Never better. How we gonna catch this bastard?"

"You nailed that huge oil company dumping pollutants offshore."

Ridge tried to grin. "Yeah. A lotta luck. And your testimony."

"Sure. But you nailed 'em. You'll get this guy too, *before* he beats and bullies someone else."

Ridge forced his eyelids up, about halfway. Looking through lashes at Patty, he mumbled, "Bullies—why I became a lawyer. To take 'em down."

"Damn right," she said.

Ridge struggled with the need to shut his eyes. Things got dark, murky. Murkier. He thought about family. Friends. Then, in what seemed seconds, he gazed over at Patty's hazy outline. She was standing now. Looking toward the parking lot.

"The paramedic's here. Thank God. You're pale, so damn pale. Stay with me."

CHAPTER 2

It was a race against time. Inside the truck, oxygen helped. And EMTs plugged the bleeding with temporary strips and head wraps. They told him it looked like the guy had tried to kill him. Ridge, now with time to think, sorted through possible reasons.

Just then, the ambulance, red lights flashing, sirens blaring, blasted up to the emergency room entrance. Yanking the doors open, the paramedics pulled his cot from the rear of the truck. It clattered as the wheels scissored down, and Ridge's ride went wobbly, to bumpy, to smooth. Within the ER, he was lifted and switched to another bed near a white wall. The paramedics had to run. Another call. Ridge thanked them, waved goodbye and waited. And waited. And waited. Nothing happened. He heard people scurrying back and forth and tried to lift his head to scan the room. But as he did, woozy got woozier. Confused, lightheaded, weak. He lowered his head again. Studied the white ceiling. Waited. Waited some more. Finally, he closed his eyes and listened.

There were people, a lot of them, and he glimpsed shadows darting back and forth, left and right. But still, somehow, he was invisible. Not really there. It wasn't the waiting; he could do patience. Not his strong suit, but he could do it. It was lack of communication. Slab of meat. Oh sure, as a legendary courtroom slayer, Ridge could have jumped up and objected, but he could no longer raise his head. Anyway, he'd been through enough military hospitals to realize waiting your turn was the thing to do. But still, without paramedics, without Patty, it was like being dumped in another world. Being alone threatened to swallow him. He thought of his cat Mister, his dog Pistol—jumping, playing, curled up. He was never alone with them nearby. He smiled, and suddenly the commotion-filled room came into focus as he heard, "What's this? Headwound. Temp strips. Clean up this blood." That—got Ridge's attention.

Next, the voice said, "Let's deaden it. Start stitching—stat." Leaning over and gazing into Ridge's eyes, a red-headed doctor added, "Stay awake, sailor."

Laying on the table, now under intense light, but still groggy, Ridge focused on the doctor's blue-gloved hand. Sharp needle. Probably painkiller, he figured, never expecting a second stab and then a third. Each punctured Ridge's head in a different area above his eyes, like injecting vodka into a watermelon, only it was his head. After a short pause, the doc poked his forehead with still another needle, asking, "Feel that?"

"Not really," said Ridge. "Kinda mushy. Nothing like those first three."

"Good." Then she pierced other areas of Ridge's forehead, now a pincushion, got similar answers, and said, "We're ready to go."

In a heartbeat, her fingers pinched a much longer, glittering needle near his eyes, like a wasp in his face and no way to duck. Yet, not wanting to lose full control, he watched—as best he could. She slowly stitched across his forehead, just above the eyebrows. As the point penetrated a third time, Ridge's back seemed to roll on the bed. Slowly, involuntarily, shoulder to shoulder. Then back the other way. The doc pulled her needle down, level with his eyes. To see further, Ridge peered left into a nearby hallway. He fixated on a white disc-shaped lamp suspended from the ceiling by a long slender pole. It swung slowly—toward the wall and then back again, quicker.

Someone said, "Quiet. Earthquake."

Ridge's back rolled some more; the lamp swung harder, faster. Why didn't it crash into the wall? Damn, realized Ridge, the walls are moving too. The hospital's on rollers. His eyes shifted frontward to the blue suture thread running from his head to the eye of the needle. The doctor seemed to freeze it in midair as Ridge continued to roll away from it. How? Then he knew. She was moving with him, involuntarily, on the same roller coaster.

The doc stared into his eyes. "We're not done, but I'm gonna cut the suture thread."

Someone else said, "It's over. Slow-roller. Google says 4.2…not sure where."

Ridge's surgeon turned her head toward the voice. "Aftershocks?"

Everyone stayed absolutely still, silent. Eventually a voice said, "Clear. Let's get back to work."

The doc gazed down at Ridge. "How you doing?"

Ridge riveted on her green eyes, just above the blue mask. "Good. Just life in L.A. I guess. Let's get this done."

"You got it."

Ridge watched the shiny needle as its point penetrated his skin over and over—spongy pressure, sometimes sharp. Local anesthesia wearing off, but he said nothing. Quicker it was done, the better.

"The scar might blend into the furrow line on your forehead," the doctor said. "Eventually disappear. If so, maybe no plastic surgery." Had it with surgery, thought Ridge, gritting, and waiting for sharp pain each time the needle pierced his flesh.

Finally, the surgeon said, "It's over. Twelve stitches. Still with me?"

"I'm good. Can I go now?'

"Sorry. You'll need a CT scan and you'll be our guest overnight for observation. Standard operating procedure with head injuries."

"Lovely."

"Could've been worse. I'm told you kept pressure on the wound and took a swim in the marina. That helped to control blood loss."

"It wasn't my idea to take a dip."

The doctor laughed. "No, I imagine not. How 'bout Percocet for pain?"

"Sure."

Next thing, Ridge was laying on a cart, watching ceiling tiles and blinding lights whiz by. Orderlies shook, twisted, and turned the go-cart, hallway after hallway.

"Where's the fire, guys?" said Ridge.

"Shift change," said an orderly from behind his head. "Earthquake slowed things down."

"Got it," said Ridge, gripping both sides of the cart, like a bobsledder streaking downhill.

He finally reached a room with a large coffin-like machine dead center. Intimidating, yes, but he'd been through worse. After the scan, the orderlies returned with their cart. On his back again, more ceiling squares and lights flew by until he reached another room, bright, small, and stuffy, like a white-washed prison cell, but with odors of antiseptic. After slipping into a blue hospital gown, a pillowcase with armholes and slit back, he got in bed, a bit depressed, and stared at the ceiling.

Minutes later, he brightened when a nurse came in, cuffed his arm, and said his blood pressure was near normal. "Does my heart good," said Ridge. The nurse laughed. Then, after taking more Percocet and downing some green Jell-o, Ridge tried to think. He focused on his wife, Jayne. Out of town—business trip. Big presentation in the morning. He'd call her afterwards. The office? In the morning. Exhausted, Ridge rolled over to sleep.

But sleeping was always hit or miss. Too much to forget. He knew others had it worse. Veterans. Brothers and sisters. Thousands already diagnosed with post-traumatic stress disorder. He was lucky. No formal diagnosis, yet, despite some flashbacks, night sweats and a few days, now and then that were damn hard to get through. But he didn't *need* treatment. Limited resources should go to those in real pain.

As he finally started to drift off, he thought of the maniac who bashed his head and tossed him overboard. What case? Which new client? Why? And why did Ridge's intuition, that nagging feeling, gut level, tell him this was all about much more than one case.

CHAPTER 3

Time to make it happen. So, on a bright blue Monday morning, in the San Diego area, Calvin Hess and his assistant tugged open the huge, tinted glass doors of the Native American casino, Barona. Hess jerked his head back, signaling his assistant, a young man in his early 20s, to follow. Then they entered the dark, din and dinging of the cavernous game room. Hess whispered, "Lesson One: Killing flies cleanses the world." He turned left and walked along a blue wall to the brass cashier cages. Hugging the next partition, he and his assistant passed a row of shiny, pulsating slot machines without gamblers. "Not many people. Still early," said Hess, stopping near a still-covered roulette table with no one around. Like a hawk hunting a mouse, he peered left and right across the dimly lit room. Finally, he spotted the judge's white hair and ruddy complexion. His Honor was sitting toward the rear, busy at blackjack.

"Can't help himself," said Hess. "Recruited him in Vegas. The courthouse loved him. But blackjack and alcohol made recruitment easy. He became our *first* federal judge. But now, since transferring to San Diego, he won't cooperate."

The assistant turned to Hess. "How do we handle this?"

Hess stared at him. "Lesson Two: Never tolerate traitors. Think Dante. He assigned turncoats to the innermost circle of Hell, closest to Satan. Flynn—the filthy fly—deserves the same. And as with the other judges, I studied this one. Loves freedom, above everything. Rip it away, and he's half done."

The assistant looked hesitant. "How?"

"We planned, now we execute. Lesson Three: Never, ever, leave a trace. Like eagles, we swoop in, snatch the fuckin' eggs, and disappear. It's all about planning. Precision. But enough training. Right now, go wait in the truck. I'll take it from here."

As his assistant turned toward the door, Hess put on sunglasses, hunched at the shoulders and headed to a blackjack table near the judge. He sat down, to keep an eye on him, pulled a hundred-dollar bill from his coat pocket, slid it to the dealer and asked for chips. After an hour of playing, Flynn ordered another O.J and Stoli and said to his dealer, "My lady, keep those beautiful cards coming because soon, real soon, I'll have to take a break. After sixty, nature calls much more often."

Hearing that, Hess stopped playing, pushed away from the table and walked to the very back of the casino, turning down a long white hallway leading to restrooms. Near the end of the corridor, he strolled into the Men's Room, marked *Hombres*, and washed his hands. No one here, he thought. Hess took off his sunglasses, slipped on tight deerskin gloves, and parked inside a stall, ticking time away.

Eight minutes later Flynn arrived. He rushed to a urinal, put his drink on the white porcelain top of the next one to the left and did his thing below. Then he yanked his zipper and reached for his drink. At that moment, Hess wrapped his arm around Flynn's neck, like a nutcracker, yanked the judge up and away from the urinal and choked off his air. Hess moved so quickly he caught the judge's glass with his left hand before it could fall and shatter. Continuing to choke with his right arm, he dropped the glass in a nearby trash can. Then he dragged the judge, now unconscious, to the bathroom door. Hess whipped a small wedge from his pocket, stooped, and jammed it at the sill. Straightening up, he spotted himself in a long mirror by the sinks. He had a six-foot frame of rock-solid muscle, broad shoulders, and stamina, even in his late 40s, to bench press 350 pounds. On top, short dark-blond hair, combed straight down at the sides. No fuss. And from far away, by stooping his shoulders and lowering his head, he looked like any older man. Yet, up close, with a cold stare and pallid blue eyes, he intimidated like a gunfighter about to pull iron. Not a *pretty boy*, he thought. Never the fuck wanted to be.

Hess quickly turned, reached into Flynn's pocket, and pulled out the judge's Volvo keys. Dropping them in his own pants pocket, he then pulled four items from the deeper pockets of his navy pea coat: A small roll of two-inch wide red stucco tape that left no visible residue, two long plastic zip ties, and a folded navy duffel bag. His cheeks creased in a quick smile as he smothered the judge's mouth with the tape. Then he cuffed Flynn's hands behind his back and feet together with the ties. Hess cinched firmly, but not enough to leave marks. Then he opened the huge duffel bag, rolled the judge's body into it, and hauled the bag upright. Stuffing the tape roll in the bag, he turned to the door, pulled the wedge out and slipped it next to the tape. Hess yanked the drawstrings closed. He grinned a bit while patting the Glock 9-millimeter pistol stuck in his rear waistband under his coat. Ready to go.

Hess heaved the bag onto his shoulder and opened the door. He stooped a bit and turned right, down the hallway. In his knit cap, pea coat, T-shirt, and jeans, he looked like a typical industrial worker in Southern California. Who would ever guess he had a fuckin' judge in the bag and a Glock 9 at 6 o'clock?

Hess casually glanced back and forth as he walked through the huge delivery doors and out into the rear parking lot. No one saw him, and to his surprise, his choke hold kept Flynn unconscious longer than expected. Without a word, he dumped Flynn in the trunk of the judge's car, got behind the wheel, and signaled his assistant to follow in the truck. They were headed to a pre-selected spot, an hour east of San Diego, deep in the San Jacinto Mountains.

§

A half hour later, the judge began to thrash around in the trunk. So what, thought Hess. Who's going to hear the bastard at 60 miles-per-hour? Turning up the volume on his favorite radio show, he heard, "National healthcare? It's for sissy radical-left bleeding buttholes." Hess cracked a smile, thought about how much he loved that show and continued his drive into the mountains.

When they arrived, no one was around. As expected. It was a remote area serviced only by one two-lane paved forest service road. Hess signaled his assistant to wait. He maneuvered the judge's old Volvo far off-road into a thicket of huge pines—trees so dense their trunks and branches created a curtain, shutting off the outside world. On one side, just another sunny day, but in the thicket—dark, dingy, damp. Hess, always one with nature, loved it. He got out and opened the trunk. Then he heaved the bag up and threw it on a ground of rocks and wet pine needles. Flynn, inside the bag, tried to stretch out. "Dammit." Hess kicked the bag, "Stay still, or I'll put a bullet in your head."

The judge continued struggling but, rather than shoot him, Hess helped the poor guy out. Opening the bag, he pulled Flynn up and out from behind. He bent down and ripped the tape from the judge's mouth. The man sat motionless for a second. Then with a roaring red face, he cranked his neck to look back at Hess. When Hess saw the judge's eyes, he knew Flynn thought all was lost.

"Calvin Hess," Flynn choked out.

Hess felt his teeth grind. His lips tightened. Only his mother or his wife ever called him Calvin. "Stow it, Flynn. Just, Hess."

"Hess," said the judge.

"Enough small talk. You had two chances in Vegas. And only because His Eminence insisted. Personally, I would have finished you at the second get-together. You should remember, we're on deadline. Less than three weeks to pull everything together. But look—water under the bridge. In America, three strikes and you're out. So yes or no. That's all I wanta hear from you." Hess glared. "What's it going to be?"

"Why in God's name are you doing this?"

"Why, why, why—always has to be a damn reason. Look, we need real justice. For everyone. Rules set. Followed. No surprises. No deviations. No stinkin' juries. It'll change America."

"Rules? How are you following rules?"

Hess squinted. "Me? I don't have to follow them. I just have to fix the damn system. But also," Hess shrugged, "truth is, I love what I do. And get paid well to do it. It's the American dream."

"But why me? Why now?"

"Because you failed. Didn't follow directives. Showed no allegiance. And bottom line: We can't tolerate that. Look, I understand why you're upset. But if we make an exception for you, what can we expect from the others? You're the example. I've got to do what I have to do."

"You're fuckin' crazy."

Hess grinned. "Not crazy, just highly motivated."

"You piece of horseshit," Flynn blurted out as he began to struggle for his life. "People depend on me. Take His Eminence and shove the sonofabitch where the sun won't shine. You motherfu—."

Before Flynn could finish, Hess bent down, hooked Flynn's neck with his right hand, and choked him silent. Hess stood, shook his head, and whispered, "Didn't think you'd cooperate." Then he thought about his dead wife and child. He reached into his coat pocket and pulled out his green laser pointer. Kneeling on one knee next to Flynn, he slapped the judge until he began to revive. As the judge's eyes opened, Hess fired the laser pointer into his right eye. The man's eyes instinctively squeezed shut, but Hess pulled Flynn's left eyelid up and fired again.

"I can't see," Flynn screamed. "Christ, what have you done? I can't see!"

"One final point, Judge Flynn. Blind justice ain't no fuckin' justice at all." It was just temporary, flash blindness but Flynn didn't need to know that. Hess choked the judge senseless with an arm hold, covered Flynn's mouth with red tape, and stood, disappointed with the next part of the plan. Not that it wouldn't work. He'd devised the plan, after all, so he knew it would work. But Hess was disgusted with Flynn, wanted to do him right there. Smash his head. Bury him so far, so deep, no one would ever find the asshole. But no. His Eminence wanted his death to look like an accident or suicide. Just like the others. So Hess dragged the judge over to the Volvo and stuffed him into the front passenger seat. As planned, he drove the car further east down the road, with cliffs to his right, until he got to a nearby curve. Halfway around, he drove straight off the road onto the shoulder. It was perfect. A slight downhill near the cliff's edge. He put the car in Park, left the engine on and brake off. He'd picked that spot carefully. Remote. Sharp curve. Steep cliff. Jagged rocks below.

Hess got out of the Volvo and pulled Flynn still unconscious from the car. Lifting him under the arms, he carried the judge to the other side and stuffed him quickly into the driver's seat. He clicked Flynn into his safety belt. For realism. Then cut off the plastic ties at the judge's hands and feet and pulled Flynn's arms forward. Finally, he peeled the red tape from the judge's mouth. He then leaned down across Flynn and put the transmission back in Drive. Pulling himself from the car quickly, he shut the door, stepped around the back and pushed the vehicle forward with his gloved hands.

"Sayonara sucker." Peering over the edge, he watched as the Volvo careened down the cliff. With thuds, it crashed into boulders, somersaulted several times, and smashed into rocks below. "Shit. Shit." Dust and debris were strewn everywhere, but Hess walked away grumbling. "No fuckin' fire. Wanted him to light up like the Fourth of July."

He then bent over, picked up a fallen pine branch, and swept away any trace of his presence. Next, he walked about fifty yards further east on the road and turned into the forest where his assistant had parked the truck. Hess went over to the truck and told his assistant to shove over. He jumped in and moved the truck to the edge of the road. Then he said, "Lesson Four: Watch how it's done." Pulling out a rake from the truck bed, Hess groomed the area back to the parking spot, eliminating all tire marks and footprints. But just then Hess noticed the ants. Large red ants—like those in his ant farm back at the house. They always stuck together, like family. Hess loved them. Why not? They worked hard, asked no questions, and followed their leader—no matter what. Stooping down, he spotted three he had mistakenly stepped on. Dead. Didn't deserve it. The right corner of Hess' thin lips rose. He gulped and his eyes welled a bit.

He pulled himself together and searched left and right on the ground. Pleased to see they were the only ones not scurrying around, Hess made three one-inch holes in the dirt with his index finger. Then he placed each tiny body in its own grave, covered them with soil and words of regret, and walked back to the truck.

He jumped in behind the wheel and turned to his assistant. Glaring, he didn't need to say the words, didn't need to tell him to forget about that last part. Hess backtracked west on the road to where he and Flynn had briefly talked things over. Again, using his rake, he eliminated all tire marks. Foot tracks. And any other evidence on the ground that he, Flynn, or the Volvo had ever been there. Pleased to have completed the mission, but still sad about the ants, Hess decided to ride down off the mountain and grab an early lunch—a huge burger, maybe two, and large fries—at the first fast food restaurant. Flynn went well, but killing the ants sucked. He needed something to get back on track.

As Hess drove along the flat streets searching for food, his assistant was eager to talk. "First time I've been in your new truck. Nice. Really nice."

Glad to get his mind off the ants, Hess smiled. He loved his 1950 three-quarter ton Chevy with rounded fenders and pristine leather seats. "Yeah. Added two fifteen-gallon tanks. Retro style, latest Nav system and, of course, police monitor."

"Sweet."

"Bet your ass."

Hess turned up the police radio. "Gibberish. Cops here are idiots. And the park rangers with the Yogi Bear hats? Even bigger idiots. Total assholes."

As Hess steered left toward the freeway entrance, he spotted a Big Burger Restaurant, swung a hard right, and pulled into the drive-in lane. After ordering, he pulled into a parking space to sit in the truck and eat.

"It smells terrific," Hess said on a deep inhale, "especially the fuckin' fries." He sank his teeth into the Double-Double Burger, like a lion devouring a downed zebra, and listened to a rescue call by a helicopter on the police monitor.

Minutes later Hess lowered his burger and stared at the monitor. "Goddamnit. It's Flynn. The fucker survived."

CHAPTER 4

The clock was ticking. An alarm buzzed in the next room jarring Ridge from a deep, deep dream. Sweat coated his neck and upper chest. Disoriented, he moved his head slowly, spotted the black and white wall clock. *Tick. Tick.* 9 o'clock. He blinked and tried to think, clear his head.

Monday morning.

Hospital room.

Redondo Beach.

USA.

Like finding the way home.

To Ridge's left, a nurse with glasses, a furrowed brow, and flowered scrubs scribbled a note on a chart. She looked up and smiled, picked up a mirror from the breakfast cart and handed it to him. Ridge lifted the glass to his face and winced. A raccoon with frontal lobotomy stared back. Ridge counted twelve stitches across his head and studied the areas around his eyes—plum, burnt orange, going black. Nice. Ridge handed the mirror back. "I'm a mess. The sweaty hospital gown…sorry."

"We'll get that all cleaned up," the nurse said in a reassuring tone. "But first, have some breakfast. And I've good news for you. Your scans look good."

"That's something."

"By the way, a well-built white man in his early 20s with a bald head asked about you early this morning. Do you know him?"

"Strange. Not ringing bells. What'd you tell him?"

"That there's no morning visitors' hours today. He mentioned he had to get to work anyway, and just wanted to make sure you were OK. I assured him things were fine."

"OK, but still weird. Maybe he mixed me up with someone else?"

"Maybe. But now you should have your breakfast."

"Yes, ma'am. I'm on it."

After eating, Ridge decided to assess his situation. Looking in the mirror with fingers to his forehead, he whispered, "OK, minimal swelling. No broken nose. No cracked skull. All in all, not so bad."

"Not bad indeed," said the redheaded doctor as she entered the room. "You're a lucky man. A few more consultations, and you can probably leave today, around 2, *if* you promise to go slow and easy."

Ridge's military time at hospitals, and later as a lawyer with injured clients taught him a big lesson: No matter how good the hospital, unless a loved one stands by like a hawk, get the hell outta there. Too much room for error. Too much confusion. And anyway, hospitals sucked. Ridge smiled and said, "A deal. Thanks Doc."

"Should we call anyone? To tell them you're here?'

"No thanks. I'll do that."

"OK then. By the way, your clothes have been laundered. They're in the closet." The doctor waved and headed toward the door, pausing to look back to Ridge. "Don't forget now—take it slow."

"Roger that."

After washing his face and neck, Ridge made two calls: The first to his wife Jayne. He knew her presentation was over. She picked up right away. So he jumped right in and explained his latest exploits.

"Jaynie, really, I'm fine. A few stitches, but I'm headed home soon."

"What are you not telling me?"

"I need to call the office right now to get a ride home, but I promise I'll explain everything in more detail later."

"Do you need me to come home?"

"Absolutely not. There's no reason to short-circuit your business trip." But Jayne being Jayne, pressed for more information—information he didn't want to get into over the phone. "Sweetheart, you stay put and do your job. I'll be fine as soon as I get out of here."

"Call me right away when you get home and we'll talk more then," she said, "and I'll decide whether to come home or not. No matter what, I'll be back on Friday. Then, if everything is *really* OK, I'll return here Sunday afternoon.

Ridge smiled. "Fine, love ya." He'd learned years ago never to argue about such things.

Next, he phoned Katarina Adler, his office manager. Kate could run the place on her own, which was fine with him because administrative paperwork was not his thing. But he needed to make sure his associate lawyers and paralegals had everything under control.

After discussing some pressing issues, Ridge asked, "Anything else boiling over?"

"The rest is good here."

"Super," said Ridge. "Thanks. Is Kapow around? I need to talk to him about our new cases."

"Why do you call him Kapow?" asked Kate. "Because he's good-looking?"

He laughed. "Terry? Hardly. You know we go back a long, long way and so does the nickname. It's an old joke. Pao—pronounced p-o-w—pow. And, you know, he's kind of a dynamic dude. Like Batman or Superman. *Pow! Wham!* Get it?."

"That's pretty lame, but OK. Wanted to ask for a while."

Ridge's right eyebrow raised, squeezing the sutures in his forehead. "OK, but is he there?"

"No. He's out in Palm Springs—with one of his associates."

Terry was Ridge's investigator. Although he worked mainly for Ridge, he ran his own shop with two junior investigators.

"Then can you pick me up at Redondo Memorial Hospital? I'm getting released around 2 p.m."

"Hospital? Why are you in the hospital?"

"I'll tell you when you pick me up." Ridge didn't want to explain about the Hulk and the Harbor Patrol rescue just yet. Instead, all he said was, "Someone wants us to drop one of our cases and tried to use a little physical persuasion to get his point across. I ended up with two black eyes."

"Gonna do it?"

"What?"

"Drop the case."

"Of course not. We've always stood for equal access. Blind justice. For everyone. Every time."

"Just checking. Now, about your eyes, that's why God made sunglasses and next time, try ducking."

Ridge grimaced, then smiled. "I'll remember that. But can ya pick me?"

"Sure."

"And please, don't forget my shades. Upper left drawer of my desk."

"You know how people say you look like a younger version of that actor, Tom Selleck? But without the mustache. Now, I guess, it'll be Lone Ranger, without the mask."

"Funny ha ha, Kate. Sunglasses please."

"Roger that, *mon capitaine*."

As Ridge hung up, his surgeon entered the room with another doctor in tow. "Mr. Ridge meet our staff psychiatrist. Because of your head trauma he wants to run a standard head-injury protocol."

"Good morning." Ridge stuck his hand out for a shake and instead was handed a pen and a clipboard.

23

"I'm sure you'd like to get out of here as soon as possible, so if you're ready, let's begin. Just follow the instructions at the top of each page. I'll return in about an hour." The pysch turned and bolted out the door. Ridge loved his bedside manner. Abrupt, but pointed. He pulled over the bedside table, rearranged his pillows, and went to work filling out forms, answering questions, checking boxes, and responding as quickly as possible to essay questions. Then, the ink blots. Right side up. Upside down. Sideways. Ridge described what he saw as efficiently as he could. He was wrapping up when the shrink barreled back into his room.

"Ready, Doc, but got to tell you—most of the ink blots looked like spiders or blood blotches. Do that on purpose?"

"No, Mr. Ridge. Just luck of the draw. Actually, eye of the beholder. A blood blotch to one can be a soda spill to another or a sparkling sun. Look, you seem fine, but the protocol requires an interview based on your written responses. I'm jammed today. Rather than make you wait to get out of here, I'd like to refer you to a colleague outside the hospital. You can call her later and make an appointment anytime over the next two weeks. She'll be expecting you."

Seeing an escape route, Ridge said, "Roger that, Doc. Will do."

After the psych left, Ridge studied the black and white business card he had given him: Marilyn Peters, M.D., Ph.D., Associate Professor UCLA, 2020 20th Street, Suite 600, Santa Monica. Nice name, thought Ridge, and a whole bunch of letters behind it. But just the same…not looking forward to this. Not at all.

Ridge rolled out of bed like a soldier on his last day in a combat zone. Cautious but raring to go. He slipped off the pillowcase gown, got on his clothes, and put the card in his wallet. Finished with paper hospital slippers, he swapped them for the leather sandals Patty had retrieved from the boat for him, along with his phone, and sat in the chair by his bed, checking text messages and waiting for Kate. Getting antsier by the minute, he almost jumped when his phone rang.

"Eric, good news," Patty said. "But first, how are you?"

"You found the bastard who did this?"

"Not that good. We're checking with everyone on the docks, the marina office, the parking lots. Nothing yet. So far, your Mr. Hulk came and went like a ghost. But seriously, how do you feel?"

"Nothing broken. You were right about the twelve stitches. But tell me the good news. I could use some."

"A question first. Did you have a dinghy on board?"

Ridge raised his eyebrows into a stiff forehead. "Yeah, a four-person inflatable Zodiac, about seven feet long."

"Tell me more."

"We keep it at the back of the boat on the swim step—the transom. On its side, nearly vertical, using a davit system—two metal latches and two metal rods. Has a wooden bench. Wooden roll-up floor. We use it to get to shore when anchored off Catalina Island. Has a green canvas cover. Go look at it if you want."

"No can do. Gone. Only the metal latches remain, and the rods—dangling from the rear wall of the boat."

"Burned up?"

"Yeah. Did you keep a gas container on board for the Zodiac's engine?"

"Yeah. A red plastic one tied down with nylon ropes. On the swim step. But we used most of the gas on our last trip."

"Well, the container's gone too."

Ridge stared at the phone. "Shit."

"Right. Mr. Hulk set the Zodiac and gas container on fire."

Ridge shut his eyes. "Don't tell me. With the candle from the deck table."

"Gone too. Everything on the swim step burned away. That's the fire we fought last night. The rubber Zodiac and plastic gas container went up like a flaming funeral pyre."

Keeping his eyes shut, Ridge lowered his head. "Well—what's the good news?"

"Heat rises. It all burned upward. Damage to your boat is minimal. Plenty of scorching, soot, discoloration on the swim step and rear wall, but operationally your boat is probably fine. I mean—get a marine engineer to confirm this—but mechanically it should be good. Looks like no fire damage forward of the transom wall."

Ridge brightened. "That *is* good news. Harbor patrol is obviously terrific."

"Tell it to the politicians, *before* the next budget cycle."

"You got it."

"Later then," she said. "I'll call with new news."

Ridge ended the call and stared down his phone. What was that fuckin' maniac after? Drop what case? Why? And, who the hell is he?

CHAPTER 5

Time was of the essence. Listening to the police monitor, Hess knew park rangers instigated Flynn's rescue and that local police were responding. As Hess turned the frequencies on the monitor, he heard: "Thank God the vic was in a Volvo, seatbelt on, he came through." Hess' stomach turned sour. Then the emergency medical technician in the chopper reported: "We have strong pulse. ER personnel standing by."

Hess stared at the radio, mumbling, "Tell me, tell me, damnit. Tell me fucker."

Then it happened. The chopper pilot reported his estimated time of arrival: "ETA Medford General, ten minutes."

"Got it," said Hess, pulling out his local maps to see the big picture. "We don't fuckin' fail this time."

§

At Hess' command, his assistant had Googled the Medford hospital near San Diego for information about it. When they arrived around noon on Monday, he and Hess circled the main buildings. Medford General stood eight stories and covered a square block, counting the nearby medical office buildings. The hospital was small by California standards, but large enough for a full ER Department. The main building, white and boxy, had long, squatty dark windows for energy conservation. Built in the late

90s, it supported the San Jacinto Mountain area and surrounding communities. Not fancy, but functional, and according to a local news story *understaffed*.

Hess parked his truck in a visitor's space and monitored the police band. His heart raced. Not nerves. Excitement. He turned to his assistant. "Commando training emphasized planning everything—to a gnat's ass. And I've taught you that. But this is different. A one-in-fifty mission requiring improvision. First, you develop a barebones plan. Then react spontaneously to unforeseen situations, conditions, and people. And as a combat medic, I learned to read people. Assess conditions. In life and death situations. You understand?"

"Yes sir."

"Bet your ass," said Hess, thinking how he really fuckin' loved his work. Really. The surge in his loins was testament to just how much he loved it.

Importantly, prior to this mission, Hess had researched Flynn thoroughly. The judge had an adult son, Patrick, overseas in Afghanistan. Knowing that, Hess dialed Medford General from his cellphone, blocking his number with *68. When they answered, he posed as Patrick. They confirmed Flynn was still alive and would be out of surgery in a couple of hours.

"Not only that," said Hess to his assistant, "but the blabber-mouth volunteer said, due to extensive head injuries, Flynn was in an induced coma. The doctors immediately induced it with meds to keep Flynn stable, until lab and other test results got back. When ready, they'll bring him out of coma using other drugs. But she couldn't tell me *when* Flynn would be revived. We'll have to act quickly, once he's out of surgery."

"What room will he be in?" asked his assistant.

"*That* the bitch didn't say. I'll call back."

The same woman picked up and again Hess said he was Patrick. "By the way," she said, "you have an interesting accent. Thought with a name like Flynn it would be Irish if anything. Sounds more Russian or something."

Hess did speak with a slight Finnish accent, reflecting the childhood he spent in Finland before his parents emigrated to the United States. Other people had told him it sounded Russian.

"That's right," Hess said with a ready lie. "Mom originally came from Russia. We all lived there until I was 16. Old habits die hard, I guess."

"Oh no, nothing's wrong with your accent. It's interesting. I expected an Irish brogue, that's all."

"Well—will you help me with one more thing?" said Hess.

"Sure, if I can."

"I'm at the airport now, rushing to see my father. I don't want to get lost or delayed, but just in case, where will they be taking him after surgery?"

"He'll be on the sixth floor, but he won't be assigned a room until after he gets out of surgery. Just check with us, main desk, when you get here. But Patrick, just so you know, shift change is at 1 p.m. and things can get rushed. Better to arrive before or after, so everyone's on-station to meet you."

"OK, thanks. Appreciate it, really."

Big-mouthed bitch, Hess thought. She gave him what he needed and he felt better about the situation. The plan, coming together. Now he needed to kill time until Flynn got to his post-op room, and shift change began.

"This whole mess ruined lunch," he grumbled to his assistant. "Hell...didn't even finish my first damn burger. Everything's stone cold." Hess pulled out of the hospital parking lot, and trolled town looking for another drive-in burger joint. "Flynn isn't going to mess up lunch. No goddamn way."

§

At 12:45 p.m., the sun was bright. The air crisp. Hess, bent over for stealth, entered the hospital wearing a white T-shirt, jeans, and brown contacts to hide his pale blue eyes. His Glock 9 was strapped just above his ankle, under his jeans. A switchblade and supple deerskin gloves tucked in his pockets. He was ready. He studied the building directory. Took the elevator to the basement, he turned left out the doors, and followed signs to the laundry. The huge white room smelled of soap and chemicals. Luckily, he found what he wanted, almost right away.

It's a damn good thing orderly jackets are so fuckin' baggy, he thought. He moved down the racks to larger sizes and found one that closed loosely around his chest. Finally, he located a matching light blue orderly cap. Perfect. Dressed for deception, Hess headed up to the sixth floor. He arrived at 1:05 p.m. and whiffed the lingering scent of antiseptic. Then he quickly determined Flynn's room by simply passing through the central nursing area. Only one nurse on station, huddled over a computer at the rear wall. The other staff members were jabbering in various hospital rooms briefing replacements about shift change. No one even looked at him. The name Flynn, and that of his nurse, Amanda, were grease-penciled in the slots next to Room 621 on the big glass-wall chart. Hess slowly turned left, saw the Men's Room sign down the hall near Room 621, and turned around, strolling the opposite way.

Walking down the near-empty hallway, away from 621, the open door of Room 603 beckoned. An older woman, lying in bed, had a plastic respirator mask strapped across her face; eyes firmly closed. The stand on the far side of her bed had intravenous bags hanging all over it. The plastic tubes leading down to her body were a cabling nightmare that even Hess couldn't fix. No one besides the old lady was inside, outside or around Room 603. Hess searched the hallway for signs of life. Finding none, he slipped silently into the old woman's room. Switching several tubes to different bags, with gloved hands, did the trick. Hess watched her vital signs go south, removed his gloves, and ducked out of the room. He slipped into the hallway and headed back toward the central nursing area. When he got there, the computer monitors were sounding. Two nurses stopped talking to each other and turned to face the Room 603 monitor. By the time Hess neared the Men's Room across from Flynn's Room 621, "CODE BLUE-STAT" blared over the loudspeakers throughout the sixth floor. As Hess expected, several doctors and nurses came scrambling out of Room 621, just as he entered the Men's Room.

Hess counted to ten. He left the Men's Room and cut across the hall to Room 621, silent, like a wisp of smoke through an exhaust fan. No one was there. No one—except John Flynn—on the bed, eyes shut, IV tubes connected. Slow, steady respirator-breathing. Hess' plan snapped together on the spot. And carrying it out was easier than expected. In her Code Blue rush, one of the nurses had left a syringe on the table near Flynn. Not just any syringe, but a 20 cubic centimeter syringe with a long needle. That sticker was a weapon-of-choice.

The carotid artery ran up the right side of the neck and was especially vulnerable to a long needle at the upper region, where it saddled the jugular vein. Day after day, Hess and his colleagues had trained to locate the carotid artery in the upper neck of various victims. If that portion of the artery were properly injected with 20 cc's of air, death would occur in a few minutes. Sometimes much less. And the cause of death was untraceable. The carotid artery simply carried the 20 cc's to the brain and caused stroke or heart attack. If you injected the neighboring jugular vein by mistake, results varied, because the vein carried the air to the heart where it might or might not cause death. But I don't make mistakes, Hess assured himself.

In addition, though, you had to push the plunger on the syringe rapidly to get a 100% death rate. Hess considered himself an expert at doing so. Turning to Flynn, he put on his deerskin gloves and located Flynn's carotid artery. Next, he picked up the 20cc syringe.

Hess pulled the plunger full back. Then, as he had been trained to do, he pulled back a bit more on the plunger to add another cc of air, ensuring death. Hess positioned the needle with his right hand and, without hesitating, stabbed Flynn in the neck. Nice shot. As Hess plunged the deadly air into Flynn's carotid artery, he cracked a smile and whispered: "That's 21. Game over, John. Blackjack, baby."

Hess left the room. With head down and rounded shoulders, he shuffled through the hospital to the parking lot. Blending in. Every turn. As he jumped behind the wheel, he glanced at his assistant. "Now—we focus on the others. First, the judges."

"Second, the lawyer. Can't forget him," said his assistant.

"Right. We're on deadline. The Summit's breathing down our necks."

CHAPTER 6

Ridge was more-than-ready to leave. And antsy to get out of the damn wheelchair the orderly insisted he sit in until his ride arrived. At 2 p.m. sharp, Kate, a petite Latina, brunette and street-smart, pulled up in front of the hospital lobby, hopped out of the car, and handed him jet-black Ray Ban sunglasses. Ridge stood, gave the orderly a crisp 'thank you' handshake, and put the glasses on. Aviator frames. Appropriate, thought Ridge. After all, I *am* a pilot, and bonus time: they're just right for covering black eyes.

Kate slipped back in behind the wheel as Ridge got in on the passenger side, buckled up, and flipped down his visor. Mirror, mirror on the wall. Most of the bruising was covered, but the stitches showed above the frames. Nothing he could do about that. "Except for twelve stitches, I look pretty normal," he said.

"Normal is what normal does. Where to?"

"My apartment."

"No way," said Kate. "You need a complete checkup by your internist at UCLA." When Kate got ideas like that, she was hard to turn around. So, Ridge agreed to see his doctor—if anything got worse. She insisted. He insisted. Back and forth, back and forth until he finally convinced Kate to drop him at the apartment because he needed to get some rest.

Ridge and Jayne had only recently moved to the apartment. It had been Jayne's idea—sell the house, buy the boat Ridge had always wanted, and alleviate the stress of commuting, which too often fed into his nighttime struggles with PTSD. At first, he thought he'd miss their house in Westwood, but nope. Not with the marina so close. Ridge loved boats; Jayne didn't. She couldn't even swim. But they were both glad they'd made the move. They ended up choosing a corner apartment, with balconies to the west for sunsets, and to the north for the coastline—the Queen's Necklace that ran from the Beach Cities to Los Angeles Airport and then around to Santa Monica and Malibu. The apartment was big, not fancy. But the views were to die for.

Ridge took the elevator up to the fifth floor, and as soon as he got inside the apartment, Mister demanded Tasty Tuna. Mister, their rescue cat, had had the good sense one day to walk up to Jayne, with bright blue eyes and deep dark tabby swirls, and purr. The rest was history, and now Mister ran the house. Well, he and Pistol duked it out on a daily basis as to who was top cat—or top dog—in the pecking order. But Pistol was being boarded since Jayne was out of town and Ridge thought he'd have to do some business travel while she was gone. So, Mister truly ruled the roost this week. So be it. Ridge opened a can, fed Mister, and made a ham sandwich for himself. He headed to the north balcony packing the sandwich and an Amstel Light. As he lay in the chaise lounge, thinking about the Hulk and the hospital, Mister jumped on his lap, shared some ham, and burrowed in for a siesta. Ridge was damn jealous. If only he could rest—*really* rest—like a cat.

And then he heard the *thrum* and slowly turned his head toward the corner of the porch where Jayne had set up a bright red plastic feeder and several hanging geraniums. Two hummingbirds, each not much bigger than a shot glass, sporting translucent wings and an inch-long black bill, like a slender plastic straw. It was amazing the kind of noise their wings made. The first had a shimmering rose-red neck and head. Remarkable. When the head twitched, it all turned bronze-green. Probably male, thought Ridge. Wing span… about five inches. Then the bird stuck its bill deep into the feeder and hovered like a miniature chopper. Meanwhile the other tiny bird, with brown, green, and cream coloring, seemed to be building a teeny nest of fuzz in one of the geranium pots. Remarkable. But also, somehow, very restful. Moments later, still thinking about hummingbirds, he conked out.

§

He woke with a jolt, as Mister bolted from his lap like a small cougar. Ridge took a few seconds to orient himself, and then focused. A red sun was setting in a sky drenched by layers of baby blue, pink and burnt orange. Beautiful. After watching it drop below the horizon and wink goodbye, he walked into the living room where he found Mister swatting at a piece of white paper flat on the entry floor. No doubt, slipped under the front door. He stroked Mister and grabbed the paper. On it, scrawled in black magic marker, were the words: "WE'RE WATCHING. DO IT OR DIE." Ridge, still holding the note, ran to the door and crouched. He yanked it open and searched left and right in the hallway. Nothing. Then rising he checked the elevator and stairwell. Nothing.

"This is shit," he growled, as he called Terry Pao's number. No answer. Ridge left a voicemail: "Kapow, 7 p.m. Monday. Got to talk, pronto. Need help." Then Ridge stared at his phone. On silent. Two voicemails waiting. The first was Kate saying she was having trouble getting hold of Terry. The second was Jayne, checking in. Ridge called Jayne first, because, well, he was no dummy. But he didn't mention the note, just that he was feeling better.

"If you keep that up, I'll fly into L.A. at noon Friday."

"Perfect. Terry and I can pick you up at LAX. That way, we can all go to lunch at the Blue Grill."

"I'm good with that," she said and signed off with a "Love you."

Ridge nodded. "Love ya back. See you soon." Then he hung up and tried Terry again. Still nothing. He whispered, "Come on,

Terry. I *need* you." Mister responded, rubbing against Ridge's lower leg, and giving out a long, long purr.

§

At 9 p.m., sitting on the sofa, staring at a blank TV, Ridge's thoughts turned to his son, Sean. He'd been a marine with the 15th Marine Expeditionary Unit. In March 2003 during the invasion of Iraq, the MEU, attached to the United Kingdom's 3 Commando Brigade Royal Marines, secured the only deep-water port in the country. During battle, Sean died trying to rescue two other marines. Never stopped fighting, they said. Ridge closed his eyes and lowered his head. "Tough never quits."

At that moment, he decided to go check out the boat. Secure it and see if maniac left some evidence behind. Anyway, he damn well needed to do something. Needed to take back control of the boat. He went to the bedroom and changed into jeans, a dark shirt, and a black windbreaker. Then he opened the closet safe and took out his nine-millimeter Beretta pistol. Black. A 92F semi-automatic. "Safety's on," he whispered to himself. Ridge double checked it anyway. He touched the tiny safety lever with his thumb to make sure and slammed a 15-bullet magazine into the handle.

He'd qualified as an expert in both handguns and automatic weapons before going to war. He even got a green, yellow, and baby blue ribbon for it, a ribbon that looked good in his collection. But that was long ago. That's why over the years, he and his daughter, Jenn, had spent plenty of time at firing ranges. She was now a deputy L.A. district attorney and Ridge insisted she know how to handle a weapon. Even Jayne, who didn't care for guns, had joined them a few times.

Ridge tucked the Beretta at the small of his back and grabbed a long flashlight. Turning to Mister he bent and rubbed under the cat's chin. "Nighty-night, buddy." Ridge opened the front door, checked the hallway, and locked the door behind him. He rode the elevator to the ground floor. When it opened, he searched left, right, and left again, crossed the entry area, and exited through the main entrance.

Beautiful night. Fresh, clean air. Stars twinkling. Low lights lit the walkway to the ocean, but he turned left and crossed a huge sand lot with the Pacific pounding to his right. It was sometimes used for weddings on weekends but was empty now. In the white sand, Ridge clicked on the flashlight, and headed straight across and through the marina parking lot to Dock C.

Approaching the boat, Ridge switched the flashlight to his left hand and grabbed the butt of his gun with his right. Everything was quiet. Looking around, he stepped over the siderail and peered beyond the rear wall at the swim step. No shit scorched. Wow.

Just then—a click, like a hammer thumbed back on a .38, and images of a hair trigger. Ridge twisted 180 degrees toward the front cabin and crouched. The sliding door was slightly open. Ridge pulled his weapon. Flipping the safety off with his thumb, he yanked back the slide and chambered a bullet. He brought flashlight and pistol together, right over left hand, straight-arming them at the cabin. Surrounded by dark, Ridge listened. Nothing. He stood and stepped forward. Silently, he slid the door open and pointed gun and light dead ahead toward the main bed below the bow. Nothing. Without hesitating, he crouched again at the cabin door and spun the gun and light left toward the small kitchen area. No one. He whirled right toward the table area. Again nothing. Zilch. That left—only the closed-off rear sleeping area and head, inside the cabin.

Now or never. Ridge slowly stepped inside. Still no noise. Still dark—but shadows from the portholes painted everything. Turning left, he squatted and listened. Nothing. Then he shoved back the curtain on the rear sleeping area and pointed the Beretta straight ahead. Still nothing. Ridge straightened up, twisted around, and rushed forward to the closed bathroom door. He kneeled, hesitated a heartbeat, then flung the door open and pointed the gun and light inside. Ridge turned left, then right. Nothing.

Only then did Ridge finally blow out some air. He stood and mumbled, "Boat's mine."

The tension easing, the pain from his face made itself known. He found the bottle of aspirin in the bathroom, dry swallowed a few, and began to search for evidence. On his first pass, he came up zilch. So, he searched again. And again. Until finally, he was truly able to breathe.

CHAPTER 7

When Ridge woke, the dial on his IWC dive watch showed 9 a.m. He rubbed his eyes. Made it to Tuesday—slept straight through the night. Easing out of bed, he reached for the Beretta he'd kept under his pillow—safety on, muzzle pointed away—checked the safety again and set it on the built-in bedside table. He loved sleeping on the boat, the easy, gentle rocking like balm for his soul.

Once he was up and truly awake, he put on his favorite blue swim trunks and a red zippered sweatshirt, and picked up his Beretta. He unlocked the white fiberglass door to the outside. Sliding it open, he turned right and then left. No one. Quiet. Too quiet?

Up on deck, he looked rearward to the stern, squinting against a bright blue sky and brilliant sun. It mirrored on the water, and he spotted silvery sea bass running a foot below surface. Ridge pivoted and rushed back into the cabin. He grabbed his shades and traded the Beretta for his rod and reel.

As he started back out, a loud voice shattered the stillness, "Ahoy, or whatever! Eric! Where the hell are you?" Bending to look through an oval porthole, Ridge saw his investigator, Terry Pao, standing on the dock. Dressed for business. Even wearing a tie.

Ridge bellowed from the cabin, "He's gone. Try his phone."

Terry shot back, "You forgot to turn on your damn phone. I've been trying since 7 a.m."

"OK, bring it on board."

As Terry maneuvered, head down, over the siderail, Ridge popped from the cabin. "Where the hell you been, compadre?"

"Hunting down a dirtbag who beat his wife in the Springs. Guy got physical, broke my phone so I broke his jaw. Everything's good now."

"That karate stuff works, huh?"

"You bet." Terry straightened up and stared at Ridge. "Whoa. Kate told me it was bad, but you look like shit."

"Thanks, pal. What else did Kate tell you?"

"About the Hulk, the Harbor Patrol rescue, and that I should get you to an internist."

Ridge frowned. "Ain't happenin'. But we need to figure out what case that maniac is fired up about. He said 'a new one'. And last night, someone shoved a note under my door saying, 'We're watching. Do it or die.'" He shook his head and looked down at the rod and reel in his hand. "A guy could get beaucoup paranoid around here."

"No shit." Terry shed his blazer and walked to the stern to peer over the rear wall. "Your swim step is burnt toast."

"It can be fixed."

"You think?"

"I think."

"Then, how about some coffee?" Terry took a seat at the shiny white outside table near the cabin door.

"Hang on." Ridge ducked into the cabin and switched on the pot he had readied the night before. 100% Kona. When had he become a coffee snob? Ridge picked out two small plates and selected two large ceramic mugs. "Here," he said, handing them to Terry, "while you're doin' nothing, set the table. And think—think about what case could've caused that psycho to come after me."

"Well, we usually have a dozen cases going at any one time. But he said a new one, right?"

"Yeah," said Ridge from the cabin.

"With moving the offices, we've only brought in two new cases recently. And we haven't had a chance to work up either. But that's where we should start."

"Agreed."

"The first is a wrongful death. A judge, I believe. Strange circumstances. We'll meet with family members on Thursday. More, I just don't know."

Ridge came out of the cabin with a plate of bagels, some butter, and a knife. "Do you know what judge?"

"No. But it's down in Orange County."

"Talking about OC, wasn't the other new case for your Uncle Cho—who lost his lawyer?"

"Right. That one I know something about. Last Wednesday you had Kate file a substitution of attorney on-line. Then I met with Uncle Cho in Orange County, for lunch, a couple of days later—on Friday."

Ridge ducked back into the cabin, saying over his shoulder, "Anything for a free lunch, right?"

"Hell, I ended up paying. But as always, if Uncle needs help, nephew travels. It's the Laotian way. At least in my family."

"Speaking of family, didn't you have a date recently? How'd that go? At 42, you ain't getting any younger."

"Most of us don't luck into a Jayne in high school."

Ridge brought out a carafe of coffee and a small carton of half and half and poured. "Maybe it's just you can't give up freedom—doing what you want when you want."

Terry grimaced. "Can we not have this discussion? Finding a soulmate ain't easy for most of us."

"After twenty years as an investigator, you think you'd have an advantage. But try slowing down. Not running a thousand miles an hour. Sometimes by slowing down, you catch up to yourself."

"OK Yoda. I'll think on it. But right now, let's get back to Uncle Cho."

Ridge took a swig of coffee. "We were talking about lunch in Orange County."

"Yeah. When I arrived at the Vietnamese restaurant he chose, he was super upset again. Didn't calm down until the shrimp pho. You know—hard to fling the arms around, eat soup, and tell your story at the same time."

Ridge smiled. "I get it. Uncle Cho is a bit short-fused. I know we usually look before we leap, but helping relatives and friends has always been the exception."

"And we usually live to regret it, but I hope not this time."

"We'll see." Ridge started scraping butter over one half of a bagel. "What's it all about?"

"Well, Uncle Cho, he of the short fuse, told me—"

A loud splash, like a body slapping water. Close. Both men froze. Ridge looked up and out. Then something whacked the back of the boat. Shook it. Both men bolted to their feet and then stood, stock still, listening. Heard nothing. Not even the squawking of seagulls. Ridge stared hard at the rear of the boat. Still nothing. Just glare from the morning sun. The vibrating stopped and Ridge stepped out from behind the table and moved, cautiously, toward the stern. Terry held up a hand, then reached down, released the button and pulled his .38 snub nose from its ankle holster. He looked at Ridge and nodded. "Now."

CHAPTER 8

Ridge sucked in a deep breath and stepped slowly forward, looking, listening, waiting to feel something. But nothing. He finally reached the stern, stopped. Looked over the rail.

"Tommy?"

The nine-year-old, from two boats south, sat upright in his yellow plastic kayak just below Ridge. "Sorry Mr. Ridge. Derek jumped from the kayak. I couldn't stop it from hitting your boat. But wow, it's really a mess back here."

Ridge exhaled and smiled. "We're gonna get it fixed." Then he turned to Terry. Ridge moved his hand up and down, palm to ground, like dribbling a basketball. Terry slipped the .38 back into its holster and secured it. Then Ridge looked south of the boat. There was Derek, Tommy's eight-year-old brother, ten yards out. Floating on a body board.

Little Derek jumped off and held it up. "Mr. Ridge. Hi! Saw this board in the water. Thought it might be yours. The kind you keep near your dock box."

"It is," said Ridge. Then he turned toward Terry, now standing. "It's my other one. Must have fallen in, Sunday night, with all the commotion." Pivoting back to Derek and Tommy, Ridge said, "Keep it. It's yours now."

Both boys beamed, and said together, "Thanks Mr. Ridge!"

"Just one thing," said Ridge. "Be careful with that plastic bubble. It can crack, if it's hit hard by something." Both boys nodded, with wide eyes, as only kids could. Ridge waved goodbye and headed back to settle in at the table.

Terry squinted. "What about fingerprints? Maybe the hulk touched both."

"On the board? Not after 36 hours soaking in salt water, and an eight-year-old—all over it."

"Right."

Ridge went back to slathering butter on his bagel. "So, where were we?"

"Uncle Cho."

"OK. What's the story?"

Terry pulled off his tie and relaxed back in the seat. "Originally Uncle Cho got sued for implanting a defective mesh, called Ringstone, during a hernia operation."

"Right. He's the surgeon."

"Yeah. The mesh was supposed to hold things together—internally. But it was a defective design. It popped, tearing up the patient inside, which led to a painful death."

"I remember reading about the Ringstone Mesh. Hundreds of lawsuits filed. People maimed or killed all over the country. But Ringstone, Inc. simply went bankrupt. Escaped liability, right?"

"Right, leaving hundreds of patients suffering or dead, and doctors holding the bag. But my uncle, for one, felt guilty. Ringstone had wined and dined him for weeks. Paid for two cruise seminars to get him to be among the first to use the mesh. Uncle Cho felt he should have researched more and been entertained less."

"Did your uncle settle with his patient's family?" asked Ridge, biting through a bagel.

"Yeah, that's the thing. He wanted to settle with the widow and her two young children. But his insurance defense lawyer kept pressing the case."

"Oh shit, don't tell me. The insurance company didn't want him to settle because they also insured hundreds of other doctors who used the Ringstone Mesh. Didn't want to set a precedent that could lead to other lawsuits and other payouts?"

"Exactly. And Uncle Cho, being Uncle Cho, hired another lawyer, on his own, to file suit against the insurance company."

"On what grounds?"

"He asked the judge to disqualify his insurance defense lawyer because he had a conflict of interest."

"I see," said Ridge, slowly nodding. "A conflict between doing what the insurance company wanted and what his client, Uncle Cho, wanted."

"And because of the conflict, Uncle Cho asked the judge to order his insurance company to pay for another lawyer, one with no prior or pending work for any insurance company. In that way, the lawyer's advice could truly be independent of the insurance industry."

Ridge put his bagel down and made a T with his hands. "Whoa. Time out. That's the 'Silent Conflict'. Always bothered me. Can impact anyone with insurance."

"The silent what?" Terry put his coffee cup on the table.

"A multi-billion-dollar bombshell. Something few lawyers or judges ever mention."

"I don't get it." Terry refilled his cup.

Talking through a mouthful of bagel, Ridge explained. "As you know, all insurance defense lawyers in America—and we're talking hundreds of law firms and thousands of lawyers—owe their livelihoods to the insurance industry. It pays them. It makes or breaks them. The insured, like your uncle, is the lawyer's client; but the insurance company remains his principal."

"Like having two bosses."

"That's right. And every day some insurance defense lawyer somewhere faces the tension of two masters—anytime doing something, anything, on a case might benefit the insurance company to the detriment of the client. That's a conflict—pure and simple."

"Like what?"

"Like not spending enough money on investigation or discovery. Like hiring cheaper or fewer litigation experts. Like continuing to litigate a case—say your Uncle's, which should really be settled, because the insurance company is worried about setting precedent for other cases. Or even settling a case that should be continued to limit future expenses. Almost every aspect of litigation."

"I get it," said Terry, undoing the top two buttons of his shirt. "But where does the silent part come in?"

"The bottom line is no one ever talks about these conflicts. If they did, it could cost insurance companies big time. I'm talking billions. They'd have to hire independent lawyers for their insured drivers, homeowners, businesspeople—all their insureds."

Terry nodded slowly. "And insurance companies would have little to no control over the independent lawyers. They'd always do what's best for the client. Which might not be best for the insurance industry."

Ridge flashed a grin. "Money and control—two sides, same coin. Called power. That's what it's all about in the insurance world, amigo." Just then Ridge heard something on the dock and turned. "Holy shit."

"Hulk?" Terry asked, pulling his leg piece as a big guy in a black diver's suit and mask, carrying scuba tanks, marched down the finger dock toward them.

"No. Hold it." Ridge huffed out a laugh, waving at the diver, who now waved back. "It's Mike. Takes care of boat bottoms in the marina."

As Terry holstered his pistol again, Mike walked closer and said, "Hey, okay if I do the bottom now? Needs scraping and some new zincs."

"Sure. By the way, have you seen any other divers in the area lately, especially at night?"

"Don't work at night. Too dangerous, too hard to see. But no. I haven't noticed any other divers in the area for a long while."

"Thanks. Just wondering."

After Mike put on his flippers and tanks and jumped in, Terry picked up his coffee cup with both hands, hesitated a long time, and finally said, "Eric, I know it's spooky right now but, getting back to Uncle Cho, looks like I've got a personal problem. Going to have to call in some chips."

"You certainly have 'em coming. You've pulled me out of countless fires."

Terry frowned. "I thought on Friday Uncle Cho's case was a relatively minor deal. To calm him down, I sort of promised— No, I did promise, without talking to you, we would charge ahead with his case. Now I see that the whole damn insurance industry may line up against it. I swear, had I known, I never would have encouraged him. But it seemed the only way, at the time, to make him happy."

"Terry, Terry, Terry…I would *never* have encouraged him. The case could drag on for years and, not that I care, but it could make us the target of revenge by the insurance industry in every case we have against insured defendants. The real question though is how your uncle would pay us for all the litigation costs and attorneys' fees. It's crazy."

"Well, you see, I kinda promised we would switch from an hourly fee to a contingency fee."

"You did what? You know we don't get paid in a contingency case, unless money damages are recovered, a verdict, settlement, something. Your Uncle Cho will only get a court order—words on paper—deciding the issues. If no money is recovered, the fee is zero."

Terry squeezed his eyes shut and pinched the bridge of his nose. Then he glanced up and said, "We've done cases *pro bono* before. For special clients. And, after my parents were killed,

Uncle Cho raised me. Not only that, but he certainly can pay some fees and costs."

"Terry, no doubt, Uncle Cho *is* special. And it might be the right thing to do—but taking on the insurance industry in a 'no fee' case could be a quick trip to bankruptcy. Look, I'll ditch this quiet day on the boat—my head feels fine anyway—and let's try a meeting with your uncle. Maybe, together, we can put our arms around this somehow."

Terry's face brightened. "Eric, you the man."

"Kapow, no promises. But let's give Mike room to do his job and go to the apartment. You can call Uncle Cho. I can get changed. Then hopefully we'll go see him. Orange County, right?"

"Anaheim. Behind the orange curtain."

"Curtain?"

"On the other side, in OC, where everyone lives structured lives in structured communities. Like a real-world Disneyland."

Ridge smiled. "I could use some structure about now—maybe even a little Magic Kingdom."

"Be careful what you wish for, buddy."

"I hear you on that."

§

As Terry and Ridge stepped onto the dock, Terry whipped out his phone and started making calls, almost walking into the sharp edge of an anchor before Ridge pulled him back. "Kapow, heads up, man. Docks are dangerous. And don't I know it. Make your calls at the apartment and we can avoid more paramedics."

Shaking his head, Terry shut down and holstered his phone. After closing the dock gate, they crossed the parking lot and Ridge saw Terry's car. Not the Prius, which he used for stakeouts and blending-in assignments, but his black ZR-51 Vette. A real machine.

"Since we're headed to Anaheim to see your Uncle, you drive. OK?"

Terry grinned. "Least I can do."

"Damn right." said Ridge, thinking, OC. New cases. Wondering what's really behind that orange curtain.

CHAPTER 9

When they got to the apartment, Ridge decided to shower and change while Terry, with Mister on his lap, fired up his laptop and started making calls. Twenty minutes later, Ridge returned in a black sports coat, pale yellow shirt, and black trousers.

Terry closed his laptop. "Arrangements made, Batman. Ready?"

The next issue was getting into the Vette. It was perfect for Terry's 5-foot 9-inch 160-pound athletic frame. But Ridge always felt like he needed to be surgically implanted. Never one to give up, Ridge sucked in a breath, squeezed into the leather passenger seat, tucked his knees, and struggled with the seatbelt. Once strapped in, the ride was a dream—until the freeway. Ridge had been a fighter pilot. He could take Gs. Sure. But Terry had a lead foot and breathtaking steer that defied gravity.

Shooting down the freeway like a starship, Terry explained his prior phone calls. "Uncle Cho wants to meet at that same Vietnamese restaurant in Anaheim. I told him about your stitches and shades—so no surprises. I made reservations. 1:00 p.m."

"Sounds good. But can we make it by 1?"

Terry smiled. "Watch."

§

Clear sailing at first. But as they approached Orange County on the 91 freeway, it all went to hell, bumper-to-bumper. Frustrated and annoyed, Terry jumped off at first opportunity and used surface streets. When they finally entered the restaurant, at 1 p.m. exactly, Terry's Uncle Cho was waiting, all 5-foot 3-inches of him. He weighed no more than 140 pounds but looked as tenacious and hard to cross as a bull in heat. Uncle Cho sported gray hair and a gray mustache to match and wore a dark thin-lapelled suit, narrow black tie, and white shirt. Like someone off a TV series, he had his medical bag and a black bowler hat on the chair next to him.

After introductions, Terry's uncle came right to the point, "You need to look hard into this case."

"Well, it'll be expensive," said Ridge.

"Contingency" replied Terry's uncle, looking down at the menu.

"But, Uncle, it could be *very* risky," said Terry.

"Contingency," said Cho, without looking up from the menu.

"But Dr. Pao, we might end up having to take on the whole insurance industry," Ridge said, hoping to reason with him.

"Contingency," said Uncle Cho, now staring over his eyeglasses at Ridge.

"OK, OK. Contingency," said Ridge, closing his eyes and dropping his head into his hands.

Then Terry's uncle smiled for the first time and looked back down at the menu. "The food is good here. You'll like it."

Ridge drew in a long breath and let it out slowly.

Terry looked between Ridge and Uncle Cho. "It is good."

"Very good," said Uncle Cho.

After they ordered, Uncle Cho turned to Terry. "What happened to my old lawyer? Why did he quit on me?"

"He didn't want to go forward with the case," Terry said.

"Favorite nephew, I know that. I meant why?"

"We don't know," said Terry, "but we'll look into it."

"Good," said Uncle Cho as the waiters brought the food. "Very good. So let's eat!" After garlic beef, tiger shrimp, and Chef's Rice, Uncle Cho and Terry seemed happy. Uncle Cho, of course, got his way. As for Terry, he was probably just glad to stay a favorite nephew, thought Ridge. Then as a surprise bonus, after they all put down their chopsticks, Terry's uncle picked up the bill.

After saying goodbye to Uncle Cho, Ridge and Terry headed west toward the beach cities. Minutes later they hit real rush-hour traffic, the apocalyptic L.A. freeway type. "Here we are," said Ridge, "in the world's biggest parking lot with 400 horses under the hood."

Terry threw up his hands. "It's L.A., man."

As they creeped down the freeway, every so often, Ridge watched Terry kick it into second gear, followed always by a shift back to first or a stop. Ridge used the time to call Kate.

"Are you taking it easy, like the doctor told you?" said Kate. "Remember your heart. You just got that stent last year."

"Easy?" replied Ridge. "We're stuck in traffic. This is downright boring."

"Good," said Kate. "Then let's talk business."

An hour later, Kate finished updating Ridge on what had been going on at the office. Finally Ridge said, "OK Kate, we're approaching the beach cities. Terry will drive me straight home. Then he'll take off. My plan is to chill out tonight and tomorrow. But Thursday, Terry and I will meet with the family members about that new wrongful death case."

"It's on the calendar."

"OK, but in the morning please email me what you and the crew worked up on it. I'll forward Terry what he needs. Ciao now. Have a good night."

"Take it slow and take it easy," said Kate as she hung up.

Ridge ended the call as Terry glanced again in the rearview mirror. "I could be wrong," Terry said, "but since we left the restaurant, I keep seeing a black Toyota Supra in the mirror. Might be following. Single guy. Wearing some type of cap, but no beard. No mustache. And no license plate out front."

"How can you tell he's following us? Mostly it's been stop-and-go straight-ahead traffic. No?"

"It's a gut thing. I'm jumping off at the next exit. We'll find out." Soon they were rolling on a black four-lane undivided boulevard headed north, with palm trees on both sides and almost no traffic. "There he is again," said Terry. "About two blocks back. A white guy in a black baseball cap."

"Let's speed up. See if he drops back."

Terry ran it up to 50 miles per hour. "He's sticking there. Two or three blocks back. I'm gonna spook him."

"Roger that. No cars around. Everyone's on the damn freeway."

Terry slowed to 40 mph and watched the Supra get a little closer. Then he said, "Hold on." Terry pulled his foot off the gas. Threw the Vette into neutral, yanked up on the handbrake and whirled the wheel full left. Spinning through ninety degrees of turn, he pushed the handbrake off, slammed the Vette into first gear and hit the accelerator. Ridge's head, like a shotput, was wound up and hurled backwards. Terry shifted higher and Ridge stared straight ahead as they accelerated head-on at the front of the Toyota.

"Shit," Ridge breathed out as Terry veered right whisking by the Supra like a gale force wind. A second later, Terry took his foot off the accelerator, pivoted left again through a 180-degree flip turn, and accelerated straight ahead. Ridge's neck crackled as it flung back. Terry quickly swerved right, aimed dead-on at the rear of the Supra, and pointed at the glove box. Inside, Ridge found Terry's long-nosed Smith and Wesson Model 67 .38 Special revolver. Quite a weapon. Ridge pulled it out. Held it in his lap facing forward. Terry accelerated again. But as he closed in, the Supra took off with smoking tires like a dragster on a speedway.

"Damn," said Ridge, as he peered at the rear license plate covered in plastic, "discolored from sun. Can't read the plate numbers." Terry floored the accelerator. Ridge, glimpsing a sign whizz by, shouted,

"Construction ahead!" Terry hit the brakes. As they decelerated, they watched the Supra smash through orange cones near a group of workmen. Then it disappeared down the road in a dust storm.

"Next time," said Terry.

"Next time." Ridge rubbed the back of his neck. "After I get outta traction."

Terry nodded and turned toward the freeway. "Nice quiet afternoon we're having."

"Just what the doctor ordered."

"So," Terry glanced at Ridge, "who the hell was that guy?"

"And what the hell did he want?"

CHAPTER 10

On Tuesday afternoon, Hess decided it was way past time to get out of San Diego. Driving north on the 405 toward Santa Barbara. he stopped near Redondo Beach to pick up his assistant. After a few more miles down the road, from out of nowhere, his assistant spoke up.

"So what's the key to making your missions successful?"

"Blending in," said Hess without hesitation. "Disappearing into the background. *Always* critical. Never forget Adolph Eichmann. He operated free in Argentina for years. Not only because he was a genius, but because he looked like any other man as he walked the streets of Buenos Aires."

"I see. Can I ask another question?"

"Go head."

"You don't smile much. What do you love to do most, besides work?"

Hess raised his eyebrows then stared straight ahead. "I want to travel. Really travel. Once all aspects of the Raven Society are in place."

"To see different people. Different places?"

Hess scoffed. "Not people. They ruin shit."

"I see," said the assistant. "Know what you mean. When the mines closed in West Virginia, my father hit the bottle, then he had the car accident, leaving mom, me, my four brothers and no income. As oldest, I took off for California at 10. Could have been a real adventure, but I had to beg cross country. Took five years, met all types. You're *absolutely* right, people ruin shit."

"Unless," said Hess with a small smile threatening the corner of his mouth, "they're Raven Society or our friends."

"Of course."

"Now enough," said Hess. "No more talk. I want to listen to my show."

The rest of the drive up to Santa Barbara took about two hours. Not bad for a Tuesday afternoon. As they approached the big house, Hess told his assistant to gather the others for a 7 p.m. meeting. "All hands, on deck."

"For sure."

"You bet your ass."

§

At 6:30 p.m. Hess sat with a scotch, neat. He needed a break to assess where they were and where they were going. Although Hess posed as groundskeeper at the estate, his most critical jobs were security and teaching six young men—now ranging from 18 to 21 years old—to do the will of the Raven Society.

All six were fine physical specimens, each stood close to six-feet tall and boasted muscled bodies from daily workouts in the weight room, but they remained inexperienced. With their hair shorn to the nub and piercing brown or blue eyes, they looked like soldiers, but they lacked maturity. Not Hess' fault. He taught through strict discipline and dogma. Did a terrific job. And they now exhibited strength, dedication, and allegiance—like the best attributes of a great ant colony. An Army of Ants. But it wasn't easy. They were young men, not ants, and Hess had to deal with their libidos— their damn sexual drives and desires. He had considered lacing their food with saltpeter— potassium nitrate—supposedly used in prisons and some military theaters to suppress libidos. But Hess always did his homework, and discovered it was a myth. No science evidenced that potassium nitrate—fine for fertilizers, fireworks or rocket propellant—had any effect on libido. Hess, left on his own, had to dig deep. But never one to give up, he learned that a certain combination of antidepressants, statin drugs and blood-pressure medication—all easily available on the dark web—could do the trick. Mixing the resulting powder into their food and drink created needed focus by wiping out the sexual urges, any runaway teenage passions, and the risk of mixed allegiances. All for the greater good. And for giving the Raven Society, after additional training, their first squad of "Watchmen"—21st-century enforcers with strength, loyalty, endurance, and dexterity—perfect soldiers. Perfect security.

Hess glanced down at the blue face of his steel Rolex. 7 p.m. He finished his scotch, lowered his glass, stretched up and walked into the next room. All six young men were standing at attention. "At ease," he said.

The oldest Watchman dressed like the others in a tan shirt, matching slacks and polished boots was first to speak. "Herr Hess, as always, we are here to learn." Hess liked what he heard, and doing what he rarely did in their presence, he briefly smiled. His Eminence had given them the names One, Two, Three, Four, Five and Six. And One, the oldest, had always been Hess' favorite. Even during their early training, as young teenagers, One had been strongest and most determined.

Hess turned to One. "Of course, of course. Next, I'm going to teach you how to carry out missions alone. Solo. That way, we multiply our assets. As you know, I've been training you with the Navy SEAL syllabus. The same program I used as Western Training Officer for special operatives of the National Socialist Group, our nation's greatest neo-Nazi organization. And just Sunday, I myself used those techniques—in a solo mission."

One's blue eyes gleamed and he seemed to straighten his spine even more. "Herr Hess tell us how, please."

"As always, start with planning. Do your homework. I soak up my subjects. That way, I twist them the way I want. Before my Sunday night attack, I became intimate with the background of the target—a lawyer—as well as his movements, location, and methods of escape. That gave me needed flexibility."

"How did you study his background?" One, again.

"The internet is great. Lawyers have websites. Love to talk about themselves. Then there's photographs, news articles, reviews, and things they've written."

Two spoke up this time. "Why was that all necessary?"

Hess gave Two a sharp glance. "I *said*, for flexibility. His Eminence insisted that I not kill the target, this time. The mission was only to put fear of God in him. And this lawyer loves control. So, the best way to hurt him—take it away. My approach was under water, but the physical attack demanded stealth. It would have been simple, if only I could have used my knife. At night, a knife is fine for killing, but error-prone otherwise. Too easy to sever an artery or impale a critical organ. Remember: We *never* tolerate mistakes."

Hess stared at each Watchman in turn, to make sure everyone had focused on those words. Then he continued, "To just stun him, I took a body board near the boat. Slammed it in his face. But the shit was so weak, he started bleeding. I made sure he was conscious, ordered him to fuck off the case, and threw him in the water."

"And next?" said One. "What happened next?"

"Not unexpectedly, he hid like a coward, and I had to teach him a lesson. He kept a gas container on board for his Zodiac, sitting up, attached to the swim step. Not much gas, but enough. I sprinkled what was left on the Zodiac. Lit it with a candle the idiot had on the deck table."

"To burn the boat?" asked Two, his brown eyes wide as walnuts.

"No—I said a *warning*—like a burning cross. I simply picked up my tank on the dock and escaped under water. Before leaving the parking lot, while Harbor Patrol responded to the fire, I got in my truck and left the scene. Warning delivered. Mission accomplished." As Hess finished, the young men, starting with One, clapped. Cracking his face, ever so quickly, to smile again, Hess said, "And I commend One who completed his first solo mission earlier today— shadowing and stalking that same SOB lawyer with his Supra."

Two, looking surprised, said, "Sir, what about me—on Monday? Checking on the SOB at the hospital and slipping that note into his apartment?"

Hess' face turned to stone. "Relying on what some nurse said is *not* checking on someone. But at least you did get that note under his door—without being caught. Fucking amazing."

Two lowered his head. "Thank you, Herr Hess."

Hess continued, "The lawyer's been warned now. He does what we want, or I'll finish him. And soon, all of you will be ready to carry out solo missions. I swear, within three weeks, you will *all* be ready, or else." Hess resumed his stone-cold expression. He looked at each Watchman in turn and said, "Now, you have work to do. Dismissed. Except One. You standby."

CHAPTER 11

Hess had told One it was critical they discuss certain things later Tuesday night. Before that meeting, in his bedroom at the big house, Hess stood alone and bare-chested. staring at the mirror. He raised both arms, posing like Atlas holding the world. The muscles in his shoulders, upper chest and arms rippled and bulged. And then, there they were. On each side of his chest, beneath his armpits, at heart level—his Totenkoph tattoos, or what Americans called Death's Heads. Each—a human skull with multiple fractures at top, missing eyes, blank nose and a full set of grinding teeth. Crossed thigh bones behind. They still looked awesome, and he was glad he had put them where he did. They were his, and his alone. With shirt on or arms down—they were stealth. Hidden.

Only after he had added them did he learn that, besides today's neo-Nazis, the SS-Totenkophverbande had used the same symbols on their uniforms. They were the ones who ran the concentration camps. Hess disapproved of the camps. They broke up families and that was impermissible. That SS revelation began Hess' migration toward the political left, leading to today, His Eminence, and the Raven Society. Make no mistake about it, neo-Nazis were still friends. But not family. Hess shook his head and slipped on his black t-shirt. Then he sat down at his desk.

His room was spacious but spartan. Good example for the Watchmen, especially because the rest of His Eminence's house was so god-awful grandiose. Hess kept a single bed with white sheets, a taut green blanket, and square corners. His beige walls were blank, except for the framed 8x10 photo of his dead wife and child—centered three feet above the head of his bed. There, to remind him each night, so he could maintain proper perspective every day. In addition, Hess' 35-gallon ant farm sat against the wall opposite the foot of his bed. Family was everything to Hess and had to be kept close. To the left of the farm, Hess had a five-drawer wooden dresser. To the right, a five-foot-by-five-foot metal bookcase filled with medical, legal, and history books. On the dresser top, he stored food and supplements for his ants and the large magnifying glass he used to study them. Hess didn't want or need anything else, with one exception. He kept a grand old wooden desk at the center of his room. It used to belong to His Eminence, and the black leather executive chair had come with it. Hess had also put two wooden chairs in front—for visitors.

One knocked at 9 p.m. as planned. Hess gestured for One to take the chair on the right. Between them, on the desk, sat a big black coffee cup full of green-laser pointers. Another reminder. Next to the cup sat stacks of papers related to the human traffic business. He hated paperwork. He was no goddamn accountant. So, for fun, he used expended 50-cal bullets, shrapnel, and collectible pistols as paperweights.

Hess eyed One. "Any questions?"

"Just a few. What if the lawyer doesn't back off?"

"Like with Flynn, we raise the heat. If that doesn't work, we lower the boom. Lawyers have accidents too, you know."

"I get it."

"Right. And talking about lawyers, I have another mission for you. This time with Three and Four."

One twitched in surprise. "What about Two?"

"Not ready. I want the three of you to rifle the lawyer's office. I've got the address. Do it within the week. At night. Then put everything back, exactly as found. No trace."

One seemed confused. "Of course. But what are we looking for?"

Hess flashed a grin. "Treasure." One's eyes glittered, and Hess continued, "Not in a chest. In file cabinets. They're full of cases: Jones versus Boeing, Hernandez v. Toyota, like that."

"What about computers?"

Hess fleered. "Waste of time. Full of passwords, codes, and other gibberish. But lawyers seldom put real security on their front doors or locks on their file cabinets. Idiots."

"What cases are we looking for?"

"Those with wealthy corporate defendants. And big, important legal issues that could cost the defendants a fortune."

One looked worried. "But how will we know?"

Hess snapped his fingers. "Easy. You look at the case folders labelled 'Pleadings' and 'Discovery'. Use our high-speed cameras. Click away on the latest 'Complaint' and latest 'Answer' under Pleadings. That way, we'll know the issues, who the defendants are, the courtroom, and what judge is involved. Then photograph the 'First Set of Interrogatories' and 'Defendant's Responses' in the Discovery folder."

One, trying to write everything down, squinted. "What are interrogatories?"

"Questions to the corporate defendant. The responses will tell us what we need to know about the corporation. And the person who signs and verifies the responses will be our primary contact."

"Contact?"

"Right. If the case is big enough. To see if they're interested in our services. If so, we negotiate a price, work on the judge, and get the right decision for each client. Like goddamn lawyers, we can't have too many good clients. This is a great, new way to generate them. When it works, and it will work, His Eminence will be pleased. Then, we can raid law offices all over the state. Hell, all over the country. We'll develop more lucrative clients and efficiently target judges. To maximize income."

One was overwhelmed. His eyes bulged and he swallowed hard. "I see."

Hess slammed his fist on the desk. "Remember One, this is still a business. With more money, comes more control. With more control comes more power to change the shit system we have today. It's for the greater good. A grander America. To fulfill our vision, our destiny."

"Sir, this is fantastic. I get it. But I have just one related question."

"Go head."

"How did you learn so much about legal cases, complaints and the rest, to come up with this plan?"

"Early on. Got involved in a case. About wrongful deaths. Needed to be straightened out. But that's a story for another day."

"Understood. Will that be all for now?"

Hess placed his hands flat on the desk. "No. There's more. It's time I explained other aspects of the operation. Everyone needs a backup, even me. I plan to go on to greater things in the organization. Someday, maybe soon, I'll need a replacement."

One stared at Hess. "I'm honored. Truly honored."

"Then shut up and listen."

As if backhanded, One lowered his head. "Of course."

"Head up," Hess commanded. "I took you on the Flynn mission for training, and I'm sure His Eminence will be pleased with the results. He'll also love my scaring the shit out of that lawyer on Sunday night. Perhaps, I hope, that'll make up for the bad news. About the teenagers. But I swear, people will fuckin' pay for those delays."

"Won't His Eminence understand the delays?"

"They've never been this bad. For five years, like clockwork, every three months I've selected at least six teenagers from the various sources. Runaways, orphans, the kidnapped, the homeless, the lost, the abandoned. I have contacts throughout Los Angeles who provide the best healthy ones—most between 15 and 19 years old, like His Eminence wants."

One looked up toward Hess. "Did your sources quit?"

"No way. Every one of them was carefully recruited and well-paid—workers at hospitals, funeral parlors, foster homes, and orphanages, even some cops, pimps, and yes, petty criminals. Until recently it all worked. I kept a steady flow of candidates coming. I indoctrinated each group myself. Then I would always bring the best to His Eminence, who with my help divided them into three categories: Objects of sexual pleasure, physical trainees, and rejects."

"I was slated for the PT group at first," said One proudly.

"That's right. And those in the PT group go on to become mercenaries, bodyguards, and private police for dictators, oligarchs, and anyone one else who can pay our fees. Or Russian-roulette players in the betting parlors of Asia. Even kickboxers in fighting rooms around the world, where people bet 24/7 on who will live and who will die. On the other hand, the candidates talented enough, in different ways, go on to first-class escort businesses, private massage rooms, sex clubs, internet sex services, brothels, even wealthy homes to serve as sex surrogates for the well-to-do. The dark web makes this all possible. Even easy."

"What about the rejects?" asked One.

Hess flinched a smile. "We find them places, especially in Asia, as field hands, miners, and servants. Regardless of group, though, no later than ten weeks after arrival, I make sure all of them are moving in the global market. Human trafficking has become big business in the 21st century—thanks to the web, porous borders, nonstop corporate and private air traffic, container ships all over the globe and easy-to-obtain high-quality fake documentation. In our case, most of our product is shipped to South America or Asia. But all are used up, all that is, except the few, like you, chosen each year for security training."

One looked directly at Hess. "Thank you for that honor."

"Certainly. I choose well in every category. For example, His Eminence always seems happy with those I earmark for escort services. But—and this is highly confidential—it worries me that sometimes he reaches out to certain ones before we can get them into global traffic. But then rank has its privileges, I guess."

"A lot of Presidents have shown indiscretion in that regard," said One.

Hess lifted the corners of his lips trying to smile. "No doubt. But look—you also need to know, in addition to security and training, I directly supervise Three and Four. They do all the accounting related to the human trafficking. Both, it turns out, left home at sixteen after private schooling, met on the road and love numbers. And let me tell you, each year profits have increased, making His Eminence more and more pleased. Last year, alone, it brought in millions. Millions. Even the rejects were sold for top coin in certain countries."

"Amazing."

"You bet your ass. But lately, here's the problem—my sources have been slow to deliver. At start of this year, because there were less than six worthy prospects, I had to skip a class. That rightfully made His Eminence angry. But as I explained to him, the success of our enterprise depends on quality, not quantity, and I had to teach my sources a lesson, rejecting all candidates until they improved raw product. His Eminence seemed to understand but was still clearly upset."

One nodded. "Understandable."

"Yes, of course. And I promised His Eminence it would never happen again. Now, we must make sure it *never happens again*. Even if we have to kill a source or two to spread the word. One, I swear, next month's candidates will be better, damnit, or else."

One shifted in his chair and bit the corner of his lower lip. "Herr Hess, L.A.'s a huge place. Why not collect our own candidates? Teach those bastards a lesson."

Hess cracked a full smile. "Why not? Goddamnit, One, you *are* learning. Why not, indeed. Let's do just that."

CHAPTER 12

Despite resting all day Wednesday, Ridge was running late. He met Terry in the Marina lot near the apartment at 9:15 on Thursday morning for the trip to Orange County on their other new case involving a judge's death. Three squawking seagulls fluttered overhead, the sky glittered, and sand blew briskly across the black asphalt. "Morning compadre," said Ridge. "Sorry I'm late. Got directions?"

"Took 'em from Google and loaded the address in the Vette's nav. We'll take the 91 to OC and exit at Oppenheimer. Parallel the freeway and then follow Mohr Drive north into Anaheim Hills—until we get to 6120, the judge's house."

When Terry and Ridge reached the freeway, they headed east into a blinding sun, and Ridge said, "Did you see the news articles Kate emailed yesterday?"

"Sure did. I didn't realize it was Judge Millsberg who died. Wasn't she the judge in that OC case we finished last year?"

"Roger that. And more importantly, a special judge. She had the three graces—sensitivity, humility, and empathy. Juliet Millsberg made every lawyer welcome in her courtroom, and just loved being a judge. She often said she was but a civil servant on the public payroll, trying to do the best she could."

Terry nodded. "The type of judge we all need."

"Damn straight, my friend. Damn straight. Did you see Dan got assigned to investigate her death?"

Dan was Detective Sergeant Dan Thompson, a crime scene investigator they had worked with before.

"Sure did, and I gave him a call," said Terry.

"How did Dan get involved? He's LAPD. The judge is from Orange County. No?"

"OC called him because of his rep in crime scene photography. Their guy was on vacation. And later when Judge Millsberg's family asked Dan to recommend a civil litigator, he offered your name at the top of a list of three. I hope we can help."

"Me too, but we'll see," said Ridge.

"Oh, by the way, I told Dan about your head and eyes. He agreed to explain it to the Millsbergs, so no one's surprised."

"Good. I never wanta tell that story again."

"Oh, I also mentioned the car chase. But without a license plate, wasn't much Dan could do."

"Understood."

About an hour later, after some thrilling moments on the freeway and the twists and turns of Mohr Drive, Ridge and Terry arrived at 6120 Mohr Drive. The house was set back into the canyon, only a black gate and brick posts faced the street. The gate was open, and an LAPD squad car sat at the end of a 100-foot narrow driveway. Near the bumper stood their friend Dan Thompson, dressed in his LAPD uniform, and a young blond-headed man in his early 20s, in jeans and a blue polo shirt. Terry pulled up next to the squad car and jumped out, as Ridge pried himself from the Vette, wishing it were a convertible. Dan then introduced them both to Justin Millsberg, son of the deceased Judge Millsberg.

"My condolences," Ridge said. "Your mother was truly one of the good guys."

Justin's throat worked, swallowing hard. "Thanks, Mr. Ridge. I'm hoping you can help me understand exactly what happened. And why."

"Me too," said Ridge.

"Sergeant Thompson has been great explaining the findings to date and is here today closing out the crime scene," Justin continued. "He told me earlier you're a trial attorney who prosecutes lawsuits against corporations, governments, and other defendants. Do you think you can help me?"

Ridge glanced at Terry and Dan. "I'll do what I can. But I need to know some facts first."

"If Justin wants," Dan said, "I can summarize the facts for you. And I'd like to get Terry's thoughts on what we've got. The facts are, to say the least, strange."

"Great, let's go around back to the terrace." They followed Justin along the side of the house to a large flat backyard, surrounded by canyon hills on three sides. The sun was high and the lawn was green and lush, with a line of lemon and orange trees arranged in a semi-circle at the base of the hills. A cement patio ran behind the house, spread with outdoor furniture. After they all sat down at a large rectangular table near a barbeque set-up, Dan began.

"Last week, on Monday afternoon, Justin was at school and planned to spend the night with a friend. Judge Millsberg apparently went bike riding when she came home."

Terry broke in. "How do you know that?"

"We found her bike in the garage, on the rack behind the judge's SUV. The vehicle itself seemed fine. It's one of those new imports from China. The Grand Sport from Chin Motors. The bike, however, was a different story. Dented and scratched all along the right side. Later we discovered the judge's face also had scratches. Top to bottom."

"Where did you find the judge?" asked Ridge.

Dan narrowed his eyes, a sure sign he was annoyed. "Guys, give me a chance, and I'll give you the facts. She was found dead on Tuesday morning in the guest room next to the garage with her back on the bed. Nothing unusual physically, except the scratches on her face."

"Cause of death?" Terry asked.

"Looks like carbon monoxide poisoning. Justin arrived home early Tuesday morning. When he opened the garage door, he found the judge's SUV in the garage, engine running. Carbon monoxide built up, passed across the small hallway, and saturated the guest room."

Ridge was hardly ever speechless—after all he was a lawyer, but dumbfounded he blurted out, "Dan, sorry, but hold it. Stop. Did the Chin SUV have a keyless remote ignition system?"

"Yeah, and the remote control was found in the judge's pocket. Apparently, she never shut off the car before lying down in the guest room."

"Dan, that's similar to a case I had with Judge Millsberg a year ago," said Ridge. "It seemed my client died after leaving his car on in the garage. He had the remote in his pocket and it looked like he walked away without shutting the vehicle off. But we downloaded the black box on board and found out the car had in fact been turned on after he left the garage."

"After?" said Dan.

"Right. Turns out the casing on the remote was defective. The start button protruded above the rest of the case, making it easy to inadvertently start the vehicle if for example you sat or laid down on the remote-control unit."

Dan's eyes went wide. "You're kidding."

"Unfortunately, no. Carbon monoxide saturated my client's small house, and he died overnight. You know, manufacturers compete to make their engines as silent as possible, and often you don't even know if the engine is running when you're in the car, let alone elsewhere in a house."

"That's for damn sure," said Dan.

"Bottom line," said Ridge, "the manufacturer should have analyzed and tested the fob to ensure the start button didn't stick out beyond the casing and, as a further safety measure, installed a loud-warning chip in the remote to warn the driver that the engine was on if he or she got more than ten feet or so from the vehicle. But to save time, to save money, or because of plain old apathy, it didn't do either."

Justin spoke up at that point. "Mr. Ridge, I think my mom told me about your case. I'm a first-year law student at UCLA, and she used it as an example of potential dangers from new products and related theories of liability. Before your case, she'd never heard of such a thing."

"Neither had I." Ridge shook his head. "I don't know if it's blessing or curse, but I always seem to get the cases no one has heard of—like the unstable SUVs back in the 90's that were too tall and too narrow and rolled over if they got sideways on the road. Until I, and some of my colleagues across the country, started winning those cases, no one believed there was a risk."

"We believe today," said Justin, his voice tinged with righteous anger.

"Now most people understand the dangers associated with unstable vehicles and stay away from them. As a result, manufacturers have been making cross-over vehicles which offer the convenience of an SUV, but are shorter, wider, safer. Those design changes have saved lives."

Dan rubbed his chin. "Wait a minute. Here's what I don't get. If Judge Millsberg knew of your keyless-remote case, how could she fall victim to the same danger? Why would she get out of the car, lower the garage door, and go lie down in the nearby guest room with the remote in her pocket?"

"Well, her remote may look different but have a similar defect," said Ridge. "We can test that later. But right now, my best guess is she must have been dazed from that bike accident you mentioned, had the remote in her pocket, and didn't hear the engine start when she laid down on the remote device. Look, clearly all the facts aren't in. Let's start by seeing the garage and the guest room where the judge died. And I'd like to study the SUV and its remote too."

Dan stood and the others followed his lead. "Officially this is no longer a crime scene," he said. "That's why I told Terry yesterday that it'd be easier to show you than tell you the details."

"Justin, is it OK if we take photos?" Ridge asked. "Terry's got his camera."

"Of course."

§

Forty-five minutes later, they gathered back in the patio area. Ridge turned to Dan. "Did you find any other physical evidence?"

Dan shook his head. "None."

"What about pathology? When will we get that?"

Dan smiled. "Happy to report, the amazing Dr. Sanchez is on it."

Ridge smiled. Timothy Sanchez was among the best medical examiners nationwide, if not the best. He held a medical degree and a Ph.D. in biomedical engineering from the University of Wisconsin in Milwaukee.

Justin raised his hand like a schoolboy. "Who's Dr. Sanchez?"

"He's on part-time contract as a coroner with Los Angeles and Orange Counties for crime scene investigations and pathology studies," Ridge said. "He also practices as a private consultant in cases where L.A. or Orange counties aren't parties. We've worked together for years."

"Thank you." Justin smiled. "That's terrific."

"He's our number one choice as expert whenever 'cause of injury' or 'cause of death' is an issue, which in product liability cases is almost always. Most manufacturers defend product design lawsuits to the hilt rather than ever admit a defect and open themselves up to a tsunami of cases and what could be billions in liability payouts."

Ridge turned to Dan. "When will the good Dr. Sanchez have his report ready?"

"He did the autopsy last week. But needed to leave town afterwards. So yesterday I set up a meeting with him for tomorrow morning at the morgue. You and Terry can attend as family representatives—if that's OK with Justin."

"Mr. Ridge," said Justin, "I would really appreciate that." The young man's eyes glistened and he cleared his throat. "I...I lost my father three years ago in a car accident. Now, my mother. Truth is, I'm not doing so great right now. "

"Consider it done," said Ridge.

"And I almost forgot," said Justin, "I've got to tell you— I'm really, really sorry. I jumped the gun and gave your name to a *Orange County Register* reporter last Thursday. Before we had a chance to meet. But with Sergeant Thompson's recommendation and my call to your office on Wednesday, well, I just got ahead of myself."

"Oh, no harm, no foul," Ridge said. "Seriously, don't worry about it."

"One other thing," Justin continued. "My mom's memorial service will be Saturday evening at 7:30 p.m. at Rolling Hills Cemetery. I know it's short notice, but I would love if you and Mr. Pao attended. I've already invited Sergeant Thompson, but he'll be on duty in L.A."

Ridge glanced at Terry who gave him a quick thumb's up. "Thank you, Justin. We'll be there."

§

"Shit, there's a black Supra. Two cars back." Ridge leaned forward and reached into the glovebox for Terry's pistol. They'd been on the road for a while, headed back to the Beach Cities, and Ridge had been staring at the passenger side mirror.

"Easy big fella," Terry said. "Been watching him. Two people in the car, and it's got a front license plate. Not our guy. And to prove it—they just flashed their right blinker to exit up ahead."

Ridge let his head drop back against the headrest. "Sorry. Guess I'm a little spooked."

"A whack on the head and a stalker can do that."

Ridge wagged his head left and right in short shakes, like a wobble-head doll. "Just not used to this, I guess."

"That's because we're in the business of using the justice system to help people. Not spending time watching our backs."

"Amen. Hey, by the way, don't forget to use the Prius tomorrow morning. After meeting Tim at the morgue, we pick up Jayne. LAX. 12:30. And no way we all fit in the Vette."

"Got it. I'm really looking forward to Tim Sanchez. If anyone can figure out exactly how and why the judge died, it's him."

Ridge nodded. "I sure as hell hope so."

"Dr. Sanchez—the Answer Man."

"Roger that. Would be nice if he could tell us who the Hulk is. Or why that dumbass driver was tailing us."

Terry smiled. "He's good, but I'm not sure he's that good."

CHAPTER 13

Friday morning, 10 a.m. sharp, Ridge and Terry arrived at the cement-colored Orange County Morgue with Starbucks in hand. Dan, waiting in the marble lobby, frowned at them. "No coffee for me? And with all I do for you guys."

Terry shrugged. "You keep saying you want to ditch caffeine. Now's a good time. And, while you're at it—the donuts should go too." He patted his flat stomach. "Anyway, we're almost finished. You know how it is, no food, no drinks downstairs."

"Life on high, death below," Ridge intoned.

Dan rolled his eyes. "Then chug-a-lug, boys. Sanchez is waiting."

Terry and Ridge gulped down the last dregs of their coffees, tossed their cups into the nearest trash can, and headed downstairs to the morgue. When the shiny elevator doors opened, they were hit by darkness and a strong antiseptic smell. Then Dr. Timothy Sanchez materialized in the hallway, his white smock giving off an ethereal glow.

Short, only five-foot-three, stocky and sporting a deep tan, Sanchez had brown eyes and silver-streaked brown hair. He gave them a huge smile and opened his arms as if to hug all three men at once. "The three musketeers together again. What an honor. Good to see you, but look, we've got to move fast. I have a meeting at 11, and you need to see what we call evidence down here." He pointed to the camera case Dan carried. "That could prove useful."

Sanchez turned to lead the way but caught a good look at Ridge removing his sunglasses. "What the hell happened to you? Looks like Frankenstein meets Rocky Raccoon. You OK?"

Ridge once again explained the Hulk story as Sanchez led them through the swinging metal doors. A cold breeze and stiff scent of chemicals met them. Two customers, each on their own metal table, were draped in white sheets, everything covered except for toe tags. Other bodies along the wall were stored horizontally, head-first in three-high stainless-steel lockers. Dr. Sanchez unlocked one of the lockers, hit a remote, and a body on rails slid silently out toward them. Then he pulled down the blanket, pointed at the judge's face and explained: "Here's the key. You see all those vertical scratches on her face? Presumably from a high-speed bicycle accident. The marks on the bike told us the judge crashed sideways so we figured she skated across the ground headfirst. But it doesn't match up. Look closer. The scratches should be wider at the forehead and narrow down toward the chin. They do the opposite. Dan, go ahead and take some close-up photos."

When Dan stopped clicking, Tim continued his explanation. "Next, I examined the clothing the judge had on at the time. Here, let me show you. We still have the evidence bag. All the torn threads and marks on the front of her jacket, blouse and pants go in the wrong direction. A person that crashes sideways off a bike doesn't slide feet first. Something is wrong. The physical evidence doesn't add up."

After Dan shot a dozen close-ups of the judge's clothing, spread out on a nearby stainless-steel table, Dr. Sanchez added: "Another thing, we carefully studied the bike. No marks, none, except on the front wheel and scratches along the right side from ground contact."

Ridge interrupted. "Isn't that what you'd expect in a bike spill?"

"Not this one. Look, the front wheel took a hard hit. Cut the tire, banged in the wheel, and drove it into the bike frame behind. At that point, the biker's going up and over the handlebars. Yet no marks on the handlebars, none at all. They never hit the ground. Also, a bike that takes a front wheel hit like that doesn't just plop over on its side. You'd see scratches and other marks in more places around the bike."

Ridge fiddled with his sunglasses. "Where does that leave us? How about cause of death?"

"Definitely carbon monoxide poisoning. No question about it. And that's why the D.A. cleared the case. He didn't want to launch a criminal prosecution based just on scratch directions or a lack of marks on a bicycle, especially when the bike accident didn't cause death. To use his exact words—that will never get us beyond reasonable doubt even if we had a suspect, motive, and opportunity, which we don't."

Ridge glanced at Dan and Terry, then back to Tim. "Raises more questions than answers, doesn't it? Anything else strange?"

Tim tapped a finger on the metal table. "Only one thing I can think of right now. The level and saturation of carbon monoxide in her system is extremely high. Carbon monoxide is colorless, odorless, and tasteless, and mixes evenly with air. It enters the blood stream through the lungs and displaces oxygen needed by the body. Prolonged exposure to low concentrations can kill. But so can shorter exposures to higher concentrations. The judge sucked in huge concentrations—so much carbon monoxide her brain exhibited severe damage before death. It's strange, considering the garage was thirty feet from the bed where she was found. I simply don't know what to make of that."

Then Dr. Sanchez's cellphone buzzed. He answered, turned back to them and said, "Sorry. I need to vamoose, guys. Next time."

§

After goodbyes all around, Dan left to make his way along the freeways toward his office in downtown L.A., and Terry and Ridge headed to LAX to pick up Jayne. Westbound on the 91, Ridge got a call from Patty Barnes at Harbor Patrol with good news and bad.

"Good news first?" she asked.

"Sure."

"We've got a witness who was in the public parking lot on the night of the Hulk attack. He remembered a big guy in a wetsuit getting into some type of pick-up truck. The engine roared when the driver started the truck, so it probably has a lot of horses under the hood. But pitch dark, the witness couldn't see much else. Except, when the truck's headlights were switched on, weak lights at the rear illuminated a black license plate with yellow lettering, the type of California plate used in the 60s and before."

Ridge's pulse pounded at his temple. "You've got a license plate number?"

"Not quite. He said the plate had "MAN" on it. But, and here's the bad news, he couldn't remember any numbers."

"You try to run the plate? It's gotta be vintage, right?"

"I had a friend at Redondo P.D. run it. But the search for active vintage plates came up empty."

"Still, it's something. Thanks, Patty. As always."

He ended the call and immediately called Dan, hoping L.A.P.D. had access to more databases on vintage plates. The 5 Freeway to L.A. had moved much faster than the 91, and Dan was already at his office."

"On it," he said. "I'll call as soon as I know anything."

Ten minutes later, Ridge's phone rang.

"Sorry, man. Ran it through two different state-wide systems. Turned up nada."

§

At 12:30, Jayne stood outside Southwest luggage in a white blouse, black pants suit, and stylish low-slung heels. The outfit went nicely with her auburn hair and hazel eyes. Of course, Ridge thought everything went nicely with her auburn hair and hazel eyes. Most importantly, she was smiling when Ridge and Terry pulled up. In fact, she was in a good mood, which improved once she got a look at Ridge's stitches and black eyes and was satisfied he was on the mend.

They sat by the window at the Blue Grill, a table with a view overlooking the marina and breakwater, and, for the first time since the Hulk incident, Ridge felt on a roll, like things could only get better. The place was a favorite and they loved to watch the surf break and the birds dip and soar. After they placed their orders, they watched five birds in formation, each with a 7-foot wingspan, and a foot-long conical beak ending in a blood-red tip. Two split off to soar lower, like gliders. Three remained high. A minute later, one of the high birds tucked into an 80-degree nosedive, nearly straight down. It smashed into the water like a depth charge. After the stupendous splash subsided, the big bird popped up through the water's surface. Ridge saw a fish slide down its throat and then pointed to a second bird up high. It rotated into another dive, over 80-degrees, straight down. This time the crash reverberated through the window. The bird stayed submerged for minutes. When it popped up, Terry, Jayne and Ridge watched a fishtail disappear down its beak.

Ridge turned to Terry and said, "Now that's teamwork. Two of 'em fly low and sight the fish. The others up high make the kill. Why they don't break their necks hitting the water is beyond me. But the real mystery is, how the hell do they communicate?"

Terry laughed. "Got to be eye contact."

"Or maybe wing signals?" Jayne offered.

"Probably a little of both," said Ridge. "Now, we need our own teamwork. How do we get a name or address, knowing only the first three letters of a vintage license plate? You guys are the computer whizzes. Time to shine."

Terry and Jayne bantered about Google, HTML, JavaScript, and URLs, and then continued to talk computereze for the next ten minutes. As they soared in their own world, Ridge went in for the kill on his fish chowder.

"I know," Jayne said suddenly. "I've got a friend in Phoenix, Phyllis. She runs a data storage firm. Twenty-five years ago, when we started out, it was called a 'service bureau' and stored and retrieved computer data for businesses and government agencies. Today—the exact same thing, but in a huge desert warehouse with endless rows of equipment for storing data—you know, the 21st Century Cloud. Anyway, she has public-document storage contracts with various states. I remember Phyllis telling me once it took weeks and weeks to scan California's DMV documents."

Ridge grinned. "Go get 'em, Wonder Woman."

Jayne and Terry left the table to call Phyllis, while Ridge finished his chowder and started on to his Mahi-Mahi fish sandwich. Like the red-beaked birds, Jayne and Terry did recon; he ate the fish. Couldn't get much better.

About an hour later, they finished lunch, and Terry dropped Ridge and Jayne back at their apartment. Jayne unpacked and made follow-up calls to Phyllis while Ridge fed Mister. Moments later, Jayne busted into the kitchen. "Call Terry. Pay dirt! No name. Records were too old, too scattered, too incomplete. But we got an address—from 50 years ago. It's at least a place to start. Back then, California plate "MAN 659" was sent to 66 Sixteen Road, Goleta, California."

"Fantastic!" He pulled Jayne in for a kiss and thought about Hulk. Tough never quits—you piece of shit. Next stop, your goddamn doorstep.

CHAPTER 14

Friday night was a good time to harvest L.A.'s children. So, rather than kill a source, to prod everyone into better service and products, Hess decided to teach by example. He'd show the bastards he didn't need them. Better to hit where it really hurts, in their fat wallets, than spill the blood of just a few.

He had told One through Six to meet him at 6 p.m.

"Tonight," said Hess, "we hunt. Seek prey. Dress in black suits, with white shirts and black ties, like missionaries. Three, you and Four package small boxes of food, just snacks and treats, in two large sacks."

"What'll we do with them?" asked Three.

"Give 'em away," said Hess. "You and Four travel with me. One, Two, Five and Six will be another group. We'll visit skid row in downtown L.A., then the construction area near the University of Southern California, where the city is building the railway and freeway interchanges. Posing as ministers of God with food for the needy, we'll ferret out candidates—the homeless, the runaways, the lost and the abandoned. Then we'll take the best. So bring plenty of sacks, rope and red tape."

"Why the construction area near USC?" asked One.

"Because teens feel safe there," said Hess. "They group together in make-shift tents, behind the construction fences. Every Friday night after the crews leave. We'll join them. Provide handouts. And return later to corral the best. Now let's get going."

§

At 9 p.m. on a chilly, moonless Friday night, the ministers of God hit skid row in downtown L.A. It was slim pickings. Hess found the few little snits worth talking to grabbed the food packages and ran. So much for God's message. Luckily, the construction area near USC proved far more rewarding. Hess ended up bagging two boys about 16-years-old. One and his crew sacked three girls, ranging 15 to 18 years in age. All five were taken back and herded into a special room. There, Hess had Two untie them, and rip the sacks from their heads. Then Two retied their hands with plastic ties and put more red tape across their mouths. Finally, Hess sent the Watchmen back to the big house and sat alone, in a chair, watching. For most part, the new students sniffled, whimpered, and sobbed. One guy and two girls just wouldn't shut up, so Hess got up—and did what had to be done. A hard slap to the boy's face did the trick.

But the other boy—he seemed special. With long blond hair, he sat silently, legs crossed Indian style, staring at Hess. Not a word, not a sound, not a blink, even when Hess slapped the first boy. Interesting.

Eventually they all shut up and curled into fetal positions. Some slept. But not the blonde boy. He just lay there and watched Hess, with deadpan eyes. Intriguing. Hess got up again and tied the blond boy down. A test of sorts.

The boy did well, lying there silently, staring at the ceiling regardless of what Hess said or did. After ten more minutes, Hess untied him realizing, despite some looks of disdain, this special boy had the strength, resolve, and focus to be a Watchman. His Eminence would love it, thought Hess. It'd put them closer to their goal.

CHAPTER 15

Saturday was a day off for Jayne and Ridge. The marine engineer Ridge hired to inspect and sea-test his cruiser had cleared the boat for operation late Friday afternoon, so he and Jayne packed breakfast and went down to the dock.

After Jayne's initial shock at seeing the scorched and discolored swim step and rear wall, they boarded and decided to search for some peace and quiet. Soon, they were idling along Palos Verdes, a beautiful, forested peninsula jutting into the Pacific south of Redondo Beach. As they floated along the west side, Ridge marveled at the steep red cliffs, speckled greenery, and coves, with rocky beaches, that peppered the shoreline. Sometimes he and Jayne anchored in one of the coves, but this morning they simply shut down engines and drifted, about a half-mile out.

Good choice. While setting the table for breakfast, Ridge and Jayne wandered into a huge pod of dolphins. Ridge recognized them as nearshore bottlenose. Hundreds of them, swimming directly at the bow, leaping in and out of the water. Half to the right, half to the left. With large black-button eyes, bottle-shaped noses, shiny skin, and best of all—smiley faces—each was beautiful. The cutest though were baby dolphins swimming tight formation with their moms. But most amazing were other adults rising from the water, performing pirouettes, as they twirled 300 feet away. Showoffs.

As the last one passed, Jayne said, "Darn—we didn't use the camera."

"Next time, kid. We'll just keep this one in our heads, instead of on a chip."

"Just for us," Jayne said softly. After a few moments of silence, just listening to the peaceful slap of waves on the hull, she turned to him. "Let's take the boat in and pick up Pistol."

Pistol—half Lab, half Chow-Chow, with a purple tongue to prove it—was the black, 45-pound rescue who wrangled with Mister for dominance. It was all for show, though, as Mister and Pistol were often found occupying the same clump of blankets or curled together in Pistol's doggie bed. She'd been boarded since last Saturday, but with Jayne back, Ridge thought why not?

"OK," he said, "let's break her out."

Pistol was a special dog. When a pup, a worthless wahoo had thrown her from his pick-up while speeding down the 405 Freeway. A woman behind stopped and brought the puppy to a vet who saved her life. Then they took her to a no-kill rescue mission in the Valley, where Jayne and Ridge, one fine Sunday, saw the little black-puddle of a dog and adopted her. What they didn't know was the Chow DNA and pick-up experience would combine to create a 45-pound alpha-dog, with few equals. In fact, Pistol was expelled from two training schools in a row for fighting with every bully dog bigger than her. With little choice, Ridge and Jayne turned to a doggie psychologist—after all it was L.A. Following months of therapy, more directed at Ridge and Jayne than the dog, they realized Pistol would never graduate from any damn dog school. Instead, they would live with a terrific guard dog, one that would never attack a friend or smaller animal. But beyond that, all bets were off. Big dogs. Bad guys. Beware.

§

When they got Pistol back to the apartment midafternoon., Mister went nuts—purring, rubbing, and weaving in and out of her legs. Clan's all here, thought Ridge. Everything's good. Then he remembered Terry would be picking him up in just a few hours to go to Judge Millsberg's memorial service.

"Sure you don't want to come?" he said to Jayne.

"No. This is something you and Terry should do. Anyway, you're in great spirits and I'm thinking of heading back to San Francisco tomorrow afternoon if that's OK. Duty calls."

"Pistol and Mister can keep me safe while you're gone. But the memorial service is near 23rd Street Landing. Terry and I were thinking of grabbing dinner there after the service. Want to join us at the restaurant?"

"I'm going to do laundry and review some things for Monday morning's presentation. I figure I can take the 1:00 back to San Francisco tomorrow and then return home Monday night."

At times like this, Ridge was glad they lived only a few minutes from LAX. "No problemo. Done deal. Should we get breakfast near the Manhattan Beach Pier beforehand?"

"Sounds like a plan."

As Jayne went to start her laundry, Ridge started developing another plan. Ever since she discovered the license plate's Goleta address, it was burning in his mind. Sunday afternoon Jayne would be back in San Francisco. Terry would be down in San Diego, finishing another stake-out with his associate. He wouldn't be back until Monday morning. Why waste a perfectly good Sunday afternoon? Why not fly away? Solo. Just to look around. A little reconnaissance, seemed like a perfect way to spend the day.

CHAPTER 16

Terry picked Ridge up at 6:30 p.m. as planned. Jayne kissed him goodbye and assured him she'd spend the evening curled up with Mister and Pistol and would probably go to bed early. Less than 40 minutes later, they arrived at Rolling Hills Cemetery, located on the lower bluffs of Palos Verdes Peninsula.

After passing through the gates, Terry and Ridge joined a long line of cars waiting near the Spanish Chapel where the family had set up a reception to celebrate Judge Millsberg's life. The cemetery grounds were park-like with flat-to-earth headstones, green everywhere and black winding roads, grassy slopes, tall trees, and harbor views. Peaceful. Beautiful, really.

Once parked, they were directed to a large but charming hacienda-type building with a central courtyard just to the left of the Chapel. Inside, the main room had café tables with white tablecloths and chairs all around. Wine and cheese bars were set up in two corners, and tables of hors d'oeuvres were placed throughout the room. In the background, on low setting, they played the judge's favorite songs. Ridge immediately recognized "The Impossible Dream" from *Man of La Mancha*, "I Dreamed A Dream" from *Les Mis*, and "Memories." from *Cats*.

With a drink in hand, he studied those around him. Most notable was a group of judges from Orange County. Actually two groups: Four in long black robes, and the others in dark suits, much like the ones Terry and Ridge wore. Ridge knew all the judges, either directly or by reputation. The four in robes were the royal core of the Orange County Courthouse, led by Chief Judge Christian Gimuldin. The others in suits, standing separately, were the ones Ridge hoped would get assigned to his cases. They ranged from Millsberg-like to merely conservative in their judicial demeanor and attitudes. No agendas. No decisions based on prejudices rather than facts and evidence. Agenda justice is no justice, he thought.

He turned and focused on the four black robes. Watching them, anyone could conclude two things: All were closely bonded, like brothers, and three responded quickly to the call of the fourth, Judge Gimuldin, who was standing center in his trademark bow tie and black robe. In fact, rumor had it Gimuldin even showered in a black robe. He seemingly wore robes at all times, in his office, in the hallway, everywhere, even when rules didn't allow it. The related rumor was he used the robes to hide his stacked heels. Allegedly, the judge sported a much shorter and fatter body under those robes and masked it with two-to-three-inch heels and the flowing gown. Right or wrong, one thing was certain: When he robed up for an event, so did his three brethren. Lock step. All the time.

Now, they headed toward a table of food. In their long robes, they seemed to slide in unison across the room, like penguins without the waddle. In an opposite corner, a large flat screen TV was on, surrounded by three sofas. Ridge headed that way.

The TV, hooked to a DVD player, cycled through photographs of the judge's life—high school, college, the Army, her time as a lawyer, and her many years as a judge. The presentation included photos of family vacations, social events, and the judge's hobbies—fishing and bicycling. Ridge sat on a sofa watching the show, while Terry talked with another investigator nearby. Then a long-time lawyer friend sat down next to Ridge, Elliot Green.

"Eric, it's been awhile. How goes it?" Elliot was a trim man in his late 40's, who stood 5-feet 8-inches and had dark Mediterranean features. "Sad thing about Judge Millsberg, huh? Everybody's stunned—especially after Judge Flynn's recent death in San Diego."

"Judge Flynn? I didn't know him, unfortunately, or about his death. But losing Judge Millsberg has been shock enough. By the way, how are your fights for rights going?"

Elliot Green had been a civil-rights lawyer for twenty-five years. One of the best in L.A. and an activist for the LGBTQ community. He basically lived in court, especially the federal and state courts in downtown L.A., and the Santa Ana division of federal court in Orange County. Most of his cases involved civil rights, disability laws, and the like. He was also something of an expert on the personalities of judges in and around California.

"So what's with the dark shades? And are those stitches? What happened?"

As Ridge gave him his stock reply and lowered his sunglasses, Elliot's eyes widened.

"I hope the other guy looks worse," said Elliot.

Ridge shook his head and frowned. "Not really." Then, they both smiled and began to share memories about Judge Millsberg.

"No matter what," Elliot said, "Juliet Millsberg was always fair." Then he pointed discreetly at Gimuldin and his three brethren, still sliding around the room as a unit in their long black robes. "Now that group is the exact opposite of Juliet Millsberg. Gimuldin is a piece of work. He rules the roost. Doesn't even bother to show up on Mondays and most Fridays. which screws up trying a case in his courtroom. But he couldn't care less. Too busy working on his deep tan—especially now that he's between trophy wives."

"What's it like to try a case in his fiefdom?"

Elliot leaned toward Ridge. "Just finished another trial in front of him. Did you know, before his appointment to the bench, he had never tried a case as a lawyer? Never. Spent twenty-five years defending public utility companies in administrative hearings. But to hear him now, you'd think he invented trying cases in front of juries."

"That bad?"

Elliot nodded. "By the way, have you ever been in his chambers?"

At that point, Ridge asked Elliot to step away from the couches. He was tired of whispering, and he didn't want the wrong ears overhearing what was said. They each got a glass of wine and strolled out to the far end of the central courtyard. Ridge turned to Elliot. "OK. Tell me about his chambers."

"Huge," said Elliot. "When you walk in—an enormous desk in the far corner. But here's the thing, the desk has a false front all the way to the floor. It hides the fact the desk and his chair are elevated on a platform. There's also a ramp hidden behind the desk. He uses it to ascend subtly to his throne, I mean—chair. That way, when he directs lawyers to take the visitors' seats in front of his desk, they feel like midgets, gazing up at judge on high. It's one thing in a courtroom, where the judge sits higher than everyone else, that's for decorum and safety. But in a private office—so he can look down on lawyers? That's just sick."

Ridge was going to agree, but Elliot, on a roll, continued, "I just hired an associate who spent two years as Gimuldin's law clerk. Each summer Gimuldin selects two graduating law students as full-time researchers for two-year terms. Supplements his permanent research clerk who's been with him for about ten years. All three are paid of course by taxpayers—a perk of the office."

Ridge tipped his wine glass at Elliot to slow him down and said: "But that's not unusual. Chief judges are assigned law clerks to help with research, drafting opinions and other duties."

"True. But get this. My new associate tells me the permanent researcher is named Henri. Gimuldin hired him because, before law school, he was a sous-chef at a famous French restaurant in Napa Valley. Gimuldin even has a special deal with the manager of the court cafeteria. Henri works in a designated portion of the kitchen, preparing lunches for the judge and his guests."

"Next to hospital food, court cafeteria food ranks worst in the world."

"Not this food," said Elliot. "Haute cuisine. Served through the back elevator, complete with large silver covers on trays to keep things hot. According to my associate, the judge's two-year clerks do the serving. They get special training from Henri, even as to how to pull the silver covers off the main dishes in unison and, get this, announce "Voilà." Tricky, too—it can require both hands for two covers, especially at the big table with multiple guests."

"The big table?"

"Oh sure—that's right, you've never been in his chambers. Look, as you enter, to the left is a massive 12-foot wooden table surrounded by a dozen high-back chairs. Each chair supposedly has the judge's family crest carved at the top. During the day it's all theoretically used as a research table, but at lunch—the black tablecloth and napkins come out. My associate tells me the black decor contrasts nicely with the crystal, silverware and silver serving dishes kept nearby in the wooden cabinets, beneath the bookshelves."

Just then, as Ridge was trying to visualize the whole thing, Terry came over and politely interrupted them. "Boss, shouldn't we think about leaving."

Ridge introduced Terry to Elliot, and after handshakes said, "Terry's right. Time to go. But thanks, Elliot, for bringing me behind closed doors. Always love to hear about my tax dollars at work. Later amigo." Ridge and Terry then bid good night and thank you to Justin Millsberg and his aunts and headed to the car. As they got in, Terry said, "Next stop, 23rd Street Landing. Too bad Jayne's not going to join us."

"She said she was going to crash early, so we're on our own."

"Like old times."

§

The Landing in San Pedro was one of Ridge's favorite restaurants. Right on a wooden pier overlooking the commercial fishing boat slips. Talk about fresh. The Landing got its fish straight off the boats and its clam chowder was to die for. Not only that but its long dark wooden bar was the best in SoCal—no question. Everything from Anejo Tequila to the greatest Irish and Canadian whiskeys. It was already 10:30 when they arrived and headed straight to the bar where they drank, talked to other patrons, and popped peanuts and chips until 1 a.m. when they finally decided to order some food to soak up the drinks.

CHAPTER 17

Seventeen miles away, Two, who had excelled at climbing during training at Hess' mountain camp, used handholds, grappling hooks, and rope silently and efficiently to scale the five-story building. On the cement balcony, he got out special tools to open the sliding glass door. It was a dark night and pitch black inside the apartment. He crouched, keeping a low profile, and reached for his mini-light to switch it on when a jungle-cat *yowl* sliced through the air and something attached itself to his face, smothering and stabbing at the same time.

As claws ripped his eyes, he grabbed the thing, pulled it from his face tearing flesh along with it, and flung it across the room. Just then, he heard a low growl like a sound from the bowels of hell, and sharp teeth clamped on to his groin and held fast. Two yanked out his gun. Shot the dog. Stepped over it and rushed to an inside door, barged through, and found himself in an empty den. He turned, went to the next door, and kicked it in. An office. The computer room. His face was bleeding. He could barely see. All he wanted was to double over and vomit from groin pain. But goddamnit, *no!* He *could* not fail. He *would* not fail.

Running back out to the main room, Two threw open the next door. Pitch black. Then, "Get out!" Next a blast. The flash blinded him. His body was thrown back from the force of the bullet as it ripped a hole through his chest. *Fuck!* He staggered back. His knees buckled. But instead of falling, he hunched over. He forced a turn and hobbled quickly to the balcony, expecting another shot any moment. But none came. He grabbed the rope, flipped over the balcony and slid the five stories to hit the ground hard. Hands raw, nearly blind from the scratches to his face, and bleeding like a stuck pig from the wound in his chest, he struggled to his feet and took off stumbling down the beach.

CHAPTER 18

Ridge's phone rang at 1:30 a.m. Not good. He set his fork down and put the phone to his ear.

"There's been a break-in. I heard the animals attacking, then a shot. I reached for the gun in your nightstand and ducked behind the bed. He smashed in two doors, then burst into our room. I fired. Hit his chest. He staggered back. Then out. Gone. I called 911. But Eric, he shot Pistol!"

"Jayne—holy shit—are you OK?"

"Yes, yes, but after losing Sean in Iraq—I thought I'd never touch a gun again. Then, with the blast and Pistol's yelping, I was on automatic. I called 911. Oh, God. I think I shot someone."

"You did good, baby, real good, but can you bring Jenny into this call?"

Ridge was up and moving, heading outside. Out of the corner of his eye, he saw Terry on his feet, signaling for the check. The calls merged and Ridge quickly explained to his daughter what was happening and where he was. Luckily, Jenn's condo was in Manhattan Beach, only a mile from Jayne. They all three stayed on the phone until Jenn arrived to find Jayne outside, holding Pistol wrapped in a blood-soaked blanket. Ridge, through her speaker, said, "Jenn—I called the vet's emergency service. Hermosa Beach on PCH. They're waiting. Go!"

Then he heard Jenny say, "Mom. What happened?"

Ridge said, "Jenn—she'll explain on the way. Go. Please go."

When he hung up, the cellphone started shaking slightly in Ridge's hand. He dropped his arm, hiding it. Then, a sharp pain. Upper left chest. Momentary. Ridge ignored it.

Terry stepped up beside him. "I paid. I'm getting the car."

Ridge just nodded. "I'm calling the police."

Moments later, as the Vette tore out of the parking lot, Ridge reached into the glove compartment and pulled out Terry's gun, thumb running over the barrel as if it would sooth him. "Whacking me," he said with a growl. "That's one thing. But breaking into my home, attacking my wife, shooting my dog? This is Holy War."

"Copy that." Terry took a corner on squealing tires and stomped on the gas again. "A goddamn fucking Holy War."

§

At 2:15 in the morning, the doctor, looking tired and solemn, came through the white door into the waiting room. Ridge focused on the man's eyes but couldn't read them.

"One lucky dog," the vet said.

Jenn squeezed her mom's hand. "Thank God."

"The bullet went right through. No organ damage. You can see her for a few minutes. But she's sedated. Gotta stay that way for a few days while stitches set. We'll know, by Tuesday noon, when she can go home."

"Thanks Doc," said Ridge putting an arm around Jayne. "Please show us back to her."

After visiting Pistol, Terry and the three Ridges split up. Terry headed home, and Jenny drove Ridge and Jayne to the apartment where the police waited. Their home was a crime scene now and blood was on the carpet and on the walls. Mister was in hiding and officers were taking photos and trying to get prints. They had the rope and grappling hook in an evidence bag and a mini flashlight that the intruder had dropped in the bedroom after being shot. All in all, it was a mess. After the police were finally done and they'd given their formal statements, Jenn went home, and Ridge and Jayne went to bed in the guest room.

Eventually Jayne stopped shaking, but Ridge couldn't let go of her. Holding her tight, he said, "You still planning to go back to San Francisco?"

"I think I need to. You know me. I need to work to get my mind off bad stuff."

"Yeah. I know you," Ridge whispered. "I'll get you to the airport and you go do your thing and then you come right back here. Promise?"

"Promise."

Two hours later, lying in bed and still staring up at nothing, Ridge decided to bail on the sleep thing. Instead, he pieced together his plan for a step-by-step aerial reconnaissance of 66 Sixteen Road in Goleta.

§

At 11 a.m. on Sunday, Ridge dropped Jayne at LAX and headed home to change into his flying stuff, make final arrangements, and pick up his satchel, a weathered black-leather bag with a ballistic-nylon fabric interior and long shoulder strap. He'd modified it years ago to carry his Sig Sauer pistol to and from the target range near LAX. The bag had a form-fit padded pocket for the Sig, and smaller internal compartments to hold four magazines and extra ammunition. The forward side closed with a Velcro strip that ran halfway down. By leaving it open, Ridge could grab the handle of the Sig, and slide it out without a problem. In California, it was legal to carry a pistol in such a case, with no magazine in the gun and no bullet in the chamber. And using the satchel was a convenient way of carrying all the pieces in one easy package. Ridge's Sig was a P229 model that shot .357 hollow-point bullets from a 10-round magazine. Compared to his 9mm Beretta, the Sig was smaller. Lighter. And packed a bigger wallop. He was more accurate with the 9mm though. Probably because its barrel was 25% longer. But the Sig's portability was hard to beat especially with the satchel. Might become critical—one never knew.

He checked his Sig first. Good to go. Then he donned beige cargo pants, white flannel shirt, and a chocolate-brown leather jacket. Putting his tan ball cap on his head, Ridge focused on the mission and phoned Torrance Airport. He usually rented airplanes at either Santa Monica or Torrance but preferred the latter. The skies over Santa Monica and the airport itself were often saturated with air traffic. Torrance was far less busy, closer to Redondo Beach, and getting in and out was much easier.

So, Ridge arranged to rent a blue and white Cessna 172SP at Torrance, a high-wing single-engine airplane with fixed-gear, but fast enough to get him up and down the coast in about 40 minutes each way. He also called Goleta airport and arranged a rental car. The trick was to get a vehicle with a navigation system. It was easy to get lost up there with the winding roads, especially in the mountains. And then there was the general lack of road signs, which Ridge always thought intentional to discourage tourists from motoring around. People in the Santa Barbara area, even Goleta, coveted their privacy. A big reason many moved there from Los Angeles.

On the map, Goleta was just above her sister cities of Santa Barbara and Montecito. Above—geographically, but not in other ways. Goleta was the stepsister of the group. Both Santa Barbara and Montecito were picture-perfect Mediterranean-type cities on sheer mountain coastlines, with residences that ran from expensive to obscenely expensive. Goleta had mountains too, deep forests to the east, and coastline to the west, but only flat lands in-between made up primarily of industrial parks and middle-class homes.

Ridge liked Goleta, it was a bit bohemian. But it certainly lacked the Mediterranean flare and smell of money in Santa Barbara, and more-so Montecito. On the other hand, Goleta had a nice little airport. Easy to find. Just north of the campus at University of California/Santa Barbara.

Ridge left Mister some Tasty Tuna, picked up his gear, rode the elevator to the underground garage, and jumped into Jayne's black Infiniti sedan. He had a mission. Needed to get to Goleta, do his thing and return before nightfall.

Pulling the Infiniti from the garage, Ridge gazed at a strange, hazy glare, and thought, Shit. Overcast. The marine layer—moving in. He bent his neck further to look straight up and focused on low gray clouds. Only a few breaks. And heavy mist and blacker puffs, like cannon plumes, to the west. Not good.

After parking at the general aviation lot, Ridge hoofed to the Base Ops Building and then beelined to the Flight Planning Room, way in back. Opening the door, he stared at... empty. Stale smell. Dark, only dim glare from two windows at the rear. Ridge flipped the switches and heard, "No lights. They're out."

Peering to the back of the room, Ridge found a guy, hunched over, sitting on the well-used leather sofa near the Coke machine and restrooms. "What?" said Ridge.

"No lights. They're out. Waiting for the electrician."

The guy stood up and walked haltingly toward Ridge. About six feet tall, white, muscular build, maybe early 20s. Blue knit cap, shaved hair at the sides or bald, wearing a Grateful Dead sweatshirt and jeans. The 12-foot flight planning table with glass top covering aeronautical charts, mapping Oregon to Mexico and east to Vegas, sat between them. Ridge moved forward. Slightly. To his end of the table. Grateful Dead shifted slowly to Ridge's right, then bit by bit moved along the side of the table. Halfway, he stopped, said nothing, stared wild-eyed at Ridge.

CHAPTER 19

"What?' Ridge said.

"The jacket. The jacket, man. Brown leather aviator. Been lookin' and lookin' for one just like that."

Ridge pulled his black satchel closer. "J. Pierson and Company. On-line. 300 bucks."

The guy didn't move closer. Instead, he pulled pen and crushed paper from his jeans and started writing. "Thanks, man. I mean it."

Ridge relaxed a bit. "When will the lights be back."

"Not sure, but I'm Ruben—new here, training to be a mechanic on the General Aviation line."

"I'm Ridge. I fly in and out a lot."

"Hey man, good to meet you. They're doing flight planning now out of base ops. Until we get the lights back. That's your best bet."

Ridge stepped forward and shook Ruben's hand. "Glad to meet you. I usually fly the white and blue 172."

Ruben smiled. "Cool, dude. I'll keep an eye out for ya."

Turning to the door, Ridge said, "Appreciate it, man. See you later."

Ridge hurried to the front of the building and entered the Base Ops Room. After hellos to people he knew, he checked the weather, happy to learn the gray skies broke up ten miles west over the ocean. So, he filed an IFR to VFR-On-Top flight plan. He'd use his instruments to punch through the clouds and then fly Visual Flight Rules to destination. Happy to be on his way, Ridge walked briskly out to the bird with his checklist, satchel, and necessary paperwork. After pre-flight checks, he jumped into the blue and white Cessna and headed to the runway. As he approached the black top, he radioed the tower, "This is Cessna 3-2-1 Alpha, about to take the active, requesting a couple of minutes extra at end of runway."

"Roger that 3-2-1 Alpha, no traffic, take 3. Cleared for takeoff."

Ridge clicked the microphone two times. "Roger that. 3-2-1 Alpha, cleared for takeoff."

Ridge checked visually left and right and left again and taxied into position for takeoff. Plenty of civilian pilots finished their engine run-up checks as they rolled down the runway. But Ridge did it the military way, coming to a stop, feet on the brakes, and running full up at a stand-still. The theory was: If something went wrong during run-up, better to have more runway ahead, and less behind. Ridge liked that idea .

The run-up went without a hitch, and off he went. He punched through clouds and got further clearance straight up the coast. Beyond the overcast deck, the world burst into a fresh, crisp, glorious blue. An almost blinding sun. No clouds. Ridge pulled out his Ray Bans, slipped them on and thought how lucky he was. Below, the sun reflected across the marine layer creating a deck of bright white puffy cotton stretching for miles. As advertised, near the ten-mile point, the sea of cotton became an ocean of blue-green sparkling water. Same world, different perspective. Beautiful.

Thirty minutes later Ridge reached the sun-drenched orange roof tiles and creamy stucco buildings of Santa Barbara. Just as he remembered, the Goleta Airport was easy to spot from the air. Couldn't miss the UCSB campus. He glanced toward the beach. Normally, after landing, he grabbed lunch at The Café on Goleta Beach. Great fish tacos. No time for that today, though. He was on the clock. This morning's donut and coffee would have to do. So, Ridge made his approach, and landed—a squeaker. He taxied to the chocks outside the Ops Center, shut down and checked out his rental car—a green Toyota 4Runner. He grinned when he saw the navigation system ready-to-go.

Strangely, though, when Ridge entered the address, the computer only allowed him to pick numbers between 1 and 50 along Sixteen Road. 66 wasn't in the database. Never one to give up, Ridge typed in 50, figuring he'd wing it to 66 from there. Sixteen Road ran out of a flat industrial-park area, way up into the mountains. Eventually, it bent right, and the pavement turned to compact dirt. Ridge was deep in thick forest, glad to be driving the four-wheel-drive Toyota, when the friendly gal in the computer said: "You have arrived at your destination."

Looking around, he saw no structures, no addresses, and no side roads. Seemed to be no 50 Sixteen Road. Ridge began to think the database was keying off property records reflecting some contractor's dream for future development. With few options though, he continued to travel east on the road, finding higher mountains, deeper forest. Suddenly, a side road. Swinging his vehicle to the right, Ridge followed the rutted dirt deeper into the woods. Until he came to a chain-link fence. Six-feet high. Old. And rusty. The gate was open.

The fence ran around two buildings. A dilapidated wood cabin, and a more dilapidated barn—that looked 100 years old. Seeing no signs of life, Ridge crept his vehicle up the long crushed-stone driveway. Toward the cabin. Still no life. He called out. No one home. Ridge pulled the 4Runner slowly to the back of the barn. Nothing there. He parked out of sight from anyone in front and grabbed his satchel. He loaded a magazine in the Sig. Flipped the safety off. And left the Velcro side open. Bending the law a bit, he put the satchel over his left shoulder, intending to draw with his right hand, as he approached the cabin on foot.

It was old. The porch was bigger than the rest of the structure. Looking through the window, Ridge saw one main room and a stone fireplace. A sink and black stove sat in a corner. The furniture, what little there was of it, was beat up and circa-1950. Seeing no signs inside of recent life, Ridge reached into the outer pocket of his satchel and pulled out a small digital camera. He snapped interior photos of the cabin through its small dusty windows. Stowed his camera. And turned toward the barn. Termites had eaten most of the outside planks, and the structure had never been painted in its life. The two large doors were unlocked. Slightly open. Ridge pushed, ever so slowly. They creaked. Inside, Ridge found—well, an old barn and musty, moldy straw everywhere. Including ancient bales on the second level. Dated tools. Pitchforks, shovels, and saws, leaning against the stalls and walls. A big rusty red tractor, built in the 1960s, was parked at the center. Near a block-and-tackle device, probably used to lift the tractor's engine in and out for maintenance. There was a big old generator on the other side of the tractor, more tools scattered on a nearby wooden table, and not much else.

Then Ridge's eyes focused on something weird. In the far corner of the barn. A stand-alone room. Rectangular structure with fibrous weather-proofing panels nailed to the outside walls. And the roof. And the door. The only openings, besides that door, were a few slit windows. Near top of the structure. Ridge turned and reached into his satchel. Pulled out his camera. Clicked 360-degrees of photos. Then, tucked the camera and re-focused on the room.

The padlock for the door sat on the floor. Easing the door further open, he found more weather-proofing panels. Nailed to the inside walls. And the ceiling. And, near center of the room, eight large dog cages. Four cages, stacked on a bottom row of four other cages. Each measured 3x3x3. Had its own lock. And seemed almost big enough for a person. Then there was a cot along one wall. And a large wooden box, apparently used as a table. Both were placed near an old stuffed chair in the far corner. The room smelled of stale sweat. But still no signs of life.

Most of the metal dog dishes, inside the cages, were caked with some kind of dried food. There was still a little water in the bowls but it was dirty. Behind the cages, a tarnished brass faucet stuck out of the ground on a 4-foot stem. Had a 10-foot black hose attached. But surprisingly, no dog food bags. Anywhere. Then Ridge reasoned, weatherproofing—inside and out—makes sense. The crappy barn couldn't keep out winter rain or summer heat. And the panels also work as soundproofing if any dogs act up. But a cot? The chair? What the hell. And where are the dogs? Where in fact is anyone?

As if answering, out of nowhere, came the rumble of a truck on the crushed-stone driveway out front. Ridge made sure he could easily reach the butt of his Sig. He moved to the barn door. With his right eye pressed against a separation in the wooden slats, he watched two men jump from a beat up, jacked-up, brown pick-up. Each looked about six-feet tall, fit and around 20. Each wore a beige hunting jacket and matching hunting cap with sides down over their ears. More importantly, each carried a huge rifle strapped to the left shoulder. Without words, both sauntered to the cabin. Climbed the porch. Opened the door. And vanished inside.

Time to get outta Dodge, before the twins get upset. Ridge pulled his Sig. Gently moving the slide back, he chambered a bullet. Holding the weapon down and along his right leg, he crept out the barn door, noting the front gate on the chain-link fence still stood open. He tip-toed backwards around to the 4Runner. Got in. And silently as possible started the rental with his left hand, holding the pistol in his right. Eyes plastered on the corner of the barn, Ridge slowly rolled forward over dirt and grass, until just before the edge of the structure. Then he put the SUV in reverse. Negotiated a slow U-turn. And rolled quietly around the corner of the barn, backwards. He cranked his neck to see toward the cabin and continued to roll rearward over dirt in front of the barn. When he reached the crushed-stone driveway, he steered clockwise until the 4Runner was centered on it. Backwards. Facing the cabin. That way, if the twins heard him crushing rocks, and stormed from the cabin, rifles blasting, he'd have straight-on shots with the Sig. On the flipside, if either twin or both nonchalantly opened the cabin door and got surprised by Ridge, he could throw the SUV in 'Drive,' tuck the gun, and feign being a lost soul looking for directions. That was the plan anyway. Good, bad, or ugly.

Centered in the gravel with his eyes forward, riveted on the cabin, Ridge gradually backed down the long driveway. Crushing stones. One pop a time. Staring hard at the cabin door. Breath on hold. It seemed forever. And ever. And ever. But he finally reached the gate. No storms. No surprised twins. No gun blasts. Ridge twisted his head, and slowly backed out onto the public road. Hoping. Listening. Hearing nothing. He looked again toward the cabin and let out a long sigh. Ridge put the 4 Runner in Drive and headed to the airport, wondering, *What next?*

CHAPTER 20

Two had to do something. Now parked in the Santa Barbara area, he hadn't left his car since the shooting. Scared shitless. Like when he was little—3 years old—and his father started beating him. He'd hid in closets. Heart pounding. Behind chairs, head down between his knees. But it always ended the same. He was always found. Always caught. Always beaten. For six years, Two could do no right. He tried—oh, how he tried. Then he ran away. For good.

Now Two looked at his hands. At least the bleeding had stopped. But by 6 p.m., he decided, no choice. Got to tell Hess. Sure, Two could cover the chest wound. But not the eye. And anyway, he needed a doctor. Now. Or he'd die. But still…he feared going to the big house. Instead, Two headed for the barn.

He arrived near 7 p.m., saw no one, and went directly to the cage room. Sitting in the stuffed chair, feeling depleted, Two wondered, What have I done? Just wanted to show Hess I could solo. Better than kiss-up One. Planned everything to a gnat's ass. I knew the woman would be alone. But no one, not even Hess, could have known she had a bobcat and a damn wolf-dog in her apartment. Talk about sick. Who the hell does that? She's friggin' nuts. And who in damn hell could know she'd have a gun? Just then, Two peered down, through his good eye, at the bloody rags pressed into the bullet wound in his upper chest. He eased the pressure, which decreased pain, but then blood began to pool. He pushed the rags back, deeper into the wound. The excruciating pain returned, but nothing, absolutely nothing, felt like the fire in his right eye. Two hung his head and, well, gave up. Rocking slowly side-to-side, he picked up his cell, and called Hess.

§

Hess arrived around 8 p.m., with One and Three. As they entered the barn, Hess yelled, "Two, for Chrissake. How many times have I told you. Close the damn gate. Leave it open again, I swear—I will eat out your heart. What's going on? Where the hell are you?"

Moments later Hess stood in the doorway to the cage room, the other two Watchmen behind him. Two staggered to his feet and hanging his head, mumbled, "Here, Herr Hess."

Hess immediately shoved Two back into the chair, told One to get the medical kit from the truck, and ordered Two to explain. As Two recounted his story, Hess' eyes bulged, and his face flushed redder and redder. By the end, Hess was seething with anger. He barked, "Unbelievable. You asshole. A fuckin' failure. A damn embarrassment to me, His Eminence and all your ancestors. I should kill you now. Be done with it. But I, unlike you, know discipline. I'll call His Eminence. Let him decide what the hell to do with you."

Hess instructed One to replace Two's bloody rags with compress bandages, and to do and say nothing else. Hess then left the room and called on his cell from inside the barn. When he returned, he spit toward Two, and directed the other Watchmen to lay Two out on the cot. Then, looking down on Two, he said, "His Eminence has decided to spare your life. Despite my urging otherwise. But no doctors. I'll do what has to be done."

Reaching into his black medical bag, Hess pulled out a bamboo stick. He shoved it sideways into Two's mouth, shouting, "Bite down." Then, Hess went back to his medic bag and pulled out one of the hypodermics. He loaded it through a vial and jammed the needle into Two's upper chest. He then loaded the needle again and moved it toward Two's right eye. As the needle point came closer, Two fell unconscious.

§

Two awoke hours later, still on the cot, with the other Watchmen and Hess nearby. His right eye was covered, and he had bandages on his chest. The other Watchmen gazed at Hess who glared at Two.

"You're a lucky son of a bitch. First, you live by the grace of His Eminence. Second, the bullet hit no organs and came out cleanly. And, by the way, so did your right eye. His Eminence felt it best to take the eye, rather than deal with a detached retina or optic nerve damage—which is probably what you had. Thirdly, you'll be returning to the big house, but only after just punishment. We've got important work to do. Failure cannot be tolerated."

Then the other Watchmen lifted Two and followed Hess out of the room. They hoisted Two with pulleys attached to the block and tackle in the barn. Hess had set it up the typical way: Two was suspended vertically, about a foot off the ground, with arms and legs stretched by chains at 45-degree angles. The chains were cinched to plastic shackles on his wrists and ankles. Once up, Two slowly turned his head to the left and down. With his left eye, he saw Hess pick up a tool from the wooden table.

Hess approached Two. "As I've told you again and again, His Eminence is far too lenient with you. All of you. Here, that same leniency saved you. But your unauthorized actions were fuckin' intolerable. They won't happen again. And this—is so you never forget."

Suspended in mid-air, Two turned his head right, looked down, and stared out his left eye. He watched Hess slowly reach up with wire cutters, toward the shackle on his right hand. Two cranked his head further right and up a bit, just in time…to see the tip of his ring finger fall to the ground. He tried not to make a sound, but a whine rose up in his throat. Then everything went dark.

CHAPTER 21

At 11 a.m. on Monday morning, Joshua F. Censkey, impeccably dressed in a gray suit with his trademark red silk tie and matching hanky, and sporting perfectly coiffed blond hair, sat atop the world. He and his huge semicircular desk seemed to float above the other downtown L.A. buildings, with the majestic San Gabriel Mountains to his back. The rest of the views through his floor-to-ceiling windows were also drop-dead gorgeous, with the Pacific Ocean to his left and, on a clear day, three different mountain ranges to his right. Joshua never closed his vertical shades, which kept his office blindingly bright. People would always squint as they looked at him behind the desk, and every newcomer to his corner office on the 67th floor of the Library Tower simply stood in awe. And why not, he was awe-inspiring. And the setting kept clients, employees, and anyone else in his presence intimidated, which was all that mattered.

Joshua reached over and hit the button on his intercom. "Amanda, send in Ryan, please."

Ryan Stacey was his personal assistant. In his early 30s, Ryan was already a standout at the company. In fact, Joshua became sure early on that Ryan had decided to hitch his star to Joshua's wagon. Smart kid. But it meant hard work and long hours, which probably led to Ryan's divorce. Yet through it all, Ryan never wavered. Always there. Ever trustworthy. And most importantly, he had become Joshua's confidant. Even the gods, need someone to talk to—now and again.

Ryan knocked.

"Enter."

As Ryan opened the door, Joshua watched him squint and smiled inwardly. He then motioned to one of the white leather chairs in front of his desk. "Close the door and take a seat."

As always, Ryan carried his laptop, and took long strides as he crossed the huge office to his chair.

"Ryan, what I'm going to tell you is top secret." Joshua cleared his throat and waited for Ryan to acknowledge the statement.

"Yes, sir," Ryan said with a nod.

"I'm not getting any younger. Mid-fifties now. I need to think about my legacy. So, I've decided to work with you on my memoir. I'll talk extemporaneously. You take notes. I'll edit them later. Any problem?"

Ryan immediately opened his laptop. "No, Mr. Censkey. I'm honored."

"I'm going to start with an overview of how I got where I am today. Ask questions if you must. I want to make sure you understand."

"Will do."

Joshua had thought of starting the book at his birth. With something about his parents. A lot of stories about great men began there. But that would lead to elementary school. Grades 2 to 8. When they picked on him. Chased him after school. And how he never got selected for any team. Bullshit. No one cares about that— or them. And stupid high school—the football guys always making fun of him. Things didn't really settle down until college, when he realized looking like a winner was the critical thing. But then— some unmasked him anyway.

"Where do we begin?" Ryan said, clearly eager to get started..

"I don't think you know this, but back in the '80s, I made my living as a California lawyer. But, as fate would have it, one day the California State Bar came down on me like a ton of bricks."

Ryan stared at Joshua in disbelief. "Why?"

"Because they could. Bureaucracy at its worse. They subpoenaed my bank records and then alleged I used client trust funds for outside investments."

Ryan shifted in his seat. "Did you fight them?"

"Why bother? Rather than go through a long, one-sided State Bar trial, I copped a plea. And the assholes disbarred me."

"What did you do then?"

"With few places to turn, I went into finance, investments, and ended up in hedge fund management in 1990. The good part was I got in at the ground floor. New high stakes gambling with other people's money, people who wanted huge profits. There was no bad part. I was a natural."

"What about the State Bar and your disbarment?"

Joshua scoffed. "They were out of it. No one in hedge funds cared about my background. The only thing that mattered was that I made deals and the deals paid big. At first, I did what I had to do to keep things going. Then in 1992, I made some big bucks with a few lucky hits. I was on my way, Joshua F. Censkey, Hedge Fund Manager."

Joshua looked out the window for a moment and thought to himself. *And that's when I learned money meant respect.*

Ryan, shifting again in his seat, sat straight up. "What happened next?"

"I knew I could make more of my success, so I combined my backgrounds. True, I couldn't act as a lawyer anymore, but I still knew about lawsuits. I also knew that catastrophically injured folks, most times, couldn't afford to take on giant corporate defendants."

"You used that how?"

"Well, corporations simply spent injured victims into the ground. Legions of lawyers, expensive experts, and motion after motion in court. They dragged litigation out, knowing the injured person was already out-of-work, crushed by medical bills, and unable to support self or family. Soon the victims and their lawyers ran out of money, and had to go away, or settle for next to nothing. They needed a hero."

Ryan smiled. "And you became that hero, right?"

"Right. And in 1994, I started JFC, Justice Finance Corporation, to funnel hedge fund money to catastrophically injured people with meritorious lawsuits. In that way, the victims, who were often destitute, could afford to live and fight the giant corporations through trials and appeals. The problem, however, was that, in most states, including California, the law prevented a non-lawyer from investing in a lawsuit and sharing in a client's recovery. Only lawyers, subject to State Bar regulations, could do that."

"Why?"

Joshua shook his head. "The self-serving states said they didn't want unregulated, private marketeers moving in, taking advantage of injured victims, and fanning litigation for profit. I, for one, thought it was all grossly unfair. And Ryan—if you haven't already, you'll soon learn something about me. I'm nothing, nothing at all, if not a world-class free-market thinker. Write that down."

Ryan typed then moved to the edge of his seat. "So, what did you do?"

"At first, I reflected on lending hedge fund money to lawyers, instead of their injured clients. Then the lawyers could, in turn, reinvest in the lawsuit and lend needed money to their clients."

"What happened?"

Joshua pursed his lips. "Unfortunately, most of the lawyers got bogged down in the details of my forty-page contract and refused to sign. They groused about allegedly exorbitant interest rates. It got old. Once again, small-minded lawyers and ill-thought-out laws hampered my free-market thinking."

Ryan typed something in his laptop. "What did you do then?"

Joshua's smile was like a beacon, even in the overly bright room. "One day, the light came on. If I couldn't legally *lend* money to catastrophically injured people for a percentage of their recoveries, why couldn't I just *purchase* a property right in the lawsuit? If the injured party lost the case, my property right would be worth zero. But if they won, they would have lots of money. And my contracts could force an automatic resale of the property rights back to the injured party for a predetermined amount, based on a "schedule of payments" fully detailed in footnotes on page 38 of my contract."

Ryan cringed. "What did all the lawyers say about that?"

"No laws or regulations even addressed such a deal." Joshua smiled again. "None outlawed it. I don't think anyone had even thought of the idea before. So there were absolutely no regulations limiting how much I could charge in my "schedule of payments." Bottom line: No law stopped me from taking big, rightful profits through my JFC contracts. Not only that, but I could legally market my product directly to disadvantaged, severely injured people who needed help. And then use my finely tuned marketing skills to make the deal. It was a thing of beauty—for me and the free market."

"Sounds like it," said Ryan, nodding his head, then smiling. "Got to tell you, I'm so happy to be working here. Before I was always nose to the grindstone and getting nowhere. Yes, a Harvard MBA, and at 26—CCO of a Fortune 500 company, but miserable. Really miserable."

Joshua twitched. "CCO?"

"Chief Compliance Officer. In charge of making sure the company complied with all federal regulations. And yes, it was as bad as it sounds. Worse. I was trapped in a 200K-a-year mind-numbing corporate job. I hated it. Then, I read that article about you in the *Wall Street Journal*. And well, here I am, ready to work as hard as I can and learn as much as possible from you."

Joshua cracked a smile, thinking to himself, *I wish I had ten more like him.* Then, he stared intently at Ryan. "And you will. You will. I promise. Follow me. Do as I say, and a whole new world will open up. But right now, let's get back to my memoir. Where was I?"

Ryan looked down at his notes. "Using hedge fund money. To buy up property rights in lawsuits brought by desperate, severely injured people. Brilliant."

"Yes. And with only hedge fund money at risk, I was able to pull in huge fees, and still kick back principal and a minimum of 25% to 30% extra to the hedge funds. That's all hedge fund investors care about."

Ryan was typing like a madman. "Did anyone ever question the contracts or challenge the set up?"

Joshua twirled his silver and gold Mont Blanc pen. "At first, a few courts questioned me. About the arrangement. But by putting money in a few critically placed judicial hands, as charitable contributions, I was able to set early precedents—opinions in my favor. My lawyers used those precedents to convince other judges my property-right contracts were valid. In fact, one key ruling established that my contracts did not violate lending-law limitations on maximum chargeable interest rates, because I was not lending money, just purchasing a piece of a potential transaction and then reselling that piece to the original owner."

"Sweet."

"Yes. Life was sweet. In our society, Ryan, the only real need is money. Everything else follows. And the sky was the limit on what I could make. Better yet, by continuing charitable contributions to the private foundations of certain judges who helped with earlier precedents, I was able to network my hedge-fund-investment cases into courts that basically ensured a win. Everyone was happy. Everyone was making money."

"Wow," said Ryan.

Joshua placed his pen on the desk. "Of course, don't mention the networked judges in my memoir. But play up the philanthropy thing. Big time."

Ryan nodded his head. "Of course. How long did this arrangement go on?"

"Things went well. Extremely well, for a little over six years. Then in 2000, through no fault of my own, hedge fund money started to dry up. Dot-com bust. Worse yet, despite the cases in front of my networked judges, I had arranged too many other deals that ended in lost lawsuits. Truth is, I never was much of a litigator. Of course, leave that out of the book too. But I had real trouble seeing whether a lawsuit was destined to go down the tubes. And by then I had an L.A. lifestyle that required major bucks. And my company, Justice Finance Corporation, had significant overhead."

Ryan stopped typing and looked up, concerned. "What happened?"

Censkey shifted and sat taller in his chair. "I hung on for some years. Sheer skill and cunning. But finally, everything came down like an avalanche. I thought about going to friends in high places, but unfortunately there weren't many left. In fact, none, except a bunch of networked judges I'd been providing funds to on a regular basis for years. So rather than give up, I leveraged that end of my business."

"Leveraged how?"

"Since the 1990s, I'd contributed hundreds of thousands of dollars, if not more, to private charities designated by my judges—you know, private foundations, non-profits set up by them, closely-held corporations, like that. Even election committees. But here's where my true genius came in. If those judges could help ensure hedge-fund-investment cases resolved for the injured victims, why couldn't they do the same for the other side?

"What do you mean?"

Censkey pointed his finger at Ryan and shook it. "Why couldn't I flip the process on its head? Make hedge fund loans—or underwrite—the corporate defendants.

"Wow," said Ryan.

Censkey chuckled. "Corporations understand risk. If I'm putting my cash on the line—not theirs—they can fight supposedly injured people tooth and nail without putting a dime of their investor's money at risk. They lose, I lose. They win, I win. They pay me back at an interest rate high enough to compensate me for putting *my* money at risk, especially as more and more lawsuits resolved in their favor. Like spending money on insurance. A sound investment. In the end, I won, the judges won, and corporate defendants won. A perfect world."

Ryan stopped typing for a moment to move back in the chair. "Where did your clients come from?"

Joshua peered at his own reflection in the mirrored back of his desk clock and straightened the knot on his tie. "Interestingly enough, most came from the insurance industry itself. They were paying to defend high-stakes litigation and were the most interested in ensuring the outcome of certain cases, cases that might set unwanted precedents and open the floodgates to even more litigation in other cases. If I could ensure the outcome, they wouldn't mind the exorbitant interest rates. So, I renamed JFC, Joshua Finance Company. The rest is history. Now, JFC is a multi-million-dollar company, and I'm, well, a very rich man."

"What a story!"

"Right. And it ain't over yet. It's still work in progress. And you'll be part of it."

Just then, Amanda said over the intercom: "Mr. Censkey, a representative from Chesterfield Insurance is here to see you."

"Ryan got to take this. Our biggest client," said Joshua. "Look, the next chapter will deal with a mess called the Silent Conflict, but we'll get to that later. In the meantime, handle your notes carefully. Our eyes only. Got it?"

"Got it," said Ryan as he closed his laptop and stood to leave.

Censkey smiled. "Show the Chesterfield rep in, then get back to your day."

"Will do," said Ryan.

§

The meeting with the Chesterfield man was short, not sweet, and very much to the point. The guy, in a black suit, black shirt and black tie, didn't even squint as he entered Joshua's office. He just stood there, eyes hard and focused, and told Joshua that Richard Chesterfield wanted a sit-down with him that evening at his Santa Barbara estate. Joshua agreed. Truth was he didn't have a choice. Richard Chesterfield scared the shit out of him. Always.

Joshua spun his big leather chair around to face the window. Maybe he could send Ryan in his place. Problem was Ryan didn't know Chesterfield, and, more importantly, Chesterfield didn't know Ryan. That's what Joshua got for being paranoid and keeping his biggest client to himself. Well, what the hell. Wasn't Joshua the boss? He'd talk to Ryan after lunch, tell him he was coming down with the flu—or something like that. He strummed his fingers on both arms of his chair and stared out at the mountains. "I sure as shit don't want to see Chesterfield. No fucking way."

CHAPTER 22

Ninety miles away, in Santa Barbara County, Hess sat proud as a preening eagle at the big table. His Eminence, twenty-five feet away at the other end, was dressed in a luxurious dark velvet robe and sat in a seat more throne than dining chair. The regular Monday lunch at high noon, a tradition for years, was the only time he and His Eminence ate alone together. It was a time for updates, strategy, and planning.

Hess always marveled at His Eminence's presence—his regal posture, perfectly styled graying hair, stern demeanor, dark piercing gaze, and even his deep, rich tan. This man can save America from itself, Hess thought. *With my help, of course.*

Just then, His Eminence's dark eyes grew darker. He frowned. "What in God's name are you smiling about? Stop it, for Christ's sake."

"I've got good news."

"All right, but stop the goddamn smiling."

"As you know, our regular suppliers have been slow to provide candidates worthy of our training and worldwide marketing. So, Friday, we took matters into our own hands. We collected five fine specimens, three girls and two boys. One of the boys has golden hair and seems special, a potential candidate for Watchmen training."

"How many in training now?" His Eminence scowled at the servant who placed a plate before him.

"We have five at camp, all between 17 and 19," said Hess. "This boy would complete our second squad. Then, they could take their places next to One through Six."

"Interesting." His Eminence waved off the food with a look of disgust and glared down the table at Hess. "Why haven't our teams come back with fresh venison lately? You know I love it. I thought you trained Three and Four as a hunting team, and Five and Six as another? It's been weeks."

"I'm sorry," said Hess. "The drought conditions this past winter reduced the number of deer. We keep trying. One team or the other goes out every Sunday."

"Send them both out until they get something."

"Will do."

"About the new lad, I've been waiting for this type of news. Let me spend some time with him this afternoon. If he's worthy, put together an immediate ceremony. That way, we can relocate him to the camp, right away, for training."

"Will do," said Hess.

§

Later that afternoon, Hess and One sat alone in the huge kitchen near the intercom waiting for His Eminence to ask for the boy. One turned and looked directly at Hess. "Sir, do you know anything about His Eminence's past?"

"Of course. I always do my homework."

"I was wondering if you could share some of it with me. For my homework, so to speak."

Hess hesitated but then told himself that he trusted One. He was the best of the whole lot. Eager to learn, and second in charge of security. It made sense for him to know. "All right, but this is strictly confidential. Your ears only. Understood?"

"Understood."

Hess leaned back in his chair, his fingers steepled together. "His parents were rich. Idle rich. Idle, except when they abused him." He drew in a breath and let it out. "Some people are not fit to be parents. For all the money they had, His Eminence's parents treated their children like, well, animals. I suppose the emotional abuse started early, but the physical abuse really began when he was ten. Same thing with his older brother, James, who took his life at 15. His Eminence, on the other hand, learned to survive. The abuse made him more resilient. He learned from it. Drew inspiration from it. He came to understand that life is all about natural selection: zebras and lions, fish and bigger fish, even humans. It's a food chain where those at the top thrive and those below get eaten. Those who exploit and those who are exploited. All life is divided into one of those two groups. And remember, we—" Hess motioned between himself and One "— are not zebras. We are lions."

"Understood."

"Thank Goodness, His Eminence learned to be a lion early. He practiced on small prey first. Hamsters and the like. His parents, content with their own perversions, kept thinking the hamsters were running away. Never looked for the pieces buried or hidden all over the property. Later, when he realized his parents were burning through their money and, if nothing was done, little would be left for him, he knew he had to act. When they were found, police ruled it a double suicide."

One's face clouded, but Hess continued, "His Eminence ended up with the real estate, jewelry, and enough cash to finish graduate school. The rest he built on his own. Just like with those hamsters, he thrived by manipulating, exploiting, or eliminating those in his way. A win-win for everyone. Because, you see, everyone has a role to play. The strong survive." He shrugged. "The weak don't. Just like on the savannah where lions rule."

One's brow furrowed. "So, why did His Eminence form the Raven Society? Where does it fit in?"

Hess stared at One. "His Eminence *and I* formed the Raven Society. A cabal destined to usher America toward a greater future, a future based on strength. At first, to structure it, I studied Nazi occult groups. You've heard of the Schutzstaffel or protection squads, commonly known as SS, right?"

"Of course."

"Heinrich Himmler, SS Reichsfuhrer, was obsessed with secret societies, occults, and rituals, and he modeled the SS on the Teutonic Knights."

"The Teutonic Knights?" One's eyes grew wide. He scooted to the edge of his chair.

"A secret society in Germany. Turned itself into a military order to fight the crusades in the 11th century. They carried their insignia of the Black Cross into combat for more than two centuries. Now think, One. What is a swastika—other than a black cross rotated 45 degrees with each end twisted further right?"

"I never thought of that."

"And there are more parallels, but then I realized the Nazi death camps broke up families. That's never OK, except for very good reasons. So, His Eminence and I eased away from the Nazi heritage. Neo-Nazis remained our friends, but not our soulmates. That didn't change the fact that we needed a secret society. It was key to creating a better America through much-needed social justice reform.

"Why?"

"Right now, One, the justice system is a game. A crapshoot. That needs to be changed from within. The Raven Society's goals are to increase efficiency and add certainty and predictability to the system."

"But how do you do that?"

"We start with judges. Ensure we get the decisions we want, decisions that reflect the need to build a society in which the strong prevail and the weak are, well, weeded out. In time, we'll expand our influence, take in lawyers and law student groups across the country. Within five or ten years the Raven Society will be self-perpetuating. We'll have created a behind-the-scenes network with the ability to shift the law and judicial decisions to where they should be. No more games, just results."

One was quiet for a moment. "I see, I think. But why choose the raven as a symbol?"

Hess smiled. "Ravens are incredibly smart, among the smartest of all birds. They're powerful, territorial, and are associated with mystery and death. They tower over their lesser brethren—like the crows and magpies of the world. Yes, they're basically loners—one or two at most—but when banded together in larger numbers, they inspire awe and fear. That's why a group of ravens is called a conspiracy. On top of all that, they're manipulative, opportunistic, and flexible. They're not birds of prey who just hunt meat, but rather they can survive on seeds, grain, and berries when fresh or decaying flesh is unavailable."

One nodded. "So, they're survivors."

"Exactly. They do what it takes to thrive."

One was quiet for quite a while, obviously thinking over all Hess had said. "OK. I think I understand. Just one more question, please?"

"Go ahead."

"Why does the Raven Society just target judges? What about juries? Don't they get in the way?"

Hess laughed, a rare sound that jangled in the room. "Goddamnit One, that's three questions. But definitely three good ones."

One's cheeks actually flushed at the unusual compliment. "Thank you, Herr Hess."

"First, judges can manipulate jurors, who look up to them— figuratively and literally—as the most important neutral person in the courtroom. So, judges have outsized importance during a trial. They can easily turn a jury against one party or the other with pre-trial orders, evidentiary rulings, facial expressions disapproving of a party or her witnesses, general attitude toward a party, her witnesses or even her lawyer, tone of voice, and other tricks. And if those tactics don't work, there's always the appeals process where other judges—without the bother of jurors being involved—simply overturn the jury decisions."

"But what about truth?"

Hess stood and stared down at One. "Truth? Truth? Truth is defined as what serves the Society. Don't ever forget that."

One stared at a spot on the floor between his boots. "Yes, Herr Hess."

"Look, it's simple. Power in the judicial system rests with judges. That's why we must control them."

One glanced up quickly and then back down at the floor. "But how do we do that?"

"Well, there are only so many judges for sale. Greed goes only so far. After that, we coerce, threaten, exploit. As His Eminence likes to say: Find weaknesses; impose your will."

At that very moment, the voice of His Eminence thundered through the intercom. "Bring the golden-haired boy." Hess rushed to his study while One fetched the boy from the basement. When Hess arrived, the velvet drapes in the room were drawn, and the only light came from the single desk lamp to His Eminence's right. "Sit him there," His Eminence pointed at the left chair in front of his huge desk.

Four minutes later, after One brought in and sat the boy, he and Hess silently left the room. Hess was smiling. Again, he was ahead of things. He knew the golden-haired boy would be worthy and therefore he'd already made arrangements for a Tuesday night ceremony in the Great Room, right after the Board meeting. He had notified the participants, directed One and the other Watchmen to set up the room, and ordered the vestments prepared by Two and Three. In their earliest ceremonies, Hess had argued against using vestments, but His Eminence insisted. "Makes everyone feel part of a special team," he had said. "After all we can't control facts, but we can control feelings. That's why cults work."

§

Hess was summoned back to the study twenty minutes later. The room was still soaked in dark shadows, but the velvet curtains had been retracted. His Eminence, sitting in his black leather chair with its gold-plated seatback, turned to look at Hess as he entered the room. The boy, standing now, staring straight ahead, said nothing.

"He is worthy. Prepare him and make arrangements for the ceremony. Tomorrow, 9 p.m., after the Board meeting. I want everyone there."

CHAPTER 23

Ridge hated staff meetings. Too much talk. Not enough action. But like birth and death, they were part of life, and it had been too long since the last one. So, at 4:15 p.m. on Monday afternoon, when Terry returned from San Diego, Ridge gathered everyone—lawyers, paralegals, staff and interns—in the conference room.

Kate summarized case activities over the last two weeks and reviewed the upcoming week's calendar, while Ridge answered questions and posed others to the team. Ridge broke up the meeting at 5 p.m., but asked Terry to stick around.

When everyone had gone, Ridge sat down across the table from Terry. "Don't be blabbing this to Jayne or the others, but yesterday I flew up to Goleta. To check out 66 Sixteen Road."

"You what?" Terry jumped to his feet and slapped his hands on the table. "Solo? You've finally gone out of your goddamned mind. How many times do I say it? Unnecessary risks get people hurt."

Ridge motioned for Terry to sit down. "Sometimes, compadre, taking unnecessary risks is necessary. We've got to know more about that address. It's the only lead to Hulk and what the sonofabitch is up to."

"For God's sake." Terry groaned, rubbed his forehead, and sat back down heavily in his seat. "You couldn't wait for me, or Dan, or someone to go with you?"

"You were in San Diego. And Goleta is way outside Dan's jurisdiction at LAPD. Anyway, it was just to look. That's all. But one thing led to another and, well, I have some photos to show you." Using the overhead digital projector and drop-screen in the conference room, Ridge went through the pictures with Terry, explaining each. When finished with the photos, Ridge turned to Terry and mentioned the two guys and guns.

"Jesus, you fucking idiot. Two guys with rifles? You could have been killed! Sometimes you make me so goddamn mad."

"Calm down. Forget the rifles. Let's talk about what you, Super Sleuth, see in these photos."

Terry sighed. "Not much, other than someone liked dogs. Not to cuddle, maybe, but to hunt? Maybe they kept hunting dogs in the barn? That's not so unusual."

Ridge leaned his elbows on the table. "Maybe, but you know what my first thought was? The cages reminded me of the ones used in Southeast Asia by both the Communists and the CIA to soften up prisoners. Before the hard questions."

"CIA? But they can't operate in the U.S."

Ridge raised his eyebrows. They both knew that since 1981, the CIA could collect foreign intelligence information on U.S. soil. No harm, no foul. And since 9/11, the CIA could conduct specific counterintelligence activities within the United States. Today, they were an integral part of the FBI's terrorism task forces in more than 50 U.S. cities, including L.A.

Terry leaned forward. "What? Do you seriously think the CIA is involved with anything at 66 Sixteen Road?"

"No. Just mentioning that the dog cage arrangement, without dogs, looked familiar."

Terry nodded slowly and looked at his notes. "Okay, keeping that in mind, let's get back to the evidence. I did spot a few suspicious things."

Terry picked up the projector's remote and went back to the first photo. "First, look at the inside of the door. It has two bolt locks up high near the top. Why two? Why any? Why high up on the door? I mean—the locks are located in a way that only a very tall person could reach them. Why?"

Ridge raised his eyebrows. "Go on."

"Unless they're really smart dogs, one bolt lock four feet from the ground should do the trick, don't you think?"

"OK. What else?" Ridge said with a nod.

"Well, sometimes it's what you don't see that's important."

"OK. What don't you see?"

"I expected to see dog fur in the cages at least. Or on the cot and stuffed chair. Look closely," Terry pointed at the photo. "See any? Unless they have a giant vacuum hidden in the room someplace, that makes no sense."

"Two bolts up high and no dog hair. Got it."

"Got what? Bottom line is we have no idea where we are in all this. We don't even know if that address is real or connected in any way to the Hulk."

"What's your recommendation?"

Terry clicked off the projector. "I need to do some serious homework. On the ground in Goleta. No direct confrontations. I'll just drive up tomorrow, nose around public records, and maybe talk to a few cops."

"OK, and I'll stay put until you get us something more to work with."

"Roger that—I hope."

Ridge checked his watch. "Hey, it's almost 5:30. Let's get an early dinner. Then afterwards, I'll pick up Jayne at LAX."

"OK. And if you promise to stay out of trouble, I'll pick up the tab."

"Roger that," said Ridge, crossing fingers behind his back.

CHAPTER 24

Joshua Censkey had to do something. The clock was ticking. So, at 5:45 p.m. on Monday, sitting behind his big desk in downtown L.A., he asked Ryan to come into his office .

The young man stepped in and Joshua surveyed him. Tall, good looking, smart. He was a good right-hand man and Joshua trusted him. Still, he felt bad throwing this potential shit storm in the boy's lap. "Ryan, I hate to do this to you, but I'm not feeling well."

"Really? You're never sick. Was it something you ate for lunch?"

"Maybe. Look, I know it's inconvenient, but I've got a critical meeting tonight with our biggest client and I can't show up sick but I can't not go, either. What do you say to being my representative? Find out what the client wants."

"Me?" Ryan was beaming. "I'd be honored."

Joshua exhaled. The hardest part was over. "Don't be too honored," he said with a short laugh. "Dick Chesterfield is the biggest Dick since Richard Nixon. Maybe more so. He's the Almighty God of the insurance industry. He knows it and he acts like it. And he takes no prisoners. He has more influence and surrounds himself with more muscle than a Mafia Don."

"Richard Chesterfield?" Ryan's eyes went wide. "Is he really Mafia?"

"He's more powerful than that. Remember the dot-com bust in 2000? Chesterfield, at the center of insurance and banking, had invested too heavily in upstart online businesses and was headed down the tubes along with all the other businesses going bust. Chapter 11 was definitely in his future. But he single-handedly convinced both Republican and Democratic administrations to bail out his insurance conglomerate. Too big to fail was his mantra."

"Was it? Too big to fail?"

Joshua nodded. "Probably. If Chesterfield went belly up, pension programs, annuities, money markets and more would have crashed across America, even skyscrapers."

Ryan looked stupefied. "Skyscrapers, how?"

"Who do you think owns them? New York, Chicago, L.A., every big city."

"Banks?"

"Banks *and* insurance companies. If one goes down, the other goes down. If they both go down, everything they own—including skyscrapers—goes to seed. Richard Chesterfield's empire touches every part of the economy. He's a zillionaire now. American Royalty."

"How did you first meet him?"

"Six years ago, when we renamed ourselves, Joshua Finance Company. Chesterfield became our first and biggest client. Still is. The man is a control freak, so when we explained we could minimize his corporate risk profile and ensure favorable outcomes by tapping into our judicial network, he signed on immediately."

"So, where's the downside? The more we meet with him, the more business, right?"

"First of all, Chesterfield is a Royal Ass Pain, with capital letters. Worse, like I said, he's a control freak. No—he's out-of-control. Say the wrong thing, look at him funny, and it's over. The business, maybe even you. Like I said, he surrounds himself with muscle."

Ryan blanched. "Mr. Censkey, I don't think I'm ready for this. What if we went together this first time?"

Joshua stood and went to stand by the window, looking out toward the ocean. "That would go over like a lead balloon, which might be attached to us just before the splash. When Chesterfield orders someone to report to him, that person better not show up with company. It's one thing if I checked into a hospital and sent you in alone, but for us to show up together—that would be a train wreck. And asking him if you could come along would be useless. At this point in life, he almost always stays at his mansion. Meets with as few people as possible. Has no interest in meeting more."

"Mr. Censkey, it sounds like Chesterfield won't be happy with anyone but you. I'd be a poor substitute and it sounds like it would really, frankly, piss him off."

Joshua braced a fist against the giant window and lowered his head to rest against it. "You're right. Unfortunately, you're exactly right."

§

The drive to Santa Barbara took almost two and a half hours. Joshua approached the giant black gates, glad he'd driven his new Jaguar. Anything less and he'd look like a pauper pulling up to the huge house. Then Joshua spotted a small black panel on a post at the side of the gate. He stopped next to it and rolled down his window. Before he could say anything, a deep voice bellowed: "Who shall I say is calling?"

"Mr. Joshua Censkey. I have an 8:30 p.m. appointment with Mr. Chesterfield."

Joshua thought the panel looked interesting. Solid black, no buttons, and a tiny red video-camera eye. He hoped they couldn't see the sweat beading on his brow. Then, the huge gates swung open, quiet as a whisper, and Joshua pulled forward. As soon as he passed them, the gates slowly closed behind. Lasers, Joshua figured.

The driveway, a quarter mile long, ended in a circle around a six-deck fountain. It would have looked ostentatious at the Louvre. But somehow, it fit here. As Joshua pulled up to the stairs leading to the mansion's massive doors, he got out, and pocketed his keys.

Sweat trickled down his back and he was thankful for his dark suit coat.

"This way." A valet appeared out of nowhere and Joshua nearly jumped out of skin.

"Thank you," he managed to reply, and then followed the man through the doors, down a cavernous hallway to a gigantic dining room. At one end of a huge table that seemed half the length of a football field, sat Richard Chesterfield. Mid-60s, distinguished, graying hair and deeply tanned. Without getting up, he pointed— directing Joshua to sit at the opposite end, about thirty feet away. He was eating dinner. Looked like prime rib. No, more like half a cow.

Chesterfield gazed up from his plate with dark eyes. "Censkey, would you like some wine?"

Before Joshua could say yes, a huge arm swung out from behind him, placed stemware, and poured a Napa Merlot from the bottle. Obviously, thought Censkey, Chesterfield isn't gonna share the 'good stuff' in the crystal decanter near him. Nevertheless, lifting his glass, Joshua saluted, "Mr. Chesterfield, to your health!" Sipping, he said, "Ahhh. Delicious. Thanks so much."

Chesterfield gazed up from his plate and scowled. "OK, Censkey. Cut the crap. And don't get too comfortable. We have business. What's going on down south? My people tell me some judge may rule against us on the Silent Conflict issue. That's a neutron bomb about to go off in the insurance industry. It could take us all down. We've already taken some critical steps to protect our interests, but this is what I want to know: How did you let this get fucking out-of-control?"

Joshua could feel the sweat running down his sides now. The hand holding his glass trembled and he carefully set the glass on the table so as not to betray his fear. "Mr. Chesterfield, I assure you, I don't know anything about this."

"That's the point, Censkey, you should know everything about it. That's why we pay you. My people also tell me there's a new lawyer involved. Take care of it. My security team has other pressing matters. Bottom line is that you better start pulling your weight or we'll have no need of your services."

Censkey glanced at his fingers, still trembling on the stem of his wine glass. "Understood."

"Let me make this clear Censkey: If we lose on this issue, it could cost billions. Maybe as much as the bail-out money I had to sweat out of the government after the dot-com crash. This isn't a matter of easy come, easy go. It's still rough out there financially. Since the crash, our sales have been in the toilet. And let me promise you, that's where you'll be, headfirst, if I hear more about Silent Conflict issues. Got it?"

Joshua felt weak. Lightheaded. Pulling himself together somewhat, he looked up and said, "Mr. Chesterfield, I swear, I'll get on this right away."

"I don't ever want to have to call you here again. And if we lose the Silent Conflict issue, you'll find yourself in a cage and you won't like it. Now, get the hell outta here."

Two escorts—well-dressed goons—lifted Joshua by the armpits and dragged him out of the room. His legs were shaking, but he managed to walk himself toward the door. Behind him, he heard Chesterfield slam a hand on the table and swear. "I'm done. That motherfucker has to go."

Has to go? What did that mean? That he had to leave his property? Or…go as in…*Shit*. Go as in….

The Jag still sat at the foot of the steps. The goons watched as he got in and, as he reached to pull the car door closed, one of them bent down and smiled. "Goodbye, Mr. Censkey."

CHAPTER 25

Jayne's Monday evening flight was right on time. After she stowed her bag in the back seat, and they both buckled in, Ridge pulled away from the curb and looked over at her. "Hate to tell you this, but we'll be back here tomorrow."

"Why?"

"A hearing Wednesday morning. Federal court in Phoenix. Kate reminded me today at the calendar meeting. I guess, with the last two weeks of crazy, it slipped my mind."

"Are you ready?"

Ridge cast her a look. "You know me, I was born ready."

She rolled her eyes. "Right."

He chuckled and reached out to take her hand in his. "Luckily, I got everything ready last month, before the judge delayed the hearing. All I have to do is review my notes and some key documents at the hotel in Phoenix."

"What time do you need to be at the airport?"

"One. But will you be OK alone? You want to stay at Jenny's? Or have Terry stay over? The apartment's been thoroughly cleaned, but still…"

"I'll be fine." Jayne squeezed his hand. "What could possibly go wrong?"

This time Ridge rolled his eyes. "Right."

§

Terry had gone home after Monday evening's dinner with Ridge. About 9:30, watching TV, he remembered he had to complete monthly billings and some case reports before heading up to Goleta the next day. So, he jumped in the Vette and drove the fifteen 15 minutes back over to the Ridge Law Offices.

After using his key to get in, he walked to the kitchen to make a cup of Keurig coffee. With no one else in the office, he left the lights off, other than the few 24/7 fire bulbs, and strolled with his coffee to the Vault. That's what the associate lawyers and paralegals called the small conference room, in the back next to the copy room. It had no windows, but Terry loved to work there. It was isolated, private, and the extra wall insulation deadened sound, just like the copy room next door. Once the door to the Vault shut, it became its own world. The room had a table for six, black leather swivel chairs, and a wooden side bar with drawers full of paper, pens and other supplies. Terry also kept two beige file cabinets in the corner. Always under lock and key, they held his personal financial and cases-in-progress files.

Terry spread his files in distinct piles from one end of the table to the other and immersed himself in his work. Like Ridge, once he got into something, he couldn't let go. Hours later, he glanced at his watch. Holy shit. It was past midnight already. Terry gulped down the dregs of his cold coffee and promised himself just one more hour.

At 1 a.m. Terry opened the left file cabinet. Put some folders away. He paused. Froze. A shuffling sound. Outside. Maybe Kate? Or an associate working crazy hours? He crept to the door and turned the knob. "Kate?" No answer. He pushed the door further open, into the darkness, and stepped into the hallway. "Shit." Dancing flashlight beams. Two guys. Black-stocking masks. A split second later, a shadow from his left and Terry's world went dark.

§

When his eyes fluttered open, Terry shut them immediately. Knee-jerk reaction. Things turning. Dizzy. He tried again. This time, he opened them slowly. His eyelids let in light. Not much. Still dark. Quiet. His head ached. Sprawled on the floor in the doorway, his only thought, *What the hell?* He lifted his left arm and looked at his watch. 1:30. Gazing around, no one. Still very dark. And silent like a tomb. What the hell happened? Flashlights. Black stockings. Damn. He moved his left hand to the side of his head. Touched it, with fingers only. Pain. Hurt. But nothing, thank God, was wet. Moving his left hand slowly across to his eyes, he focused on his fingers and muttered, "No blood."

He struggled to his knees. Looked out—and searched the office as far as he could see. Still nothing. No one. Just dark. And quiet. So he pulled himself up using the edge of the door. Got to his feet, turned and wobbled inside the Vault to the table. Swirling both hands round and round through papers, he finally found his cell and called Ridge.

§

"This is too coincidental," Terry said as soon as Ridge arrived. "Gut tells me this has something to do with the Hulk, the car chase, and the attack on Jayne."

"I agree."

"But I'll be damned if I know what."

Ridge drew in a long breath and looked around the room. "Me either."

"I checked the whole damn place," Terry said, "but I can't see that anything's missing. Nothing out of order."

"But how do you feel?" Ridge looked Terry up and down. "Dizzy? Concussed?"

"Stupid. Just sat here while two or more guys had their way with the place."

Ridge snorted. "Shit happens."

"Not to me, Kemosabe," Terry said with a grimace. "But at least I figured out what they hit me with."

"What?"

Terry pointed to a thick hard-covered book on the floor near the Vault door.

"Damn," said Ridge. "That's my copy of the Standard California Codes. Has only four of the 29 code sections, but the most popular ones. It's gotta be four inches thick."

"I felt all four inches of it."

"Most people use the digital versions, but I like the feel of the top four in one volume."

"You would." Terry rolled his eyes. "Me? Not so much. Whoever hit me probably had to use two hands to swing the damn thing."

Ridge laughed and looked at his watch. "It's two in the morning. Shouldn't we go to the ER?"

"And spend hours waiting for them to tell me I got bashed on the head, but I'm gonna be fine? No thanks. Let's just lock up. Not worth calling the cops now. Nothing seems missing, and I need to get some shut-eye. But in the morning, you and Kate should re-check the files around the office. Make *sure* everything's in place. And then please, ask her to file a police report. Breaking and entering. Assault. Battery. Robbery. And anything else you can think of ."

"OK."

"And one more thing. Have her order a new edition of the California Codes for you—this time, in soft cover."

"Roger that."

CHAPTER 26

On Tuesday morning at 9 a.m., Ridge and Kate searched the entire office. Nothing missing. In fact, nothing seemed disturbed, except Ridge's copy of the Codes and some individual folders, within case file drawers, that Kate found slightly out of place. "But that could just be lawyers, paralegals or interns," said Kate, "replacing folders in the files without paying attention. Truthfully, I'm always reminding them to do it right—so we can find things when we need them. It's an on-going battle."

Ridge grinned. "One I know you'll win in the end. In the meantime, please file that police report. I don't think it'll go anywhere, but at least we'll have a record of the B&E. Also make sure they check the cover on my copy of The Codes for fingerprints. They'll probably come up empty. Gloves. I'm sure. But still…and Kate, one last thing, let's change the locks on the outside door and add a dead bolt."

"Got it. Did Terry get a doctor to look at his head?"

"Don't think so. He said he was fine. I know he was in a rush to get up to Goleta today. But when he calls in, don't hesitate to remind him. A check-up won't hurt him."

"You know I will."

Ridge smiled knowingly but said nothing.

§

By noon, Ridge was back home getting ready for Phoenix. He packed his overnight bag with his suit, his laptop and files, a baseball cap to hide the stitches, and his aviator sunglasses. His blackened eyes were now a pleasant shade of purple, and even that was fading quickly. Still, it wasn't pretty.

On the way to the airport, Jayne reported that she'd called the vet and that Pistol was holding her own, but that Pistol, being Pistol, was restless in her cage. Worried about infection, the doc decided to keep her sedated until her stitches were fully mended. "She probably won't be ready to come home until Friday," she said.

"Can we visit her tomorrow evening, when I get back?"

"I'll call the vet and ask. I miss the crazy thing," Jayne said with a laugh. "Doesn't seem like home without her."

After a goodbye kiss at the curb that knocked Ridge's baseball cap sideways, he asked Jayne to call and check-in on Terry. "He's probably in Goleta already but tell him my return flight should get in at about 4 tomorrow. If he can pick me up, I'd like to get his updates on the Goleta trip and the Millsberg case, and make sure he's OK—with my own eyes."

"Will do. But if Terry can't pick you up, I'll be here. I don't start my next gig until Thursday." She reached up for another kiss, this time holding his cap in place. "You have a great flight and a helluva a day in court tomorrow. I'll be spending the night with Mister."

He smiled and touched the tip of her nose with a single finger. "You two take care of each other."

Ridge entered the terminal, snaked through security, boarded, and took his seat. Just as the flight attendant said: "All electronic equipment must be shut down," Ridge's cellphone vibrated. A text from Jayne: *Terry didn't answer. Left vm. Will try again later.*

Ridge powered down his cellphone and started looking for gold in the hearing docs.

§

After landing in Phoenix, Ridge took a taxi to the hotel, and arrived at 4 p.m. After checking-in and putting his clothes in the closet, he turned back to preparing for the hearing. It was scheduled for 10 a.m. but Ridge decided he'd arrive at 9. The case before his hearing involved a challenge to the CIA's authority to conduct certain operations on U.S. soil. Having just had that conversation with Terry and since he'd once worked with the CIA, Ridge wanted to hear the arguments. In addition, it was always helpful to see the judge in action and witness his or her demeanor and attitude with other attorneys before your case was called.

Of course, Ridge's focus remained on his client. It was a critical hearing in a drop-dead case-over motion for summary judgment brought by a defense contractor in a military air crash case. Ridge represented the family of the pilot who died after his plane caught fire and he tried to eject. When he had pulled the triggers on the ejection seat, nothing happened. He crashed in the desert, some twenty miles south of Luke Air Force Base in Arizona. The post-crash investigation determined that a solid-rocket motor in the ejection system had fizzled due to a design that packed too much explosive in too small a space. No question. The design was defective. Everyone, including the defense, agreed on that point. Easy case to win, right? Wrong.

Federal law gave the government immunity, a free pass, for a defective design that killed a serviceman, in war or peace. In fact, the military contractor responsible for the "nuts and bolts" design could get a free pass too. Even if Ridge showed that the manufacturer put profits before safety, failed to test adequately, and was motivated by greed, the same immunity applied to the contractor, with only few exceptions, whenever a defect killed a serviceman. Such was federal law, as first declared in Boyle v. United Technologies, a case that went all the way to the Supreme Court. Motions to dismiss had been brought by defense contractors ever since Boyle was decided.

This particular Boyle motion, all 1,500 pages of it, was filed by the defendant contractor to end the lawsuit and leave Ridge's clients, the pilot's widow and their two small children, with little recourse. Happily, Ridge's firm enjoyed one of the best records in the country proving that the few exceptions under Boyle applied in their cases. They had already won 12 out of 12 Boyle motions brought in 12 different federal cases across the nation. But this was case 13. And each case had different facts, a different judge, and its own challenges. So, Ridge couldn't ask one of his associates to cover the hearing. Next to actual trial itself, this was the most critical event in any military air crash litigation. Life or death for the case. Justice or not for the widow and her two fatherless children.

CHAPTER 27

It was time. At precisely 6 p.m. on Tuesday, Hess began administering LSD-laced sedatives to the Golden-Haired Boy.

"Because of this and my other arrangements, this evening will be a great success," said Hess to One

"For sure," said One.

"Bet your ass. A lot of pomp. A lot of circumstance, a lot of theater. And nothing will go wrong."

§

At 9 p.m., all six Watchmen, Hess, and every member of the Raven Society's Executive Committee, including prominent businessmen, judges, lawyers, TV and radio personalities, and wannabe celebrities, congregated in the Great Room wearing elegant gowns. Their ceremonial garb—only used on special occasions—looked something like Ku Klux Klan robes of old, but black rather than white, and far more expensive, exquisitely tailored, and exclusively fabricated of 150-point worsted wool and cashmere. Their matching hats weren't cone shaped, but oval, flatter in front. The tops were sliced near the head, at forty-five-degree angles, higher in back. The crown itself looked like a ski slope, Hess thought, or a shorter, stylized-version of Cardinal hats in the Roman Catholic Church. Whatever. He loved the robes, the hats, the ceremony. Everything.

At one end of the huge, dark room stood the Great Fireplace, big enough to walk into, and where a roaring, crackling fire was now going strong. Soft orange glows flickered, bounced and danced around the room. Three-foot candles on giant pedestals surrounded an altar in front of the fireplace, and large wooden tables along the surrounding stone walls were laden with fine red wines, loaves of crusted bread, exotic cheeses, and a favorite—raw beef tartare, draped in egg yolks. The aroma of food, especially the soft French cheeses and fresh baguettes, blended perfectly with the smokey oaken notes of the fire. The din of the conversations, with its ebbs and flows, heightened the energy in the room. Everyone was having a grand time, as usual.

At exactly 9:30, One and Three ushered the Golden-Haired Boy, clad only in a dark silk robe, into the room. He stumbled a bit—the drugs always put initiates in a slight stupor—and his teeth worked against the thick, black braided cord tied around his head and stuck in his mouth. On Hess' command, they lifted him onto the altar and strapped him down. The boy turned his head toward the small table next to the altar where an array of twinkling knives and other sparkling tools sat on black velvet, then he looked up at the ceiling He lay motionless, silent, but his now wide-eyed stare disappointed Hess.

An instrumental version of "God Bless America" began playing softly over the speakers. The participants stood. His Eminence entered, dressed like the others, except in blood red rather than black. When the music stopped, he sat in a throne-like chair behind the altar, raised his hands, and addressed the group. "This evening, this young man will join the elite. The few chosen to train, defend, and sacrifice their lives, if necessary, to perpetuate what we build. Let God be our witness. Begin."

At that command, Hess slowly rose and approached the altar. Using large sheers, he cut the boy's hair. Two scooped the locks from the floor, surreptitiously mixed them with fine powder of iron filings and aluminum and magnesium shavings to cause gold and silver sparks to flare when he threw them into the Great Fireplace. Several let out impressed oohs and ahhs as everyone clapped. Then, at the nearby table, Hess selected a two-foot razor knife and sharpened it on a leather strop with long, graceful strokes. With knife in hand, he slowly approached the boy. The flames from the Great Fireplace reflected off the blade. In the tension of the moment, it seemed magical. Alive. Hess leaned over and ceremoniously shaved off what was left of the boy's hair. Then he slipped on a heavy glove and walked slowly to the fireplace. He smiled, drew a red-hot branding iron from the flames and walked back to the boy. On cue, Two threw more powder into the Great Fireplace, causing huge flames to erupt. His Eminence nodded to Hess. "Let it be done."

Relying on local anesthetic administered earlier through injection, Hess opened the boy's robe and pressed the branding iron into his skin, just below the navel, until the sizzling stopped. It was perfect. A profile of a glorious raven's head, the brand was a smaller version of the Society's emblem engraved on the stonework of the Great Fireplace. Lifting the iron high above his head with both hands, Hess intoned, "It is done. Another soldier borne to the Raven Society." At that point he pulled the cord from around the boy's mouth, and everyone in the room shouted and clapped— except the boy. Instead, he turned his head slowly to the side, toward His Eminence, and threw up.

Moments later, for just an instant, Hess caught the boy watching His Eminence with a fierce, hateful, burning stare. A stare he had only seen once before, during a combat interrogation. Just before the tortured son of a bitch died.

CHAPTER 28

Just back from his Goleta trip, Terry was in his apartment on the Esplanade in South Redondo, an area known as Hollywood Riviera. He was cooking pasta and putting notes about the Goleta trip on a yellow pad. It was around 9 p.m. when the doorbell rang. He stepped to the door and peered out the peephole. Ava Best. Wow. They hadn't spoken in over six months.

Terry threw open the door and pulled her in for a hug. "Ava, my God. How are you? Everything OK? What are you doing here?"

"What do you think? I'm here to see you."

"Of course, of course, come on in. I was preparing pasta for dinner. I've got a salad. Wine. Want to share?"

"I'm hungry, but not for pasta." She turned to lead him down the hall, toward where she knew his bedroom was.

"Wait. Let me turn off the stove."

Ava Best was the girl next door, California style. Blonde, 5-foot 7, hazel eyes that turned green, blue, or brown depending on the light, and a trim, athletic body. Terry had known her for almost nineteen years. Met as undergrads at UCLA. Her name had been Ava Thompson then. It had been love at first sight. But then on again, off again. Ever since their first date. Most of the time, Terry was sure he loved her. Sometimes he was sure Ava loved him back. But all the time, he was sure they would never work. They were ying and yang. Oil and water. Bad medicine.

She was 41 now and working as a TV reporter for local Channel 5 News. She'd married once, but it lasted only two years. She and Terry had even been engaged once. But that ended in two months. Ava was, first and always, a career woman. Nothing got in the way of that.

She grabbed him by the hand, tugged him back to the bedroom, and started unbuttoning his shirt, kicking her shoes off at the same time. Then she paused and slowly, slowly, slipped her black dress over her head.

Terry, always cool and collected, nearly choked. "Jesus, Ava. You've got nothing on."

"No need for anything else." She slipped his shirt off his shoulders, pulled the sleeves over his wrists, and let it fall to the ground. Then she dropped to her knees and looked up at him, her hands on his belt. "Time to get you out of these pants."

After shedding Terry's clothes, she stood and walked him backward, then pushed him flat on the bed and crawled over him, straddling his hips. Her skin was warm. Roses and musk filled his senses. Leaning over him, she kissed up his body until she found his lips. Terry worked to catch up, pushing his hands through her hair and pulling her to him. Her body undulated above him. Slow. Then slower. Fast. Then faster. Then harder and deeper. Her skin gleamed with perspiration. Terry gasped for air, his eyes rolled back in his head, and he cried out as his mind went blank.

At midnight, he woke up and looked at Ava sleeping soundly beside him. She was in his bed. Again. Maybe his luck was changing. Then again, maybe not. He slid out of bed, trying not to disturb her, and then headed to the night-cloaked living room to pour himself a glass of red wine. He leaned against the kitchen counter, swirled the wine in his glass. He'd always loved her, but he'd never fully trusted her. Not then. Not now. He sipped his wine, stared out the window, and wondered what the hell she was up to.

CHAPTER 29

The ejection-seat hearing in Phoenix went much longer than Ridge expected. But as usual, because of all the issues involved, the judge didn't make a decision on the spot. Instead, he took the matter under submission. Ridge figured the judge planned to dwell on it, a week or so, and then send out a written order explaining his decision.

When he arrived back in L.A. late Wednesday afternoon, Jayne picked him up. "What's up with Terry," he asked. "How's he doing?"

"Good. Talked to him by phone this morning. Seemed in a great mood."

"And how are you?"

"Tip top."

Ridge smiled. "OK then. When can we see Pistol?"

"We can head over there now. The doc still thinks she can come home Friday to recuperate at home. But he emphasized that it was a close call and that she won't be back to her same old tricks for quite a while."

"All this is going to cost us. Big time. Mister too. Pistol will want to be fed first, pampered always."

Jayne smiled that wonderful smile of hers. "Lucky we have Nurse Mister. He'll stick to Pistol like glue."

On the way to Hermosa Veterinary Hospital, Ridge made another call, this one to GringoMan, their favorite Mexican restaurant in the Beach Cities. He ordered take-out: a barbeque chicken quesadilla for himself, and machaca and eggs for Jayne and

Mister. Mister loved the shredded beef scrambled in eggs. And no doubt he'd need his strength to ride herd on Pistol.

When they got to the hospital, Pistol was lying in a recuperation cage, still on medication. But when she heard Ridge's voice, her head rose slightly, and she started a slow, loud pathetic panting. Pistol, the Drama Queen. Ridge responded to her act, stroking her head and slowly rubbing her belly. Then without a warning Pistol jerked her head and jumped up, almost out of the cage, into Ridge's arms.

The vet tech rushed forward. "Take it easy! She still has stitches."

Ridge eased Pistol back down, whispering, "Good girl, but no canon-balls for a while."

Pistol seemed to understand, and laid back on her side, while Ridge continued to stroke her skin and whisper sweet nothings. Then, he and Jayne told Pistol they'd be back soon. As Ridge closed the cage, Pistol lifted her head, whimpered, and placed her head back on the pad, with a long, deep sigh. The vet tech stared up at Ridge.

"Not to worry. Drama Queen. I'm sure you're taking good care of her, but she's always gonna put on a show." The tech smiled and made some distracting noise while Jayne and Ridge quietly made their getaway.

§

An hour later, Ridge, Jayne, and Mister ate their GringoMan on the north balcony, wondering at the lights along the coast. It was a beautiful night. Reflections from the beach cities stretched over the ocean like beams of sparkling light. As Ridge pondered them, his eyes drifted to the hummingbird feeder at the corner of the balcony. He rarely saw the hummingbirds at night, yet there they were.

"Looks like our friends are back." Ridge stood and slowly approached the corner of the balcony so he could see the feeder better. "With the ninja attack last Sunday, I thought they'd move out for good."

"Not with that nest she built."

Ridge peered at the tiny tight-knit round nest nestled in the geranium pot. "How the heck do they build such a perfect structure? The outside diameter is little more than half a toothpick in length."

Jayne, Ms. Hummingbird-Expert, got up to stand by his side. "They're Anna's hummingbirds."

Ridge blinked and looked down at her. "Whose?"

"No. That's the name of their species. Anyway, the female builds the nest. She uses fuzz, then threads it with spider silk stolen from webs. Finally, she reinforces the outside with seeds and bits of moss."

"Amazing. Does this mean babies are on the way?"

Jayne smiled. 'Soon, I think. Usually, two eggs per clutch."

"Clutch?"

"Litter to you, Pistol, and Mister."

"Got it. And now, with babies on the way, we definitely need to keep this place safer."

"Which reminds me," said Jayne, "I forgot to tell you that I arranged for that security alarm system we've been talking about since moving here. The installer should arrive in the morning. Alarms on all windows, both sliding glass doors, and the front entrance. Also, two 'panic buttons,' one in the front room and one in our bedroom. If we push either one, Redondo P.D. will dispatch a squad car. I've decided not to shoot people in the future. I'm sticking with my day job."

He pulled her into his arms and tucked her head beneath his chin. "Shooting people is no fun. Been there, done that. I don't want you to ever be in that position again." He kissed the top of her head. "Remember those bolts I bought at 24-Hour Depot for the sliding glass doors? I'm going to install them before I go to bed."

Jayne groaned and looked up at him. "I love you dearly, but every time you start a home project, it goes south fast. I was hoping to get some sleep tonight. It's already nearly eleven."

Not to be discouraged, Ridge said, "You will. In security. Not to worry. I'll handle this."

"That's what you said last time, and we ended up calling a plumber on a Sunday morning."

"This is different. Promise. You relax and I'll take care of everything."

§

At two in the morning, Jayne opened the bedroom door and walked into the living room to see Ridge on his knees in front of the glass door. "How's it going?"

"There's something wrong with these templates. It's impossible to line up the holes at the center, so I went back to 24-Hour Depot for larger bolt systems. I re-drilled the holes, but the damn things still won't line up—on either set of doors."

"Let me look."

"No, no, no. I've got it."

"Eric, let me look."

Ridge sighed. "OK already. Be my guest, but—"

Jayne shot him a look, and Ridge stood and went to pour himself a double shot of Anejo Tequila, his favorite. Jayne was right, although he was loathe to admit it. He was shit at home improvement projects. He watched for a few moments as his beautiful, extraordinarily competent, good-at-everything wife studied the problem. Then he took another sip of his drink and headed into the bedroom, figuring he'd check on Mister and kick back until Jayne figured out that the Depot Bolt System template was indeed deeply flawed.

CHAPTER 30

"Good morning, sleepyhead. It's 7:30."

Jayne watched as Ridge blinked his way to consciousness and pushed himself up on the pillow. He'd ended up falling asleep on the covers with his clothes on, empty tequila glass in his hand. Jayne had set the glass on the bedside table and slipped in under the covers on her side of the bed. She didn't think Ridge had moved once all night.

She held out a cup. "Have some coffee."

"Thanks." His voice was like gravel. "Must have fallen asleep."

Jayne laughed. "Ya think?"

"Don't worry, I'll take the 'Bolt Systems' back to the Depot this morning. And give 'em hell."

She sat on the bed beside him and patted his leg. "No need. The bolts are in and working just fine."

He groaned and wiped a hand down his face. "How long did it take you?"

"About twenty minutes per door."

He let his head fall back on the pillow and shook it in resignation. "How about I make it up to you by fixing my world-famous pancakes?"

Jayne laughed and bent to give him a kiss. "A perfect trade."

Ridge dragged himself into the kitchen and poured a second cup of coffee. Slugging down half of it in one gulp, he pulled out the mixing bowl and utensils and prepared to start his pancake ritual.

Then his cellphone vibrated and the theme from *The Good, The Bad and The Ugly* filled the kitchen. Terry.

"Been talking to Dan," Terry said as soon as he answered. "The Millsberg Investigation Report will be out later today."

"What'll it say?"

"He wants to discuss the results with us in person. He's getting off night shift at 8 a.m. Wants to meet in Hermosa at 9."

Ridge checked his watch. "Where in Hermosa?"

"Where else? The Ocean Café. And this time, he said you pick up the bill."

"Fair enough. And once Dan is done, you can update us on your Goleta trip. That way, more bang for my buck."

After ending the call, Ridge found Jayne finishing her coffee on the porch. "Bad news. My world-famous pancakes must wait. I need to meet Dan and Terry at the Ocean Café. The Millsberg report is out. Want to come?"

"I would, except the alarm guy will be here within the hour. I'll settle for cereal and the *L.A. Times*. By the way, I know Terry has a surprise for you about Goleta, but he swore me to secrecy. You'll have to ask him."

"Great, keeping secrets from your husband?"

Jayne blew him a kiss. "Every marriage needs some."

§

When Ridge arrived at the Café, Terry was waiting. They walked in together and took their favorite booth in the far corner. That way they could each sit with their back to the wall, looking out at who comes and goes at the restaurant. Old habit. Defensive posture. Like gunfighters of old. And, yup, they all knew it was a bit paranoid. But it was always best to see who's coming at you.

The Ocean Café was a favorite meeting place. And a time machine. With its long counter, red booths, refrigerated glass enclosure by the cash register where homemade cakes and pies teased customers on the way out, the place was a snapshot of the 1950s. The walls were decorated with ads for tiny-screen TVs, transistor radios, phonographs, box cameras, ringer washing machines, and tank-like Detroit cars. The shelves fixed near the ceiling held vintage toasters, waffle cookers, mixers, and other cooking utensils.

A big white board featuring daily specials in grease pencil hung behind the counter. And the specials actually changed each day. Best of all, everything on the board or the menu was always fresh, homemade, and delicious. As soon as Terry and Ridge sat, Robert, one of their regular waiters, brought coffee, OJ and ice water. When Dan arrived shortly afterwards, they ordered. Ridge decided on Jack's Omelet, with diced turkey, feta cheese, garlic chunks, salsa, and flour tortilla. Terry ordered a garden-vegetable omelet. Dan, who announced he was finally cutting down on donuts, ordered coffee and a piece of lemon meringue pie.

After a fork-full of pie, Dan began. "Look guys, more than ever, everything I say here is confidential. Krug is on the war path again. All 6-foot 2-inches, two-hundred and fifty pounds of pure ornery."

"OK, OK," said Ridge. Both he and Terry knew what a bear Lieutenant Krug could be. "Mum's the word."

Just then, Terry nudged Ridge's left arm and glanced pointedly toward the door. Two white guys, 20ish, athletic builds, with similar dark glasses and black baseball caps, sauntered into the café. Each about six-feet-tall, each wearing brown shirts, jeans, and black boots. Faces, clean-shaven. No tatts. They slowly scanned the café, left and right, as if looking for someone. Ridge and Terry smiled and focused on their food.

Dan said, "What?"

Terry squinted both eyes. "Car chase?"

Ridge raised the right side of his lips, as if chewing on something. "Or Goleta twins?"

"That too," said Terry, slowly dropping his right hand. Below table. Closer to his leg piece.

They watched as Robert walked over to the two men. "Guys, sorry. Tables full right now. Want to wait outside? I'll send free coffee out to you."

"No sweat man," said one. They turned and walked toward the door.

Robert said, "Black right? They turned again, both nodded, and went outside. As Robert walked toward Ridge's table to get coffee from the nearby stand, Ridge motioned to him, "Hey Robert, those two regulars?"

"Every Thursday morning. Like clockwork."

"Thanks." Ridge exhaled and turned to Terry. "False alarm."

Dan looked lost. "What?"

Terry said, "We thought both looked like the guy from the car chase. Or maybe two hombres Eric met in Goleta. But no go. So, tell us. The Millsberg Report."

"OK. Here goes. The report comes out at 11 a.m. today. But as part of the CSI team, I got briefed yesterday. Bottom line: Accidental Death. But the background I got later from a buddy on the OC team proved a lot more interesting."

After a bite of his omelet and a swallow of coffee, Ridge said, "How interesting?"

Dan swallowed another fork-full of pie. "The word is the Assistant D.A., Rob Jones, rushed to judgment on this one. But not before he and Dr. Sanchez got into some long, intense arguments. The good doctor wanted a continuing investigation because of open questions he documented in the draft report about injury patterns, CO saturation levels, and physical evidence. In fact, the draft report had concluded: 'Death by Suspicious Circumstances. Possible Accidental Death or Suicide.'"

Swallowing some broccoli, Terry said, "Suicide? Where'd that come from?"

"With the permission of Judge Millsberg's family," Dan went on, "the lab guy stripped out the data on the hard drive from her home computer. Turns out she had something of a gambling problem. First on-line, then Vegas. She owed nearly $100K at the time of her death."

Ridge broke in. "Judges make good money. A hundred grand is plenty to owe, sure, but no reason for suicide. Not for someone like Juliet Millsberg. Don't believe it for a second."

"That's what ADA Jones said," replied Dan. "He used prosecutorial discretion to slam the book shut on the whole case, replacing the draft report with a final that concluded: 'Accidental Death.' No mention of suspicious circumstances. Not a word about suicide."

"OK," said Terry, "but that doesn't answer Dr. Sanchez' open questions, does it?"

"No, it doesn't," said Ridge, "and I hope the ADA didn't throw out the proverbial baby with the dirty bath water. I agree with Sanchez. Something's not right here."

"Terry, let's talk about Goleta," Ridge said, "Jayne tells me you have a surprise for me. By the way, I'm assuming you've been keeping Dan up to date on our adventures?"

Dan chuckled. "Assault. Break-ins. Shootings. Car chases. Aerial reconnaissance. You guys certainly keep busy."

Terry washed down the last of his veggies and eggs with orange juice. "First, I talked to a lot of realtors and came up zero. So, I called Jayne, our resident computer expert, for help. She searched Santa Barbara County property records back to the beginning of time. And that did help, big time. She discovered that Sixteen Road divides federal land that Teddy Roosevelt set aside for public use in the early 1900s. In the '80s, part of that land was sold to a private company, Coast Development, Inc., who subdivided it into fifty lots centered on Sixteen Road. But that's as far as Coast got, before going belly up in the recession of the early '90s. The land reverted to the feds and, except for hunters and squatters, remains untouched today. Virgin forest, including the areas north and east where you found the old cabin and dilapidated barn."

"Where does that leave us?" Dan asked.

"Turns out," Terry said, "I took a trip out to the old barn and found, well, what Eric found. But because it was a second look, I searched deeper."

Ridge, thinking about how wonderful his wife was, perked up. "And?"

"I scrutinized the dog-cage room. Sure enough, no visible dog hair in the cages, on the nearby cot, or imbedded in the corner chair. Then I lifted the large wooden box which looked like a table near that chair. It hid a trap door."

"A cave or passageway?" asked Dan.

"Neither. An outhouse. A huge hole in the ground with shit at the bottom. It seems to be where someone threw dog dung over the years, although I've got to say—it looked big enough for use by people."

Just then, Todd Valentine entered the café. A reporter for the *L.A. Times,* Todd was a distinguished-looking Black man in his 60s with a short beard, penetrating brown eyes, and a medium build. Ridge had known him since the late '80s when Todd reported aerospace stories from Southern California, including cutting-edge stuff about Hughes Aircraft Company, Rockwell International, McDonnell Douglas, Northrop, and others. Then in the '90s, when aerospace slowed down, Valentine switched to investigative reporting and never looked back. Today, Todd was the quintessential investigative reporter. In fact, he was everything a reporter should be—a knowledgeable, crackerjack thinker with relentless focus. Ridge's type of guy.

Ridge waved Todd over. Being less paranoid than the three of them, Todd sat opposite Terry, with his back to the crowd. Ridge introduced him to Dan and Terry, and communicating silently with knowing looks, Ridge asked them if they should bring Todd into their 66 Sixteen Road mystery. Getting agreement, almost imperceptible head nods, Ridge asked Todd if he had time to help out with a little problem.

During the rest of breakfast, Ridge brought Todd up to speed on the Hulk, the license plate, the cabin, the barn, and the attacks on Jayne and Terry. As Ridge knew he would, Todd soaked up the information and immediately agreed to help. As the meeting broke up, Ridge thanked Todd and "officially" welcomed him to the team.

With the Fourth Estate—power of the press—on our side, Ridge thought, you can't hide much longer Hulk, baby. We're coming at you. And bringing fire and brimstone with us.

CHAPTER 31

Joshua Censkey sat brooding at his desk. It was late afternoon, and he wished he had a Westside office. Sure, the views from this office were great, but Westside had cleaner air, closer ocean, and the streets didn't roll up at 6 p.m. like downtown. But the insurance companies, funding banks, and central courts, at the heart of his business, were all here, and so downtown he stayed. At one point, he'd contemplated opening a satellite Westside office, but unknown to everyone, he couldn't take on extra overhead. Everyone thought he was filthy rich, but no one knew about all his recent losses. Damn Hollywood.

A few years back, flying high with his judge-network business, Joshua had decided to diversify. Being from L.A. that naturally meant the movie business. But Joshua, not being an idiot, knew he needed a special angle. L.A. is full of losers who put their own money into legitimate productions and ended up broke. And Joshua was no loser. So, he invented "ghosting". The basic idea: Make a low budget movie. A couple of million max, using his hedge fund dollars. Guarantee one million to a fading star—someone with a name everyone recognized from years of stand-out work—but whose phone had stopped ringing because of drug use, alcohol abuse, advanced age, or all three.

Joshua figured the Fading Star would only have to shoot one or two scenes. A still from that best scene would then be used on posters and a DVD cover box, with Fading Star's name, in big letters, plastered all over them. The movie itself would always be a formula flick, with no-name actors, maybe some vampires or zombies, and of course sex and murder. That way, production costs would always stay below an additional million. Joshua called the process "ghosting" because the Fading Star was on the cover and in a scene or two, but the film itself had no substance. A ghost, so to speak. The genius of the idea was using the Fading Star's name and image to sucker people into watching the movie, or at least buying or renting the DVD. Then when sales and rentals tapered off, Joshua could pull the movie off the shelves, and repackage it for Europe and Asia. Profit after profit, with few additional expenses.

For his first film, he selected Stan Diller as the Fading Star. Diller had had a promising career. Early reviews likened him to Brando or DeNiro. He won several New York Film Critic Awards. Then, a terrible agent and too many drugs took Diller down. He dropped out for five years, made a come-back in two or three "A" films, and then started settling for second-fiddle roles in "B" grade movies. Even though he had a loyal fan base, who dug his anti-hero persona, Diller's phone stopped ringing. That was, until one day, when Joshua Censkey called.

Diller's agent, of course, told Diller to go for it. And sure enough, Diller made a million, minus his agent's ten percent, for a couple of days of work. The film, released in only eight theaters nationwide, went to DVD almost immediately. But Joshua brought in two million from DVD rentals in America alone. Then two million from sales and rentals in Europe and Asia. And so, the hedge fund got its two million back, plus forty percent, and JFC pocketed most of the rest. Economics at its best.

With success in hand, Joshua did two more ghosting productions with Diller. But then the internet reviews on all three DVDs caught up with the actor. With his career in shambles, Diller ended up shooting himself one night in a dark lonely Hollywood bar. Yes, it was tragic, but Joshua reminded himself Diller had been unstable from the beginning. Anyway, by then, Joshua had located four other Fading Stars, and productions continued. The idea was to double production, double profits, and everyone would be happy.

Then, streaming internet movies started killing DVD sales and rentals. At the same time, the word spread throughout Hollywood, then Europe, then Asia about what they called "less-than-stellar work at JFC Productions." Soon, the whole scam tanked. Joshua, who then had twenty ghosting films at various stages of production, had no market, and no choice but to cover thirty million in hedge-fund investments already sunk in those films. If not, the hedge-fund masters would have cut off their funding for his day job, the judge network. And no matter what, Joshua couldn't let that happen.

And so, Joshua's Hollywood career ended, leaving him light on cash and heavy on brooding. But, worse, he now had Chesterfield all over his ass. If he lost the insurance company account, how would he pay off the judges? And if the network broke down, well, he'd be toast.

Joshua hit the intercom. "Ryan, can you come in for a moment?"

Ryan had barely shut the door before Joshua started in. "I haven't mentioned it before, but Monday night was a disaster. Chesterfield is mad as hell at us for not keeping the lid on the Silent Conflict case in Santa Ana."

"What did you tell him?"

"Well, for God's sake, I didn't tell him we knew about it. I just assured him we'd fix it. He didn't say it in so many words—he didn't have to—but he made it crystal clear he wouldn't lay out money, especially millions or billions, for independent lawyers anytime his regular insurance-defense lawyers faced a conflict."

"Conflict?"

"Between what's best for his insurance companies, and what's best for their client. No way that was ever going to happen."

"Did you tell him we already have an operative working the problem?"

"No. Chesterfield wants results. Yesterday. If he thought we knew about the problem and were just dinking around looking for solutions, he would have taken off my head. Maybe quite literally. We need results, now. Or it's over."

"I'll get on it."

"You better. That damn case by that sonofabitch doctor, Cho, Pao, or whatever the hell his name is. It better get reassigned to one of our network judges. Right away. I don't care how."

Then Joshua spun his chair back around toward the window, obviously dismissing Ryan. And he promptly began brooding again.

§

Joshua ended up staying late at the office. Brooding takes time. But by 8 p.m., he'd had it. He locked up and rode the parking elevator down to his reserved spot on level 2. His mouth, very dry. Then, suddenly, "Bing." The elevator stopped and the shiny stainless-steel doors slid open. Lights low beyond. Really damn low, thought Joshua. With the price of parking, why can't the fucking building owners pony up a few more bulbs?

Then, Joshua remembered. The soda machine. Seven feet high. Just left. Outside the elevator. It pulled him, like a magnet. Joshua turned, took a few steps and leaned over, peering into the glass front. Caffeinated drinks. Plastic bottles of filtered tap water. Shit. Not first choices. But damn thirsty is damn thirsty. Joshua looked down at the price in small print near the cash insert. $5 a pop. Outrageous.

Joshua backed up. Stared at the front of the machine. Then—a scuffing sound. Up high. Near the ceiling. Joshua raised his head. What...the hell? A guy. Burlap sack. Top of the machine. The guy pounced. Sacked Joshua's head. Joshua's chin slammed his upper chest. Dust filled his nostrils. Couldn't breathe. Dark as hell. Mouth, throat—sandpaper. Then, a rope. Wrapped his head. Again.

And again. Cinched his neck. Joshua tried to call out. No sound. The guy lifted him. Threw him to the ground. Joshua moaned at the impact. A fist slammed into his stomach. Joshua doubled over. Pain. Then, light. Stars popping in the darkness. God, vomit? Joshua conjured up drowning inside the bag. He choked back spew. Like chugging vinegar. Then, more rope. Wrapping his hands. Wrapping his ankles. Tying him off. Fast.

A vehicle screeched up. A door swung open. Big hands clamped down. Grabbed the scruff of Joshua's neck and smashed into his groin. Lifted him again. Up, up. And flung, as if shot from a cannon. Then he landed. Jaw and knees slamming into something hard. Air flushed from his lungs. He slid forward into a hard stop, a wall or something. He heard a slam and a clang. What the hell? Was that a tailgate? Was he in the bed of a truck?

"Fucker pissed his pants."

"Disgusting. We'll teach him manners when we get to the barn."

And then the truck doors slammed shut and someone stomped their foot on the accelerator, sending the truck careening, tires screeching, straight toward hell.

CHAPTER 32

Friday turned into a crazy, busy day in Redondo Beach. Before he went to the office, Ridge and Jayne picked up Pistol at 7 a.m. and got her home and to bed right away. Mister curled up with her, and soon both fell asleep. During breakfast, Jayne explained the new alarm system. "It's unobtrusive and works well. We tested it with Redondo P.D. yesterday."

"Installation go smoothly?" asked Ridge.

"Smooth enough. They sent two installers. An experienced guy in his fifties and a young assistant, early twenties. The assistant followed the older guy around like a shadow. Nice enough young guy. I felt sorry for him. I think he must have been in a car accident recently."

"Why do you say that?"

"Eyepatch over his right eye. A bandage around his right hand. He moved slowly, almost like an old man. Strangest thing, though, was how Mister acted."

"Strange how?"

"When the young guy walked in the door, Mister started yowling, like guttural wailing. His fur stood on end, his tail shot up, and he started turning in tight circles near my feet. The guy with the patch jumped behind the older guy. Begged me to put Mister away. Said he was allergic to cats and, as a result, they hated him."

"That's a new one," Ridge said. "What'd you do?"

"Put Mister in the den. But he kept pushing and scratching at the door. Making these unearthly sounds. Demonic. Until they left. Then, he seemed OK. Go figure."

"Probably, the guy with the patch hates cats and Mister, as only Mister can, sensed it. You know, it's his way or the highway."

"Still, it was weird," she said. "He's never acted that way before."

"Well, hopefully they'll send out a different guy if anything goes wrong with the system."

§

When Ridge arrived at the office, things continued crazy, busy. He had to start the day with a 9 a.m. teleconference with a Court in Nebraska, and then took a call from Todd at the *L.A. Times.*

"Eric, you owe me. I spent yesterday afternoon and evening tracking things down. Got nowhere with the Goleta address. But could have a lead in the Santa Barbara area."

"Fire away," said Ridge.

"Well. Coming up zero with newspapers, databases, and internet searches, I turned to on-line court records. Since the Hulk told you to get off the case, I searched your name as attorney-of-record."

"That's why they pay ya the big bucks. But not to burst your bubble, we tried the same thing. Came up empty."

"Figured that too," said Todd. "So, I narrowed my search to new filings. Found you recently substituted in as attorney-of-record in Pao v. Constant Coverage Insurance Company in the Santa Ana courthouse."

"Right, that's the case I took for Terry's Uncle Cho."

"Well, I went on a quest with that. Took me hours, but I tried to link 'Constant Coverage' to the Santa Barbara area."

"And?"

"Got a hit. Constant Coverage is a subsidiary of a company called 'Friends Insurance, Inc.' Part of an insurance conglomerate called 'King Field Enterprises.' Headquarters on the island nation of Nevis. Part of the Dutch West Indies in the Caribbean."

"OK, and that led where?"

"Well it led me to learn everything I could about King Field Enterprises."

"Don't tell me…they have branch offices in Goleta, California?"

Todd laughed. "No, nothing's that simple. But the character behind King Field Enterprises is an insurance mogul at the top of the food chain. Name is Richard Chesterfield. And guess where Richard lives? Right. Santa Barbara."

"Tell me the address, and I'll send you flowers."

"It's 100 Royal Hill. But make it chocolates. I've got a sweet tooth."

As soon as he hung up, Ridge asked Kate to get Terry on the phone, and to send chocolates to Todd. Just then, another incoming call came through.

"Mr. Ridge," the voice on the other end started, "I'm John Gryme of Words & Gryme, attorneys for Constant Coverage Insurance Company in the Pao case."

"Good morning, Mr. Gryme. What can I do for you?"

"Please, call me John. As you know, with Judge Millsberg's death, this case is waiting reassignment to a new judge. But we, here at Words & Gryme, have already fully evaluated this matter. Although we see absolutely no merit or chance of success for Pao, our principals are businessmen."

"As executives of Constant Coverage, I assumed that would be the case."

Mr. Gryme didn't miss a beat. "As businessmen, Eric, my principals have decided to offer you and your client the money they'd spend anyway on the cost of defense."

"Well, that wouldn't be much, would it John? I mean since Words & Gryme has determined it's a meritless case anyway, right?"

"That's true, Eric. But you know as well as I do that even frivolous lawsuits cost money to defend. We here at Words & Gryme leave no stone unturned in defending our clients, and we estimate our cost-of-defense at $200,000. That's our offer. Take it or leave it, Mr. Ridge. But I'm sure you realize it's a great deal for you and your client."

"Well, thank you, Mr. Gryme, for your invaluable insights and the offer. But my recommendation will be to reject it—although the final answer, as you know, will come from my client, Dr. Pao. I'll get back to you next week with his decision but please, don't get insulted if the answer's X-rated."

"Wait a minute then. Maybe we should talk—face to face?"

"About what?"

"Maybe we'll see your side better, and vice-versa after a short get-together. Off the record."

Ridge wanted to decline the offer as the waste of time it would inevitably be, but he had a duty to Uncle Cho and the court to at least explore settlement. So, what the hell.

"When and where?" said Ridge.

"How about next Monday evening? A drink, just one drink. Say at a bar near you?"

"My office is about a block from the Il Forno Italian Restaurant. Has a quiet bar on the left as you get inside. What time?"

"Say 6 p.m.? I'll bring along my senior associate on the case, Sasha Kachingski. She knows the facts."

"Sasha who?" asked Ridge.

"Kachingski. Like the sound of money—Ka Ching—with a ski at the end."

"OK. 6 p.m.," Ridge said, shaking his head. "See you there."

Ridge hung up and Kate appeared in his office doorway. "Kate, before I forget, please calendar a 6 p.m. meeting next Monday on the Pao case with attorney John Gryme of Words & Gryme at Il Forno. And Google him. Get me some background on him and his firm. And oh yes…a senior associate named Sasha Kachingski—like the sound of money with a ski at the end. Ask Terry for help if you need it."

"OK. But Eric, I've got something important to tell you. Judge Sayor in Phoenix just issued his decision, on the Boyle Motion, in our ejection seat case."

"Already?"

"Yes. And we lost. He threw the case out!"

"Shit." Ridge was flabbergasted—which didn't occur often to 'Mr. Never-Let-Em-See-You-Sweat.' But by rights, plaintiffs should have won. Ridge couldn't understand it. God. They had the law. The facts. Even emotion on their side. "OK. Go ahead and forward me the opinion. Can't wait to read the sucker."

§

After twice reviewing each and every word of the written opinion, Ridge remained, well, flabbergasted. Didn't even seem to be written by Judge Sayor, who Ridge knew from other attorneys and from reading his earlier decisions to be a thorough, thoughtful judge. The opinion was fragmented, full of errors, and to be kind, totally illogical. Seemed the decision was made first, then someone pieced together just barely enough reasons to justify it. It invited appeal. But just the same, it was what it was. The case had been dismissed.

Ridge called his client, the widow of Lieutenant James, and gave her the bad news. He promised he would file the appeal right away. Wanda James, as always, sounded gracious. But Ridge could tell from her voice, she was heartbroken. When Ridge hung up with Wanda, he called his associates and key paralegal into his office. They immediately started planning the appeal. This was wrong. It had to be fixed. And, no doubt about it, it was a clear abuse of justice.

After his staff left the office, Ridge sat, stared at his pen, and wondered aloud, "This stinks to high heaven. What the hell caused Sayor to do this?"

CHAPTER 33

Late Friday afternoon, Ridge had to disappear. The day was getting to him. So, at 4 p.m., he called Kate from the parking lot. "I forgot about a personal meeting outside the office. I'm running late, but if you need me, call my cell." Before Kate could ask questions, he added, "Have a terrific weekend."

That worked. Always positive—or at least always trying to be positive—she said, "You too! Take it easy now."

"Roger that." He cut the call and jumped into Jayne's Infiniti, borrowed for the day, and headed to Santa Monica. Earlier, with a pit in his stomach, Ridge had called the psychiatrist on the card from the hospital. He'd promised the hospital shrink he'd follow-up and complete the head-injury protocol, and his two weeks to get it done had run out. He hated the very idea of it, but had to admit that maybe, just maybe, a session with a psychiatrist could do some good. Might help with the flashbacks or migraines. Either way, it was a twofer. He'd complete the protocol and her nurse had agreed to remove his stitches.

Dr. Peters kept her office in a white low-profile medical building along 20th Street in Santa Monica. Near St. John's Hospital. Ridge pulled into underground parking and took the elevator to the lobby level. Crossing a courtyard full of bright yellow and orange flowers, including some terrific Birds of Paradise, he worked his way to the next set of elevators. After checking the building directory, Ridge exited the elevator on the sixth floor, and found a bronze wall with water slowly cascading down into a narrow trough built into the floor. Calming. By design, no doubt.

A few minutes later, peeking at his watch, Ridge signed in with the receptionist. 5 p.m. Right on time. "Good start," he mumbled and then told himself to stop talking to himself.

After a short wait, he was ushered in to see the nurse and was thankful that removal of his stitches turned out to be a piece of cake. Now for the hard part, he thought, as the nurse showed him into the doctor's office.

Dr. Peters got up from her desk, a large glass table with shiny steel legs, and extended her hand. "Good afternoon, Mr. Ridge. Marilyn Peters. I see you were referred by Redondo Memorial to finish up your head-injury protocol. Great to meet you."

In her late 40s, Dr. Peters stood about 5-foot 9 in heels and had long brown hair pulled up in a sleek, professional-looking bun. With an attractive face featuring eyes the color of almonds and a pleasant smile, she wore a stylish black pants suit and a white silk ruffled blouse under her jacket.

"Hi." Ridge shook her hand and asked where he should sit—in one of the black leather chairs in front of her desk or in one of the two modern armchairs to the right? The armchairs were positioned catty-cornered to one another, and Dr. Peters seemed headed there.

"Oh, I'm just getting some tea," she said as she pointed toward a server table beyond the armchairs. "Sit where you'll be most comfortable. Some tea, coffee?"

"Coffee, black, would be super." Ridge took the nearest chair in front of her desk. Keeping his distance couldn't hurt and the ocean view in the window behind her desk was calming. By design, no doubt.

As she took her seat, she put her tea and Ridge's coffee on coasters, perfectly positioned on the glass desktop which was empty except an open laptop computer, a small flower vase with one red rose, and two carefully placed stacks of white paper, a notepad and three professional journals. "Your wound looks great," she said. "Hardly any scarring. And that will only get better over time."

He nodded. "But there's more to this protocol than a look at my stitches."

Peters pursed her lips then smiled. "Right. Yes. I reviewed the forms you filled out at the hospital. We just need this interview to complete the protocol."

"OK. Ready, willing, able."

"Let me start with—your age?"

"Early fifties." It wasn't that Ridge didn't want to own his age, just that he didn't see the need for the shrink to know it to a specific date and time.

The doc tilted her head. "You look younger."

"Good genes. Got 'em at Tommy Bahama."

Peters' eyebrows rose. "Well, your sense of humor is intact, more or less. But look, I have good news. Your tests came back fine. Relax. We just need to complete this interview."

"I thought you said good news."

"Funny. Look, what I want to do is follow up on a few notes from the hospital. The first says you're a combat veteran. The second documents a restless night at the hospital."

Ridge sat back in his chair. "Guilty as charged."

"Do you think your restlessness was due to the head injury? Or have there been similar episodes in the past?"

Deciding he liked Peters and, since he was here, he might as well be frank, Ridge answered truthfully. "Yes. To both."

"What similar episodes?"

Ridge looked down at the floor. He let out a sigh. "Fact is, there've been problems, now and again. For a while. Headaches, insomnia, even flashbacks. To combat."

"Combat?"

Ridge looked up. "Southeast Asia. CIA. Secret War. Laos and Cambodia."

Peters again tilted her head, but then bit her lip. "Since I'm somewhat younger than you, I have to ask, how extensive was this secret war?"

"Per capita, Laos became the most bombed country in the history of the world. Still is."

Peters nodded. "How long have the flashbacks been going on?"

"Oh, about four years or so," said Ridge. "Started around 2001."

"9/11?"

Ridge stared at her. "Well, I was in New York City and headed to a late morning deposition in Midtown Manhattan. But I didn't get there. And I never related any of that to my flashbacks."

"With post-traumatic stress or PTS, unrelated events can trigger flashbacks to earlier times. Even years or decades earlier. Especially if those experiences were combat related. Have they been getting better or worse over the last couple of years?"

"It isn't getting better," said Ridge, "especially over the last couple of years. But look Doc, I need to be frank. I've never been to a psychiatrist, except in hospitals during short consultations. I don't really think therapy can help me. It's something I need to work out myself."

"How's that been going? I mean, it's been years."

He shrugged. "Like I said, not getting better."

"What if we start slow? I've reviewed your medical records. But I still need to get a better sense of you and any specific issues involved before I complete my evaluation. Remember, everything here is confidential. Let's start with your background. What's your ancestry?"

Ridge took a sip of coffee. "Half French. Half Spanish. All-American."

"What about your immediate family? Are your parents alive?"

"No. My mother was a World War II war bride, from Paris. A nurse, then a homemaker."

"How did you feel about her?"

Ridge smiled. "As a child, light of my life."

Peters made a note. "Your father?"

"A graduate of World War II, D-Day, then an artist. Designed embroidery for dresses, blouses, shirt logos, military patches, like that."

She looked up. "How did you feel about him?"

"He, ah, got angry a lot. From the time I was two until about twelve."

"Any siblings?"

Two younger sisters. All of us brought up in New Jersey. We were what they called middle class, living paycheck to paycheck."

"Did your father get angry with your sisters?"

Ridge looked down at the floor. "Not much. Not like me."

"What was it like with you?"

Ridge raised his eyes and looked at Peters. "Used his leather belts. Strapped me. Below the neck."

Peters' eyes grew wider then narrowed. "What did you do."

"Ran. Hid. But if he caught me, I never cried. For ten years. And then he stopped."

Casting her eyes down, Peters said, "Did you ever figure out why he beat you?"

"Emotional triggers—I won't get into now. But basically, he wanted to control me. I wouldn't let him. Simple. But let's switch subjects."

Doctor Peters lowered her pen. "OK. When did you meet your wife?"

Ridge smiled and pictured Jayne at home now, sitting on the porch, listening to the thrum of the hummingbirds. "High school sweethearts. Our daughter is a deputy district attorney in L.A. We had a son, Sean, but he died. Two years ago. Iraq."

"Your forms indicate you had heart issues last year."

"Right. Pains. Needed a stent."

"Do you feel that was related in any way to your son's death?"

Ridge stared into his coffee cup. "Don't know. But probably not unconnected."

"OK. Let's return to your background. Your education?"

Ridge looked up and smiled. "I got lucky. Got an academic scholarship. New York University."

Peters took a few more notes. "And after NYU?"

"Pilot. Air Force. Then a lawyer. Brings you right up to date."

"That covers the basics," she said. "But I'd like to get some additional details. Something more to work with. Let's try this. First, let's move over to the armchairs. That'll be more comfortable than staring at each other across a desk. OK?"

"I knew it could come to this," said Ridge, with a half-smile. "Sure. I'm willing to try." Peters headed to the nearest armchair with her tea, a pen, and a pad. Ridge took his coffee to the other armchair.

"Mr. Ridge. Get comfortable, please. Remember what's said here is strictly confidential. So, let me ask you, what do you think of war?"

CHAPTER 34

Ridge nearly choked on his coffee. "War? What do I think of it? Frankly, I try not to."

"That's fair. But what is your attitude toward it? As a concept."

"If you're asking me to define it, I can tell you that it's struggle for control of people, of resources. Just like all conflicts—in all aspects of life. Isn't it always about control? One way or the other?"

"One could argue that. Did you know you tend to answer questions with questions?"

Ridge smiled. "I do? I'm a lawyer. You gotta give me a break."

This time Peters smiled. "OK. Any other personal thoughts about war?"

"Oh, I have all sorts of thoughts about war. For instance, all wars are framed by an 'us versus them' mentality. I know that seems obvious. But it's more than that. It's us versus 'the other.' And going to war taught me a universal truth: All wars are started by someone spouting about the greater good."

Peters leaned forward. "Greater good?"

"Yeah. But what the greater good is for some is likely to be the greater bad for 'the other'."

Peters picked up her pen and wrote something. "How do you feel about that?"

"In war, I think the proverbial 'others' always end up being soldiers, allies, resistance fighters, and collateral damage. Including innocent civilians. In Southeast Asia that amounted to millions upon millions of people, dead or maimed, on all sides of the conflict."

Peters slowly nodded. "You've obviously thought about this a lot. But let's focus in on you. Tell me about a combat experience that's played over and over again in your mind."

Ridge raised his cup and took a drink. Then, he looked up at Peters. "Probably my third mission. CIA. Laos."

"Tell me about it."

"We were flying unmarked, camouflaged O-2 aircraft. Visual and photo reconnaissance missions."

Peters looked up from her notepad. "O-2 aircraft?"

"A twin-engine low-flying spotter aircraft. Push-pull engines— one in front and one behind. Nice thing was if bullets or rockets took out the front engine, it could fly all day on the rear."

"Did you fly alone?"

Ridge shook his head. "Generally, someone was in the right seat. Either to operate the camera pod or help with visual recon. But on this third mission, I was alone, and things got ugly. Fast."

"How?" Peters leaned forward and concentrated her gaze on Ridge. "What got ugly?"

"Well, Laos itself was beautiful. Flying low in the valleys, we were surrounded by gorgeous, towering green mountains. Long, glittering waterfalls. Where I was that day, the Mekong River snaked through the jungle. I knew when the valley twisted back to the river, my destination, Muang Phong, was just a few miles ahead. Intel photos from the previous day showed a charming city centered on multiple bridges spanning the Mekong, something like Paris on the Seine."

"Sounds lovely," said Peters.

"And then it wasn't. What I found was less than half a city. The buildings east of the river were leveled...blown up, burned out, blackened, and still smoldering. I also saw NVA—North Vietnamese Army troops with black uniforms and flat coned hats, kicking and prodding hundreds of people across the bridges to the west side."

"What did you do?"

"Shoved in throttles and climbed to gain altitude, see more, and perhaps make radio contact with friendlies. At about fifteen hundred feet, I radioed call sign, latitude, longitude, and the 'needs help' code. No answer. Nothing. From CIA ops or Air America pilots. So, I circled higher and spotted a plane down. A T-28, used by CIA-contracted pilots out of Thailand."

"T-28?"

"Really a single-engine trainer aircraft. But modified to carry machine guns and shoot the hell out of ground targets. This one, though, had the hell shot out of it. As I looked down trying to find the pilot, the trees seemed to separate. Won't ever forget it. That's what it looked like. A huge orange fireball blossomed. It was a 23mm radar-controlled gun. I yanked, banked to get the hell out of there, but the exploding 23mm shell took out part of my right wing. Down became my only direction."

"And…?" asked Dr. Peters.

"My bird strafed treetops, cartwheeled, and hit the jungle floor. I survived, but my left ankle got mangled, like being shocked by live wires. I got outta the cockpit, grabbed my AR-15 rifle and dragged myself away."

"And then?"

"Yeah. My adrenaline was pumping, and I managed to crawl about thirty yards. Began burying myself in jungle growth, happy that survival training in the Philippines taught me how to disappear. But then I realized, my bandolier with extra AR-15 magazines and my .38 Special pistol were still in the plane. The prospect of being an NVA prisoner-of-war in a bamboo cage somewhere didn't set well. So, I got up and tested my ankle. Sprained, not broken, and I hobbled back to the plane. My hands were on the .38 when, well, all hell broke out."

Peters leaned forward. "What happened?"

"NVA troops, crashing through the jungle, straight at me. Then, a helicopter appeared overhead. Whirl winds thrashed down, and the pilot hung out the left side firing a machine gun at the NVA. Another crew member, on a dangling rescue line, fired his gun to the right. Using my left hand, I opened up with my AR-15 into the charging NVA. Then I blasted at the others with the .38 in my right. When the guns stopped and the black smoke cleared, I counted nine NVA dead. The chopper lineman simply slipped a loop under my arms, and up we went."

"Who was in the helicopter?"

"The crew was Hmong. Part of thirty thousand Laotian mountain people who, with CIA-backing, fought our secret war in Laos."

Peters looked perplexed. "Hmong?"

"People who emigrated from south China. Late 1800s. Settled the northern mountain regions of Laos. They cherished their freedom and saw communism as a threat. The CIA recruited them to fight the Communist Pathet Lao and NVA. They became loyal allies, and fought bravely, fiercely. Always." Ridge tried to keep the emotion out of his voice, but those last words ended on a wobble.

The doctor carefully placed her tea on the small glass table to her right and turned back Ridge. "How did that Hmong pilot ever find you?"

"He'd picked up my earlier distress call. Hmong crews flew over Laos frequently for that purpose. Unfortunately, my rescue pilot and his crewman died just two months later during another rescue of a U.S. pilot." Ridge tapped his fingers on the armchair. *Rat-a-tat-tat. Rat-a-tat-tat.* "Bottom line, I'll never forget them. Or the Hmong people. But, as you may or may not know—given that you're younger than me—for what some American bureaucrats thought was the greater good, in 1975 thousands of Hmong were left stranded at Long Tien, CIA Headquarters in Laos, waiting for promised American evacuation planes that never came. Instead, the Hmong were executed by Communists, drowned trying to cross the Mekong River, or died disease-ridden in refugee camps. That image hasn't left me. Frankly never will."

Dr. Peters picked up her tea cup again, took a sip, and looked at Ridge. "Do you feel guilty about that?"

"Sure. Don't you?"

Ducking the question, Peters looked down at her notes. "OK. I can see why the sleeping problems. Have you had any extended nightmares, detailed flashbacks? Where events seem to be happening again."

Ridge started to feel uncomfortable. "Time to time. Over the last four years, especially lately. Yeah."

"Any physical cues or symptoms, before or after a flashback?"

Ridge, startled, composed himself, took a sip of coffee. "Funny you ask. It's been bothering me for years and it's kind of weird. Often before a flashback, my feet—especially the bottoms—get warm. Hot, really. And after the flashback, I wake up abruptly, in a sweat. Sometimes my upper teeth ache. Other times, my ears seem to burn. Go figure."

Peters scribbled a note, her lips pursed. "Could be elevated blood pressure. Supine position? I'd have to know more about your particular situation. By the way, what did you do after the war?"

"Left the CIA. For reasons I don't want to get into now, other than saying: Anything extreme can turn evil."

Peters wrote something down. "So don't ever push to the edge—is that it?"

"No. Always push to the edge. Just be careful not to go over it."

The doc stopped taking notes. "So what did you do after the CIA?"

"Returned to the Air Force. But it was different, stateside. I flew as a functional test pilot. Tested jets after major overhauls and in-flight emergencies that supposedly were fixed."

Peters' eyebrows drifted up. "Dangerous? No?"

"Dangerous, yes." Ridge downed another gulp of coffee. "But not like combat. It could get exciting, though. Unanticipated spins, engines that burn out during afterburner climbs, canopies that separate at Mach One speeds. That sort of thing. When you could, you brought back the bird. They adjusted it. You flew it again. Until it was safe for other pilots."

Peters crossed her legs, one foot gently swaying up and down. "Why not dangerous like combat?"

"Just me and the machines. Not head-to-head."

"No enemy?"

"That's it. And then one day, I decided to try law school. Become a litigator. At 28, I started at the College of William and Mary. Williamsburg Virginia. GI Bill."

"Why the law? Did you have a goal as a litigator?"

"Absolutely. My goal is justice. Real justice. For everyone."

Peters took down a note. "Why William and Mary?"

"That's easy. First law school in America. 1779. For me, at the core of the American dream. It seemed right for three years of study, self-examination, and thinking about what makes our country what it is. And then I graduated. The rest, as they say, is history."

"The rest," Dr. Peters said, "will have to wait until next time. And, Mr. Ridge, I do hope there's a next time. But for now, our time's up, and I have another patient waiting. I'd like to schedule our next meeting for about two weeks from now. I do think I can help."

Ridge started to back pedal. "Hmm…have to check my calendar first. Then I'll call your receptionist. But really, thanks for your time today. I appreciated it."

§

As Ridge sat in the car, hands on the steering wheel, staring out the windshield at nothing, he mentally catalogued everything she'd asked, everything he'd answered since he'd stepped into Dr. Peter's office. Bottom line, she seemed like a nice person. Competent. Good listener. But....he couldn't bring himself to commit. *I don't know. I just don't know.*

He started the car and headed up the ramp of the underground garage. Once he hit daylight, he decided. *I don't have time to do this now. Too much on my plate. Attacks, break-ins. People getting hurt. Shit. And the James ejection-seat case shot out from under us. I need to get that all fixed first. Then, maybe, maybe think about the rest.*

CHAPTER 35

At 6 p.m. on Friday, Joshua Censkey woke up in a dog cage. Drugged. Disoriented. He started to call for help. Then, reconsidered. Musty, moldy odors choked his nostrils. The room, hard to see in the dark, looked like the inside of a tomb. When his eyes adjusted, terror swamped his mind. He saw other dog cages. A cot. A well-used armchair. And fiberglass weather-proofing panels—on all walls and even the damn ceiling. He tried not to make a sound, but he must have moved, must have been heard—or seen? Cameras? The door to the room swung open. An overhead light switched on. A huge guy, with pale, pale blue eyes, strode in. Two younger bald-headed men behind him.

The big one pointed at him. "Keep your goddamn mouth shut." To the other men, "Put him on the cot."

To get out of the cage, Joshua decided to cooperate fully. What other choice did he have?

The two bald men opened the cage door and dragged him out, picked him up by his arms and feet and swung him up onto the cot. He didn't dare move a muscle, but the two younger guys held him tight anyway. Then the big man looked down at him. "Open your mouth." *What?* Joshua felt the panic rising in his throat as the big man produced a stick and jammed it sideways between his teeth. *Christ!* Then the two baldys produced a couple of lengths of rope and proceeded to tie him to the cot, cinching his head so he had no choice but to look straight up at the ceiling. All three lifted him and the cot and placed Joshua's head directly below a faucet sticking up out of the floor. The big guy twisted the faucet. To a slow drip. First one drop hit the middle of his forehead and slid down into his eye. Then another. And another. Joshua couldn't see anything but the ceiling and the faucet and the tiny balls of water as they slowly beaded and fell. The door slammed shut, and he was alone. *Drip. Drip. Drip. Drip.*

Joshua tried to move. But it was no use. The ropes were taut. No play. In fact, they cut him in so many places, any movement ramped up the pain. Meanwhile the damn faucet continued to drip. Slowly. Relentlessly. Soon Joshua's head ached. Then a migraine settled in. Throbbing pain throughout his head. Like an abscessed tooth. His eyes started to sting. They watered. Mucus-like tears pooled at the corners. He kept his eyes closed tight and the images he saw…he couldn't unsee. *I'm in hell.* Losing his mind, drip, by drip, by drip. Forever, it seemed.

Then finally someone entered the room. Heavy steps. The big man with the pale eyes came into view. Leaned over. Yanked the stick from Joshua's mouth. In a voice that sounded like Satan, he growled out, "You will tell us. Now. Each and every judge in your network."

My network? Who is this guy? Shit…whatever the bastard wants. "Of course, of course," and then in a desperate play, "There are too many. I can't remember them all, but the list is at my office. Let me go. I swear. I'll get it to you immediately. Every name, address, phone number. Everything. Anything you want."

"I want it all. Now."

"I swear. Just give me some time. You'll get it all!"

The big man straightened and turned to speak to unseen others who'd entered the room. "Bring him." Then, leaning over again, he jammed the stick back into Joshua's mouth. "Bite down."

Joshua bit down. Then three bald men untied him and lifted him from the cot only to lug him through the door and into a barn.

He watched with horror as they attached chains to his body. Wrists. Ankles. And a pulley turned. Joshua's body stretched toward the rafters. Every bone, every joint, about to break. When he finally hung vertically, chin to chest, about a foot off the ground, the big man reached for the collar of his shirt and ripped the fabric, buttons popping, exposing Joshua's chest to the cool air of the barn. Then the man pulled out a shiny stiletto knife, held it up for Joshua to see, and sliced into Joshua's chest. Frantic, Joshua tried to see how deep the knife went and what the man carved. His brain registered an 'H' and then an 'E'. But what did it mean? Bleeding, exhausted, and more afraid than he'd ever been in his life, Joshua pushed with his tongue and the stick dropped from his mouth. He sobbed. "My God—stop. I have what you want. Here. Just please. Stop."

The big man barked, "Where?"

"My pocket. Left pants pocket. I'll get it. Just...let me down."

One of the bald guys reached into Joshua's pocket. Pulled out a cellphone. He threw it to another bald man, turned to Joshua and shouted, "Tell him how to access it."

His body shook, writhing in pain and terror, he nodded frantically. "Yes, yes, let me down. I'll show him. Please!"

"No. Tell him first. You lying sack of shit."

Following Joshua's directions, the bald-headed guy eventually hit the correct buttons. He got through the passwords to the network list. By then, Joshua was ready to pass out. He begged and pleaded, but the men ignored him, focused on the cellphone. *I don't want to die in a barn hanging from a goddamn rafter.* He must have passed out momentarily because his eyes flew open when the pulley began to turn. Finally, feet on the ground, Joshua knew, only the hand of God had saved him. His whole body flushed with a strange sense of elation and thankfulness. He started to speak, to thank his captors, but the big man shoved the stick back into his mouth and slammed the rank bag back over Joshua's head. Blind and suffocating, he felt hands on him, tying his hands and legs. Someone pushed him to his knees. He stayed there, swaying, trying to stay upright, but then he could hear the men leave, and he collapsed sideways. Wrapped himself into a fetal position. Frozen in fear. Just a lump of flesh on a smelly, dirty barn floor.

§

That night, two bald men returned. Joshua heard their footsteps. They stopped beside him. One of them ripped the bag from his head, and he blinked against even the dim light. They yanked the stick from his mouth. Stuffed a rag in it. Then picked him up. Carried him outside. And threw him once again into the back of the truck. This time feet first. He landed on his ass, his head banging hard against the metal of the truck bed. The two walked around and piled into the back of the cab. The big man and another bald-headed guy were already in front. Joshua looked around. To his left, in the truck bed, sat a six-person inflatable on its side, with a 25-horsepower engine laid behind it. They took off. Windy, like falling from an airplane, thought Joshua. But at least, thank God, not the barn.

Then the truck stopped. Near a dark beach. Two of them carried Joshua. Loaded him into the boat, launched further into the waves and jumped in. The big guy steered. About a half mile out, they stopped. Tossed Joshua overboard. Then motored off.

Joshua, out of time and out of luck, had only two things going for him. First, while on the barn floor, he had loosened the ropes on his wrists and ankles. Second, he had been on the swim team at the University of Southern California. Before USC got around, that is, to expelling him, unfairly he felt, for allegedly cheating on exams. Putting those thoughts behind him, Joshua worked the ropes off. Spit out the rag. And swam for his life.

About thirty minutes after being dumped at sea, Joshua washed up on shore at a small tree-lined cove. Exhausted, he sprawled out and then blanked out on the rocky beach. When he awoke, just after sunrise, he saw two girls, jogging along the cliff line above. They spotted him. Said something to each other. Then dialed their cellphones.

Joshua concluded they were probably calling 911. With everything else shit, he sure as hell didn't need cops. Joshua pulled himself up and crawled like a lizard into the nearby woods. Through a clearing, he saw buildings. And a sign. The UC Santa Barbara dormitories. No students around though. Probably sleeping off Friday night parties, thought Joshua.

He got up. Crossed a lawn and sneaked into the first dorm, through a back door. To his left, the students' laundromat area. Again, no one around. But clothes spun slowly, over and over, in one of the dryers. Hopefully, men's clothes. Pulling open the dryer door, he got his first break. He yanked out grey sweatpants, a blue UCSB hooded sweatshirt, and a pair of white canvas Sperry Docksiders. He quickly stripped, dressed in the stolen goods, and jammed his clothes into a trash bin. Then he made his way to the quadrangle. Lucky break two, he found a wall phone in this messed up world of cellular everything. Joshua smiled, picked up the phone, and dialed.

"What did you say?"

"Collect call for Ryan Stacey from Joshua Censkey," the operator repeated. "Do you accept the charges?"

"Ryan," Joshua broke in, "accept the damn charges! This is an emergency."

§

As Joshua waited for Ryan, the fast-food restaurants on the quadrangle beckoned. He would have killed for a McDonald's breakfast sandwich and coffee. But without money, he just sat and waited. And contemplated the last 24 hours. And how glad he was to be alive and how messed up his life had become. Then, he had an epiphany, and big decisions followed, tumbling over one another like rocks in a landslide.

Sure, he'd used up all his liquid assets to pay off the thirty million in Hollywood debt. And he'd been fucked over by his number one client, Chesterfield. Not to mention, getting kidnapped, beaten, tortured, dumped at sea to die, and worst of all, robbed of his judge list. And he was an idiot for never backing up the damn information he'd kept on his cellphone, his only copy detailing the lives of each of the twenty-five judges on his list—including name, court, phone number and address, family issues, addictions, porn site use, embarrassing events, and other useful data. The information was his fallback position if money ever became an issue. Now, it was all gone. Leaving Joshua, well, shit out of luck.

So that's it, he thought. Enough bullshit. Only God knows what could happen next. Time to exit. Stage left. Wash his hands of Chesterfield. Those goddamn money-hungry judges. And all the Hollywood jerks. Most of all, whoever or whatever sent those hounds of hell who stole his list. First, he'd get Ryan to start liquidating everything. Then Chapter 11. Stiff everyone he owes. Fuck 'em. Meanwhile, he'd be long gone. Safe. But where? Gotta be far away. Somewhere he could make a new start.

Just then, another brilliant idea struck him. Bolivia! Butch Cassidy and the Sundance Kid had tried it a century ago. Their timing was off. Definitely off. But Joshua had a terrific sense of timing. And four years of Spanish in high school. In fact, Bolivia needed someone like him. Someone who thought outside the box. Someone who could interact with the power elite. Make them stronger. Richer. Still more powerful. In short, what Joshua had done for America, he could do for Bolivia. And, without all the bullshit American laws and lawyers in his way, he'd do it bigger. Better. Faster.

As soon as Ryan arrived in his Land Rover, Joshua demanded a hundred bucks. Without getting in, he turned and ran in his hoodie to McDonald's on the quadrangle. Then with enough egg sandwiches to feed most of China, Joshua hopped into the SUV. Between mouthfuls, he barked instructions. In fact, Joshua didn't stop eating. Didn't stop talking. Until they reached L.A. His last words to Ryan before getting out of the SUV were, "God bless, Bolivia! Get ready. Here we come."

CHAPTER 36

Ninety miles away in Redondo Beach, Ridge sat enjoying the late Saturday morning air on his west balcony, glad he had installed Malibu glass. The 3x3 clear panels kept the wind out, while spacing between them let salt air in, and prevented a Florida-room effect that broiled brains in direct sun. With the wind blocked, Ridge read the *L.A. Times* without papers flapping back, forth, and sideways. Sure, he could have used his laptop to read news online but, especially on Saturday mornings, he loved the feel of paper with his coffee. The scent of ink went well with his Kona blend. He even liked the black smudges on his fingers. Scrolling the web just wasn't the same.

Jayne was in the kitchen feeding Mister and Pistol, who was feeling much better. In fact, the previous night, Pistol was running around in the den, according to Jayne, until Ridge came in. Hearing him enter, Pistol stopped short. Laid her head on her paws. And cast pathetic, soulful eyes up at Ridge. But after some play-acting and a chew bone, Pistol forgot herself. Jumped for another treat. Her gig was up, and Drama Queen knew it. So, this morning, not bothering to fake it, Pistol ran to Jayne for breakfast, leaving Ridge alone with his coffee and paper.

As he leafed through the Business Section, Ridge came across an article that made his heart skip a beat and then pick up at a faster pace. The picture showed a 21st Century version of the O-2 aircraft he'd flown in Southeast Asia. High wings, twin booms, and a rear-propeller-powered engine. The headline read: New Spy Plane –

With or Without Pilot. The article explained that a new aerospace start-up, called WingX, had developed a plane which could be either piloted or radio-operated from the ground. They dubbed it 'WebBird'. Test flights were being flown at Dryden Flight Research Center on Edwards Air Force Base, near Palmdale, California. Palmdale was about two and half hours north of the Beach Cities, no traffic. Then Ridge read something else, and got really excited. The Chief Test Pilot was none other than David Lake.

Dave and he had met in Southeast Asia. Over the years, they'd tried to stay in touch through holiday cards and letters, but in the last five years, their contact had become sporadic at best. Ridge didn't even know Dave was in California. He put down the *Times* and picked up his laptop. The number for WingX popped up. And even though it was a long shot on a Saturday morning, Ridge dialed his cellphone. They answered.

Ridge went from receptionist, to press relations, then to WingX at Dryden, and then to another receptionist. Being a persistent guy, he pressed forward. Eventually, the Dryden receptionist agreed to give his cell number to Chief Pilot David Lake. A few minutes later, it rang.

"Is this the one and only Eric Ridge?" David's voice was as familiar as if they'd spoken yesterday.

Alone on his porch, Ridge's face broke into a wide smile. "Only if this is the infamous Dave Lake."

"Bet your bippy it is!"

They caught up quickly on the big-ticket items—family, friends, health and what each has been doing with his life. Then, to Eric's delight, Dave said, "Hey, we're having a major test flight today. Really a demonstration. The press will be here at 2. Why don't you come up? If you do, I promise a personal tour after the demo flight. Whatta ya say?"

"Yes, absolutely," said Ridge. "Mind if Jayne tags along? She'll love that computer flying from the ground."

"More the merrier, but, just so you know, I'll be flying stick and rudder in the air. She'll have to watch some young techies fly it remote. I don't get the same sensations, the same feel, the same smells sitting in an armchair playing with a joystick."

Ridge nodded, "I can only imagine. See you at 2."

Jayne jumped at the chance to accompany Ridge to the demonstration. So, Ridge called Torrance Airport and arranged for the same Cessna 172SP he'd rented the previous Sunday. Then, a few calls later, and with David's assistance, Ridge got clearance to land on a salt flat at Dryden. Weather checked and flight plan filed, Jayne and Ridge took off at noon. Once at altitude, Jayne noticed that in her rush she had left her cell phone at home.

"Not to worry," said Ridge. "We have radios in the bird and my cell phone is right here."

"I just hate to forget things."

"Baby, all that matters is that you're here with me."

"Don't patronize me, big boy."

"Oops."

§

Around 1:15 p.m., the vast salt lake, bone-dry, solid with spider-web cracking, and blindingly white, stretched beautifully in all directions right up to the crystal blue horizon. Knowing exactly where to land was easy. The press planes and WingX birds were already chocked in a row south of the landing zone. David sent a WingX truck out to bring Ridge and Jayne to Ops Center.

After the demo flight, Dave and Ridge grabbed some coffee, while Jayne and a bunch of reporters had fun in the control room watching a remote-control operator fly WebBird with a monitor and joystick.

"The real joy is being in the bird," said David, as he sat down at the cafeteria table with his mug of fresh coffee. "When you hit top speed at 230 mph, she sings." He smiled and shook his head in wonder. "And she's got a helluva voice."

"What else can she do?" Ridge asked, as he took the seat next to Lake.

"Well she's G-limited because of her long narrow wings. But she more than makes up for that with other qualities."

"Like?"

"Flies at thirty-thousand feet for up to forty hours. Uses power from solar panels. And shoots close-up video coverage of the ground. She also has high-powered radar and can listen in on phone conversations with the touch of a switch, on-board or remotely. And if needed, get this, she can strap on missiles. Quite a gal. A cheap date too, compared to other drones, robotic jets or spy planes."

"I'm a believer. She's got it all."

Just then, a distinguished, silver-haired man in his 70s rolled up to their table in a wheelchair. Ridge almost dropped his coffee.

David, shaking the man's hand, introduced them. "Eric, this is Jack Miles. He's Program Manager for WebBird and Director of Research and Development here at WingX. Jack, Eric Ridge. A good buddy from Southeast Asia. Saved my life once, big-time."

Ridge reached over, shook Jack's hand, and said, "Pleasure."

As David turned to get himself some more coffee, Jack winked at Ridge and whispered, "Been a long time."

Ridge smiled and winked back.

CHAPTER 37

Leaving Dryden, the forecaster had predicted "severe clear" into Los Angeles. And that it was. They could see forever. Mountains. Lakes. Cities. Beaches. Ocean. It was a spectacular flight.

"Do you remember me talking about Jack Miles?" Ridge asked as they approached Southbay.

"He was your senior CIA contact in Laos, right?"

"Yeah. The first time we met was in Paksé. Did I ever tell you about it?"

Before Jayne could answer, the plane's engine put out five or six ugly, ugly coughs. Then, suddenly, it quit. Ridge looked around. Checked instruments. Attempted restart. No go. A second try at restart. Nothing. Ridge grabbed the radio: "Torrance Approach: Mayday, mayday, mayday. This is Cessna 3-2-1 Alpha. Engine out."

"Cessna 3-2-1 Alpha, this is Approach. Go ahead."

"At 2000 feet. Tried two restarts. No joy. Two souls on board. Setting up emergency landing. Headed west. Five miles north of Torrance Airport."

"Roger, 3-2-1 Alpha, copy. No traffic in sight. Good luck."

Ridge turned to Jayne. "Cinch your belt. I see an open farm. A field, within glide distance. Furrows running our way. Should be OK. Straight down the tracks."

"Got it," said Jayne, cool and collected as always. Ridge always figured that both her parents dying young and living with a combat pilot did that to her. "Try another restart?"

"Why not?" He checked the instruments. Tried again. Zip. Nada. Nothing. "No luck. Get ready. We're goin' in."

"OK." She reached out and squeezed his arm. "Get us down safe, Batman." God, Ridge loved this woman. He was going to nail this damn landing just for her.

"Winds crazy," he said suddenly, feeling the gusts all the way down to his bones. "Damn. Glide path's gone. We're headed at those houses. South of field. No way we can do that." Ridge raised the nose and stretched the glide. But then with little choice, he banked left away from the houses. The plane dropped like a rock. He leveled wings and brought the nose up slightly.

"Oh my God. Powerlines, straight ahead. 12 o'clock."

With no other option, Ridge pulled the nose up to hop the lines. But it killed airspeed. The wings rocked. Then the entire plane wobbled in a death dance, edging disaster. A stall, then a brick. Pulling in air through his nose, teeth clenched and breath held, Ridge froze everything. The wobbling increased. Ridge held steady. Steady. Steady.

Finally, he sensed—through his butt—that the plane had cleared the powerlines. He nosed the aircraft over. Rolled right a bit to increase speed. And tricked the deadly stall. But as he leveled wings, the bird plummeted toward the ground, like a kite in a downdraft.

"Open field. Shit! Crisscross to furrows."

Down they fell, like sliding on a rope. Sucked into the ground. At the last second, Ridge yanked the nose up, hard. A desperate attempt to plant the wheels, minimize roll out, avert a cartwheel. Or worse. Thank God. It worked. The furrows—less deep than they looked. The dirt, wet. The plane slammed into the ground. Rolled forward. Jolted to a stop. Ridge and Jayne lurched forward in their seats, thrown toward the instrument panel and glass. But the seatbelts locked. Everything went quiet. Dust settled. Ridge, coughing, turned to Jayne. "You OK?"

"Yeah." She blew out a shaky breath. "We'll have belt bruises for a while." She pushed hair out of her eyes and looked at Ridge. "Next time, Batman, try to use a runway."

He laughed. "You got it."

Ridge unlatched his door, jumped into the mud, and ran around to the passenger side. When he rounded the tail, Jayne, already on the ground, looked directly in his eyes. He stopped. She lifted a fist to her heart, tapped her breast three times. Ridge, holding her gaze, did the same. Then, she was in his arms, and he was holding onto her as if the last time.

Finally, they stepped away from the plane, and Ridge called Approach Control on his cell. He reported safely down. Minimal damage. Then he called Operations Center at Torrance Airport advising them of the forced landing. A landing Ridge figured was caused by someone screwing with the fuel control system. But he wasn't going to say that just yet.

"We'll come get you and bring a truck for the bird," said Ops.

"OK," said Ridge. "The only damage looks like a bent prop. Wings, fuselage, and gear are muddy, but seem good."

"We'll send Ruben with the truck. He'll be with you in about forty-five minutes."

He turned back to see Jayne, standing in the open field, arms wrapped around herself and head tilted back as she watched a flock of birds dip and twirl overhead. He swallowed hard. A muscle in his jaw twitched. His fists clenched. His heart pounded against his ribcage, and he worked to steady his breathing,

Everything started with that damn attack. Outta nowhere. Stitches and black eyes. Set the boat on fire. And the maniac screamed at me to drop the case. But we can't even figure out which case. Not that it matters. No way we'd drop any case for that SOB. Then a break-in at the apartment. Jayne had to put a bullet in some fucking Spiderman wannabe. Pistol shot, almost died. The office broken into. Can't even figure out what was taken. And Terry ends up on the floor. Unconscious. Then a judge makes an inexplicable ruling that kills one of our cases. The widow and her children are left with nothing. No husband. No father. No justice. And I…I can't get any sleep, day or night. Now the plane, just quits. 2000 feet up. *Goddammit. Goddammit to hell. It's outta control. I mean, it's all really out of control.*

At that point, Ridge swore to himself. This was the second time in a week that Jayne could've been killed. He was damn well going to do everything in his power to make sure there wasn't a third.

So, he decided to call Terry. Tell him about the forced landing. But while dialing, his cell phone went dead. Battery out. Kaput. Ridge looked at the sky. *Isn't anything going to go right?* Then he pulled in a deep breath and caught himself. It was just a coincidence. Shit happens. Batteries run down. But one thing was clear to him, the forced landing was no goddamn accident.

CHAPTER 38

At 6 p.m., Terry headed to Santa Barbara. He'd called Ava to tell her he had to work and would have to skip Saturday night. She wasn't too happy with that. Since she'd shown up at his door unexpectedly, things had been…weird. Thursday, wearing a short black negligee, she'd insisted on sleeping over. Yeah, the sex was terrific, but then last night, Friday, she'd asked him to make the trek to her house in Hollywood Hills. When he got there, there were enough candles burning to fill Notre Dame Cathedral, and her perfume…wow. It was a wonderful fragrance, but maybe, just maybe, a bit too much of a good thing.

She'd also made dinner. Terry's favorite, vegetable lasagna. She served it with a Monteraponi Chianti Classico Reserva DOCG, one of his favorite wineries in the heart of Chianti. After dinner, the outside jacuzzi, the lights of L.A. twinkling to the horizon, champagne cocktails, strawberries with whipped cream, and still more candles. Then talk turned to marriage and babies. Well, at least Ava's talk turned to marriage and babies. Terry choked on a strawberry and said nothing. It wasn't that he was against marriage or kids, and any guy would be proud to have Ava as a wife. But this was too much, too soon. Especially after not hearing from her for six months. It was strange and Terry needed space and time to think. And, well, he was feeling a bit smothered.

So, he'd told Ava he had to work Saturday night, and now he had to make good on that. Ridge and Jayne had headed north earlier to see a buddy from Southeast Asia. So, he figured it was time to follow-up on Todd Valentine's lead and check out 100 Royal Hill, Santa Barbara. A road trip with the Vette would clear his mind. Hopefully, he'd decide what to do about the beautiful woman he'd loved half his life. Passionate, focused, and, frankly, scary.

§

Terry took the back way, Vista del Mar along the ocean, to Pacific Coast Highway through Malibu. In the 'Bu' he stopped for a bite at the Fishnet Café along PCH. Rustic outside-tables, the salty smell of ocean air, fresh fish fried, grilled, broiled or anyway you liked. The bonus? A dead-on view of sunset surfers at ocean's edge. Perfect. In fact, Terry hated to leave. But duty called: 100 Royal Hill. After following the Bu coastline, north of Ventura, he caught the 101 Freeway. It took him straight into Santa Barbara. The Vette's nav system got him the rest of the way, through town and into green hills. About 8:30 p.m. he got to the big iron gates.

A voice from a black panel near the fence said, "Can we help you?"

Terry, using his enormous investigative talents, feigned a response: "I'm looking for 80 Royal Hill. A little lost. Can you point me in the right direction?"

"Back down the driveway," said the voice, "turn right and it should be south of us, on the hill, about a mile or so."

Terry thanked the voice and pulled a K-turn to head back the way he came. He scanned the 8-foot ivy-covered cement walls surrounding 100 Royal Hill. Saw the rotating black panels, each with a red video-camera eye. They popped out every fifty feet or so along the top. The only question left: Did the cameras surround the whole property? Only one way to find out.

Later that night, Terry returned. He parked the Vette off road. In a flat-forested area about a quarter mile from the gates. He had on black coveralls, a black baseball cap reversed on his head, and a black backpack with a flashlight, infrared camera, and mini night-vision goggles. He also carried his .38 Special, a Smith and Wesson Model 66. And extra ammunition—three speed loaders in a black shoulder strap for snapping one at a time into his pistol, allowing six extra shots each. Staying in the thick forest, he walked the walls either side of the gates, realizing the video panels were indeed positioned all around. Best bet: Get to the wall, across the clearing, by crawling between cameras, and hope the field-of-view overlap obscured his presence.

When he reached the wall, it was simple to hoist up and over. He dropped silently to the ground on the other side. Through the nearby trees, a large circular structure came into view. About a football field away. Making his way, tree to tree, Terry approached. Low and slow. Reaching the structure, he peered in at the bottom of a window with black blinds. Shit. Something straight out of Disneyland. At the center of the room, a guard with his Doberman Pinscher sat at a circular console in a high-back swivel chair. Surrounded by three-hundred and sixty degrees of video screen, above the blinded windows. From that vantage point, the guard could monitor the entire perimeter outside the walls of 100 Royal Hill. Only lady luck could explain why Terry wasn't detected as he crawled through that clearing up to the wall. Of course, always better lucky than good. But then never press when you get a gift. It was time for a graceful exit.

Just then, a huge oaf with muscular arms grabbed Terry from behind. He jackknifed an armlock around Terry's throat. The oaf jerked Terry's head back, yanking under his chin. Terry glimpsed his attacker by rolling his eyeballs back into his head. Fortunately, Terry's backpack created separation at chest level. So, he kicked back, connected with a shin, and stomped down on the man's instep. Hitting pay dirt loosened the grip on Terry's neck. But just an instant. Terry pulled away, spun, jumped, and side-kicked the big shit in his temple. The attacker staggered slightly. But a split second later lunged forward, metal pipe in hand. Smashed Terry in the ribs. Solid hit. But Terry had already been back-pedaling. As soon as he regained breath, he kicked the pipe from the oaf's hand. Then Terry spun 360 degrees and landed his heel in the attacker's face. The big oaf stumbled back. Terry kicked him in the crotch. When he bent over, Terry smashed the edge of his hand into the oaf's neck. Heard the collarbone break. The man collapsed just as Terry heard a barking dog.

The guard inside yelled, "What the hell? Is that you, man? What's the goddamn racket about?" That was definitely Terry's exit cue. He ran full speed. Dog in pursuit. Terry leaped to the top of the cement fence, just as a snarling Doberman missed him and body-slammed the wall. He jumped to the ground on the other side and, despite burning pain in his chest, raced across the clearing. Hunched over. Then penetrated thick forest, smashing branches until he reached the Vette. He jumped in. Fired it up. Sped away. Back to what he thought was the safety of L.A.

CHAPTER 39

Ridge checked his watch. 1:00. Jayne slept soundly beside him, but he'd been staring at the ceiling or the inside of his eyelids for hours. The emergency landing, seeing Lake and Miles again, thinking of Lake's test flight, too much pizza, or perhaps a little of everything, he'd been tossing, turning and tacking all night. He took a deep breath. In through the nose. Out through the mouth. Eventually he settled in. His feet went warm, as if slightly sunburned, and his mind drifted to Southeast Asia.

§

Three weeks after the Laotian missions began. Ridge and Sergeant Ed Drew were in the briefing room below ground at Ubon Air Base. Normally Hal Thomas gave the morning briefing and overnight intel reports. But today was different. His boss, Jack Miles, stood behind him. Something big was up.

"Last night our crews, flying black C-130 gunships, engaged NVA in Central Laos," Hal began. "Near the Vietnam border. In the excitement, they lost track of ground position. Chased the enemy across into the Demilitarized Zone. Gunships, using huge search beams, lit up the targets. Hmong chopper pilots, flying close support, reported something very strange. The NVA were disappearing into huge cave openings. Near Hon Son Doong, Vietnam."

"Later that night," Jack Miles broke in, "one helicopter returned. Dropped in two Hmong fighters. They followed trails through deep jungles. Found openings that led one-quarter mile below surface. Inside, the caves were enormous. At one point, two football-fields-high. A football-field across. They found huge lakes. Gigantic waterfalls. Some tunnels went even deeper. Seemed to the bowels of earth."

"More importantly," said Hal, "the Hmong fighters found a prisoner-of-war encampment. Third level of the cave. Somehow, slipping below the fence, they pulled out one French and two American POWs. Later, outside the cave, they got into a firefight with NVA guards."

Miles took over again. "Only one Hmong crewman got back. According to him, his buddy and at least two of the POWs were gunned down. He lost visual on the third POW and had no further contact before being airlifted by chopper."

Jack and Hal paused and looked intently at Ridge and Ed. "We want you two to take a couple of days," Jack said. "Photo recon the area. Get us as many close-in shots of the trails and cave openings as you can. Work a grid east to west. With photos, we can do some planning. Then if appropriate, ask Washington for a greenlight to assault the caves. Those caves are probably full of NVA troops. Armament. Stockpiles of explosives. You name it. A major attack could put out their lights for months. Maybe years. Are you in?"

Ed and Ridge eyeballed each other. Both said, "We're in."

Three days later, the Hmong helicopter from the previous firefight led them to the caved areas. At daybreak Ridge and Ed were on station. They covered the planned grid in four hours. One-hundred and fifty photographs, flying mostly in a right bank, so that Ed's camera platform could point at the ground. Ed was finishing up, clicking away like mad, when a fifty-millimeter machine-gun nest opened fire. The sky filled with white streaking fireflies. The plane was riddled but held up. Then, as Ridge leveled out, Ed caught one in his right arm.

Telling Ed to hang on, Ridge banked left, lowered the nose and firewalled the throttles to pick up speed. About one-half mile from the gun nest, about to use excess speed to pop up and separate vertically from any other guns, Ridge spotted an orange signal flag on the ground. Looking at Ed, Ridge saw he'd wrapped a tourniquet around his upper arm.

"Bleeding's stopped," said Ed. "Let's do this."

So, Ridge cranked in more bank, raised the nose, and pulled a hard level turn until he again saw the orange flag. Then Ridge leveled wings and rocked them. Dramatically left and right, again and again, signaling to anyone on the ground they saw the flag and would help.

Pulling up about a thousand feet or so, Ridge turned to Ed. Got a thumbs up. Ridge jumped on the radio. Coordinated with the Hmong chopper. They rendezvoused over the orange marker. Then the chopper went in, dragging a Hmong crewman at the end of a line. Ridge banked left. Stuck his AR-15 automatic rifle out the window. Laid down ground fire, forming a wide perimeter around the orange flag. The chopper hovered at the center. The lineman slipped a loop under the arms of a man who now stood near the orange marker.

Once the chopper cleared the perimeter, Ridge stopped firing. He pulled off station and followed the chopper back to a forward operating base on the Laotian side of the border. After landing, a medic looked to Ed's wounds and Ridge went over to the Hmong helicopter to meet the rescued man.

Dave Lake looked like a grinning skeleton. White, yellow, and blue taut skin. Hallowed cheeks. Sunken eyes. Ridge learned that Lake had been shot down and captured months earlier. Since then, NVA troops had kicked, beaten, poked, and prodded him through the jungle, eventually getting to the caves. Every few days, maybe, they threw him some left-over rice and fish heads.

Now, as Dave had his first real food in months, Ridge asked where in the world he had located an orange flag. He explained it was actually the orange-colored interior of a flight jacket he had taken from a dead Hmong crewman after they escaped the caves. He also confirmed that the two other POWs had been killed that night. To the best of his knowledge, the NVA had no other POWs in the cave system. They had only just begun setting up POW operations at certain levels of the caves. The other levels had NVA troop quarters, training grounds, dining areas, explosives storage, infirmaries and more.

Later that day, both Dave and Ed were air evacuated from the firebase to a CIA-hospital in Vientiane, Laos. Ridge had mechanics help him patch up the holes in the O-2, and flew it back, gingerly, to Ubon, Thailand. Two weeks later, during a mission briefing in their hotel basement, Ridge and Ed learned David Lake had been returned state-side. They also got a confirmed report that, the preceding night, unidentified gunships had blown holy hell out of the cave entrances near Hon Son Doong, Vietnam.

§

As Ridge's eyes opened, he smiled at lingering thoughts of exploding cave entrances. And Dave Lake's grin when Ridge first saw him, right after the rescue. What Ridge didn't understand though were other nights. Similar flashbacks. Same exploding caves. That jolted him awake with muted screams. Blood. And countless body parts—drifting above the inferno.

Shaking his head in frustration, unable to get back to sleep, Ridge got up carefully without waking Jayne. He headed to the living room, grabbed a bottle of Don Julio 1942 Tequila. Anejo. Poured three fingers in a short tumbler, and plopped down on the sofa. It was dark. But moonglow stretched across the room. When he raised the glass to his lips Ridge caught his reflection in the large mirror on the opposite wall. He moved his head left and right. Then stopped and stared at the mirror. *You're pathetic, Ridge. Past time to get your shit together.* You're in the middle of a battle, and you can't even figure out who the enemy is. Or what the battle's even about. But two things are dead certain—your family, your friends are at risk, and you, you have to get a handle on this. Sleep. No sleep. Flashbacks. No flashbacks. Doesn't fucking matter. You get a handle on this. Now.

As Ridge slowly finished off his tequila, he looked back at the mirror. Held his gaze. He thought of Sean. He thought of why he'd become an attorney in the first place. He thought of that widow and her kids. Then he put his glass on the end table. "Tough never quits," he said aloud. "We're coming at you, whoever you are. And we won't stop."

CHAPTER 40

Early on Saturday, Hess gathered the Watchmen near the Grand Parlor at the big house. It was a spacious room with priceless paintings by modern masters, beige stucco walls, four long white sofas arranged in a conversation pit, a cavernous black marble fireplace, and beige, almost white, carpeting throughout. It smelled new, unused. The Watchmen stood at the entrance as Hess approached. Then they snapped to attention.

"At ease, gentlemen," he said. "But stand where you are. We don't want to soil His Eminence's Grand Parlor. I've asked you here because there's a mission that needs doing. And one of you is coming with me. Based on merit. The rest will maintain security, here."

Hess looked at each man in turn.

"Gentlemen, this is a kill assignment—ordered directly by His Eminence." He paused, focused his pale blue eyes on One. "One, I have chosen you again to join me on this mission." The other Watchmen turned immediately to congratulate One, all except Two, who turned his eye-patched face away, exhibiting disappointment and disgust. His petulance was noted by Hess, who ignored it. For the moment.

Hess said, "One, to the Planning Room. The rest of you to your jobs. Security is 24/7 business around here. Never forget that."

§

Ten minutes later, Hess joined One at the table in the Planning Room. "We leave in one hour," said Hess. "Our destination: The Phoenix area. We'll go in my truck. That way, no traces of travel are left behind. No online reservations, tickets, charge slips. Get the idea? Wear your brown boots, jeans, a T-shirt, and your black sweatshirt with the hood. Don't forget sunglasses. The desert can murder your eyes. Bring two canteens of cold water, and a sheet of clear plastic wrap about 12-inches by 12-inches. Now get going. See you at the truck in 52 minutes."

One looked perplexed but didn't ask questions. His eyes had widened when Hess mentioned the clear plastic wrap. Despite that, Hess decided to brief him afterwards, when One had a real need to know.

Fifty-one minutes later, One joined Hess at the truck. Hess had on boots, jeans, a T-shirt, and a black hooded sweatshirt. The silence of the five-hour trip on freeways and across deserts was broken only by Hess' political talk shows, "By Far Right," and "Beyond Conservative America," and a further briefing by Hess. He told One that the target was William Sayor, a federal judge in Phoenix, and that Hess had already done all the homework. Hess knew the judge lived alone, the judge's address and directions to his house. "Sayor is a fuckin' traitor," said Hess. "We contacted him through your work at the lawyer's office last Monday night. At first, he agreed to join us. Even issued a critical decision in our client's favor. Then, almost immediately, refused to do more. The piece-of-shit actually threatened to rat us out. Little wonder, last night, His Eminence gave the order. A death sentence."

"Herr Hess, does the killing ever bother you?" asked One.

"Of course not. It's for greater good. Remember that."

One nodded. "How will we go about it?"

"Because I studied him, I know Sayor. He's a city boy, born and bred. Take him out of his element, he's half beaten. Like a fish sucking air."

§

At 6 p.m., Hess and One pulled into a drive-thru lane at a burger joint off the freeway, three hours outside Phoenix. Hoods and sunglasses on, they loaded up on burgers, fries, and soda. Hess got the 'Big Drink.' It came in a large plastic-molded cup with 'Big Burger' stamped on the side. He saw immediately that One felt sorry he had ordered only a large cola. Just a Styrofoam cup, less soda, and a cheaper look.

Hess paid in cash, and not to miss an opportunity for instruction told One, "Next time, get the Big Drink."

They ate in the truck. But not on the move. Bad for digestion. Instead, they pulled into a trucker's rest stop, two-and-half hours outside Phoenix. Parked. Near some straggly trees at the far end of the huge parking lot.

"Get comfortable," said Hess. "After we eat, shut-eye. Here in the truck. On a mission, we never leave a trace—no motel register, no charge receipts, nothing. And don't even think about using the bathrooms across the parking lot. Someone might see you. Anyway we have a big desert outside for that type of thing."

As they finished their burgers and fries, One asked permission to pose a question.

"Sure," said Hess. "Fire away."

"What did you do before the Raven Society?"

"A commando. Tier One Special Operations Force. 76th Ranger Regiment."

"Like it?"

"I did then."

One's eyes grew large. "Did you see battle?"

"Saw it. Felt it."

"Where? When?"

"That's five questions. But OK. The Persian Gulf War. '90-'91. Most everyone recalls the 100-Hour War, Operation Desert Storm.

Just one-hundred hours after U.S.-led coalition forces entered Iraq, then-President Bush, the First, declared a ceasefire and Kuwait's liberation. But few mention the lead-in. Special Operations. Non-stop all-out battles against Iraqi forces in Kuwait and Saudi Arabia. I know; I was there. A commando medic. We dealt with chemical attacks, truck-mounted Scud missiles, mortars, barbed wire, minefields. Shit, we're talking three or four of the largest tank battles in American military history. In field operations, we piled up bodies, arms, legs, feet, even eyes. As Special Ops medics, we saw and did more in a few months than most doctors do in a lifetime. And eventually, we drove the fuckin' Iraqis back into Iraq. Then, 100 hours of ground and air attacks in that pit, and we shut 'em down. All over, February 24, 1991."

Eyes wide, mouth open, One was obviously mesmerized. "But why, if you liked it, did you leave the Army?"

"That," said Hess, "is another story. But here's the Reader's Digest version: On leave, returning from a Hawaii vacation with my wife and eight-month-old son. Got to LAX around 1 a.m. Then drove home. Exited Interstate 15 and took Temecula Road south. Not much lighting along that road. I entered an intersection on a greenlight. Got T-boned. A BMW without headlights. The son-of-a-bitch ran directly into the passenger side of our car at 50 miles per hour. Killed my wife, in the right seat, instantly. And my baby… strapped into the safety seat behind her."

"My God."

"God had nothing to do with it. I ended up in a hospital— shattered right ankle. They fixed it with rods and pins after sewing ligaments together for six hours."

"What about the son-of-a-bitch in the BMW?"

"Essentially unhurt. Airbag. A seventeen-year-old drummer. Returning from a gig—drunk. On drugs. His liberal-ass divorced parents let him do anything he pleased. They hired an expensive lawyer. Got the booze and drug evidence suppressed on a technicality.

Then a liberal-ass judge let him go for time served and a slap on the wrist, as if fuckin' blind to what he did."

"What did you do?"

"Quit the Army. Started drifting. A lot of nothing. No one. Then I met the friends who changed my life. Neo-Nazis. Members of the National Socialist Group. They gave me purpose, a sense of family. And helped me file a civil suit against that drummer and his family."

"What happened with the lawsuit?"

"Another judge threw it out. Beyond the statute of limitations, he said. Not filed soon enough. And then back at NSG I eventually became Western Training Officer."

"Ever hear more about the BMW driver?"

"Let's just say, he and his liberal-ass parents died in a freak accident. Those two liberal-ass judges too."

One nodded and took a loud slurp of his drink. "I see."

"Yeah, I think you do," said Hess. "But now, I need to get something done outside. So, no more questions. Just stay put."

Dusk. The sun almost down. Hess jumped from the truck into a purple-hued desert with long deep shadows, all helter-skelter, bushes, and giant cacti, standing five to eight feet high. The nearby rocks and huge boulders, even the sandy ground, had that same violet tinge. Nice night, thought Hess, for what has to be done. Then, he turned and took a large burlap bag from under the driver's seat. Hess noticed One watching, probably wondering why he needed a bag like that for a simple shit in the desert, but the boy knew better than to ask.

By the time Hess got back to the truck, it was pitch black. One had dozed off. Hess put the burlap bag in the truck bed and got behind the steering wheel. He fell asleep himself, after setting the alarm on his black Seiko for 3 a.m.

At 4 a.m., Hess pulled the truck into another drive-thru lane at a 24-hour fast food restaurant. They got egg sandwiches, coffee, and orange juice and ate in the parking lot.

"Eat fast," said Hess, munching on his egg sandwich. "I want to be in the bastard's face, before sunrise."

CHAPTER 41

They kidnapped the judge, right out of his bed, well before the first glimmer of sun broke the horizon on Sunday morning.

The judge had a pencil-thin gray mustache, and closely cropped gray hair around the back of his head and above his ears, setting off a bald crown. He was small, thin, and looked ridiculous in his oversized black sleep mask. Wearing deerskin gloves, Hess sat at the side of his queen-sized bed. He slipped off the judge's blue sheets. White t-shirt and plaid boxer shorts, thought Hess. Shitty sissy clothing. Hess put his big right hand over the judge's nose, chin, and throat, and yanked the sleep mask off with his left hand. Sayor's blue eyes bulged. Hess tightened his grip, just enough to almost choke off all air.

As they had planned, One turned the light on at the judge's nightstand. Hess stuck his right index finger an inch from the judge's eyes and commanded, "Silence. Or you die." Hess then slipped his right hand down to the judge's throat. One plastered a six-inch piece of red stucco tape over his mouth. With no hesitation, Hess pulled the judge from bed by his throat and chin, and pushed him to One, who grabbed the judge in a vice grip. Hess crossed the room, rummaged the judge's closet, and threw out a short-sleeved shirt, hiking shorts and tennis shoes. He ordered Sayor to dress and then demanded the keys to the judge's Lexus RX 300 SUV in the driveway. Once he had the keys, Hess wrapped the judge's eyes and mouth multiple times with the red tape and cuffed the judge's hands behind his back with a strong plastic tie. He then slammed a baseball cap on the judge's head, pulling its bill low over his eyes. Then they marched him out to his midnight-blue Lexus. With his sweatshirt hood up, sunglasses on and shoulders slightly rounded and forward, for any nosy neighbors, Hess ushered the judge into the passenger seat. He then walked around the vehicle, slipped behind the wheel, and motioned One to follow in the vintage truck. The Lexus and Hess' truck crept down the driveway. Then both slipped quietly into the street.

An hour later, they stopped south of Phoenix in an isolated stretch of desert peppered by rocky terrain, low bushes, and patches of slender grass. The sun, just rising, cast low-angled red rays and long shadows across the landscape. Hess yanked the judge from the Lexus and threw him to the ground. The baseball cap fell off his head, and Hess ripped the red tape from around his eyes and mouth. Obviously suppressing pain, squinting, and trying to orient himself, Judge Sayor said, "What the hell is this all about? For God's sake, what is this?"

Hess, standing over him with a gun, cut him off. "You asshole. Traitor. This is what you get for disloyalty. You don't join His Eminence, and then quit."

"Goddammit," said the judge, sitting up on the desert floor, "I issued that opinion you wanted. Dismissed the dead pilot's case. What else do you want from me? Like I said, I won't do it again. I don't care what you tell the press about my sexual preferences. Or nights at gay bars. I don't give a damn. Tell it like it is. I won't be your goddamn puppet."

"Shut up. I don't give a shit whether or not you take it in the ass. Sit, don't fuckin' move. Stay absolutely still. Or I'll shoot you in the head and bury you so deep you'll be below water level." Pointing at One, Hess added, "That's why I brought him along, for digging."

Hess handed his 9mm Glock to One, with a wink, saying, "If he moves, if he even breathes too much, shoot him in the leg. I have to get something."

Hess then went to his truck. He returned with the molded plastic "Big Drink" cup, a stick, some wire and the burlap bag. He placed everything on the ground, and walked around the objects, putting his back to Sayor and One. Shielding them from view. Hess crouched, tied a loop of wire to the stick and lifted the bag so its bottom remained on the ground. He opened the drawstring at its top and used the stick and wire to grab and lift. Then he switched the stick to his left hand and clutched with his right. Dropping the stick, he closed off the bag with his left hand, and placed it on the ground. Hess then turned to face the others. A deadly four-foot snake writhed in his right hand. Hess then squeezed the brown and black reptile behind its flat triangular-shaped head. The snake's mouth opened wide, followed by an electric buzzing sound. Then, two three-quarter inch fangs popped from its upper jaw. Hess walked over and leaned in front of the judge.

"Judge—this is a Western Diamondback Rattlesnake. This one is a bit small; some grow to seven feet. But look, it has fine fangs." Wide-eyed, both Judge Sayor and One fixated on the deadly creature.

"You can't do this. I'm a federal judge. The FBI won't stop. They'll hunt you down. Slam you in prison. You'll rot. Forever."

"Judge, judge, judge," said Hess in a patronizing tone as the snake continued to twist like a corkscrew, "the FBI can't chase what they don't know. That's the beauty of all this. And even if, let's just say, they catch me, I'll probably skate on a technicality. You know how that works, right?"

"You son of a bitch."

Hess squeezed the snake again, just behind its head. It made a guttural sound from the depths of hell. Fangs dropped from its upper jaw. "Now notice the white and black bands, just below its rattler. That tells ya it's the real thing. A pit viper. Lethal hemotoxic venom."

Sayor glared up at Hess. "Go to hell."

"No." Hess shoved the snake closer to Sayor. The judge recoiled and One jumped back, stumbled, and dropped the Glock, tripped on a rock, and fell on his ass. Hess, turned on him, shouting, "Get up you fool. Or I'll put the snake on you, instead of this shithead. And, while you're at it, put tape back on this fucker's mouth. I'm tired of listening to him."

One jumped up, grabbed the gun, got the tape, and slammed a strip on Sayor's mouth. Then he backed up, far from the snake, and retrained the pistol on Sayor. Hess focused on the judge, who now looked pathetic, like a terrified puppy.

"You know," said Hess, shaking his head slightly back and forth, "you really should wear boots and long pants in the desert. Hiking shorts. Tennis shoes, without socks. They don't give you the protection you need." Hess pushed on the snake's head. Stooped forward. Put the snake's mouth just in front of the judge's lower left leg and let go. In an instant, the snake struck. Latched on. Planted two long fangs into the judge's flesh. Sayor's screams were muffled by the red tape over his mouth. A moment later, the snake folded back its fangs, and slithered quickly through the sandy desert to a nearby rocky area. Hess watched it go. He had a soft spot for snakes. Most of them, in his opinion, didn't deserve disdain. They only did what they had to.

Hess turned to Sayor. "Damn," he said, calling One over with a curled index finger. "Look, the snake bit the judge." As One neared, the two puncture wounds were swelling, and turning purplish-red from internal bleeding. The judge, topped over on his right side, moaning.

"Here's the thing," Hess said, "the venom will destroy the tissue around the bite. Then, attack the heart muscle. Death will follow. Oh, there'll be some intense burning pain too. But here's the real problem: Death from a single viper bite can take 6 to 48 hours. We just don't have that kind of time, do we?"

One, taking the hint, said loudly, "No. We've got to get going."

"Yes, we've got to go," said Hess. "Luckily, I have a solution." Hess turned, walked back to the 'Big Drink' cup he had placed on the ground, and brought it to One. "Here, hold this. Do ya have that plastic wrap?"

"Yes. In my pocket."

"Get it out," said Hess. "Wrap it tightly over the top of the cup. Then come over here next to Judge Sayor. Maybe we can fix all this."

Hess went back to the burlap sack, stooped down, and opened the drawstring. Slipping the wire loop over its head, he drew out another four-foot Diamondback Rattler. He gripped it firmly behind the head with his right thumb and forefinger. "You see, Your Honor, our real dilemma is we can't leave you here with two snake bites. People won't believe that. And we can't leave you alive." Turning to One, Hess snapped: "Bring over the cup. Hold it dead steady. We're gonna milk the snake."

When One was set, holding the cup with both hands, Hess brought over the second snake. With its fangs extended, he put the snake's mouth around the edge of the cup. As soon as it punctured the clear plastic, Hess squeezed. The glands below its eyes shot yellow venom through its fangs into the cup. Hess threw the snake to the ground and it too slithered away toward nearby rocks. Hess removed the plastic wrap from the cup One was holding. He took a syringe from his pocket. The big man slid off the protective covering on the needle and stuck the syringe into the cup. Pulling back on the plunger, he loaded it with deadly venom. Then he turned to the judge. Approaching with the needle, Hess said, "Your time's up shithead." Then he yelled at One, "Put down the damn cup. Hold him tight."

The judge stared up in wild-eyed terror as the Watchman grabbed him from behind. Hess jammed the needle into one of the puncture wounds in his leg and drove in the plunger, slowly, until the syringe was bone dry. "Keep holding him up," he said to One. Hess reached into his jean pocket, thinking about his former wife and son, and pulled out a green-laser pointer. He quickly opened it.

Without hesitating, he fired the light into each of the judge's eyes.

"My God, I can't see! My eyes…" moaned the judge through the red tape.

"Just a final point," said Hess. "Blind justice is fuckin' no justice."

Hess turned to One. "Let him drop."

Ten minutes later, Hess determined Sayor was gone. His lower left leg had ballooned into a purplish mass. The venom had gone to his heart. Hess yanked off the red tape, cut the hand restraints, and shouted at One, "Let's head out."

"Herr Hess, one question, please."

"What now?"

Looking unsure of himself, One said, "Why shine that green light into his eyes?"

Hess smiled. "It's green laser light. 100 milliwatts. Illegal but effective. Easy to buy on the internet. It oversaturates the eyes. Causes temporary blindness. Well, if too much, could cause permanent retina damage. But I know just how much to use, based on past experiments. That way, no trace. We don't want to leave evidence—do we?"

"No, of course not."

"Bet your ass."

Hess picked up the burlap bag and threw in the tape, the stick and loop, the cup and plastic wrap, the plastic ties, the needle, and its protective cover. Then he pointed a finger at One. "Always protect the environment. The desert is pristine. Beautiful. This plastic shit can last 5,000 years. Here, take the bag. Trade it for the rake in the back of my truck."

One obeyed and then stood silently by the truck.

"OK," said Hess, "now I'm going to move the truck back two hundred yards to the road. I want you to rake all these footprints, and the tire tracks. Meet me at the truck. Don't leave a bit of evidence showing we were here. Got it?"

"Yes, Sir," said One.

Hess stopped and looked hard at the boy. There was something in his eyes. In his tone. The boy looked a bit dazed. "Getting sentimental on me? Didn't like what you saw here this morning?"

"What? No." One looked down at his shoes.

Hess' face turned to stone. "Don't be stupid. People, like Sayor, who don't keep commitments are like flies that suck blood. So, you have to whack 'em harder. Wipe them out. Death alone isn't enough."

"Yes, Herr Hess. Sorry."

"Forget sorry. Just, move it. Do your job. We still have to wipe out other blood-sucking vermin. And we've got less than two weeks—13 days—to do it. It's all got to be wrapped up before the Sunday Summit. Understood?"

One gripped the rake in his hands and met Hess' eyes. "Yes. Of course. Whatever you say."

CHAPTER 42

Ridge and Jayne had arrived for breakfast at the Best Earth Restaurant in Hermosa Beach around 9:30. The place was a favorite. Right near the sandy shore at Pier Avenue. It had sunny outside tables and terrific omelets, and although the wait could be long on Sunday mornings, it was totally worth it.

They'd just been seated when Ridge's cell went off. "Hey, Terry." Ridge said, as he picked up. "We're at Best Earth. Just got seats. Join us?"

Even Jayne could hear Terry's laugh. "Best Earth on Sunday? Order me a spinach and feta omelet. I'll be there in less than fifteen."

"Will do."

Terry arrived, as advertised, within fifteen minutes. He had on shorts, sandals, and a blue and white Hawaiian shirt. A bit summery for springtime L.A., but not surprising. What was surprising was… "Terry, are you bandaged up under your shirt?"

"That's one of the things we need to talk about. Did you already order?"

"Yup. Food should be here soon."

"OK, so I took a little night drive to 100 Royal Hill and my visit was, obviously, not welcome." Terry proceeded to recount his evening and the run-in with the security goon. "When I got back to L.A., I stopped at the 24-Hour Urgent Care in Torrance. X-rays showed possible rib fractures, so they decided to wrap them for a few days, if just to slow me down. But I don't know. One tech said with hairline fractures, to wrap or not to wrap was always the question. Ask four doctors and they'll split two-two on whether bandages do any good. But I know one thing: they're hot and uncomfortable. So, I might unwrap myself later today. Anyway, the bruising is the worst part, and I know that needs to breathe."

The server brought their food and coffee refills. As soon as he left the table, Ridge said, "I went up there. You went up there. And we're no closer to the brass ring. Let's promise, no more solo missions. We stay a team for all future visits to Santa Barbara County. OK?"

"I'm a believer. The only thing I learned yesterday was that 100 Royal Hill is a big place with heavy security and at least one nasty dog. Next time, we bring in troops."

"Try and try again. We've come up empty. We still don't know what we're into, so we should do the unexpected. I've got an idea. But that requires a bit of background. First, let me tell you what Jayne and I did yesterday."

After Jayne and Ridge recounted the day at Dryden, the wonders of the WebBird, and their forced landing in a Torrance field, Terry interrupted, "Damnit, you should have called me."

"My cell battery was out, and it was the only phone we had. Anyway, nothing you could do. We don't even know for sure that the plane was tampered with."

Terry raised an eyebrow at him.

"Okay. Odds are great it was no accident, but we got down safe and sound and Reuben, the new kid at the airfield, came to get us."

"I think that boy has a bit of a crush," Jayne said. "He was wearing a brand-new flight jacket, just like Eric's."

Ridge's mouth quirked. "He asked about it when we first met and I told him the brand. I can't help it if I'm an example of sartorial splendor."

Terry choked on a sip of coffee. "Sartorial splendor?"

Ridge laughed and shrugged. "Anyway, here's where we are. We need to know more about 100 Royal Hill. But why risk security guards, fractured ribs, or encounters of a third kind? Dave Lake told me he's test flying WebBird all next week. Up and down the coast. Endurance runs. I'll call him later today. See if he'll beam WebBird at Royal Hill, as a personal favor. It takes video and monitors phone calls from thirty-thousand feet. Unless they have missile silos at 100 Royal Hill, we should be good."

"That's a great idea," said Terry, "if Lake will do it. I even have the coordinates of 100 Royal Hill for him. I used the new Google Maps to get the longitude and latitude of the place."

Ridge pulled out a small note pad. "What are they?" As Ridge finished copying numbers onto a pad, he glanced up and noted Terry's pained expression. "What?"

"Do you mind if I switch topics for a minute?" Terry sighed and tossed his napkin on the table. "I hate to do this to you, but I need advice. From both of you."

"Sure," Jayne said, glancing at Eric.

"Well, Ava is back. And she's...I don't know. Really intense. It's strange, especially how we left it last time around."

"Oh no," Ridge and Jayne said at the same time. Then, they listened. Terry spent the next thirty minutes bringing them up-to-speed. At the end, Jayne and Ridge surveyed one another. Ridge said, "You first."

Jayne nodded. "Sounds like a woman on a mission."

"No doubt," replied Ridge. "But why now? What changed between you two? I thought it was finally over. You both agreed to move on."

Terry rubbed both hands over his face. "Me too. I don't know. Nothing changed. We both agreed it wasn't going to work, and I was fine with that. I thought we both were. But now...it's just...I don't know. I just have this weird feeling about it all. He planted both elbows on the table and rested his head in his hands. "Right now, I'm...I'm...just not feeling well."

§

When Ridge and Jayne returned to their apartment, Ridge called David Lake. As with 21st-century instant-communication, he got Lake's voicemail. At 1p.m., though, Lake's number flashed on Ridge's cell, and he picked up. After Ridge brought him up to speed on everything that'd been going on, Dave said, "Of course, I'll help. Flying the coast for over eight hours tomorrow in WebBird. All I have to do is point and click. Unofficial, of course. But I can get close-up video and monitor the phones while I film. To stay low-profile, though, I'll limit it to 30 minutes, OK?"

"More than OK, Dave. It's terrific. We just need a lead. Right now, we've got nada."

"Consider it done, partner. We'll flush out what we can."

"Anything you can get will make us smarter."

CHAPTER 43

Ridge's First Rule of Sanity: In L.A., avoid freeways, especially during rush hours, 7 a.m. to 10 a.m., 11 a.m. to 2 p.m., and 3 p.m. to 8 p.m. Avoiding freeways was a big reason he moved his offices from Westwood to the Beach Cities. But Mondays could be rough, even near the beach and even with an easy commute. He finally reached the office at 9:30, and by 10 a.m., he was leading an all-hands meeting on the patio. It is Southern California, he figured. Might as well enjoy the incredible weather.

Everyone was seated around two large umbrella tables placed next to one another with pens, pads, and laptops at the ready. The first order of business: the ejection-seat case in Phoenix that Judge Sayor had dismissed the week before. Before Ridge could even get started on next steps, Kate jumped in. "When I called the court this morning to get information about our appeal, the court clerk started crying. She said that Judge Sayor died over the weekend, hiking alone in the desert south of Phoenix. Bitten by a snake, of all things. Found him yesterday afternoon, already dead."

"Shit." It wasn't a very articulate reaction, but it perfectly summed up how he felt about the news.

Ridge's associate, Jim Hall, who never dwelt in emotion, immediately added, "What does this mean to the appeal? I was going to start drafting the papers today." Jim was a tall, lanky, no-nonsense 35-year-old of Hispanic ancestry with dark eyes, black hair, and a crewcut short on the sides and higher on top.

Ridge turned toward him. "Draft away. The Judge's death won't affect it. We're headed upstairs to the appellate court. Remember, I promised our client, Wanda James, we'd appeal full speed ahead. This involves a national issue—whether military contractors can benefit from the government's immunity in every military crash case. So, we need a sexy opening brief that captures mind and soul. Let's get started now."

"Done," said Jim.

Ridge then glanced over at Terry Pao. "Terry, all that said, Judge Sayor's death may very well be completely coincidental, but keep an eye on the news and stay tuned to any investigation."

"You got it."

"OK, next up is Uncle Cho's case," Kate said. "Remember, Eric, you need to call him today about the settlement offer. And then get back to that defense lawyer, Gryme."

"Will do. But I know he'll reject the offer." Ridge turned to his star research paralegal, Jessie Ward, who looked more like a blocking tailback for the UCLA Bruins. "The facts are clear in Uncle Cho's case. His insurance-defense lawyer is in a pure conflict-of-interest position. Uncle Cho wants him to settle with the patient's family, and the insurance company won't let him. There're hundreds of other 'Ringstone Mesh' cases out there—hundreds the insurance company would have to settle if a precedent were set in Uncle Cho's case."

"So how do we handle it?" asked Jessie.

"They won't expect this—let's take the offensive. Move for summary judgment on the Silent Conflict issue. Take it on point-blank. Draft a brief that asks our new judge to decide, as a matter-of-law, that an insured person is entitled to a neutral lawyer, whenever his insurance-defense lawyer has to choose between him and what's best for the insurance company."

"Make it a killer brief," said Kate. "This morning we got word by email that all of the late Judge Millsberg's cases have been temporarily transferred to Judge Christian Gimuldin. He'll probably be making the decision."

"Shit." Another super-articulate reaction, Ridge reflected. "Gimuldin's a loose cannon. Jessie, call Elliot Green. He's had cases before Gimuldin and can give you hints about how to pitch the brief. Get ready for side stories though—about Gimuldin's robes, his office, and other weird quirks. Look, we're in trouble on this one. But we press on. When Gimuldin rules for the defense, we'll take that one on appeal too. Structure the papers accordingly."

Ridge took a long sip of his coffee and then turned to Terry. "Kapow, is it just me or have you noticed judges dying mysteriously, left, right, and upside down? Elliot Green told me about a Jack Flynn in San Diego who recently drove off a cliff, survived, and then died after what had supposedly been a successful surgery. Now Judge Sayor in Phoenix gets bit by a snake. And, of course, we have Judge Millsberg's death. What if this is all about attacking judges? Intimidation. Coercion."

"Damned if I know," said Terry. "There's no real evidence of that. But I'm staying tuned to all of it, as best I can. So far, both the Flynn and Millsberg deaths have been ruled 'accidental,' and a snake-bite death, although rare, seems like an accident too."

Ridge shook his head. "I don't know…and I don't like it." He turned to Kate. "Any good news this morning?"

"I've got something," said Ridge's other associate, Brenda Jameson, who sported long, straight blonde hair, striking facial features and the athletic look of the long-distance marathon runner she was. She brought an analytical mind and the persistence and tenacity of a marathoner to the job.

"What do you have?" said Ridge.

"I'm drafting the product-liability complaint for Judge Millsberg's family. Describing the defect is easy, and how the keyless remote results in the engine running and carbon monoxide build-up. We did that in our earlier lawsuit. But I need some help with pleading causation in Judge Millsberg's particular case—to make sure it's consistent with the evidence."

Terry spoke up. "You're talking about her facial scratches?"

"That and the carbon-monoxide levels."

Ridge tapped a finger on the table. "And the condition of her bike. Those things were ignored by the police investigation. The keyless remote design is defective, no doubt, but did it actually cause her death or were other things going on?"

"That's exactly what I'm wondering about," said Brenda. "And with what you just said about this Jack Flynn guy down in San Diego and Sayor suddenly dying...I don't know. My spidey-sense is telling me you might be right about the judges dying."

Ridge twisted fully toward her. "OK. Call the good doctor, Tim Sanchez. See if he'll be our consultant in the civil case. If so, retain him. Let's get his input, before we get too far down the road."

"Right," said Brenda.

Ridge and his staff went on to cover a few more cases, then the meeting broke up, and he returned to his office to call Uncle Cho about the settlement offer. It was a quick conversation. How many ways can someone say 'no'? Uncle Cho did it at least six times in four different languages, and then said little else other than he'd never give up. With that, thought Ridge, the meeting at 6 p.m. with Gryme and Kachingski will probably go fast. Better order my margarita up front, as soon as Gryme mentions a drink.

Then, breaking his concentration, Ridge got a call from Jayne. The owner of the alarm system company had telephoned her: The assistant installer, the one allergic to cats who'd helped put the system in last Thursday, was missing. He'd never returned to the office, and they couldn't reach him by phone. Company protocol called for re-coding any security systems he worked on before his disappearance. And since he was brand new to the company and had only been on a few installations, the owner himself, as a precaution, had arrived at 11 a.m. to re-code the system personally.

"Strange as that sounds, it fits with my Monday so far."

"Bad start to the week?"

"Weird start. But the last few weeks have been weird, and they just seem to keep getting weirder."

"You better take down these codes because I'll be gone before you get home. I decided to drive down to Palm Desert this afternoon."

"Oh, that's right. I completely forgot about your gig. Two days, right?"

"I'll drive back Wednesday night. Ready for the code?"

"Yup." As Ridge finished copying the numbers, Kate came into his office.

"Todd Valentine of the *L.A. Times* is on line 30 for you. He's on deadline in another matter. Just wants to pass along some information before he disappears."

"Gotta go, Jayne. Call before you leave and as soon as you get there."

"You're sounding a bit paranoid, but I will. Love you."

"Love you too." He switched over to pick up the call on line 30. "Todd, Ridge here."

"I did some more digging this morning," Todd said, "and wanted to pass it on to you and Terry before I got wrapped up in another project."

"OK, fire away. I'm ready for anything today."

"Well, it might not be important. But I noticed on-line this morning that Judge Christian Gimuldin is taking over Judge Millsberg's caseload, including your Silent Conflict case for Terry's uncle. So, because I'm an out-of-control maniac, I went back to my search routines related to Santa Barbara."

"And?"

"Again, may be nothing. But Gimuldin owns property in Santa Barbara County. A swanky address in Montecito. This may be coincidence, but when I search, I assume nothing's a coincidence. The address is 12 Oaken Drive. Just felt you'd like to know."

"Interesting," replied Ridge. "Real interesting."

"There's something else. Researching Gimuldin's name along with Santa Barbara County on some of my more arcane databases, I got an interesting hit. Way back in 1966, then-lawyer Christian Gimuldin represented a hippie commune in a federal eviction case. Couldn't find any paperwork on it except a short squib, Case No. 56-1876(RV), United States v. Luv Freedom, with a listing of the lawyers for each side and a description of the property at issue. It was a large, fenced area in a forested section of Santa Barbara County."

"Whoa," said Ridge, writing the address and case number on his notepad. "Christian Gimuldin represented a hippie commune called Luv Freedom against the United States government? Some of his friends might be thrilled to hear that. Bet he never listed it on his resume."

Todd laughed. "Bet he didn't."

"Did it say where the property was located in Santa Barbara County?"

"No. But it described the two main structures on it—a cabin and a barn. Look, gotta run now. Anything else you want me to look into?"

"Not now, but thanks. The cabin and barn thing is very interesting. And when you're circling the drain, any information helps."

After hanging up, he ripped the notepaper—now with his new security codes and Todd's info—and stuffed it in his pocket. Barn and cabin. Gotta tell Terry. As soon as I finish the Toyota brief.

Ridge pulled out his papers and began editing a long brief that had to be filed the next day in a Toyota sudden-acceleration case. But minutes later, his concentration was interrupted again. It was a call from David Lake.

"Eric, WebBird and I did that favor, regarding 100 Royal Hill."

"How'd it go?"

"I monitored the filming and phone calls real-time. Didn't see or hear anything unusual. Some talk about insurance and business matters. Not much movement around the property. But, what a house—like an English estate. Not much going on though in the thirty minutes we had. I downloaded it onto an unmarked thumb drive. Fed Xed it to your attention just now. Original version, erased. Never happened."

"Got it."

"We tried our best. Hope it helps. Talk later?"

"Later, my friend." Ridge disconnected and turned back to editing his brief. He knew he had the 6 p.m. meeting. And with Jayne gone, if he didn't get home by 7:30 to feed Mister and Pistol, there'd be two very unhappy roommates waiting.

CHAPTER 44

Ridge arrived at the Il Forno Restaurant at 6:05, and John Gryme walked over immediately and introduced himself. "I'm sitting at the far corner of the bar," he said. "Would you like a drink?" Ridge smiled inwardly. At least I'll get my drink before I reject his offer.

"Margarita, rocks. Patron with a Grand Marnier topper," Ridge said, taking the measure of the man as he followed him toward the end of the bar. Gryme was relatively short—five foot five or so—white, wiry build, late 40s, salt and pepper hair.

Climbing onto the plush bar stool, Gryme gave the order to the bartender and added, "Make mine a double scotch, Dewars." Drinks in hand, they started out with small talk—the Dodgers, the Lakers, and of course freeway traffic. Then Ridge said, "John, I talked to my client. He rejected the offer."

Gryme grimaced. "You have a counteroffer?"

"Not really. He wants to press forward."

Gryme started to huff, but then as if on cue, a striking woman with long dark hair, blue eyes, and a killer smile came up to them. "John," she said, "this must be Eric Ridge. Hi, I'm Sasha Kachingski."

Ridge sensed just a hint of perfume as she offered her hand. When he took it, he noted the handshake was warm, strong, assured. Sasha was dressed in a dark blue form-fitting suit with a light blue silk blouse worthy of a courtroom, but still certainly sexy. She contrasted with Gryme who despite his thousand-dollar Brooks Brother suit and Ivy League tie looked—well, grimy. But then they both clashed in their own way with Ridge's navy-blue blazer, open collar, and beige slacks. In fact, Ridge would have felt underdressed except—well, this was California.

Just then, Gryme stared down at his gold Rolex watch and said, "Look, I need to go. Got Dodger tickets at the last minute today. But Sasha knows the case inside out. See if you guys can reach some common ground." Without hesitating, Gryme downed the rest of his double scotch, said quick goodbyes, and was off. Sasha turned to the bartender. "A Grey Goose martini, please. Dry, thirteen shakes and two olives on the side. Thanks." Then she turned to Ridge. "I've gotta confess. I looked you up. You're a NYU grad. So am I."

At that, they launched into talk about Washington Square, Greenwich Village, Rockefeller Center, and how they both missed street-side chestnut vendors in the wintertime. It turned out she had graduated twelve years after Ridge, but New York being New York—the best never changed.

Things were going swimmingly when Sasha stared straight at Ridge and said, "Look, this is embarrassing, but I've got to make another confession. I left the case file at my condo this morning. I'd feel much better if I had it before we talk shop. I live nearby. Would you mind if we discussed the case there?"

Bells went off, whistles blew, and a perfect picture of Jayne sprang into Ridge's mind. He gulped. Then regrouped. "Sasha— can't do that. I thought this would go relatively fast, and I've got another meeting at 7:30. But look, let's set up something when we get to our calendars—your office or mine—and soon. Then, we can talk things out."

Sasha's blue eyes moved down to her drink. "OK—I get it. No harm, no foul. I'll tell Gryme you needed more time to talk to your client, OK?"

"OK."

"Then I'll just grab dinner here," said Sasha, "and look forward to our next meeting."

After goodbyes, Ridge walked back to his office thinking, better move fast to make that next meeting. It was almost 7 and Mister and Pistol expected dinner 7:30 sharp, or else.

CHAPTER 45

Monday evening, just after 7, Two sat in his car, all focus on the building across the street. He rang up the phone number for the fifth-floor apartment. No one answered. It went right to voicemail and a female voice said: "We're away from the phone right now. Leave a message at the beep. We'll get back to you." Probably, the bitch who yelled "Get out!" and then shot me, thought Two. If she's upstairs, I might not be able to control myself. But, got to remember, Hess may be right about one thing: Control. Or lack of it. That's my big problem. Gotta fix that.

7:30. Two decided to check the apartment from a different vantage point by walking around to the beachside. All lights were out. No one was home. So, he returned to his car, laid low in his seat, and continued to watch the underground-parking garage and main entrance.

§

Ridge arrived home a few minutes after 7:30. Mister and Pistol gave him a break. No complaining, which was good because Ridge was beat—maybe because of Lake's bad news about WebBird— although the mention of insurance did pique his interest. Maybe because of the Toyota brief or having to spend time with the likes of Gryme, or whatever Sasha was trying to pull. Whatever. Ridge didn't even turn on the lights. He just fed the pets, walked to the bedroom, and crashed on the bed. I'll just lay down a minute and get some dinner later, he thought, as Mister and Pistol jumped up and cuddled in next to him.

§

Back in his car, Two slipped lower in the seat. He ate the two Whoppers and fries he'd brought for dinner, while looking up every few seconds at the garage and main door. This time, he promised himself, I'm gonna do it right. He gazed again at the photo of the lawyer from the law firm's website and checked everyone entering the apartment house to make sure the yahoo was nowhere in sight. The plan was to get into the apartment at midnight and leave the lawyer and his lady a message they would never forget. The damn dog would be gone, dead no doubt. And if the opportunity came up, he wouldn't mind finishing off that goddamn cat too.

He reasoned to himself, If Hess knew I faked being the alarm-system apprentice and got their phone numbers and alarm codes, even he'd be proud of me. I did my homework. Planned it to a gnat's ass. Answered the "Help Wanted" ad at Redondo Security Lock. Became an assistant. Put the "15% Off" flyer in their mailbox. Watched the phones. Took the call. Made the appointment. It was genius. What the hell more could I do?

One got all Hess' attention. Sure, the guy was good, but he wasn't any better than he was, Two thought. "I'm really friggin' tired of not getting any credit," he muttered aloud. "But this—this will change everything."

At that moment, Two got a text message from One, asking where he was. He concocted an excuse and texted back. Then cleaned up the Whoppers and finished his fries. From that point on, he just sat and watched the garage and main entrance, while playing games on his smartphone. Incredibly, no one entered or left, except some giggling gaggles of teenagers. So much for hot night life in the beach cities, he thought, and it's only friggin' 8:45. Midnight can't come soon enough.

CHAPTER 46

Just as she planned, Terry met Ava Monday evening at 9 sharp at the Coastline Restaurant. One of the most romantic restaurants in the Beach Cities, it jutted out over the surf in Redondo Beach. At night, lights flooded white water waves, and surfers below came and went, carrying their boards, like actors in a surf movie. She'd reserved a secluded, candle-lit booth near the windows and before their entrees even arrived, her talk turned to marriage and babies. Terry tried a preemptive strike.

"Ava, you know I love you. I've always loved you, ever since our first date at UCLA. But we have to slow down. Give ourselves some time to get re-aquainted."

Ava's smiling face twisted to a pout. "Slow down? Neither of us is getting any younger. We love each other. Who knows what tomorrow brings? Especially in this mixed-up world we live in."

"We have too much history to jump back in so fast," Terry said, his voice gentle. "Especially with how it ended last time. And right now, Eric and I are working some strange cases. My hours are crazy, and I may be out-of-town a lot. I don't want to disappoint you if I can't meet your expectations right now."

Ava frowned in frustration, then pushed back her chair and stood, looking down at him. Her eyes were swimming with unshed tears and she wore an expression Terry couldn't read. "I need to go to the restroom. Get some tissues. I'll be right back. But we can work this out. I'm sure of it!"

Ava picked up her purse and headed to the Ladies Room near the restaurant's entrance. A few seconds later, a sound vibrated. Ava's cellphone. She'd had left it to the side of her plate setting. It vibrated again. And again. Terry reached over and picked it up. The display showed several unanswered text messages. But the earliest one caught his eye. It was from "Producer" asking her to "Call about Pao."

When Ava returned to her seat, she was obviously more composed. Terry was not. He caught her eyes and pinned her with a hard stare. "Who is 'Producer' and what does he have to do with me?"

Ava's eyes went wide. Her gaze flicked to where her phone had been and then to where it was now cradled in Terry's hand. He held it up and showed her the screen.

"Your phone kept buzzing."

"Terry. God." She brought her hands up to her face as if she was going to start crying.

He reached out and pulled her hands away from her face. "Tell me." Was that shame on her face? Embarrassment? Or fear? What the hell was going on?

"I swear I was going to tell you."

"Then do it, Ava. Tell me."

"He came to me a few weeks ago. A Hollywood producer with a long list of credits. Said I was perfect for the project he had in mind. He promised me, if I could help him, I would star in his next documentary."

"Help him with what?"

"Uncle Cho."

Terry froze. Every muscle and nerve on high alert. "Uncle Cho." He looked Ava up and down as if he'd never seen her before. "What about Uncle Cho?"

"He asked me to rekindle my relationship with you to learn more about some case your uncle has in court. Something about insurance conflicts related to his filmmaking."

Insurance. Alarm bells were going off so loud in his ears, he could barely hear his own voice. "And you agreed?"

"I said maybe. But Terry, you've got to believe me. When I showed up at your apartment that first night, I knew I couldn't do it. I knew I still loved you, that it was time, finally, for us to give forever a try. And I do love you, Terry. You know I do."

Terry knew Ava well enough to know she was genuinely upset. A tear trickled down her beautifully chiseled cheek bone and rested at the edge of the mouth he'd kissed so many times. He didn't want to look at her, but he couldn't look away, either. He pinched the bridge of his nose and tried to keep his temper in check. "What's his name?"

"Censkey, Joshua Censkey. But I haven't seen him since the day you and I got back together. I swear. I've ignored all his calls and messages. But, just the same, I feel guilty. And I was going to tell you. Really! I tried and tried so many times."

"I've got to go." Terry placed her cellphone on the table, face down, and stood.

She looked up at him, more tears spilling over from those eyes he could no longer bear to look at. "Right now? Terry, we need to talk about this. I said I'm sorry."

"No, Ava, I don't believe you did say that." He set his napkin on his empty plate—entrees still hadn't arrived—then turned and walked away.

CHAPTER 47

At midnight, Two made his move. It was pitch black. Good conditions. Two hadn't seen the lights go on in the fifth-floor apartment since he'd staked out the place and he hadn't seen the lawyer arrive, either. He was sure no one was home. His plan now was to enter, perhaps kill the cat, and then tear the place apart, leaving blood-red lipstick on every mirror: "Bury the Damn Case. Or You're Next." That should scare the shit out of 'em, he thought, and make this whole goddamn thing go away. He'd finally be the hero Hess wanted.

Two attacked from the rear again. With the equipment he'd stolen from the alarm company, he spliced into the alarm wiring, just the way the alarm guy had taught him, and slipped the stolen equipment in-line to enter the codes. That way, the system would stay passive when he later opened the door. Then Two repaired the splice. And using ropes, grappling hooks and handholds, he climbed up the rear balconies of the building. Spiderman again.

When Two got to Ridge's west balcony, he placed the suction cup, with a three-inch wire stretching from its center to the left of the sliding-door handle. The tip of the wire had a glass-cutting diamond head that scored a circle big enough to fit his hand through. Pulling on the suction cup brought the glass plug toward him. Perfect. Then he reached in and turned the handle. Simple, silent, effective. If only the others had any idea how good he really was.

Next, Two gingerly tugged to slide the glass door open. It didn't budge. "Shit," he muttered.

Must have put an extra pin at the top. He cursed again and reset the suction cup, made a new hole, and removed the top pin. "Perfect," he said aloud, then froze as the sound of a growling dog and that guttural, unearthly yowling from the damn cat reached him from somewhere inside. Shit. It's that cat from Hell, he thought. And a new dog! But they didn't charge at him. Must be behind a closed door. Probably the bedroom. No matter, this time I'll finish 'em both. Two cocked his .357 Magnum, planning to smear blood all over the place. He then carefully and silently slid the door open, and—shit hit the fan.

An alarm, like truck air horns, blasted away, deafening him. Red lights lit up the alarm panel like a Christmas tree on fire, and Two scrambled back, grabbed the rope, and vaulted over the balcony.

§

As soon as Mister and Pistol started making noise, Ridge was up and moving. He pulled the slide to chamber a hollow point in his Beretta, burst through the bedroom door, and dropped to his stomach, elbows propped, pistol gripped in both hands, combat-ready. Intending to shoot first and ask questions later, he sighted left to right around the room—front entrance, west balcony doors, north balcony, then back to the west balcony. Nothing. No one else was in the apartment. Alarm still blaring, he rose to a crouch and rushed to the nearest balcony. The door was halfway open. He stepped outside, gun still in position, and watched as a bald-headed ninja dropped from the end of a rope, stumbled, sprang up and ran down the beach, limping.

It was after 1 a.m. when Ridge called Terry. "Danger's over but it took a while to get things settled over here. Had to talk to the alarm company and file a police report. Not to mention calming down Pistol, Mister, and some of my neighbors. I now, probably, have more open police reports in Redondo Beach than any other person."

"Gotta make a mark in life somehow," Terry said, breathing easier now that he'd heard the whole story. "Any idea what he was after?"

"Don't have the slightest idea. But he seemed serious about it. The police took the ropes, grappling hooks, and rappelling device. But before they did, I looked at 'em. No identification marks. Maybe you can give them another look-see in the morning—later this morning—at the police station. I'll call Jayne in Palm Desert to tell her everything's OK."

"Maybe you should have her put more locking pins on the sliding doors when she gets home," suggested Terry with an almost imperceptible chuckle.

"I suppose she told you about that."

"It might've slipped out at breakfast the other day. While you were in the bathroom."

"Yeah, well. I could also have her rivet the damn thing like airplane skin. But that might interfere with opening doors."

"I've got news too," Terry said. "Long story short, sounds like some Hollywood producer type's been snooping around Uncle Cho's case. Something about insurance."

"How'd you find that out?"

"I said long story short…let's stick with the short for now."

"OK," Ridge knew when to push and when to keep his mouth shut. "Let's tally it up. My head got smashed open, the boat was set on fire, we got shadowed by a crazy guy, your ribs were broken, we had a break-in here where Jayne was attacked and Pistol was shot, we had a break-in at the office, my plane just quit in mid-air, and now we've had another break-in here. Who knows what'll happen next? We've been nothing but punching bags. Have to find out who's doing this and why. We need to put an end to this shitshow."

"Agreed. And based on when everything started going bad, it all seems somehow connected to Uncle Cho's case or Judge Millsberg's death."

"Or both."

"You know," Terry said, "there are a lot of lawyers who would bail on both cases."

"Not gonna happen. Not on my watch."

"Knew you'd say that. So, looking at what we've got, Chesterfield, Gimuldin or both are probably involved. Starting today we plug in afterburners. Solve this mess. I promise. But right now, buddy, get some sleep."

"Easier said than done."

"I know," said Terry with a sigh. "But we'll get to the bottom of this. Tough never quits."

As he hung up, Ridge headed back to the bedroom, catching a glimpse of himself in the mirror. "Tough never quits, Eric," he said aloud. "Damn right."

CHAPTER 48

Ridge jolted awake at 3. Tuesday morning. Sweat covered his skin. He pulled his eyelids open, disoriented. His eyes gritted like sandpaper. Strained, stinging. His head ached. He stared at the dark ceiling and tried to remember where he was. Finally, he realized: At home, in bed. Safe. But definitely not feeling it. His tongue tasted like a towel. He reached for bottled water on his nightstand and took a swallow. Then another. Rotating the cap off nearby Ambien, he downed a pill. Then he fluffed his pillow, put his head down, and within the hour got back to sleep—somewhat. Soon his feet got warm, then warmer and his mind slipped off to war.

§

The mission was photo reconnaissance. Ridge cinched his shoulder holster, slung the strap of his AR-15 rifle over his shoulder, and left the hootch. Jumping in the crew van, he realized it was only him this morning. First flight of the day. Crack of dawn. He drove himself to the flight line. Since it was dark, he used a flashlight to do the pre-flight inspection on his O-2 aircraft. Crouching down by the forward propeller, he flashed his light into the engine cowling. Just then, he felt a tap on his shoulder. Ridge flung around, not sure what it was, and put his light on the smiling face of 18-year old Jim Stance. Though not much younger than Ridge, he seemed like a young kid.

Stance was one of the newest mechanics. He was excited. Sergeant Ed Drew, Ridge's regular crew chief and expert photo man, picked Jim as his replacement. Ed, suffering from some type of light malaria, couldn't make the mission that day.

Stance did well, at least during the morning missions in III Corps and the Delta Region. Then about 11 a.m., he and Ridge dropped into Phan Rang Air Base for fuel and food. Jim still looked excited. They had taken ground fire in the Delta, and Ridge arranged to have some Army mechanics plug three holes in the right wing. Jim spoke to the Army guys just like Steve Canyon, Commander of Big Thunder Air Force Base. Straight out of the comic strip. He explained how difficult it was to take the thud, thud, thud of ground fire while focusing the camera and emphasized how "his pilot" couldn't go off-station until Jim clicked away on the camera and gave him the word to leave. In Jim's story, Ridge was just a chauffeur.

Oh well, he thought, the world's all about perspective. Ridge accepted his new position and focused on the bullet holes. The foam in the wing had prevented fuel leakage while they were airborne, just as advertised. And the new plugs looked good.

Afterwards taking on fuel and getting some lunch, they loaded up and pulled out to the runway for their afternoon mission in II Corps, north of Phan Rang. This sortie was different. The temperature and jungle humidity met in the high nineties. Hot and sweaty. Sticky. Bumpy. The thermals made flying feel like racing a car through a huge parking lot with speed bumps every few feet. After one hour, Jim had had it. The first time, without warning, he barfed into his microphone and all over the instrument panel.

"I'm sorry, sorry," he shouted over the noise of both propellers. "I'll clean it up—I promise." Then Jim vomited again. This time to his right onto the camera pod. Ridge reached over and whacked the back of his helmet. "Your helmet. Use your helmet!"

Ripping off his helmet, Jim threw up a third time—this one in the pot. But with the extreme heat and humidity, the stench set in, a putrid odor, like sour milk on a hot day. Which just made Jim sicker. Meanwhile, surrounded by jungle mountains, Ridge tried to figure out where to land.

"Hang in there," Ridge shouted, as Jim doubled over and barfed again into the inverted helmet between his knees. "I'll get us down."

Ridge spotted a firebase. A huge circle of reddish dirt in the middle of green jungle. Tangerine-colored powder, Agent Orange, had been used to wipe out the trees. The firebase had brownish-orange tents, two choppers and, best of all, a short roll-out metal runway for fixed wing aircraft. Ridge picked them up on FM Radio. He told the Army operator he had an emergency—an incapacitated crewman—and would be dropping in for help in five minutes. The Army radio operator cleared Ridge into Firebase Orange.

Because the metal runway was short, Ridge had to set up a steep power-on approach—an 'assault landing.' He cleared the treetops, nudged power back, and dropped like a rock. Ridge smashed into the metal runway, cut power, and jumped on the brakes. To his right, Jim had his face in his helmet, moaning. The perforated runway clanked, cranked, and sounded like it was collapsing as they rolled out.

With skill, experience, and beaucoup luck, Ridge stopped the bird before running off the runway. He shut down the props, and three army mechanics ran over. They pulled Jim from the right side, and cotted him over to the M.A.S.H. tent. Medics did the rest, as Ridge jumped out of the plane. He thanked the Army folk for their hospitality and explained the situation. Then, he looked around.

Except for the metal runway, two choppers and about eight big tents covered in red dust, there were no other structures. Three men in camouflaged fatigues walked the jungle perimeter with M-16 rifles ready. In the center of the firebase was a large dust bowl with a volleyball net. Twelve guys in green boxer shorts and little else were playing hard. Jumping, sweating, stretching, falling, and covered head to foot in orange-red dust. The rest of the men centered on Jim and Ridge.

"Welcome to Firebase Orange," said a soldier dressed in a green T-shirt and boxers. "Sorry it's hot as hell here. No air conditioning."

Always quick to pick up on things, Ridge figured out right away his host was a lieutenant. His T-shirt had "LT" printed on front in black. "Thanks Lieutenant," said Ridge. "How's my man?"

"Not good," said LT. "He's dehydrated. White as a ghost. Moaning. Needs water, and plenty, right away. That's one thing we don't have much of here at Orange. Plenty of heat, plenty of Viet Cong, plenty of red dust, but not a hell of a lot of water. We just blew away the jungle and reactivated this firebase. It's smaller than the original, and our Army engineers messed up. The underground water tank, the pump, and the spigot from the old base sit thirty yards into the jungle—thata way," he said, pointing to a narrow trail that disappeared into thick vegetation. "And Charlie knows it."

Ridge stared at the trail. Since the sun was high in the sky, he had no idea whether LT was pointing north, toward Thailand, or east toward the U.S. of A. The impenetrable jungle surrounding them seemed all the same, in every direction—green, lush, incredibly huge, and ungodly thick. "Shit," said Ridge. "Can you spare me two or three guys? I'll also need those twenty-gallon plastic jugs over there. If so, we'll get the water."

"Anytime we can help flyboys, we're in," said LT. "When the Cong start to blow us to hell, you guys save our asses from the air, every time."

Ten minutes later Ridge and two grunts with green head bandanas and M-16s strapped to their arms, called Gunzo and Habit, located the well. Ridge placed the two jugs near a brass faucet attached to a three-foot rusty pipe jutting from the ground. Less than a second later, as Ridge reached for the faucet, bullets cracked out of the jungle—from opposite sides. Ridge and Gunzo, to his right, hit the dirt. Habit, on his left, took a bullet. Through the forehead. He collapsed. Ridge crawled over, took a pulse. Then he grabbed the fallen man's M-16 and started to return fire. Gunzo, on his right, sprayed bullets in the opposite direction. Multiple screams. Yells. Running. Then things went quiet—real quiet.

Ridge and Gunzo got up, bent over, rifles outstretched. They listened. Left and right. Then they slowly penetrated trees and bush on one side of their position. Twenty feet further into dense vegetation, they found two VC, sprawled on the ground. Gunzo poked one, then the other with his M-16. They were gone. Hunched over, rifle out front, Ridge moved deeper into the hot humid jungle. Gunzo behind. Thirty more feet, thick, suffocating undergrowth and thorny vegetation gave way to a small clearing. Sweat dripping into his eyes, he stopped, straightened up, and stared straight ahead. "My God."

Instinct told him to look away. A sickly stench of rotting meat, cheap perfume, and sewage assaulted his nostrils. He shut off his breathing and closed his eyes—to escape. As he choked back the bile, he realized, it's what they want. To terrorize. Ridge refused to submit.

He slowly opened his eyes, raised his head, and tried to swallow. The things—still there. In front. Strung on webbed branches of a spreading tree. Eight human heads. Hacked. Faces the purplish-gray of rancid plums. Crudely scalped. Viciously chopped at the neck. Torn ragged flesh laced with drying russet-colored blood. Frayed black rope, through the ears, tied to branches above. Mouths sagged. Eyes, propped open with slender sticks, gazed blindly at him. Eight silent soulless stares. Stares he couldn't turn from and would never forget.

§

Six a.m. Tuesday. Ridge was up. He made coffee and checked the north balcony. The male hummingbird darted out of nowhere, straight at his head, stopped on the dime and flew round and round in vertical loops. Ridge shifted his eyes to the nest. Ms.

Hummingbird was sitting in it. Then he looked at the feeder. Empty. Ridge turned, fetched nectar from the kitchen, filled the feeder and sat in the balcony chair. The male hummingbird winged forwards, backwards, upwards, downwards, and upside down. Then he flipped upright, did a 180 and fed at the feeder. The next instant he flew right up to his better half, stopped suddenly, and seemed to kiss her—black bill to black bill. Actually, Ridge figured, he was feeding her. Then back to the feeder and back to his mate. Ridge, mesmerized, thought how right Jayne had been. Ancient symbols of joy and happiness, modern symbols of peace. Ridge sat, and watched in wonder.

Later, even with the bird show, Ridge got to the office early. On the plus side, there was something to be said for working without interruptions. No phones. No visits. No questions. No loud conversations. Like working on the moon. Or a deserted island. Surrounded by endless miles of ocean. Peaceful.

Terry barged into Ridge's office. "Oh, you're here. I was gonna leave a note. Why so early?"

Ridge shrugged. "Couldn't sleep."

"Well, I've got news. I reviewed the thumb drive Dave Lake Fed Xed yesterday. Not much on the video. But the audio picked up a phone conversation between our insurance god, Chesterfield, and someone saying the Silent Conflict issue was as good as over."

"That's news to me," said Ridge. "Our crack paralegal, Jessie, hasn't even had time to research the case yet. Maybe Chesterfield was talking to his blowhard lawyer, John Gryme. He probably plans to file his own summary judgment motion to end the case."

"Could be." Terry took a seat. "Also had talk on the audio track about the Dutch West Indies. And of all things—insuring the rulers of Yemen."

"Well, Chesterfield runs his insurance business through the West Indies, probably for tax reasons. But Yemen? Got me. Anything else on the audio?"

"Chesterfield got another call," said Terry. "About the health insurance part of his empire. I recorded that part." Terry turned on his recorder: "Tell the damn doctor and hospital associations to go to hell. Our analysts make the decisions about who gets what operation, who gets what drug, and whether generic substitutes will do. When will the fucking doctors learn? We pay the bills; we call the shots. I don't give a damn what their professional opinions are, or what they think is best for a patient. They all better start thinking 21st Century. Decisions gotta be based on fucking statistics, actuarial tables, costs, for God's sake. Look, let me make it crystal clear: I don't want to hear any bullshit about this ever again."

"Nice guy," said Ridge. "But this is just kissin' cousin to the Silent Conflict issue."

Terry put down his cellphone. "How so?"

"The insurance industry bases everything on statistics. They argue it's all for the greater good. Their line of shit goes: Sure, some patients will die, but far more will benefit from the limited resources we have available."

"Champions of Greater Good," said Terry.

"And, in that way, they put doctors in a conflict position with their patients, just like they put insurance-defense lawyers in conflict with their clients. Bottomline, they demand doctors and lawyers do what's best for the insurance company. Patients and clients run second. It's the insurance mafia at work. Every day. Everywhere."

"But where does that leave us?"

"Nowhere good. Especially since Gimuldin is the new judge on our Silent Conflict case. But listen, yesterday, I spoke with Todd Valentine at the *Times*. He discovered Gimuldin has an address in Santa Barbara County, 12 Oaken Drive in Montecito."

"Pretty high-end address, for a public servant."

"That's what I'm thinking. Maybe it's family money?"

"Would Lake beam WebBird at 12 Oaken Drive? What would we lose? How in hell could it hurt?"

"For starters, we can't keep going back to the well. It's like shooting silver bullets. Only get a few. Flip side, we don't have any other new leads worth a damn. And we need a break. Let's call and see."

When they got Dave on the phone, as expected, he hemmed and hawed. Quite a bit. But finally, he agreed. He had a WebBird flight scheduled the next day. "But tomorrow's gig has to be the last for a while," said Dave. "We can't push a good thing. Check Fed X on Thursday for the UTD."

"UTD?" said Ridge.

"Unmarked thumb drive."

"Roger that."

After Ridge thanked Dave and hung up, Terry asked if he had time to discuss a personal item. Hearing "sure," Terry described his conversation with Ava the previous evening.

"So, she was using you," Ridge said, his voice tight. The idea of Ava pulling such a stunt did not sit well, to say the least. Of course, Terry was a grown man, but Ridge and Jayne had seen him with Ava enough times that they'd long ago decided he'd be better off moving on. "If you hadn't found that text, she wouldn't have said a word. But then again, maybe, she's learned a lesson this time. Maybe now you can trust her? You've gotta decide, Kapow. But I'd say let things cool off plenty, before you make any big decisions."

Terry nodded. "Yeah, that's what I think too. Meanwhile, I'm going to check out this Censkey character. My gut tells me he's somehow involved in everything that's gone on lately, and the SOB might even lead us to pay dirt."

CHAPTER 49

On Wednesday, Ridge got up early to spend more time with the hummingbirds. Then he had court in the morning and a deposition in the afternoon. Jayne returned from her computer presentation in Palm Desert around 6 p.m., and they had dinner at the Boiling Pot near the Manhattan Beach Pier. Sitting on wooden chairs at a rustic plank table outside, overlooking the famous pier and its red-roofed roundhouse, Ridge glanced up from his large plastic menu.

"I forgot to ask. Can you meet the glass guy tomorrow morning? He needs to measure our Swiss-cheese sliding doors for new glass."

"As long as Pistol and Mister are with me."

Ridge nodded. "Always. Especially after what happened Monday night."

"Yeah. I'm getting pretty tired of strange men in our apartment."

"Well, there's always me," said Ridge.

"Mister and Pistol are enough protection during the day."

"No, I was referring to 'strange men'."

Jayne laughed. "No doubt about that." She reached out and tapped the back of his hand. "But strange in a lotta good ways."

Ridge smiled, then went back to studying the wine and beer section of the menu.

§

Lake's thumb drive arrived at 10 a.m. on Thursday. Ridge booted up his computer and called Terry into his office. When Terry arrived, Ridge clicked away on the drive. It had a video file. Ridge opened it and they both watched.

"Wow." Terry let out a low whistle. "That's quite a spread for a government employee. Especially since he reportedly only uses it on long weekends and holidays."

"Gotta be family money?"

"You certainly don't afford that on a government salary," Terry said. "Even in a down-market, that property has to be worth 10 million, maybe more. It's a full-blown estate. The main building looks like the White House. If the White House were gray."

"One thing's for sure, we need to know more about this guy. His background, his cases. If this isn't family money…"

"On it."

Ridge turned to Terry. "Before I forget, Jayne and I are taking a short getaway to Oyster Bay Resort in San Diego. Tomorrow through Tuesday. My better half says we need a break. Who can argue?"

"Best not."

"Roger that. But while we're gone, can you check in on Pistol and Mister at the apartment—once in the morning, once at night?"

"Will do."

Ridge smiled. "You're my man."

"Bet on it, amigo."

CHAPTER 50

"Shit. Goddamnit to hell." Hess kicked a rotting bale of hay, then stared at Two. "Never fuckin' rains. Only pours—it's a shitstorm. I put in the time, lots of time, training those little twits we captured near USC the other night. Then His Eminence worked on 'em yesterday, and now he tells me to get rid of 'em. All except the golden boy. That's three girls and one guy—definitely not ready for the world stage."

"Let me work with 'em," begged Two.

"One twit teaching other twits? I don't think so."

"I promise. I'll get 'em ready. You'll see."

"My idea was for you to get rid of them. But let me think. Maybe you're right."

Hess considered the situation. What he wasn't telling Two. That middle of the night, screams and yelling filled the big house. One had rushed into Hess' room, screeching that His Eminence wanted Hess immediately. Two, sleeping in the barn, couldn't have known what a disaster it turned out to be. Imagining the worst—a heart attack, a stroke, every disaster Hess could think of—Hess rushed to His Eminence's bedroom. He found two of the new girls, handcuffed together, huddled in a corner, crying, one of them bleeding from a split lip, the other with a rapidly purpling handprint on her cheek. His Eminence, with bulging eyes, a madman stare, and blood on his chin, sat in the center of his bed, sheets up, fists clutched at his waist.

"That one—with the brown hair," His Eminence pointed and bellowed. "I'm trying to teach her how to do a blowjob and she fucking bit me! Tried to bite my goddamn cock off! And the other bitch bit my lip at the same time. I'm bleeding goddamnit—bleeding! Get them out of my sight. Get rid of them for good."

Hess apologized profusely even as he motioned for One to get rid of the sobbing girls. One hauled the girls to their feet, both of them naked, and pushed them from the room saying, "It will be done, Your Eminence. It will be done." Once out of the bedroom, Hess knew he'd drag the girls down the hallway to lock them in the basement until he got further instructions.

Later Hess sent for One to come to his room. "I know this is fucked up, but we need to keep the greater good in mind. Remember, His Eminence is our best chance to save America from itself."

"He's a great man," said One, parroting the line he'd repeated so many times. "I know that."

"But this. What happened. It's not the first time. Not the first time he's allowed his …appetites…to get the better of him. No one's ever fought back before, though." He paced his room. "We gotta deal with those girls. Fuck. And how can we keep others inspired if they find out about this shit? We've got to clean it up. Otherwise all the fancy robes, all the ceremonies in all the goddamn world won't keep us on track. There's only seven days to the Sunday Summit."

§

Later that afternoon, with the girls back in cages, Hess looked over at One and Two. No one said a word. Damn it to hell. What the fuck was he supposed to do with this mess? The girls had been separated. Two different cages. Not close enough to touch each other or talk without being heard. But Two thought he could handle them? Damn. Giving Two a shot at the girls was…well, a long longshot. But why not give him his fucking chance? It's all a shitstorm anyway.

"All right," Hess said finally. "Get them ready. Give it a shot. But you damn well better succeed. His Eminence wants a real profit from every candidate we put out there. Without risk. Which means, in this case, getting them off property, ASAP."

Two, grinning like a shit-eater, started immediately toward the cages saying, "Thank you, Herr Hess. You won't regret this."

Hess, half-ignoring the twit, turned to his little black book. "Yes, yes," he said to himself, "that's it—Dubai. Always a market for American product in Dubai. "Let's go to the big house," he said to One. "I need to make some calls."

Before leaving the barn with One in tow, Hess shouted again for Two, who came running. "Yes, Herr Hess, what is it?"

"Besides finishing up with discipline, teach the students some Arabic phrases: Yes. No. How can I please you? Of course, Master. Things like that. Could come in handy—real soon. Perhaps as soon as tomorrow."

Hess then spun around and jogged with One to the truck. He climbed in, pulled his door shut and turned the ignition. "After the Dubai buy, we'll go to Camp. Finish up the training. Three told me the new boy is showing great promise. But guess he's 'golden boy' from here on—not golden-haired—since the scalping, I mean. And Four told me the other five in training should be ready soon." He headed down the rocky drive toward the road. "Maybe, just maybe, that will please His Eminence enough to get us off his shit list."

"It will," said One. "It's all coming together. But I've been meaning to ask a question."

Hess, swinging the wheel to turn onto the main highway, looked over at his protégé. "Always with the questions. Not about His Eminence, right?"

"Right."

Hess nodded. "Then go head."

"How did you arrange for that lawyer's plane to go down?"

"It's like this, when you followed the lawyer a couple of weeks ago and saw him fly out of Torrance, it gave me an idea."

"What idea?"

"You see, I have friends you haven't met. They have friends. Powerful groups in America and twenty other countries around the world. All have links to the National Socialist Group. You know—the NSG. Our American neo-Nazi friends. And most of the NSG leaders will be at our Summit next Sunday. But here's the thing, what goes around comes around. Some of these groups have affiliations with militia, nationalistic, and white supremacy groups here in America. Someday, His Eminence and I plan to bring them all under the Raven Society umbrella. Or at least service them as clients who'll pay for trial results and appellate decisions in their favor. I told you our goal is to get it all set up in the next five to ten years. By 2015 at latest. We're on fire, and the Summit this Sunday will ignite the all-important alliance with these other groups."

One shook his head in confusion. "But what does this have to do with the lawyer and his plane?"

"Everything." Hess smiled, inwardly impressed with his own cleverness. "The Raven Society and a few of our friends have tapped into a biotech hedge fund. Amazing—how those funds invest millions without doing deep dives on the details. Too quick to chase a profit to do the hard work. Anyway, we've been sponsoring ground-breaking work in bioweapons. With genetic engineering— or should I say re-engineering—of germs."

"Germs?"

"Yes." Hess glanced sideways at One, deciding how far to go to further train his star student. "Germs include viruses, bacteria, and fungi. Most of our work now is with viruses. But a while back, we had success modifying certain types of fungus."

"I'm sorry I don't understand. How are viruses, bacteria, and fungus different?"

Hess wondered if he should do more to educate the boys under his command. Some of them didn't know shit from shinola. "Bacteria are one-celled living organisms. Viruses are much, much smaller, essentially DNA shreds with protein and fatty coverings. Fungi are plant-like multi-celled substances. They're the key to the lawyer and his plane."

"Did you do this work? Are you a scientist too?"

Hess laughed. "No. I didn't do it, but I monitored it. Made sure it was done right."

"OK. So, how is this the key to the lawyer's plane going down?"

"Well, we worked with a filamentous fungus—called Cladosporium resinae. Don't let the name throw you—for decades it's been known as 'kerosene fungus' or 'fuel bugs.' It contaminates kerosene and jet fuel. Recently, they genetically modified that fungus to exist with much less water and reproduce rapidly with sufficient heat in a matter of just hours. That meant theoretically it could be used to contaminate regular gasoline—including aviation gas. But our friends needed a test bed. So that's when I volunteered our lawyer flyboy. He needed a second warning anyway—besides Two's antics—to wise him up. And the best way was to take away his control. Drives him nuts."

"How did you manage that?"

"The scientists loaded a hypodermic with the genetically-modified fuel bugs in solution. And when we learned from our contact at Torrance Airport that Ridge was going to fly again that Saturday, I visited the airport."

"We have a contact at the airport?"

"The NSG lent us a guy who went undercover there. Reuben's a mechanic, so he could help with our little experiment."

One tapped a fingertip on his leg. "OK. So, what did you and Rueben do?"

Hess noted One's fingertip moving up and down, like counting out the beats of a song. He liked the way the boy was so self-contained. Unlike Two, who was way too jittery. "I went to the Ops Center and saw on the scheduling grease board which airplane he was going to use. Cessna 3-2-1 Alpha—the tail number, you know. Then I strolled out to that plane. I checked one way while Rueben checked the other. No one was around, so I simply squirted the bugs into the fuel tank. The fungi took over from there. As expected, we learned later he crash-landed that afternoon. Mission accomplished."

"Wow. That's incredible."

"I know," said Hess with a shrug. "And with the Summit coming up next Sunday, no one—and I mean no one—can stop us now."

CHAPTER 51

On Monday, His Eminence had another appointment and couldn't make it to the regular lunch at noon. So, Hess, sitting alone, ruminated about the Camp. He'd been building it, off and on, for five years with the work and muscle of One through Six, and various trainees. It was only finished to his liking within the last year. Located twenty miles from Santa Barbara in a forested canyon of the San Rafael Mountains, east of Santa Ynez Valley, Hess had put the Camp in the middle of the San Rafael Wilderness near the desolate plateau known as Hurricane Deck. It was surrounded by miles of back country seldom visited by campers or hikers. And like the marijuana farms growing in some of the adjacent canyons, it couldn't be seen from the air—thanks to camouflage netting and thick tree canopies. Most of the foot trails into it were booby-trapped. Some with punji sticks, others with bear claws.

The Camp included a large operations tent, an underground armory for weapons storage, smaller tents for trainees, outdoor tables for seminars, a hidden helicopter pad, a target range for pistols and another for automatic weapons. A mock compound was set up for practice assaults. In addition, Hess had added two obstacle courses, a water-combat training tank, a pool covered by netting, and a man-made underwater-demolition pond. It all mimicked, as closely as Hess could manage, areas used for SEAL training in Coronado, California—training for sea, air, and land combat that many consider the most difficult military training in the world.

Hess agreed. That's why he copied it. Now, he needed someone else to step up and run it.

As if on cue, One hurried into the room. "Herr Hess, sorry to be late."

"OK, this time. Take a seat. We need to discuss the Camp. Training. You need to look at it as an instructor now, not a trainee. After Sunday's Summit, I may give you responsibility for future training. I'll probably have to spend full time coordinating with our allies."

"Of course, Herr Hess. I stand ready to help how, where, and when I can."

"Don't stand ready, sit ready." Hess motioned to a chair. "Sit the hell down. And listen closely. I want to review the new training program." One took a seat. Hess continued, "The first lesson is from a former SEAL training manual. You remember 'drown proofing,' don't you?"

One grimaced. "Sure do. In the old pool. Hands tied behind our back. Feet bound. You shoved each of us in turn from the fifteen-foot diving board. Had to swim back and forth at least a hundred and fifty feet. If anyone failed, you fished him out."

"Right," said Hess. "But in the future, tell trainees they only get two attempts. If they fail, no more tries. They're out. Darwinian, right?

"Yes, Herr Hess."

"For those that make it, I want you to test them, just as we do now, with two daily runs through the mountains for two weeks. Each will continue to carry a thirty-pound pack, and the heavy Mark-43 Squad Automatic Weapons we have. It's gun of choice for SEALs on patrol, you know."

One smiled. "No, I didn't know that."

"We want world-class commandos. Nothing less. Men worthy of serving the Raven Society and our allies wherever or with whatever is needed. To make that happen, keep using the SEAL training syllabus, but with twists. In the past, as you know, like SEALs, each trainee got only three or four hours of sleep per night during the first two weeks. Make it three weeks in the future. Get rid of the chaff. With new allies, our pool of candidates will double, maybe triple."

"This is exciting."

Hess smiled. "Damn right. Now, listen. Those who make it get to advance to the second level. Advanced scuba lessons. Helicopter operations. Ground combat maneuvers. Knife fighting. Martial arts. Sniper training."

"We got all that."

"Yes, but in three years, only you and Two through Six completed training successfully. The rest were sold off. And—yeah—five others will join you soon. And perhaps a sixth. The golden boy is excelling in every category. But overall, building security forces has gone too goddamn slowly."

"All that will change soon, right?"

"Exactly. After Sunday's Summit, with more candidates and new facilities, we'll be in much better shape. But we'll need to intensify their training. It's simple—we'll weed out weaker trainees and yet build better forces faster. That job, One, could be yours: Securing the future for the Raven Society. How does 'Director of Training' sound?"

One sat up even straighter and his smile beamed like a high-intensity flood light. "That sounds...amazing. Thank you, Sir. I won't disappoint."

Hess, about to say, 'Bet your ass,' heard a sound at the door. "Enter."

Three stood on the threshold. "Herr Hess, we've finished packing for the Camp. When you and One are ready, we can head out."

"Excellent," said Hess. "One, we'll finish training at the Camp today, tomorrow, and Friday. When His Eminence visits on Friday evening, we need to give him a demonstration he won't forget. Full combat gear. Impress the hell out of him. The graduation ceremonies before the Raven Executive Committee will be Saturday. Then, the culmination of our work. The Sunday Summit. Only five days away. The allegiances formed there will not only magnify our effectiveness, but last lifetimes."

CHAPTER 52

The weekend away in San Diego had been one of the best things he and Jayne had done in a long while. He still thought about everything going on, trying to figure out the connections and missing pieces, but the getaway gave him a chance to step back and see it with new eyes. By the time Monday evening rolled around, Ridge was almost relaxed. And then, as he was considering his dessert choices at the Oyster Bay Restaurant, his cellphone vibrated. "Damn." He pulled his phone off his belt holster and looked at the caller ID. Terry.

"I'm going to take this out front," he told Jayne. "I don't want to bother anyone."

"I'll be here."

"Terry?" Ridge said, heading for the entrance to the restaurant. "Give me a minute."

When Ridge returned, he remained standing, cell in hand, slightly shaking. "We have to go."

"We're finished here anyway. I don't need dessert." She looked up at him, his face was so intense, she took his hand in hers. "Eric. You're shaking."

He looked down at his hand as if it didn't belong to him. "Huh. Yeah. Worst since the Hulk. Doesn't matter. We've gotta go. Now. I took care of the bill."

She stood immediately. "What's happened?"

"Kate's been in a wreck. Really, really bad."

Jayne nodded once. "I'll pack. You check out and get the car."

§

Tuesday morning, Jayne and Ridge met Terry in the hospital cafeteria at 8:30 a.m. Visitors' hours started at 9:30. So Terry and Ridge had coffee. Jayne pulled a blue and white "Swiss Miss" packet from her purse and poured the brown powder into a mug of tepid water. Hot chocolate, on demand. As she stirred, Terry explained what he had learned.

"Her left arm and left leg were fractured. She took a hit to the left side of her head, but CT scans showed no skull fractures. The docs say she might develop TBI—traumatic brain injury—but it should be mild at worst."

Jayne tried to smile. "Guys, I just know she'll be OK. They don't come tougher than Kate."

Ridge smiled back. Sort of. "What did you find out about the accident itself?"

Terry lowered his coffee cup to the table. "Dan called his buddy at the Sheriff's office. Got us into the compound to look at Kate's Subaru. Like the Sheriff's investigators, we found no denting or paint scrapes consistent with impact from another vehicle. Just the wide, rounded dents from the rollover."

Ridge shifted in his seat. "Afraid of that. Single-vehicle crash, right?"

Terry looked at Ridge. "Seems so. But with no witnesses, we just don't know. Could have been someone cut her off. That orange-cone thrasher in the Supra, a couple of weeks ago, comes to mind. Or maybe she had to swerve—to miss a dog or cat in the road. Hell, it was Palos Verdes. Steep hills. And they have peacocks running around loose up there."

Jayne, sipping her cocoa, said, "What about Kate? What does she remember?"

Terry shook his head. "With the head injury, almost nothing. She was going to the office, then she woke up in the hospital."

Ridge frowned and rubbed his forehead. "Well, thank goodness, she was in a Subaru. Former ship builders. They still manufacture with the high-tensile steel used in big boats. Strongest on the market."

"Yeah. Almost no roof crush." Terry glanced at his watch. "Time to go in."

Jayne placed her cup on the table. "Wait a minute. Let's get flowers first. There's a shop, right off the lobby."

§

When they entered Kate's room, Ridge's eyes riveted on her left arm. A white cast. And her left leg. In traction. Kate was looking the other way, toward a young woman sitting next to her bed. The woman, in her early 20's, had long dark hair, and wore a brown sweater. Looked a lot like Kate. Kate stopped talking, turned toward the door and smiled. "Hey guys, meet Minnie-Me. She goes by the name Annie Gonzales, a.k.a. my niece."

Annie got up but looked down at her aunt. "Kate, you're a crack-up."

"No. I was in one. Believe me."

Ridge walked toward Kate's bed. "Wow. Still with the wisecracks. Now I know you're OK."

After introductions all around, Jayne put the glass vase and flowers on Kate's nightstand and hugged her. "Are you OK?"

Kate pointed at her left leg. "Will be as soon as they get me out of this contraption. Doctors say a month or two though until I'm back to 100 percent. Which is exactly what Annie, and I were talking about when you all came in."

"Yes?" said Ridge.

Kate pointed at him with her right hand. "You're going to need help while I'm recuperating."

Ridge raised his eyebrows. "You know, actually, I always need help."

"Exactly." Kate laughed. "And that's why Annie here is going to fill in for me. She's going to El Camino College at night. Learning to be a paralegal. And she's agreed to cover the office, during the day, while I'm gone. Whatta you think?"

Jayne moved to the foot of Kate's bed and wrapped an arm around Eric's waist. "God knows, he really does need help."

Annie laughed. "And Kate tells me I can call her anytime—in the hospital, in rehab, at home—when I have any questions."

Ridge clapped his hands. "That's it then. When can you start?"

Annie looked to Kate who nodded at her. "As soon as you give me the go ahead."

"I'm no Kate," Terry said, "but I can show you the ropes around the office this afternoon."

§

Ridge and Jayne got back to the apartment around eleven. Ridge strolled out to the north balcony to check on the hummingbirds, then hurried back inside, whispering. "Jayne...come here. Wait til you see this."

Peering into the geranium pot, they found two perfectly-round eggs, each the size of a small jellybean, sitting in the tiny nest. Ridge looked around. "But where's mama? Where's papa?"

"Fill up the feeder. We'll find out," said Jayne.

Sure enough, after Ridge topped the feeder with nectar and went inside, the two tiny birds were back. And after feeding, the female settled into the nest. Ridge turned to Jayne. "I could watch 'em all day. Really. But gotta get to the office. With Kate out, things will be different."

A few minutes later, as Ridge said goodbye and pulled the door open to leave, Jayne's phone began buzzing like crazy.

§

At noon, Ridge arrived at work. A note on his desk said Elliot Green had telephoned earlier. Ridge dialed. "Elliot, how you doing?"

"Good. Heading to court. Look—really quick—I found out this morning Judge Stevens in San Francisco died last week. Un-expectedly."

"Sorry to hear that. But I didn't know him."

"Eric, remember our talk at the Millsberg funeral? This makes the fourth judicial death we know of in just over two weeks. All unexpected. And all, so-called, accidental. A Judge Sayor in Phoenix died of a snake bite—of all things—about a week and a half ago. My friends there told me, at the time, he was walking alone in the desert. Which was beaucoup strange. Sayor was a purebred city boy. They don't remember him ever taking a hike in the desert, let alone by himself."

Ridge didn't want to jump to conclusions, but a sick feeling had taken up residence in his gut. "I knew Sayor. Judge on one of my aviation cases. But didn't know he was a city boy. Maybe that's why he got bit by a snake. Out of his element?"

"Eric. My gut tells me its more than that. Stevens allegedly fell into a moving subway train last Thursday night. But my friends in San Francisco tell me he drove everywhere. Never took the train. Makes no sense. Look, I've been doing this stuff a long time. Never heard of anything like it. Four deaths of area judges in only two weeks? It's beyond suspicious. Anyway, knowing you represent Judge Millsberg, I thought you should know."

"I appreciate it. Does anything else connect the four deaths?"

"Nothing that I know of. But look, one more thing."

"Shoot."

"Judge Moore invited me to a judicial conference last weekend. He's still trying to talk me into taking the bench."

"When you're ready, you should. You'd make a fine judge."

"But that's not it. It was the conference. Guess who made presentations?"

Ridge snickered. "Some judges?"

"Not just some. Gimuldin's three floating brethren. And they all sounded like ad men for the insurance industry."

Ridge's eyes went wide. "What do you mean?"

"The first presentation was "Insurance Matters in Your Cases." The second dealt with conflicts of interest—as in your Uncle Cho's Silent Conflict case. The charts, for both, were basically neutral, as you'd expect in a judge's speech. But what the brethren actually said sounded like they were shills for the insurance industry. Trying to indoctrinate other judges."

"Indoctrinate how?"

"When you boil it down, they were saying prior court decisions against insurance company interests were incorrect. Bad precedents, without 'real' constitutional basis. Should be disregarded in future cases. The second floating brother emphasized, over and over again, that allegations of conflicts-of-interest, whether between insurance-defense lawyers and clients or health professionals and patients, were meritless. Frivolous allegations. Bogus."

Ridge shook his head. "Bet there were no video or audio recordings of the presentations, right?"

"Right. Forbidden. Maybe they thought the charts might get outside the room, but without audio no one could really prove what was actually said."

"Makes sense. What about the third presentation?"

"It dealt mainly with tax-related cases. Again, the charts looked neutral, almost scholarly. But based on the cited statutes and cases, it was basically a pitch about why it's OK to locate insurance companies off-shore."

"Tax avoidance by insurance companies is incidental. For the greater good, right?"

"Right. You're getting the gist of the message."

"The gist is Gimuldin and his brethren are insurance industry shills."

"Yeah. But look, I really gotta run now. Late as hell. Talk later?"

"Sure. Thanks, brother." Ridge hung up, as Annie told him Jayne was on line 30. Ridge took it and was hanging up as Terry walked into his office and took a seat.

"You don't look happy." Terry said. "What's up?"

"Jayne just got hammered by a client. Some huge computer project gone sour. They literally begged her and said only she could salvage it. She's packing right now for Palm Desert and driving out this afternoon. She won't return until Saturday."

"That doesn't sound like fun. I was hoping we could have dinner together. And it's your turn to pay. But I just found out I gotta be downtown this evening."

"I'm tired as hell anyway. But look, I've got some interesting news. I just talked with my friend Elliot Green. He told me another judge, named Stevens in San Francisco, died mysteriously last week. That makes four area judges in less than three weeks. At that rate, they'll be no one left on the bench. Can you look into Stevens' death? Charge it to the Millsberg case."

"Of course. Anything else?"

Ridge smiled. "We finally might be getting somewhere. Remember Millsberg's funeral reception? And the three judges, gliding around with Gimuldin in their long robes?"

"Who could forget that sight? Night of the living dead."

"Well, Gimuldin's three floating brethren were speakers at a conference Elliot Green just attended. And all of 'em sounded like shills for the insurance industry trying to indoctrinate other judges."

Terry's eyebrows went up like dark flags. "That's interesting. I have news too."

"Shoot. I'm all ears."

"Remember the ropes and grappling hooks Spiderman left behind at your place?"

Ridge grimaced. "How could I forget?"

"On Friday, I traced the grappling hooks to a sporting goods store in Santa Barbara. Unfortunately, the buyer used cash. The trail dead ended."

"Another dead end in Santa Barbara," said Ridge. "Not only routine but seriously depressing."

"Yeah, but while there, following Jayne's research techniques, I went to Public Records in Montecito. Checked out 12 Oaken Drive. Sure enough, Gimuldin owns the property. Interestingly, he took out a permit to add three bedrooms to that already-humongous house. Strange for a guy who isn't married, no?"

"Maybe he gets visitors? Family members?"

"Maybe. The permit's been out for two months already."

Just then, Annie came into Ridge's office. "Eric, sorry to disturb you. But we got a call from a Jack Miles at WingX. He'll be in the area today. Wanted to know if you could meet with him, here, about 3 p.m. Says it's important."

Ridge shot Terry a look. "Sure. 3 p.m. works."

When Annie left, Terry said, "Too bad I've got a meeting downtown from 3 to 5 today I can't get out of. I'd like to meet Miles."

"Next time. Anything else on our Santa Barbara lead?"

"Saved best for last. Got hold of Joshua Censkey. The producer Ava talked about. Unfortunately, not with my hands, but on the phone. The guy's in Bolivia."

"Bolivia? How'd you ever track him down there?"

"Strangely enough, he called me. I found his assistant here in L.A., a Ryan Stacey, through bankruptcy records downtown. Their company just filed Chapter 11. I used a different name and Stacey said he'd give Censkey my number. Sure enough Censkey called back a couple of days later."

"What's his deal?"

Terry shook his head. "At first he tried to sell me some Bolivian treasury bonds. When he realized that was going nowhere, he opened up a bit. I mentioned Santa Barbara and that I was a private investigator, and he started spilling his guts about some attack on him by a bunch of crazies in the Santa Barbara area."

"Attack?"

"According to him, they kidnapped, tortured, robbed, and tried to kill him by tying him up and dumping at sea. Even branded him. Or sliced something in his chest while he was hanging from the rafters."

"Holy shit. That sounds like something out of a movie."

"Yeah, but that's not the best part. He said they kept him in a cage. In a barn. That's where it all took place."

Ridge shifted and sat up straighter. "Go on."

"Said the guy who tormented him was big with scary almost-blank eyes, thin lips, bony face. And, his henchmen were all bald."

"Reminds me of Mr. Hulk. And bald guys? You know, as Spiderman was scaling down his rope and running along the beach the other night, it was dark, but I thought he might be bald."

"More coincidences, huh? I'm really starting to like this asshole. At least he's talking to us. Although I think it's just that he thinks he's safe now that he's in South America."

"I hate to ask," Ridge said, "but did Censkey say anything about Ava?"

Terry grimaced. "Well, when I figured I couldn't get more out of him about Santa Barbara or the barn, I brought it up."

"What happened?"

"The phone seemed to go dead but then, after a long silence, he said he was sorry, he had been desperate and that he's now a new man. I pumped him more. He told me one of his nosy clients made him do it—pushed him. The client wanted information about you and Uncle Cho's Silent Conflict case. As a result, Censkey approached Ava, to get to you through me."

"How the hell did Censkey find Ava, or her connection to you?" asked Ridge.

"His assistant, that Ryan guy, found it all on the internet—some new service called 'face book' that he subscribes to as a Harvard graduate. And you know Ava. Any publicity is good publicity—even if it's about her breakup with me."

"Wow. Small world and getting smaller all the time. But—great job tracking down Censkey."

"Yeah. But I saved the best for last."

"Don't tell me. You got the name of his nosy client?"

"I did indeed. A Mr. Richard Chesterfield at 100 Royal Hill in Santa Barbara."

Ridge leaned back in his chair and wiped both hands through his hair. "No shit."

"No shit."

CHAPTER 53

At 3 p.m., Annie showed Jack Miles into Ridge's office. "Anyone want coffee?" she asked. "There's a fresh pot in the kitchen or pods for the single-cup machine."

"Sure." Ridge stood from behind his desk and stepped around to shake Jack's hand. "How do you like it, Jack?"

"Black's fine."

"Me too," said Ridge. "Thanks Annie."

"Ethiopian, Colombian, Kona, Kenyon, French Roast, or Dunkin' Donut? This is L.A. We revel in choice."

"Dunkin' Donut sounds good," said Jack.

"Sounds good," added Ridge.

When Annie returned with two cups of coffee, she found Ridge had moved to the black leather sofa near a glass coffee table in his office. Jack had maneuvered his wheelchair next to him. Annie set the cups on the table, and asked, "Door closed?"

Before Ridge could answer, Jack responded, "Please."

Leaving the office, Annie said, "Call if you need anything." Then she clicked the door shut.

§

"Before we get started," said Ridge, "unless it's none of my business, why the wheelchair? How'd it happen?"

"Car crash, T-10 paraplegia. Ten years ago."

"On a mission?"

"No. On the 405. Just south of LAX. Car ahead and to my left ran out of gas. The guy behind him saw it too late. Swerved into my vehicle, and that was that."

"God, I'm so sorry."

"Me too, at first," Jack said. "Considered early retirement. But I just love this shit too much. A lot of rehabs, and two years later, I was back on the job. Now I'm 90%. The other 10%, I forget about."

"Knowing you, that's what I'd expect. But look, you called this meeting. How can I help?"

"Eric, we go way back. That's why I'm here. I need your promise, no more WebBird tracking."

Half shocked, half embarrassed, Ridge put his hands up. "Whoa. OK. No more. I'd already figured I'd pushed my hand. How did you find out? Did Dave Lake mention it?"

"No. Dave's your buddy. But Eric, here's the deal, and this goes no further than this room, right?"

Ridge nodded. "Right."

"WebBird, Christ—WingX—all Company-sponsored."

"CIA assets?" asked Ridge. "To be frank, I thought there might be a connection from the moment I saw you at Dryden. But since when aren't Company assets available for use by agents?"

"Dave Lake is not an agent. He doesn't even know WingX is CIA-backed. He doesn't even know I'm CIA. Bottom line, no need to know. He's a test pilot—a damn good one—just doin' his job."

"Got it," said Ridge. "Sorry. Had the wrong picture. Won't happen again. My word on it."

"I figured that. It's why I'm here. But listen, there is another problem."

Ridge raised his eyebrows. "What?"

"You had Lake monitor a Richard Chesterfield. We know that because, unknown to Lake, Langley has coded feedback lines revealing anything picked up by WebBird—visuals, audio, anything."

"OK, again, I'm sorry. Not going to happen again, ever."

"I get that. I'm not bringing it up for that reason. Look, I don't know why you're interested in Chesterfield, but you need to know he's our agent."

Ridge almost choked. "Your agent? He's an insurance guy—actually an insurance mogul. What's that got to do with the CIA?"

"He's really only part-time. What he does in his off hours is anyone's guess. But he and his businesses have been CIA-backed for over eight years."

"That's a bunch of backing."

"Yeah, and it's one big reason the feds bailed him out when he almost went bust in 2000. He sank almost all his insurance companies' money into dot-com businesses, both on the investment and re-insurance ends. The fact is: He's an asshole, a lousy manager, and a worse corporate executive. He's wealthy today because of only two things: Millions in government bail-out money and the CIA still needs him."

"You may not want to tell me, but I've got to ask. Why?"

Miles nodded. "In for a penny, in for the rest. You might as well know."

"Know what?"

"With our backing, Chesterfield has infiltrated the Mideast high-end insurance market. His companies, mainly out of Nevis in the Dutch West Indies, insure the rulers of almost every Mideast country—and their family members, friends, and opposition. Right now, he's working on insuring all the rivals for rule of Yemen. Eric, as you know, it's all about oil and natural gas and controlling both, as best we can."

"Through insurance?" asked Ridge.

"Through information. Did you ever stop to think: Who acquires and controls more personal information about the middle-class, upper classes, and the filthy rich than even governments? People spill their guts on insurance forms—to get life insurance, health coverage, asset protection, whatever. Feed that information into the right computers, and you know almost everything about their personal life, health conditions, family assets, and—the list goes on and on."

Ridge raised both hands, palms out, fingers extended toward Jack. "But why do the rulers of Yemen, for example, need health insurance and why would they buy it from an American-owned company?"

"Because in any of these countries, rulers today may not be rulers tomorrow. And they hedge their bets—through insurance coverages, off-shore investment portfolios, you name it. And Chesterfield's companies best provide those services. In addition, think about it, healthcare in many Middle Eastern countries doesn't measure up. The ruling classes all want access to American and European health facilities for family illnesses or emergencies, and—as Chesterfield's people sell it: There's no better way to do that, than through them, if you care for your loved ones."

"So, all of the application information funnels through Langley's computers and analysts, and soon—who's who, who's got what, where and when, who has medical or other personal problems, and so forth—are all in your database. I get it."

"And that gives us otherwise unattainable, verified information about who controls what and how—from oil rights to gas leases, to terrorist-cell activities. The bottom-line Eric: Chesterfield is off-limits. Yeah, it's a little gangsta what he does, but we need him."

"I hear what you're saying."

"OK then," said Jack, nodding his head again with thumbs up. "Any questions?"

"Well, since you ask. Is the CIA involved in any way with what's going on in Montecito or Santa Barbara—the stuff on the WebBird tapes?"

Jack stared at Ridge. "Look, I checked just that with Sharon Nelson. You remember her, right?"

"Absolutely. Some amazing missions together in Laos."

"Well, she's now Western Regional Director of the National Resources Division. As you probably know, that's the domestic wing of the CIA. And she tells me there's no involvement, none at all, other than using Chesterfield as our funnel for Mideast information. And by the way, Sharon says hello, she hopes to see you soon, and it's been too long."

"Tell her, next time I'm in DC, expect a call, a thank you, and lunch."

As if on cue, Jack glanced at his watch and frowned. "Damn. Got to get back to LAX. Catching United to D.C. With the goddamn federal cutbacks, getting a private jet is harder and harder these days."

"Sorry to hear that," faked Ridge.

Miles grimaced and shook his head side to side. "Too much hassle, Eric. Too much hassle. Might be what drives me into retirement."

"I doubt that, Jack," Ridge said with a smile. "I doubt that very much."

§

At 8 p.m., back at the apartment, Ridge lay in bed, lights off, feeling like shit. Exhausted really. And it didn't help that Jayne was missing in action. But Mister and Pistol were nearby, and Ridge started thinking about Jack Miles, Sharon Nelson, Richard Chesterfield, and dead judges—Juliet Millsberg, Flynn in San Diego, Sayor in Arizona, Stevens in San Francisco and who knows who else. After dwelling and dwelling and dwelling on the deaths that just didn't make sense, Ridge began to doze off. Then, as before, his feet got warm and his mind faded to combat.

§

Before his transfer to Laos, Viet Cong mortars hit Bien Hoa Air Base—almost every night. Rocket City, Vietnam. Usually, it didn't interrupt the poker game, unless the rockets got too close. When that happened, Ridge and his buddies ducked under the table. Or, if it was really bad, they'd shout "diti mao" and rush to the bomb shelter, just outside the hootch, chips and cards still on the table. It all depended on how close was close. This particular night, it was all different.

Ridge shared his room in the hootch with his pilot buddy, Guru, already in the room when Ridge first arrived. Guru had been using the top bunk but learned Ridge hated bottom bunk. So, Guru agreed to flip for it. That's how he was—everyone's friend. Couldn't do enough for others. Always a kind word and plenty of cheer. Ridge lost the flip but gained a true friend.

That night, however, about 1 a.m. rockets rushed in. The whistling sounded so loud, so shrill that Ridge and Guru yelled at the same time, "Rockets!"

In less than a second, the hootch next door exploded. The whole world rumbled like an earthquake. Ungodly screaming. More whistling. Then—the walls of their tiny room crashed in like a train wreck. Ridge was hurled to the floor. Pitch black. Smoke rising. Guru landed on top. Arms and legs intertwined. Debris and dust all around. Then silence and the smell of gun smoke. Stale. Suffocating. Ridge was bruised, beat up, but OK. He whispered, "Guru, that was close, man. But now, get the hell off me."

No response.

Ridge pushed up and turned Guru. His face was raw meat. A bloody mass. Ridge realized he too was drenched in blood, everything running red over his face, down his neck, across his chest. Touching his cheeks and upper body with his fingers, Ridge discovered he wasn't hurt. The blood came from Guru. So, Ridge shook him. Why, he wasn't sure. He knew his friend was dead. Knew it could have been him on the top bunk. Flip of a coin. Probably better, he thought, if it were me. Guru was the better man. Ridge knew it at gut level. He pushed to his feet, lifted Guru in his arms, and carried him outside into the night, into another living hell. Full of stench. But the screaming, at least, had stopped.

The hootch next door had been two-level. It housed first responders—the med evac, paramedic and hospital teams. Now, it was shambles. Smoke and fire all around. Otherwise dark. As Ridge moved through the debris, with Guru draped in his arms, he almost tripped over the smoldering, partial remains of a nurse. Catching his balance, he saw her blackened head and upper body—still dressed in a scorched white uniform. He blinked and gagged on the reek of burning flesh and char. Everywhere. Arms and legs scattered across the courtyard. Belching smoke and hellish orange flames left and right. And everything surrounded by ghostly silence.

Then a man, forty yards away, bare-chested in only fatigue pants and boots, slowly stepped through rising vapors toward Ridge. As he trudged closer through the dark, settling dust, Ridge recognized him. A med evac chopper pilot. He had a guitar strapped around his neck and was strumming a song by 'The Animals'. Ridge knew it well. He and his buddies often yelled, top of their lungs, after a night of booze and poker, just before lights out: WE GOTTA GET OUT OF THIS PLACE! But the chopper pilot, still gradually advancing through smoke, had his head down, singing softly, slowly, over and over again, in almost a moan, *"We gotta get out of this place...outta this place...outta this place."* Then he stopped, turned and walked back, the way he had come, disappearing slowly into the murky night. His muffled words trailing off to silence.

Ridge sucked in air and looked down. He stared at the dead nurse—someone's sister, wife, mother—closed his eyes, and whispered, "My God...we're all too late. Too fuckin' late." His eyes opened and drifted to Guru in his arms. Ridge pulled in another deep breath, squeezed his eyes shut and clenched his teeth. Then his chin struck his chest, he fell to his knees, still clutching his friend, and began to sob.

Later, he stood, Guru still in his arms, and watched faint images of others in the vapory darkness. Searching. Standing. Kneeling. Weeping. Staring. Heads down. Mourning the dead engulfed in smoke and smoldering debris. Stone silent—but for tears running, soaking into the ground.

§

When Ridge woke, his watch read 9 p.m. His chest felt hollow. His teeth, at gum level, ached like hell. Everything felt like he'd been run over. He pulled himself out of bed and quietly shut the door not to disturb Mister and Pistol. Made his way to the far bathroom and downed three Tylenol. Extra Strength. He didn't know what to do with himself. He wished Jayne was here. Even if she was still asleep. Even if she didn't say a word. Still. He wanted her close. Needed her close.

So he drew in a long breath and let it out slowly. Went into the living room. Mixed some Jameson and Irish Mist and walked to the kitchen. Sitting at the table, surrounded by dark, he sipped his Irish whiskey, and fell into what he knew was depression. But he couldn't pull out. He slogged through a morass. Into a sucking hole. He could feel it grabbing at the soles of his feet and tugging. Then, pain. Soreness, bruising, aching. Tears stung. His nose tingled. Suddenly, an electric pulse passed to his left shoulder. Ridge reached out with his right hand and smothered his heart muscle. Then he froze. Waiting. But the heat of his palm helped. He lowered his head and took breaths, slow then deeper. Thinking anxiety attack, not heart attack, he repeated and repeated his mantra over and over again. "Never, ever, worry about what you can't control."

The pains slowly subsided. Then they were gone. Pleased he wasn't dying, but disgusted with himself, Ridge got up slowly, walked back to the bathroom and shut the door. He opened the cabinet. Twisted the top off a container. Sleeping pills. He swallowed one. Washed it down with his whiskey. Closed the cabinet and stared at the mirror. The past collided with the present. Ridge lowered his eyes. Gritted his teeth. And slammed his fist on the counter. "Damn. Damn it all to Hell."

Then his mind flashed to eight human heads hanging from the tree. Silent. Staring at him. And Ridge remembered. It's all about terror and control. Then he told himself the one thing he knew to be true: Can't ever let 'em win. Didn't happen then. Won't happen now.

Ridge cast his eyes back up to the mirror, sucked in a breath and addressed the man staring back at him. "What do we fuckin' have?" Again, his mind went over everything he knew. No help from Lake. No WebBird. Four dead judges. Plane quits, two thousand feet up. Assholes breaking into the apartment. Jayne could have been killed. Pistol shot. Terry, beat up. His head split open. The boat burned. And no matter what, not one lousy real break. And truth being, since the session with Dr. Peters, less sleep. More sweats. Even cases at the office—going to shit. Goddammit. Ridge's eyes dropped to the pill container. He ate another half. Chased it with some whiskey, and thought, Whoever they are, they're goddamn evil. But probably not Chesterfield if he's CIA. Although, dammit, he can't like us representing Uncle Cho. So maybe he is a part of it. But is CIA in on it? Or is it Gimuldin? The piece of shit. Can't put anything past that sonofabitch and his floating, black-robed lackeys. But how to prove it? How in the hell can we prove it?

Shaking his head, Ridge felt another sharp pain. Upper chest. Just a split second. Then it passed. Ridge lowered his eyes. Turned. And walked into the dark bedroom. He flopped on the bed, his right hand starting to shake. Slightly. He grabbed it, stopped the damn thing. Just then, Mister jumped up. Burrowed into the back of Ridge's knee. Pistol followed, stretching out close to Ridge on Jayne's side of the bed. "Thank God, thank God for you guys," whispered Ridge, as he stared at the ceiling. Burning eyes. Killer headache. Wanting to sleep. But still, he couldn't stop wondering: How? Where? When the hell does this all end? Or does it? Goddammit. There's gonna be more. *I know there's gonna be more.*

CHAPTER 54

Judge Christian Gimuldin and Calvin Hess sat in the two overstuffed brown leather armchairs closest to the fireplace in the dark cigar lounge of the Rayford Club, high atop an elegant ten-story brick building in downtown Los Angeles. The Club, started over a hundred years ago, was an exclusive meeting place for the power elite of Los Angeles. Its private members included politicians, bankers, businessmen, doctors, lawyers, and brokers, all who felt they could claw ahead by hob-knobbing, kissing ass, backroom and double dealing, and feeding off others in positions of control. Monthly dues were steep, but influence didn't come cheap—especially cloaked as networking.

With the light from the fireplace flickering in their brandy glasses, they were making small talk. His Eminence had asked Hess to drive the three hours down from the Camp, and for this special occasion, Hess sported a new haircut and wore a fine black suit, white shirt, and a blue silk tie. Hoping to blend in.

At 9:30 p.m. sharp, Richard Chesterfield joined them, lowering himself into a chair facing their direction. He held a brandy in one hand and a Cuban cigar in the other. After introductions and some chit-chat, the judge asked Chesterfield if they could all move to one of the back rooms for a private conversation.

"Of course," Chesterfield readily agreed.

When all three settled into the new walnut-paneled room, His Eminence began, "I understand your people and mine have worked together on a few projects, and that you were, at one point, loosely-affiliated with a Joshua Censkey. As were we."

"Yes," said Chesterfield. "But I believe Censkey has left the country."

"That's our understanding too," interjected Hess. "He's out of the picture, so to speak, for good. And that leaves something of a vacuum in certain circles."

Chesterfield faced the judge. "To be frank, Christian—may I call you Christian?"

"Certainly, Richard," His Eminence said.

"Well, my feeling is Censkey was something of a screw-up. But yes, his quick departure left some things unsettled."

"If you're interested," said the judge with a raised eyebrow, "I believe we can help settle those things to your advantage."

"What do you have in mind?"

His Eminence steepled his fingers and held Chesterfield's gaze. "We believe the American justice system has drifted too far left. In fact, it's broken. Utterly. My colleagues and I are determined to fix it. Before it's too late."

"I couldn't agree more," Chesterfield said. "Frivolous lawsuits, plaintiffs always crying victim, the insureds paying pitiful premiums and demanding Rolls Royce representation, it goes on and on. And pardon my bluntness, Christian, the left-wing radical judges—especially in state courts—make it worse. They're out-of-control."

"That's it, exactly," said the judge. "And my colleagues and I want to put a stop to it. You, as a premiere American businessman and world-renowned insurance professional, can join us on the ground floor, so to speak. But, of course, only if you're interested. If not, we can turn our conversation right now to any number of subjects—books, movies, sports—in fact, isn't it atrocious what's happening to the Dodgers?"

"Yes, without a doubt," Chesterfield said with a laugh. "But before we talk baseball, let me assure you, I am interested. Absolutely.

And I have things I'd like to cover with both of you. Let's get some more brandy and discuss all this in more detail."

"Of course," said the judge.

Before the evening was over, while drinking the finest cognac money could buy, the mogul, the judge, and the muscle had formed an alliance. They agreed, among other things, that any case involving potential 'Silent Conflict' issues must be buried, that certain matters involving Chesterfield's insurance groups deserved special consideration in courtrooms, and that Chesterfield's empire would provide a new source of regular funding for the judge's critical work. They also agreed, over a last drink, that networking like theirs was absolutely crucial to their shared vision for the future of America.

§

Later that evening, His Eminence was back at home, sitting in the Great Parlor with Hess. Each held another glass of brandy. His Eminence lifted his and smiled. "Chesterfield and his money are the last piece of the puzzle. No more holding back. You tell me a dozen soldiers are almost in place and that selling students will bring in even more money in the future. And thanks to that new list of judges you acquired from Censky, we could soon have more than twenty jurists in the Society—from trial judges to appellate justices. Across the country. And I know we can get others. We'll finally be able to force real change."

"And there's more good news," Hess said, the hint of a smug smile playing across his lips.

"What?"

"Our ties to the National Socialist Group are about to pay off—big time."

"What do neo-Nazis have for us?" His Eminence asked.

"I've been coordinating with them in anticipation of Sunday's Summit at the Camp. The NSG has agreed to give us access to the

Marburg virus—in the form of a new biological weapon. It's not ready yet, but soon."

The judge shifted in his seat. Seemed uncomfortable. He had told Hess his groin still had teeth marks from the bitch. Now his tongue was flicking out to touch the tiny scab where the other whore had bit him. But, largely ignoring the pain, he stared at the reflection of the fire dancing on his glass, and said, "Go on."

"The Marburg virus? Cousin to the Ebola virus. Google it."

The judge couldn't help the edge in his voice. "I don't want to Google it."

Hess cleared his throat. "Discovered in Marburg, Germany. 1960s. And studied extensively by the Soviets. A fatality rate of up to 90%. And during the Cold War, the Soviets actually built an aerosol weapon to deploy it. But when the Soviet Union dissolved in '91, the technology got sold to highest bidders."

The judge pinned Hess with a dark stare. "We don't want to destroy the world, just remake it."

"Right, but recently, using genetic engineering, the NSG—with five other groups worldwide—sponsored ground-breaking research. They're now close to modifying the virus for use in a personal bioweapon."

The judge downed half his brandy and cleared his throat. "Explain."

"The re-engineered virus will have accelerated potency, a half-life of only five minutes, and will attack only the heart muscle. They're experimenting now with an injection pen. Leaves an almost imperceptible hole when injected into the superior vena cava—the large vein in the arm that leads directly to the heart."

"So, it'll cause heart failure with minimal chance of the virus spreading?"

"That's it exactly," said Hess. "A perfect weapon for what we have to do. Traces of the virus will be almost impossible to detect after death."

"And we'll have access to it?"

Hess allowed himself a smile. "Absolutely."

His Eminence tilted his brandy glass toward Hess. "Be careful."

Hess stood and clicked the judge's glass with his own. "Of course. Here's to a memorable day."

"A memorable day, indeed," said His Eminence. "When I became a judge, I thought the rush of power—control over life and death—would be the greatest feeling I could ever have. Now, it's pedestrian. Peanuts. Now I see the way to a better America. And all because we have a perfect formula." He held up one finger. "First, exploit others' flaws." Another finger. "If that doesn't work, put the fear of God in them." Another finger. "If that still doesn't work, eliminate them."

"My God, yes," said Hess. "Control the people, control the process. But can we do it with judges alone?"

"If judges can appoint presidents, like George W in 2000, judges can dethrone them. And once we get the right autocratic president in power, we're in."

"What about Congress?"

The judge smirked. "Congress? They'll fall all over themselves, deferring to us and raking in the special-interest money we'll funnel their way. In fact, we'll create wealth beyond dreams—even my dreams. And as for the little people, the ordinary folks—we can't get greedy. Trickle down works. Keeps them in line. And if not, well, that's why we have prisons. Why we have soldiers, wars, even executions—for the greater good. After the Summit, it'll all fall in place. The path is clear."

At that, Hess, still standing, raised his glass. "To success."

The judge nodded. Then his brows drew together as he stared up at Hess. "But what about that damn lawyer? Ridge. Are he and his people still stirring things up? Snooping around?"

Hess grimaced. "He's already had two warnings—on the boat and in his plane. He doesn't seem to get it."

"You always say, three strikes and they're out, right?"

"Absolutely."

"Make it like Flynn and Sayor."

"Don't worry," Hess said. "I plan to."

CHAPTER 55

It was midnight. Halfway between Tuesday and Wednesday. Ridge still couldn't sleep. With pills and whiskey, he had hoped to get some shut-eye, but all he did was toss and turn. Thoughts of Lake and Miles wouldn't go away. So he took another half a sleeping pill. And just before dozing off, he sensed his feet getting warmer and warmer, and his mind moved to Laos.

§

CIA officer Hal Thomas, in the Ops Center deep below ground at Ubon Air Base in Thailand, finished up at the podium. Ridge, in his early twenties, was excited. He had been plucked from his Air Force Special Operations Wing in Vietnam only a week before to fly CIA missions into Laos and Cambodia. This was Mission One.

Later that evening, sitting at the big table in the Ops Center, Hal turned to Ridge. "This particular sortie is photo reconnaissance. We believe Pathet Lao are holding POWs near Paksong Laos. There's a large wooden building on the eastern outskirts of town. A red cross painted on its metal roof. But that's bullshit. A ruse. We need photos all around—before launching a rescue attempt tomorrow night."

Sharon Nelson, an African American CIA officer in her mid-twenties, spoke next. "I'll be flying your right seat, Eric, with the camera mount and high-speed film. Getting on target around 11 a.m. would be best for photos."

Hal added, "You'll also have a translator to help with the radios. That's important—if things go bad."

Ridge turned to Hal. "Could be a problem. Only two seats in the bird. One for the pilot, one for the observer or camera operator. The rest of the cockpit is filled with radios. Dead weight that already makes the plane extremely heavy for takeoff.

"We have a perfect work-around," said Hal. Just then, a knock at the door. In came Hal's assistant, with a ten-year-old Laotian boy. "Eric, Sharon—your translator," said Hal. "Mr. Pao's first name is Tee. He'll have no trouble squeezing in back, between the radios."

The boy shook hands with Ridge and Sharon one at a time, very business-like. Then he said, "When do we go?"

Hal eyed all three and said, "You take off at ten-hundred tomorrow."

The next morning Ridge and Sharon wore black flight suits the CIA had procured from the Thai Air Force. No insignia. In fact, Ridge had to leave his dog tags behind. Officially, with no U.S. military presence in Laos, tags were out. The only difference in how Sharon and Ridge dressed was that he wore a shoulder harness with a nine-millimeter Beretta. She had a waist belt that led to a leg holster with a .38 pistol strapped to her right thigh. Tee, on the other hand, dressed like a ten-year-old Laotian boy. Shorts, T-shirt, and sandals. If anything went wrong, he'd simply disappear into the background.

They loaded up and took the runway. Throttles in, they rolled and rolled a long time, and finally broke ground. Ridge waited for more altitude, and then pulled up the gear handle. During climb out, he checked on Sharon and turned to see the boy. Tee still sat in the makeshift seat belt they had strung between the radio banks, and Ridge asked, "You OK?"

"For sure," said the boy. "I've been in helicopters, but this is different—smoother—more fun!"

Flying due east, fifty minutes later, Sharon Nelson called out, "I see it. Building at two o'clock about 10 klicks. Big red cross on top."

"Klick? What's a klick?" asked Tee.

"About a mile," Ridge told him. "Cameras ready?"

Sharon nodded. "All set."

"OK, let's circle to the north. Maybe we'll hear something on these fancy CIA radios." As Ridge flew wide, Sharon turned to frequencies Hal had given them but they heard only static or silence. "Let's take it in closer then," said Ridge. "Descending to 1500 feet."

"OK," Sharon said, "but let's get some distance shots before moving in on target."

At 1500 feet above ground, Ridge banked the plane right toward Sharon to give her camera angle. He began to circle the building wide to the south. But as soon as Sharon started clicking, all hell broke loose. Fifty-caliber tracer bullets engulfed the plane with twenty or thirty streams of deadly light. They seemed everywhere. But the streaks came mainly from an area less than a klick south of the building. Ridge yanked the wheel left. He dove to get speed for a hard pull up north to escape the guns. Then, two loud clanks. "We're hit, tighten seat belts," ordered Ridge.

Then, three more impacts. The front engine died—followed by Number 2. Restarts. Nothing. Again. Zilch. Ridge feathered the props to reduce drag. He finessed the plane to a glide path to get as far north as possible. They continued to drop.

"Only jungle below," Ridge gritted out through clenched teeth. "Get set for tree impact."

Then he saw it—a river, about the width of three lanes of traffic. He banked hard. They fell like a rock. Ridge leveled wings and aimed for the river. Just above water, he pulled up, last minute, and then pushed the nose over for a level belly flop. Water sprayed everywhere, blinding him. But Ridge felt the right wing going down. He shoved the wheel full left. The bird leveled out, continued skidding like a runaway surfboard, and whacked the right riverbank. The plane leaped, smashed into the jungle, and screeched to a stop. Ridge searched frantically for fire. None. He twisted to Sharon and Tee and said, "Let's get the hell outta here."

Moments later, he grabbed the machete and followed Sharon and Tee to the ground. The sun, nearly overhead, blasted heat, but he remembered his survival training. They had to disappear. Into deeper jungle. Stay away from rivers and trails where Pathet Lao would search. As they penetrated intense growth, Ridge swung the machete lightly, to minimize noise, and tried to move westerly toward the Mekong River. But maintaining direction was a bear. The sun overhead was no help, and beneath the jungle canopy moss grew everywhere, not just on the north side of trees. Progress became slow and painful, especially for Ridge's six-foot two-inch frame. Even Sharon at five-foot-five and four-foot Tee had to crawl at times to make it through twisted thickets and around marshy bottoms.

Fighting jungle and heat, after several hours, Ridge became more and more disoriented cutting and slashing his way through the undergrowth. Sharon, with huge purple-blue bruises on her face from hitting the camera equipment during landing, fared no better. Yet despite the pain and confusion, they continued for several more hours, hacking the jungle from within.

Suddenly Ridge stopped and whispered, "Sounds ahead." All three silently crawled forward and peered through thick growth. Ridge muttered, "Goddammit, got turned around. There's the goddamn building." They all gazed up to the red cross on the metal roof. "At least it's the north side," said Ridge, glancing at the sun lower in the sky to his right. "And...."

Before he could finish, a woman screamed.

Tee stared at Ridge and Sharon. "We gotta help."

Ridge fired back. "We've got specific orders. If we go down, we get our butts out of Laos—ASAP—no delays, no exceptions."

Sharon touching the deep purple part of bruises on her face said, "We just can't ignore that scream."

Ridge, pulled inside out, stared up at the sky. Hesitated. And then nodded. "Hell. Shit on orders. It's the right thing to do."

At the building, Ridge held his Beretta ready-to-go as he peered in at the lower left of the big window. Sharon, with her .38 out, kneeled near the other side of the glass. Tee had been told to stay back—at the jungle's edge.

"Damn," whispered Ridge, trying to steel himself, "there's a guy hanging by his arms—from the ceiling. Feet off the ground. Face covered in blood. Rod or spear through his belly. Dead. Very dead." Before Sharon could respond, there was another scream. Ridge stared to the left through the window. "Two guys…knives… raping a woman." Sharon jerked her head to Ridge's left, toward a closed door. He nodded slowly, and whispered, "I've got the guy on the left."

Ridge and Sharon positioned outside the door. Kicking in together, they charged with guns straight ahead. But neither could fire—without possibly hitting the girl. So Sharon continued running at the rapist on the right, who pulled his victim closer. He threw a knife with his free hand, planting it in Sharon's left side. She continued to charge, right arm straight out, pistol in hand. When close enough she fired. Blood splattered from the man's throat as he caved to the ground.

At the same moment, Ridge dropped to a prone position. He stretched out with two hands around his pistol and put a bullet through the forehead of the other rapist. The big man collapsed with a thud. Then the woman, her nurse's uniform ripped to the waist, got up and ran to Sharon. Before Ridge could get there, she tore off the bottom of her skirt, yanked the knife from Sharon's side, and tightly wrapped the wound. Then, she pushed in to stop the bleeding, and stared at Sharon's eyes. Pointing at herself with her free hand she said, "Lani."

Just then, Tee ran up to the open door, jumping up and down. "Uncle Sand, CIA helicopter! Hurry. Hurry!" Seconds later, a Laotian man, a few years older than Ridge, stood at the door. Tee grabbed the man around the hips with a wide smile. "My Uncle Sand. But—we must hurry! Helicopter through jungle to north. Pathet Lao to south. Hurry. Hurry!"

All four followed Sand through the jungle. It was particularly hard on Sharon, but Lani never stopped putting pressure on the knife wound. Twenty minutes later they saw a small chopper, hovering above a tiny clearing, with a rope ladder hanging from its belly and its end near the ground. Tee explained that only Sharon and Lani could get in the helicopter, "No more room. Eric—you, Uncle, me—we ride ladder. Hurry. Hurry!"

Once everyone got in position, the chopper moved out fast to the north. Then west to the Mekong River and Thailand. As airflow smashed his face, Ridge hung onto the rungs with Tee above, Sand below, and Sharon and Lani safely in the chopper. He thought, *Thank God. We're outta there.* Then as he glimpsed up and down again at Tee and Sand, the wind nearly blinding him, his mind flashed to his favorite movie *Casablanca.* He clutched the ladder and whispered to the wind, "Yeah, could be the beginning of a beautiful friendship."

§

On Wednesday morning, Terry rushed into Ridge's office. "I've got a plan, and I think it's a winner."

"Go slow, compadre. Had a really bad night."

"Tomorrow, I'm investigating."

"Tomorrow? You can investigate today if you want. It's your thing, isn't it?"

"No, no. I mean I'm going up to Montecito tomorrow to investigate Gimuldin's place—12 Oaken Drive. Only piece on the board we haven't moved. We've gotta lay eyes on it."

Ridge shook his head until it hurt. "Didn't we promise each other? No more solo to Santa Barbara county. Our history there sucks. And I'm tied up with those delayed Toyota depositions downtown. The damn things are scheduled for Thursday and Friday."

Terry raised his hand to shut Ridge up. "Annie already told me. So, I called Dan. He worked weekend shift, and he's off tomorrow and Friday. He agreed to moonlight with me."

Ridge rubbed at his right temple. "OK. Give me details… slowly."

"Remember Gimuldin pulled that permit—to have three additional bedrooms built?"

"Yeah."

"Well, Dan and I will show up as building inspectors. You know, we'll say we've been ordered to make a surprise inspection for permit enforcement purposes. That should get us inside the fence, even the house."

"Isn't that bending the law a teeny bit?"

"When did that ever bother you—especially when it's the right thing to do?"

Ridge rolled his eyes. "You sure Dan's okay with this?

"It was his idea." Ridge pinned him with a skeptical look. "OK, it was my idea, but he said it was brilliant."

"Brilliant," Ridge said with a chuckle. "And what's the next part of this brilliant plan?"

"We do what we do best." Terry shrugged. "We ad lib. Take it a few minutes at a time."

"It's risky. I mean, do you really think it's necessary?"

"Sometimes unnecessary risks are necessary. You've said that yourself."

Ridge groaned. "I hate it when you use my own words against me. Tell me what the goals are here?"

"Goals? To find out what's going on inside the house. To see if there's any connection to Censkey's tormentors, the barn, the attacks on you and Jayne, the forced landing in that Torrance field, or anything else we've been hit with or dug up so far."

"Like what?"

"Like why those judges—Gimuldin's brethren—were gung-ho for insurance companies during their presentations and why four other judges have ended up dead."

"OK, OK. Good goals."

"And a good plan?"

Ridge nodded. "And a good plan."

"All right then. Tomorrow, Dan and I will take a little trip to Montecito. If things go well, drinks on you, when we return. Deal?"

"Deal. Just be careful." After Ridge's dream last night, he was feeling a little tender and sentimental toward the skinny little Tee Pao from Laos.

"Always," Terry said, with a big smile. "What could go wrong?"

"Plenty. And you damn well know it."

"You worry too much, Kemosabe."

CHAPTER 56

On Wednesday evening, Hess met with five Watchmen, including Two, in the Great Room. Hess sat in His Eminence's chair at the head of a long, ornately carved wooden table that looked like it'd been at home in some Medieval castle. One, Two and Three were on his right in high back wooden chairs, just as ornate as the table itself. The other two Watchmen sat to his left in like chairs. Six remained with the trainees at the Camp.

Hess told Two he was at the meeting because of his "decent job" readying the four recent captives for disposal. But Hess, being Hess, tempered his praise. "As you can see," he'd said to the others, "Two is once again joining us at official briefings because he finally did something right. We got decent money for the one boy and one girl, and something less for the other two girls, but that was because of their bruising. Two's efforts were somewhat clumsy, but effective, nonetheless. After he was done with them, both girls were submissive enough to be purchased as sex surrogates by the Dubai underground. At a hundred thousand each. His Eminence was pleased, and we're all glad to be rid of them."

Hess is a fucking shit, Two thought as Hess went on. I worked wonders with those little bitches. Record time. Transformed them into something they weren't. And he calls it *somewhat clumsy*. Fuck him. Then, feeling heat from Hess staring at him, Two looked up, put on a big smile, and said, "Thank you, Herr Hess, your praise is undeserved."

Hess ignored Two and turned to the others. "Moving on, except for Two, we'll all be returning to Camp for the next two days. I want to conduct even more rigorous exercises to ensure the trainees will impress everyone at the Summit on Sunday."

Two, who couldn't help himself, broke in. "What about me?"

"You," said Hess, "will not speak unless spoken to. Directly. Understand?"

"Yes, Herr Hess."

"You'll stay here on security detail. His Eminence will not be back until Friday evening, and we won't return until late Friday afternoon. Until then, you are in charge of the house. The place will be empty, so there's little chance of screw up."

"Yes, Herr Hess."

Hess went on. "I spoke with His Eminence late last night. He thinks things are going well. Before Censkey gave us his list, we had eight judges in the Raven Society. His Eminence has now taken it upon himself to make contact with seven others in Censkey's network. Six have committed to join us. Only one declined, a Judge Stevens in San Francisco, who had a bit of a pornography problem. One and I eliminated that problem last Thursday. Poor guy fell in front of a BART train. Tragic. And the ironic thing was Stevens was a friend of His Eminence. They had met years ago at a judicial conference in San Francisco. In fact, Stevens was the one who first told His Eminence about Censkey and his judges list. Once we got it, however, Stevens wanted off the list as a reward. Not smart. But there are still eighteen other names on the list, and His Eminence has tasked the Executive Committee of the Raven Society to contact each of them."

"That's exciting," said One. "Exactly what we've been working for all along."

"That right," Hess said. "Imagine thirty or more judges across the country in the Raven Society—all with authority, autonomy, essentially unbridled power in cases before them, and sworn allegiance to the Society. And then, thirty will become forty, and forty will become fifty. You get the idea. That's the future, gentlemen. And we'll be part of that—if we are ready."

One raised his hand. "What do you mean, if we are ready?"

"We must complete the training of the next squad of Watchmen by Friday, so they all graduate on Saturday. Time is short. His Eminence wants them to impress our new allies during the Sunday Summit. And in the longer run we need them to operate the larger network—keep order. Assist with enforcement when necessary. That's our mission, gentlemen. Questions?"

Two slowly raised his hand.

"What the hell is it?" said Hess.

"I heard we also eliminated a Judge Sayor in Phoenix. How'd we do that?"

"You wouldn't know, would you?" said Hess. "You were on the shit list. Couldn't participate, right?"

"Yes, Herr Hess."

"Well, you remember Judge Millsberg in Orange County, don't you?"

"Yes, of course. You made that look like a perfect accident."

Which is just what you want to hear, thought Two to himself. *Some perfect accident.* She was helpless on the pulley and chains in the barn. Then you decided to torture her some by funneling carbon monoxide from the tractor into her face. And you overplayed your hand, shithead. Millsberg died before she ever had a chance to cooperate with His Eminence. And then, based on reading about one of Millsberg's recent court decisions—while doing your goddamn 'homework,' you devised that stupid ass scheme: Faking a bicycle accident by banging up her bike. Then dragging her by her feet with your truck—to scratch up her face. Next you set her up 'perfectly' in bed at her house, with her car running in the garage, to make it look like she had fallen asleep and sucked in fumes. *All bullshit. All unnecessary.* All a waste—just because you blew the carbon monoxide thing. Nice work, Herr Friggin' Hess, you piece of shit.

Hess pounded the table. "Two! Are you listening?"

"Yes, Herr Hess."

Hess turned to the others. "As I was saying, yes, a perfect accident. The same thing with Sayor. Except that traitor ended up dead in the desert by 'accidental' snake bite. How fucking unfortunate. Right, One?" Hess pivoted toward Two. "Are you up to speed now, Two? Satisfied?"

"Yes, Sir, thank you."

"Then if you don't mind, Two, our briefing is over. Is that OK with you?"

"Yes, of course, Herr Hess," whispered Two, looking down at his feet and thinking, *What an asshole. What a huge fucking asshole.*

§

Hess was feeling the pressure of the upcoming Summit. So, at 6 a.m. on Thursday, he and five Watchmen reviewed the trainees in the Operations Tent at the Camp. With a stiff face, Hess scanned the Watchmen-in-training. "This starts your final exams. At 0615 One, Three and Four will take three of you to the target ranges. The rest will conduct practice assaults in full gear at the mock compound. Everything will be scored. At 0815, you will all run Obstacle Course B, the tougher one, in a crouch. Full gear. Four and Five will lay down automatic weapon fire—just above where your heads should be. Stay low, stay fast, gentlemen."

Three heard his cue. "What then, Herr Hess? These men crave a real challenge."

"Good," said Hess. "At 0930, we'll go on a mountain run. Thirty-pound backpacks and Mark-43 heavy guns. Upon return, we'll repeat exercises at the target ranges, mock-compound assaults, and obstacle runs. Why? To make sure your scores don't plummet after a little exercise. Then, gentlemen, we'll have lunch: K-rations and water. That way, we'll be ready for afternoon demonstrations in the training tank and the underwater-demolition pond. Again, everything will be scored. We expect your best. Don't disappoint. If all goes well, we may even take an evening run for an hour or so. Then tomorrow, we plan more of the same starting at 0400 hours. The best of you will demonstrate for the Executive Committee on Saturday and our allies on Sunday. Good luck, gentlemen."

CHAPTER 57

At 9 on Thursday morning, after being buzzed through the gate, a young, bald-headed man opened the front door. Terry, dressed in a non-descript blazer, beige chino slacks, and a white shirt with a pocket protector overflowing with pens and pencils, said, "Good morning, sir. We're Inspectors Lee and Williams. From the City. Here for an interim inspection of the construction under your permit."

"I don't know anything about an inspection. Please return when the owner's here," said the bald man.

"When will Judge Gimuldin be arriving?" asked Dan, as he shifted his clipboard and adjusted his tool belt full of levels, rulers, and other inspection essentials.

"Not until Friday evening."

"No-no-no," said Dan, looking impatiently at his cheap digital watch and the pad on his clear plastic clipboard, "we must inspect before then. It has to be done this week."

The bald man squinted. "Why?"

"Because we have schedules too, young man. Look at this," said Terry, waving official-looking documents he had found on-line. "The permit clearly notifies you that there can be interim inspections at any time without notice. That's how we enforce compliance with city code. Now, if you want us to just shut down construction and revoke the permit, fine, we can do that. Your choice."

"But construction hasn't even started yet. Can't you come back later, after it begins?"

"That's not how it works," said Dan, looking busily at his watch and pad again. "The allowable time on your permit is ticking away. You're on a clock. If we revoke it or the permit lapses, the owner has to go through the filing process all over again and it can be up to a six-month wait to get another approved. And most times the second application takes longer, especially if we write-up your refusal to grant access for inspection. Up to you—but decide quickly. We have a full day of inspections, every day."

The bald guy nodded. "OK, OK. But what would you inspect? There's no construction yet."

Dan didn't answer the question. Instead, he reached into his pocket, and pulled out some papers, briefly flashing part of his 'inspector' badge. Just enough to look official. Then he shoved it in his pocket before it could be read. "What is your name, and what do you do here?"

"My name is Two—like the number. I'm in charge of security."

"Well, Mr. Two, here's the deal," said Dan. "I'm surprised your employer didn't apprise you of the situation, but once you pull a permit in this City for any add-on construction, the City has the right to inspect anything and everything about the property. We have to make sure nothing is out-of-code—we're talking present-day code. Look at those sprinkler faucets and controllers over there. See them?"

Two looked behind the bushes near the front door. "Yes, they've always been there."

"That may be," said Dan, "but they're not tall enough. Those faucet heads should be at least twelve inches above ground—a 2003 rule. In case of flooding. They definitely look no more than ten inches high. If so, they must be torn out and replaced."

"Are you serious?" Two looked at the two men as if they'd just grown antlers.

"I'm sorry," replied Dan, "but that's the kind of thing we have to write up. Now the faster you let us get about our business, the faster it'll be over and we'll be on our way. Or we can come out tomorrow at 9 a.m. sharp with one or two other City inspectors and go over this place with a fine-toothed comb."

"Look," Terry said, sighing in commiseration with Two. "We're just doing our jobs. Just like we know you're doing yours. But this address is on our schedule today. We don't make the rules. You don't let us in now, we just come back tomorrow. And that makes our supervisor cranky. Quite frankly," he glanced at Dan, "the guy's an ass and he'll send us back out to inspect every system, brick by brick, to check for current compliance. Just because he can. Plumbing. Electrical."

Dan winced. "Wiring is always fun. Checking every receptacle in the house."

"Your choice, Mr. Two." Terry shrugged. "What's it gonna be?"

Two gave them a weak smile. "OK. Come on in, gentlemen. I think I understand now. I'm sure we can finish this up quickly today."

Once inside, Terry and Dan started with the living room—measuring, tapping, checking level, unscrewing vent covers, and scribbling on their pads. Two shadowed them. After twenty minutes, while screwing out an air-conditioning return grate near the floor, Terry turned and stared up at Two, "Look, we have to inspect all the rooms on all three floors. We can cut the time in half if Inspector Williams and I split up. Your choice, but that way we can be sure to finish today. Why don't you take Inspector Williams upstairs, and I'll finish down here?"

Two agreed, reluctantly. He mounted the stairs with Dan, who trying to keep Two occupied, talked him into helping with the measuring, leveling, and unfastening. "In that way," said Dan, "we can move things along more quickly."

Free to roam the first level, Terry was disappointed. After thirty minutes, no pay dirt. Then in the dining room, he finally spotted something strange. The big, cavernous fireplace, permanently sealed off with smoke-colored glass, had no gas logs. No grate for firewood. Weirder yet, Terry couldn't see a hearth floor within the enclosure. Looking closer, he thought a dark floor might sit lower in the open shaft. But hard to see, even with his flashlight shining through the glass enclosure. The beam got cut off by heavy carbon streaks on the inside surface of the glass.

Just then, Two came up to Terry. "Can I help you?"

Terry, surprised, answered, "No, no, just making sure this fireplace is up to code. Can I check the flue?"

As Two was about to respond, Dan called from upstairs. "Mr. Two, where'd you go? I could use your help inspecting the plumbing in the rear-most bathroom. We all want to move this along, don't we?"

Two sounding flustered said, "Sure, sure," and bounded up the stairs three at a time.

Terry, free to roam again, checked the entire first level for any type of door, steps, or down-elevator to a basement below. There were none. In fact, according to the building plans he reviewed earlier at Public Records, there was no basement. The elevator that existed serviced only the three floors of the house. The only stairwell on the first floor went up. After another half hour of inspecting the first level, Terry found nothing more unusual—except perhaps a remarkable library set up with a huge desk, leather chairs and high wooden bookshelves serviced by a sliding ladder, like the paradigm Hollywood-version of a judge's library. But the room hardly looked used. In fact, everything on the first floor seemed new or hardly used. And neat as a pin. Not that unusual I guess, reasoned Terry, for a judge—with obvious family money—who only uses the place on weekends and holidays.

Terry went to the second level to look in on Dan and Two. Dan had Two on his back under the sink in a beautiful marble bathroom off the second-story study, describing and measuring the plumbing as Dan wrote down the details. Taking the opportunity to quickly survey the second floor, Terry again found everything orderly. In fact, extremely well-ordered. And again, neat as a pin. The only unusual thing was the imposing master bedroom, which took up more than a third of the second floor. Fit for a king. Obviously, the judge had splurged when designing the master suite. The velvet curtain around his huge four-post bed must have cost a fortune by itself. And the large ornate fireplace in the master bedroom was functional—wood-burning with gas-assist, like the one in the study.

Terry returned to Dan and Two. "OK, I'm finished for now with the first floor. I'll head up to the third. Why don't you join me when you're through with the second level? Then, we'll finish up the third and go outside."

"Tell ya what," said Dan, "to save time, we'll head outside when we finish here, while you do the third level."

"I'll have to unlock my room," said Two from his prone position under the sink. "Whenever you get to it. It's the last one, way in the back, on the third floor."

"Got it. I'll holler when I get there." Terry headed up the stairwell. Again, he found nothing extraordinary on the third level—mainly guest bedrooms and bathrooms. Each looked used somewhat but clean and extremely neat, almost like military quarters. The one interesting thing was a large, mirrored exercise room with reinforced flooring, long rows of weights, running tracks, Nautilus exercise machines and stationary bicycles. The huge room looked like something you'd find at a luxury resort hotel, complete with rear deck, shower room, jacuzzi and sauna. If the judge ever invites me over, thought Terry, I'd stay at least a week. This place could be a blast.

Then Terry went to the stairwell and called Two to unlock his room. Again, nothing extraordinary inside. The only things of note were the military square corners on his bed covers. Very precise. But then Terry had seen the same thing in the other bedrooms.

Finished with the third floor, Terry and Two took the elevator down. They joined Dan outside. All three spent another hour inspecting the perimeter of the house and its grounds. Terry in particular searched for some type of entrance to a basement, but without success. Then, finally, Terry said to Two, "Inspector Williams and I are through for now. We've been at it over three hours. We need to get back to the office to compile the data."

"Compile data?" asked Two.

"Well, Mr. Two," explained Terry, "we don't carry the codes in our head. They fill ten books. And anyway, this is the 21st Century, so we enter the measurements in the computer system and a program compares our measurements and other notes to the code provisions using computerized analysis forms. If it turns out we're missing anything, we'll be sure to get back in touch with you. If discrepancies are found, we'll of course provide a report. What I'm saying, Mr. Two—when it comes to permit inspections, no news is good news. Any questions?"

Two replied, "No questions. Thanks. No news is good news. I get it."

"Thank you, Mr. Two," said Terry and Dan at the same time. Then Terry added, "Have a good day," and he and Dan got in Dan's SUV, fitted with fake government plates, and drove off. After clearing the main gate, Dan said to Terry, "Almost 2 p.m. I'm starving."

"Let's head to the Santa Barbara Pier," said Terry. Plenty of seafood places there. And won't be busy at this hour. We'll grab a secluded booth, eat, and talk."

"Next stop—the Pier."

CHAPTER 58

Dan and Terry drove right onto the wooden pier at the foot of downtown Santa Barbara. As always, fishermen cast and reeled up lines by the railings. Both sides. Tourists strolled along the wooden walkways watching boats come and go in the harbor. Luckily, Terry found a parking space near The Captain's Table. Inside, he and Dan found a secluded booth with a corner window overlooking bright blue water and seagulls swooping close to the nearby fish-cleaning stations on the dock. Dan ordered the fried fish plate with fried flounder, fried oysters, fried calamari, coleslaw, and French fries. Terry got the grilled mahi-mahi fish sandwich, without mayo, and a garden salad. Dressing on the side. Then Terry gazed over at Dan's dishes. "That stuff will give you a heart attack."

"Stuff it. What you eat," Dan waved at hand at the menu, "is all mushy. No grit."

"Gotta agree," said Terry with an exaggerated eyeroll. "True grit."

"If you're finished with nutritional advice," said Dan chewing down on three French fries at once, "let's compare notes on what just happened. That guy, Two, pretty weird. A bald head, body like Adonis, eye patch, and a loose screw…maybe two upstairs."

"No doubt," agreed Terry munching some salad. "A weird character. But the house itself—not so weird."

"Yeah," said Dan, taking a gulp of beer, "I found nothing unusual while I was with the bald guy. Big, expensive, beautiful house, but nothing out of the ordinary."

Terry sipped at his ice water. "The only weird thing is that huge closed-off fireplace in the dining room."

"Sometimes people don't want the smell of fire or smoke in the dining room. Maybe that's why it's closed off."

"Could be. But the other four fireplaces in the house were functional—either wood burning or gas logs. Doesn't seem like anyone in the house has an aversion to fireplaces. And anyway, there's a shaft, going down, where the floor of the fireplace should be. Why? And where does the shaft go? There's no basement."

Dan nodded. "I searched outside. No entrances or trap doors or anything around the house or the rest of the property leading below ground. Maybe it's just a detent or shaft in the fireplace floor that goes down a couple of feet or so to allow for more wood? Bigger logs? Maybe, for some other reason."

"Maybe. But why all the black carbon streaks on the inside of the glass enclosure? Is it a firepit of some kind?"

"Hold that thought. Here comes the waitress and the dessert menu." Dan, who patted his stomach and told the waitress he was on a diet, ordered the sherbet with coffee. Terry requested a nonfat cappuccino. When it all came, Dan looked a bit dismayed with the whip cream surrounding the four scoops in a long flat bowl. He sighed, but tried it anyway. "Not bad," he said, licking his spoon. "The sherbet's creamy. Works with whip. I was concerned, for a second."

"That's a lot of dessert," said Terry, as a lightbulb flipped bright in his head.

Dan pouted. "Can't finish it all. Too much. Want some?"

"Dan—that's it."

Dan lowered his spoon. "What?"

"The elevator. I kept thinking something was strange. Couldn't put a finger on it. Now, I get it."

Dan stared across the table at Terry. "What?"

"It's too large. It's the size of an elevator for a downtown L.A. office building. Big enough for six or more people. Why would anyone put an elevator that big in a three-story house? Dan, we've gotta go back."

"If we nose around the elevator again, that Two guy will be all over us."

"That's why we can't go back now. We need to return tonight—after dark. In the meantime, let's check into the Marriott. We can get changed and maybe take in a movie. I noticed 'The Deer Hunter' with DeNiro is playing at the Revival Theater downtown."

"One of my favorites," said Dan. "But only on one condition—we get dinner between the movie and the night mission."

"Deal."

"One more thing, Terry. No matter what happens, we've got to pull ourselves out of any mess. No cops. Or the Santa Barbara P.D. will contact LAPD, and Krug will have my ass for impersonating city officials, trespassing, B&E—you get the picture? I love my job. I don't want to give my boss a reason to take it away. OK?"

"Promise. No cops. No matter what. We're big boys, and we can handle things ourselves. Let's do it."

CHAPTER 59

Following a Thursday deposition, Ridge returned to his office at 5 p.m. With Kate gone and Annie so new, he wanted to keep a check on things. Ridge looked all over his chair and desk. No notes. Nothing. Good. He sat down, opened his laptop, and started writing emails to his staff. At 6 p.m., still alone at his desk, Ridge shut his laptop, stared at it awhile, and finally—gave up. He picked up the phone. Held it in the air. Then called Dr. Peters' number. After Tuesday night, he had to do something. And to his surprise, Peters herself answered the phone.

"Dr. Peters. It's Eric Ridge. I'm just callin' to set up that second session we discussed."

"Glad to hear it. But I have an alternative I'd like you to consider."

"Alternative?"

"At our first session, you seemed—let's say—reluctant, less than gung-ho about therapy. An alternative is conversation, especially among peers. Inner conflict is a lonely, lonely road. Talking helps. It can be that simple."

"What do you have in mind?"

"Four colleagues and I are planning a research project. Its goal is to determine the role of a group's makeup on the effectiveness of group discussions—among veterans, that is."

"How'll that work?"

"Each of us will monitor a six-person discussion group. By the way, each monitor is a military vet, not necessarily with combat experience, but we all served. And so, I think we'll be able to relate. For example, I did active duty during the Gulf War."

Ridge couldn't help but interject, "Thought I sensed a military background. Army?"

"Right you are. Anyway, one of the discussion groups will have only Navy vets. Another, only Army. The third and fourth will be made up of combat vets from Afghanistan and the War in Iraq, respectively. My fifth group will have combat veterans from six different wars— Korea, Vietnam, The Gulf War, Afghanistan, Iraq, and—hopefully if you join— the Secret War in Laos and Cambodia. What do you say?"

"What'll be discussed?"

"The groups will discuss issues they've had and related symptoms since their service. And, of course, what has helped and what has hurt. You know already, there can be difficulty sleeping, night sweats, even flashbacks. But different vets with PTS have had to deal with different problems including excessive drinking, drugs, feeling upset by things that remind them of combat, hypervigilance, loneliness, paranoia, trouble concentrating, frustration, angry outbursts, deteriorating relationships, depression and even considering harm to themselves. Unfortunately, the list goes on and on. But, regardless of the issues or symptoms, group therapy with other vets seems to be the one thing that helps most. We want to learn how to do that best, and we need your help. Are you in?"

"How long will the study take?"

"It's going to be a year-long study. The identity of all participants will be kept strictly confidential. The Veterans Administration is sponsoring the study, and we'll meet at the VA offices in Long Beach—twice a month on Saturday mornings from 9:30 a.m. to 11:30 a.m. Coffee and donuts on me. Are you in? Please say, yes."

Ridge knew he had to do something; this sounded like a great alternative to couch therapy.

"Look, Dr. Peters, fact is I haven't slept soundly in weeks. It's time I stopped running. So, count me in. When do we start?"

"A week from this Saturday. I'll email you the details."

"Sounds good."

"Glad you're in. I mean it. Welcome aboard."

After hanging up, Ridge grabbed some coffee in the kitchen. Looking at his reflection in the Keurig machine, he whispered, "Finally making progress. Kate's feeling better, and Marilyn Peters will help. I know it." Then he stepped away and thought, Maybe we're on a roll. Wonder how Terry and Dan are doin' in Santa Barbara?"

CHAPTER 60

At 4 a.m. on Friday, Terry and Dan parked the SUV a quarter mile from 12 Oaken Drive. They wore black T-shirts, black cargo pants, and black jackets, which went well with the pitch black night. Climbing a wrought iron fence at the side of the property, they dropped to the ground without a sound. Dan peered through the cut-glass panels at the top of the twin main doors and whispered, "Alarm panel's in the hall. Full of green lights. That Two character didn't set the alarm." Dan pulled out his lock picks and used them on the door. He and Terry were inside, silently, within minutes. Using mini-mag flashlights, they made way slowly to the dining room. Once there, Terry flashed his light through the glass fireplace enclosure. Still nothing visible inside the shaft. Then he noticed a turnkey to the lower right of the fireplace opening.

"Like a key for gas-assist," whispered Terry to Dan. "But no gas pipes or gas logs in the fireplace; what the hell?" He turned the key. Click. Nothing. Terry pursed his lips and turned to Dan. "Before we break the enclosure, let's look at the elevator."

Using their mini-lights, they snaked around furniture and through doorways and finally reached the elevator on the far side of the house. Terry, glad Two's bedroom sat way to the rear on the third floor, pushed the button. The doors slid open—without a sound. Something seemed different. A panel glowed—just below the level buttons marked '1, 2, 3.' Terry signaled Dan to enter the elevator with him. Then he put his fingers on the panel, as if it were a touchscreen. The digits 0 to 9 materialized. Then it requested a three-digit code. Terry tried 1, 2, and 3—but nothing. Then he tapped in 1, 2, and 0 based on the address of the house. The doors slid closed. The elevator moved—down. Terry gulped and turned to Dan. "The key musta triggered the panel. But down? What the hell?" Before Dan could answer, the elevator stopped. The doors slid open.

"Holy shit," whispered Dan.

"Holy shit," Terry whispered back.

They entered a huge subterranean chamber. Switching on larger flashlights, they saw it was surrounded by a network of stone-walled chambers connected by marble floored hallways. "What the hell is this?" whispered Dan. "Like something from a medieval castle. Look at that walk-in fireplace. The three-foot candle posts. And that altar in the middle. Is this place used for some type of church service?"

"God knows," said Terry. "And what's with that huge black symbol etched on the front of the fireplace. An eagle?"

"Looks more like a raven. It smells foul down here. Let's keep moving."

Terry and Dan lit their way out of the central chamber into an adjacent room with a long thick wooden table, surrounded by twenty or thirty high-backed leather and wood chairs. "Looks like King Arthur's place," whispered Dan. "Before the round table."

"But much more modern," said Terry as he moved his flashlight beam higher. "Look at the digital projector in the ceiling. And the huge drop-down screen along that far wall. This is a conference room of some sort."

Just then, overhead lights flipped on.

"Take a seat, gentleman," barked Two.

Terry and Dan flipped around reaching for their pistols. Two, pointing a huge shotgun, said, "Drop em'. Butt first. Then sit down. Butt first. Hands on the table. Now."

Terry and Dan placed their guns on the floor and walked toward the table. "How'd you know we were down here?" Terry asked, as he and Dan took seats.

Two smirked. "You shoulda put the code in again. Before getting off the elevator. You broke the laser beam."

"Sorry" Dan shot back. "We can try to fix it."

"Too late," said Two. "But enough chit-chat. We're going for a walk." Two pointed his shotgun at a huge door on the far side of the Planning Room. Once through it, Dan and Terry found a prison of sort. Three cells with metal bars, hard cots, open commodes, and wrist shackles attached to stone walls inside the cells. Two shoved Dan into the first cell. Terry into the next. Then he double padlocked both cells and, without a word, turned around and left the room, slamming the big door shut.

§

Two had to get his head straight, so he decided to go for a long run and let the prisoners rot. Do 'em good, he thought. Outside, the rising sun filled the sky with a golden hue, but as Two jogged the main drag, he saw clouds to the west. Oh well, he figured, bad weather was coming.

By seven, it was starting to sprinkle, and Two returned to the house. He checked to see that the two intruders were still in their cells. Then he went upstairs for breakfast. An hour later he sat with coffee in the Planning Room, at the head of the table, thinking, What am I really gonna do with these guys? If Hess finds out I let them in—I'm toast. But then who the hell are they? They're not City Building Inspectors, that's for sure. *Who cares who they are? They've got to go. Have to disappear.* Stroking the shotgun barrel, Two ran through his options. Jesus, Hess is due back late this afternoon. And His Eminence sometime tonight. These guys gotta be history by noon. Gone—without a trace. Two was resolved. No time to waste.

He marched into the Prison Room. "Get up! We're goin' for a ride." He opened Terry's cell door. Then he motioned with the shotgun for Terry to get up and out. Now. Terry took his time, and it pissed Two off. He shoved the shotgun's muzzle into Terry's back to prod the SOB. That was a mistake. In one fluid motion, Terry pivoted on his left heel, pushed the gun barrels away with his left hand, and brought his right foot up to Two's head. Surprised, Two staggered to his right. In that same instant, Terry whipped the shotgun out of Two's hands. A split second later, he flipped the gun around, grabbed its triggers, and pressed both to Two's left temple. It was over. Two raised his hands. Slowly.

"Get in the cell," Terry ordered. "Shackle yourself to the wall. Move a muscle, and I'll splatter you all over the room. Swear to God."

§

Two had no choice but to sing like a canary. Sure, he'd been trained, to the breaking point, never to say a word. He'd sworn over and over to endure all forms of torture, if necessary. But, no one could have contemplated this, not the type of torture these guys used. Cold hard logic.

"Look, weasel," Terry reasoned, "you can't win, no matter what you do. Unless you cooperate. My friend and I could just leave you here. Shackled to the wall only to be found by your boss."

Two listened intently.

"You see this key?" Terry taunted. "I'm dropping it in my pocket. And now it doesn't exist for you, ever. Those shackles are part of your wrists. What the hell are you gonna say when the judge comes back and finds you here." Terry laughed. "Some security you are. Your ass will be fired. Or, I'm suspecting, your ass will be in for something worse."

Two had no options. Getting fired would be nothing compared to what he really feared. If they left him in the cell, he was doomed.

He'd suffer whatever ungodly torture Hess could dream up. And His Eminence would be watching with approval. When Hess finally tired of inflicting pain, death would be welcome. Then it suddenly occurred to Two: His captors, who set him up for Hess' wrath, might also let him escape. These two were his only friggin' hope for getting out alive. As Terry and Dan were locking his cell door, Two blurted out, "Wait! Wait. Gimme time to think." Terry and Dan reopened the cell. They sat down on the cot opposite Two, and just stared at him. Silent. Patient. Like they could wait all day.

And then Terry sighed, "Talk, or we're outta here. This time for good."

Two, eye cast to the ground, asked softly, "What do ya want to know?"

"Who the hell are you?" said Dan. "What is this place?"

"Like I told you, I'm in charge of security here at the house. And this—this is the basement, that's all," said Two. "You've gotta believe me."

"We're outta here," shouted Dan.

"Wait," said Terry, "give him one more chance."

"Bullshit," Dan growled, as he stomped toward the cell door. Terry gazed at Two with 'what am I gonna do' eyes and said, "I tried. It's over." Then Terry stood and headed out of the cell.

Two, desperate and confused, said, "OK, OK. Look—this is where His Eminence holds the Raven Society meetings."

Terry stopped. Turned. And slowly sat back on the cot. As Dan re-entered the cell, Terry said, "Go on." Two explained how His Eminence, the good Judge Gimuldin, had created a network of judges, known as the Raven Society. They worked together to improve the American justice system. From within. Two decided not to mention human trafficking, torture, or assassinations.

"Admirable," said Terry. "Who else is involved?"

"Well some big corporate types support the Society. But I don't know any of them. Or their names."

"Who else?" Dan barked.

"No one," said Two, "just the security team."

"The one you head-up?" Dan scowled. "You expect us to believe that?"

"No, no, no. Wait." Two was afraid they would leave the cell for the last time, "I'm just at the house. Herr Hess is in charge of security."

"Herr Hess?" Dan shouted. "Who the hell is he?"

"Calvin Hess. He is—uh—Chief of Security. One big mean motherfucker."

"How big?" asked Terry.

"Six foot, maybe more," said Two, "and pure muscle. Huge shoulders. You don't want to be here when he comes back, and neither do I. I'm toast if I'm found here. And so are you. I've told you everything. Let me go, *pleeeze*."

"When is this 'Herr Hess' expected back?" Dan asked, almost spitting out the question.

"Today. Late afternoon. I'm not sure. His Eminence is coming back tonight. And if we're found here, we're fucked. You gotta believe me on that."

CHAPTER 61

Terry knew they should get out of there fast, but he wanted his canary to keep singing. He thought of his recent phone conversation with Joshua Censkey and his description of the big guy with almost-blank eyes, thin lips, and bony face. The guy who, according to Censkey, tortured him in the Goleta barn and chucked him in the ocean. "What does Hess look like? Describe him."

"Pale eyes" stammered Two, "thin lips. Scary face. Shit! I'm telling you the truth. He murders people like it's nothing. To control judges. Makes his own rules."

"What do you know about an old, dilapidated barn northeast of Goleta? In the mountains? And tell us the goddamn truth."

"That's our Farm. Where His Eminence first met Hess."

"Whoa!" shouted Dan, getting right in Two's face. "What's this His Eminence crap that keeps coming up?"

Two winced and turned his face away from Dan. "His Eminence is...well...His Eminence. That's what we always call him."

"Who's we?" Terry demanded.

"Security."

"So His Eminence is the owner of the house. It's Judge Gimuldin, right?"

"Yes, the owner."

"Jesus!" Dan shook his head in disgust.

Terry glanced at Dan but kept pressing Two for information. "Now what's this about Gimuldin meeting Hess at the farm?"

"Hess repeats the story often," Two said, speaking so fast his words practically tumbled over one another. "Hess' parents ran a commune on the Farm. Back in the 1960s. 'Liberal-ass communists', as Hess calls them. Each cheated on the other. Slept around. Traitors to one another; traitors to him, Hess says. Anyway, His Eminence became their lawyer for a while when the commune got evicted—because the forest there was federal land. He lost, and although the feds left the structures, everyone had to vacate the property. Hess, who could never stomach his parents or their friends, took that opportunity to leave."

"Then what?" Dan demanded.

"He joined various groups around the country—dedicated to a 'purer America'—as he likes to say. Years later he met His Eminence again. As Hess puts it, 'I committed, fully, to his efforts to reform America's legal system, for the greater good.'"

Dan snorted. "That's quite a story."

"It is. Because it's true," said a big man with pale blue eyes entering the Prison Room with another bald-headed guy, guns drawn. "Now drop the goddamn shotgun. And don't move a fucking muscle or you're all dead men."

Terry and Dan stared at the big guy. The scowling hulk with blank eyes was pointing a Luger at them. Without options, Dan dropped the shotgun. He and Terry slowly raised their hands. The hulk motioned with his head toward a far wall and a pegboard that held keys, cuffs, chains, and tools, and his bald-headed companion scurried across the room and returned with two sets of wrist shackles and some other items. The shackles looked much like the ones Two had on—except portable for chain-gang use. Each set had locking metal cuffs connected by a four-foot heavy metal chain.

The bald guy entered the cell while the bigger one kept his gun pointed at Terry and Dan. Then Baldy kicked the shotgun toward Hess and shackled their hands behind their backs. Next, he took out a roll of red tape. Ripped off two pieces with his teeth. And pasted them over their mouths.

The bald guy turned to Hess, "Secure."

The big man then entered the cell. Hess walked up to Two and gave him a look that would wither a poisonous spider. "Look at me, you sniveling shit." Two, still standing and shackled to the wall, stared down at the floor. Hess let out a string of expletives, picked up the shotgun, reversed it in his hands and slammed the butt across Two's face. Two let out a sound like a dying animal and then went quiet. His face flattened. Blood gushing from his nose, his body sagged, unconscious, hanging limp from the wrist shackles on the wall. The big guy turned and left the cell, nodding once at his assistant. "Lock it. Come with me."

After locking the cell, both Hess and his companion marched from the prison room, slamming the big door behind them.

§

After taking a look at yesterday's security video and working out a new strategy at the large planning table in the basement, Hess looked up at Three, still standing at attention, quietly watching Hess work. "It's a damn good thing we came back early to get the house ready for His Eminence's return tonight. But this…development… changes everything. It's a God-given opportunity is what it is."

"What do you mean?"

"We have three worthless shits so why not make examples out of them? Use them as training aids."

"I don't understand."

"We'll take all three back to Camp, where One and the others are finishing up. Then conduct a torture-training session this evening after dark. Two, especially, will serve as an example. A lesson the trainees will never forget, a lesson about how error and disloyalty will always bring down His Eminence's wrath. Then we'll interrogate the other two, and I guarantee they'll divulge who they are and why they dared come here."

"What about His Eminence?" asked Three. "Will I pick him up this evening in L.A. with the Lincoln Navigator, as planned?"

"Yes. Pick him up. But before we leave here, I'll call him to explain why our training will extend into the night. He can choose whether to stay at the house or visit the Camp. Even though His Eminence never participates, he loves to watch our training sessions." His mouth slid up at one corner in what was almost a smile. "I think tonight's lessons will be of particular interest to him. And with graduation tomorrow and the Summit on Sunday, he may well decide to visit the Camp tonight. You just be prepared to do whatever he asks."

"Of course."

"Now. Let's go deliver the news to Two and our guests."

§

Minutes before, when Hess had slammed shut the prison room door, Terry had jumped up from the cot and motioned to Dan with his head, toward his right pants pocket. Dan, struggling backwards with his cuffed and chained hands, fished the key to the cuffs out. Then back-to-back with Terry, Dan tried, blindly, to insert the key into Terry's cuffs. After some fumbling and multiple attempts, Dan connected and twisted.

The cuff-lock clicked, just as they heard Hess outside the prison room door. Terry and Dan quickly sat on the cot, and as the door swung open, Dan slipped the key behind the bedding.

"You're going with us," Hess snarled as Baldy unlocked the cell. "Get moving." With his Luger trained on Dan and Terry, Hess stood at the door as they exited the cell. Baldy uncuffed Two, still unconscious, pulled him down from the wall, and shackled his hands behind his back. After he dragged Two out behind Terry and Dan, they made awkward progress through the planning room, great room, then into the elevator and upstairs. Hess made Terry and Dan sit in the living room on the floor. Baldy dumped Two's body next to them. Reviving slowly, Two blinked his eye open and looked blearily around him. He looked like death on hold. Smashed face. Pale skin. Shirt soaked with blood.

"Go get us something to eat," Hess told Baldy. "I don't want to drive to the Camp on an empty stomach." Then he sat on the sofa and glared at Two. Pointing at the half-dead boy, he spoke to Terry and Dan as if it were a casual conversation.

"I should take care of him right now. But I'm nothing if not a model of restraint. And restraint and control, gentlemen, are always rewarded. This dimwit will be dealt with this evening. We will all watch and enjoy. And we'll take care of you gentlemen too, don't you worry. Impersonating city officials—yes, I took a look at the security video and I know how you bamboozled this idiot. Breaking and entering. Trespassing, and torturing poor Two here. You're bad people. Very bad. We'll deal with that—right after breakfast."

Baldy returned with bagels, cream cheese, and coffee. He and Hess munched away as Dan and Terry watched, Two continued to bleed, and the clouds unleashed a torrent of rain which beat against the tall living room windows. After breakfast, Hess told Baldy to go straighten up the house. As he trotted off to do his boss's bidding, Hess stared at Two again, for a long moment. Then he took out his phone.

Terry watched Gimuldin's Chief of Security stare at his phone as if trying to determine what to do next. He might well call 911—which would be good—but Terry doubted the man would want police on the premises. And he was right. Instead of calling anyone, he just stood there with his gun and phone in his hands. Still facing his three prisoners. Then, as if finally making a decision, he kept his gun pointed directly at them as he backed up toward a grouping of chairs near the furniture on the far side of the room. On his sixth rearward step, the backside of his leg struck an ottoman, the same ottoman Terry had moved to get to an outlet he said he had to test yesterday during the 'inspection'. Hess stumbled backwards, tried to catch himself without letting his gun fall, bumped into a chair—another piece of furniture Terry had moved—tripped over an end table which wasn't where it was supposed to be, and fell sideways, hitting his head on the fireplace hearth as he went down. Terry, poised and ready for any opportunity, released the cuff he held closed with his fingers, leapt to his feet, raced toward the window opposite Hess, and threw his body at it, crashing through to land on the manicured lawn, slick with rain. He rolled into a crouch, then sprang up and took off like he'd been shot out of Hess's Luger, balling the chain dangling off his left cuff in his fist as he dodged and swerved and ran for his life in the now-pouring rain.

§

Hess, shaking his head, scrambled to his feet and rushed across the room just as the other prisoner threw himself at his legs, tripping him again. This time, Hess went down hard, but he sprang up like an enraged grizzly and whacked the sonofabitch across the face with the back of his pistol. As the prisoner's head struck the floor—which was unfortunately covered in a thick oriental rug—Hess ran to the window, aimed at the running SOB, and shot, again and again.

"Goddamnit!" Three rushed in from the kitchen as Hess shouted, "I think I got 'em, but the fucker's still running. Can't chase the little shit now. Too much to do. Too little time. Maybe the sonofabitch will go somewhere, curl up, and fuckin' die."

"Will he go to the police?" Three asked.

"He can't go to the cops. They were the ones trespassing. At a judge's house, no less. Fuck him. Let's get the other two up and moving. Head back out to the Camp and give 'em both what's comin' to 'em."

CHAPTER 62

Late Friday morning, Ridge sat in downtown L.A., thinking. Some things in life were just painful, maybe necessary, but really, really painful. There was no way of getting around them. Like the dentist and a root canal. Or, he supposed, giving birth. Somewhere in-between came taking translated depositions of Japanese-speaking engineers, especially three in a row. That's where Ridge, The Great Litigator, found himself. Sometimes, he figured, you can't help but think someone's out to get you. With everything happening lately, and now this, that time was now. He was feeling trapped.

But he took solace in the fact that these depos were part of the Good Fight. Ridge's client, Heather Bautista, was one of three children waiting for a school bus when a Toyota vehicle suddenly jumped a curb. All were hurt, and doctors did what they could for nine-year-old Heather's left leg, but despite six operations and months of therapy, Heather would remain in pain and limping for the rest of her life.

The legal issue in the case was whether an all-weather mat had moved into the gas pedal and caused unwanted acceleration. Ridge also had to establish what Toyota engineers knew, at the time of the crash, about the mat's propensity to do that. The mats had been recalled afterwards, but evidence of that subsequent recall was inadmissible, in order not to discourage manufacturer recalls. So, off to translated depositions they all went. When Ridge asked his first question in English, his interpreter had to invert it, due to differences in sentence structure between the languages, and state it in Japanese. Then Toyota's translator had an argument in Japanese with Ridge's interpreter about the correct translation of certain words. When that was sorted out, the agreed-to translation was posed to the witness in Japanese.

As the witness mulled the question, Toyota's attorney interjected a belated objection for the record—which then had to be translated by the dueling translators, after which the witness could finally answer—in Japanese, of course. But instead of answering, the witness asked Ridge to repeat the question, and they went through the whole ordeal again. Then the translators argued in Japanese about how to properly translate into English what the witness said, and finally—the agreed-to English version of the testimony was spoken in English by Ridge's translator, so the court reporter could type the answer into the record. The real problem was, as was typical in these depositions, by the time Ridge got the answer in English, he had forgotten the question, let alone the objection.

After hour upon hour of this, even better minds started to gel over, and the headache pain could be tremendous. And God forbid anyone should have to use a document to pin down a witness on a particular point. The whole document typically would have to be translated by the dueling translators for the Japanese witness, before he could even start to answer—in Japanese, of course. Normally, Ridge could take it. But today he was just tired, damned tired. He somehow had lived through it all on Thursday. But this morning, the second day of the Japanese depositions, he'd rather be getting an emergency root canal or delivering a baby. Or both. At the same time. His head was pounding that bad. Maybe I could schedule an emergency teeth cleaning. He reached for his phone. He could hand this whole depo business over to Brenda Jameson, his intrepid associate. She could take over for him. She, of course, could give birth. But she wasn't pregnant. And her teeth were just about perfect. So, she had no excuses. And too, she was good, really good. She's a star, thought Ridge. *I should tell her that more often.* Honestly, he felt punch drunk. He reached for his phone to text Brenda, even though she was sitting next to him, just to tell her she was a rising star, when a text message popped up from Terry: *"Eric—need you. Trouble. Call now."*

Terry. All Ridge's alarm bells started clanging in his head. He leaned over to ask Brenda to take over, and she nodded and gave him a smile full of youthful exuberance. Ridge hurried out of the deposition room and called Terry from the hallway. No answer. He left a voicemail telling Terry he got the text message, and that Terry should call him back or Ridge would keep trying. He peered back through the glass doors to see Brenda was beaming as she put documents in front of the witness. He knew then that she'd finish the depo as well or better than he could. It was best to leave her to it, so he went outside to try Terry again.

§

It'd taken Terry less than five minutes to sprint back to Dan's SUV. Glad he'd taken the driver's seat that morning, Terry reached into his pocket for the key to the Nissan Pathfinder. Once inside, he'd grabbed his cellphone and started to call 911. But then he hesitated, thinking, *What do we really have?* We trespassed onto a judge's property. Broke in at night, with guns, no less. His security nabbed us. Then we shackled the security guard to a wall. Everything else was hearsay or deniable. 911 wouldn't work. Instead, Terry had texted Ridge a brief message.

Now, waiting for reply, he used his left hand to feel under the driver's seat. There it was. Taped to the bottom. Dan's back-up piece. A holstered Glock 9 and extra magazines. Terry strapped on the brown shoulder harness, checked to be sure the Glock was loaded, and stuffed the magazines into his cargo-pants pockets. He then started the Pathfinder and pulled away, cranking in a U-turn, to return to 12 Oaken Drive. About a block later, a big black Lincoln Navigator shot by, going in the opposite direction. Didn't look like there was anyone in the passenger seat, and after it passed, Terry slowed. Approaching the house carefully, he saw the gate closing, just as a vintage pick-up truck turned out of the driveway and accelerated down the street. Terry followed at a discreet distance. The truck turned off the 101 onto 154 heading up toward San Marcos Pass. Staying two or three cars behind, Terry followed it over the pass and down into Santa Ynez Valley. I doubt he's going wine-tasting, thought Terry, as they approached a location used in the movie *Sideways*.

Terry trailed the truck past the movie location and onto the turnoff at Los Olivos for Figueroa Mountain. He lagged back as the truck slowed somewhat to make the turn. The road up the mountain was steep and winding. Terry was able to stay out of sight behind the many curves. Near the top of Figueroa the pickup turned onto a dirt road that led west toward Zaca Peak. It raised a whirlwind of dust. Again, Terry stayed back, keeping the truck's dust cloud in sight without raising his own. They went about four miles toward Zaca Peak when the dust cloud settled. Terry moved in closer. The truck had left the road to turn onto a grassy track that led north. Terry had camped in the area several times, so he had a cursory knowledge of the countryside and knew there was nothing out there.

"Where the hell are you going?" he said aloud. He had no clue.

CHAPTER 63

Driving his beloved vintage truck, Hess followed the grassy track for several miles which led into a deep canyon. From there, he climbed a side ravine onto the rocky plateau known as Hurricane Deck. It was desolate. Which was why he put the Camp, his destination, in the midst of the San Rafael Wilderness. No roads. Only this jeep track, created back in the 1950s by uranium prospectors.

The Forest Service, undermanned and underfunded, never patrolled the country beyond Figueroa. And no one ventured into the wilderness north of Hurricane Deck. Knowing that, Hess had found the ideal location for the training camp. A deep canyon—with all-year water supply—at the base of the Sierra Madre Mountains.

Now, following the jeep trail, Hess was feeling good—really good. Only two days to the Sunday Summit. And tonight, His Eminence would visit the completed Camp for the first time. But what to do with the two shitheads in the truck bed? Two would be put on display. Tortured in front of the other Watchmen. No one betrays the Society. But what about the other guy? What was the best way to deal with him? So many choices. And had he put a bullet in the asshole who escaped? Too bad there was no time to hunt the bastard down.

He was sure he hadn't been followed but paused a couple of times anyway to look back. No one. Nothing. So he continued his slow progress over rocks and ruts, knowing his huge tires let him move much faster than the Lincoln Navigator that would bring His Eminence out later that evening.

CHAPTER 64

Well behind the vintage truck, Terry paused to text Ridge: *In deep shit. Surveying the situation. Hold tight.* A message came back almost immediately. *Roger that.*

He peered through the windshield, studying the terrain, trying to figure out where to leave the Pathfinder. He felt he'd have to go ahead on foot. The jeep track cut across the desolate plateau for about five miles. Then down to a river bottom. Beyond the river, the ground rose, and the track led up into mountains higher than those in the coastal range. Leaving the Pathfinder in the river bottom, concealed among trees, would be best, but it would mean a helluva hike. On foot, though, he'd have a better chance of staying out of sight.

Decision made, he left the Pathfinder downstream in a thicket of willows, waded across the stream and followed the track about two miles up a steep slope. Then he saw it. The entrance to a deep canyon, inside the spurs of the mountain range. Terry advanced slowly.

After miles of traveling cross country seeing no one, what Terry found in the canyon blew him away. He scrambled further up the slope and ducked behind a huge boulder. Peering out, he witnessed a whole shitload of activity below. It looked like a military camp. Huge. He made out target ranges, obstacle courses, and tents all around a big pond formed by a dammed-up stream. One tent was considerably larger than the others. Probably the Operations Center.

The vintage pickup was parked in front of it. As Terry watched, the big man pushed Dan from the pickup bed. Then he pulled out Two, dropping his limp body next to Dan. Terry took out his cellphone to call Ridge, but—no signal. Text failed too. *Damn it.* Terry glanced up and saw dark clouds moving in over the mountains. Bad weather, bad service, so much for it never rains in Southern California.

He went back to observing the camp. Terry counted eight people moving around—all dressed in green camouflaged fatigues. Two of them carried what looked like ammunition from an underground bunker to east of the Big Tent. Staring harder to the south of the Tent, Terry saw a helicopter pad—covered by green netting that blended with the trees. These guys don't fool around. Genius, really, hiding a camp this big in these mountains. Then Terry tried his cellphone again. Still no signal. No texts. Nothing. He hustled further up the mountainside, hid behind a tree and held his phone high, reaching for the stars. Finally, a signal. Intermittent...at best. But going with what he had, Terry touched "Favorite Numbers" and hit one. Ridge's cell began to ring.

§

Ridge sat at his Starbucks table in downtown L.A., still nursing his cappuccino and trying to decide whether or not to order another one or go back to the deposition. He was worried about Terry and Dan, but there wasn't much he could do until—his cellphone rang. Terry's ringtone.

"What the hell's going on?"

"We're in deep shit out here."

"Where's 'here'?"

"Here is someplace in the mountains northeast of wine country—way behind Santa Barbara. I'm about three-quarters of a mile up a mountainside. Just emailed you longitude and latitude using Google. I'm looking down on some type of hidden military camp. Dan's down there. In trouble. A guy named Hess has him. I think he's the Hulk. And he's the one killing the judges."

Ridge stared at his phone. "Military camp? Holy shit."

Terry quickly brought Ridge up to date on everything that had happened. "I escaped but the big guy kept shooting," said Terry. "A lot of ducking, zig-zagging, and beaucoup luck got me the hell out of there. And, I think, the rain threw off his aim. But bottom line is Dan's down there with Hess and the guy's out for blood."

Ridge stood, knocked over his cappuccino. "Holy shit. Sounds like Gimuldin and the three floating judges are running some kinda weird society to control other judges. And I bet they're the ones who want us to drop Uncle Cho's Silent Conflict case. But what proof do we have?"

"None—other than what Two said. That's the kid's name. And he'll change his tune once Hess gets through with him."

"Let's call 911 anyway."

"Can't. No real evidence and remember, we were the ones who broke into the judge's house. Anyway, Dan made me promise that if anything went wrong, we'd handle it ourselves. He doesn't want to lose his job at LAPD. And you know his boss, Lieutenant Krug. He'd can him in a heartbeat just because."

"OK. OK. What's happening now?"

"Now, I'm watching from behind a boulder up above the Camp. Eric, I'm really worried about Dan. There's about ten of 'em down there, and I think Hess is a psycho."

"He is. Believe me. Look, I'm on my way. I'll grab a plane at Torrance Airport and get up there. But it's going to be three or four hours, at least, by the time I get to the airport, fly up there, grab a rental car and find you. But that's still quicker, way quicker than driving from L.A. to Santa Barbara on a Friday evening. That could take past midnight."

"Roger that. But either way it'll be dark by the time you get here. So, make sure you arrive with some serious help, not alone.

Ten on two are bad odds, no matter what. Wait! I just had a great idea. My uncle and his sons could meet you at the airport."

Ridge stared at his phone in disbelief. "Uncle Cho? We don't need him. We need a show of force."

"Not Uncle Cho! Uncle Sand. The ex-Hmong fighter, remember? The lineman on CIA choppers. And you remember his sons, don't you?"

"Got it, yes, of course," Ridge said, thinking, *How could I forget any of them?* Sand had saved Ridge's ass in Laos again and again. His twin sons—Terry's cousins, Trong and Tam—were in their early-20s by now.

Terry continued, "Uncle Sand has been training them in the traditional ways of fighting for over fifteen years. They're strong as hell and even smarter. The latest generation of Hmong fighters. And they'll be more than happy to get in the fight for Uncle Cho. And to save my ass and rub my nose in it as a bonus."

"That's a lot of motivation. I'm sold. Have them meet me at Torrance Airport in two hours. About 6 p.m. Hopefully, I'll have a plane ready to go by then. And Terry, I'm bringing my satchel and Sig. Maybe my 9-millimeter too."

"Dress for success, buddy. I have no idea what to expect, but it won't be good. And watch the weather. Black storm clouds rising fast here."

CHAPTER 65

As soon as Terry hung up with Ridge, he called Uncle Sand's house. No answer. Damn it all to hell, thought Terry. I don't have his cell or the twins' numbers. Maybe Uncle Cho has 'em.

Terry called Uncle Cho by speed dial. But his uncle turned out to be in one of his moods. Rather than just give Terry the numbers, he insisted on knowing what was going on. Terry pleaded. But then he realized it was gonna be easier just to fill him in on the details. Anyway, Terry's cell signal was going intermittent. So after explaining what was happening, Terry agreed to let Uncle Cho contact Uncle Sand and the twins.

"Make sure they get to Torrance Airport on time," said Terry.

After Uncle Cho assured him it would happen, Terry hung up and turned his attention back to the camp. He couldn't see Dan, or even that poor sap, Two. Terry assumed they were both still in the Big Tent, where he saw Hess and the others drag them while he was on the phone.

§

Getting his butt from depositions in downtown L.A. to Redondo Beach on a Friday afternoon was hell. A big goddamn headache and Ridge was so hyped up and worried and anxious that it was tough keeping his cool. He was, once again, like in a bad dream, creeping down the freeway in a 400-horsepower road chariot. This time it wasn't Terry's Vette, but his own baby—a black Porsche 911 with turbos, rag top, and six-speeds forward. Ridge couldn't help but love having to clutch every few seconds in stop-and-go traffic. So very practical. But late on Friday afternoon, it didn't matter what car he drove because L.A. traffic was the same— freakin' unbelievable. So, as he crept along, he used the time to call Charlie Dunkle, of Dunkle Aviation at Torrance Airport, to explain what he needed.

"Eric," Charlie said before Ridge could say a thing, "we got in the report on the Cessna you brought down in that field. Turns out it was fuel bugs."

"What?"

"Fuel bugs," repeated Charlie. "A fungus, known as Cladosporium resinae."

"Is that the stuff we called 'kerosene fungus' in the Air Force?"

"That's it."

"But I thought that only affected jet fuels—and only in tropical areas."

"We did too. That's why we called the FAA. They brought in the National Transportation Safety Board to investigate the whole thing. NTSB confirmed it was fuel bugs. Much less common in aviation gas than jet fuel, according to them, but it can occur in avgas. The inspectors showed me the brown sludge in your fuel system. And the smell—oh my god—putrid, like sulfur."

"Shit. What happens next?"

"They investigated the avgas fuel supplies here at Torrance. And up at Dryden. Found nothing. So, the report concludes that the root cause of fuel contamination is 'Undetermined.'"

"Undetermined?" Ridge slammed on his brakes to keep from hitting the car in front of him. "You're kiddin' me. That's not very satisfying. But what about the bird?"

"We went into the fuel system including the tanks. Removed all visible growth. Not a pleasant job, let me tell you. Then we applied a biocide throughout, to kill any microbes. Good news: Everything was inspected and approved. The plane's back on the flight line."

"What about costs?" asked Ridge, as he shifted into second and crept forward again.

"All covered by insurance. But if you feel like giving a bottle of your favorite tequila to each of the three mechanics who did the cleanout, I'm sure they'd appreciate it."

"You got it," said Ridge. "I'll have my secretary send over three bottles as soon as possible."

"Super. Get it to me, and I'll get it to them. By the way, you knew Rueben, right?"

"Sure. He was the one who picked us up."

"He really helped my three mechanics with the cleanout. Was extremely interested in the whole operation and what the fungus did. Even took notes and pictures."

Ridge smiled. "Well then, I'll make it four bottles of tequila."

"No need. Rueben quit right after that. Disappeared. Hated to lose him."

Ridge frowned. "Sorry to hear that. He wasn't with you very long."

"It's how it goes. Get someone good, and then they take off."

"Again, sorry for the whole mess, but thanks for all you did. The fourth bottle will be for you. But now, I need to switch gears. I'm in a helluva pickle. Need a bird to fly up to Santa Barbara. This evening."

"This evening? All my planes are either gone or committed to other pilots. Even 3-2-1 Alpha. It's the weekend for chrissake."

Ridge bit his lip. "But, it's kind of an emergency. I've got to get to Santa Barbara tonight. Can you check with the other rental guys at the airport? Please call my cell if anything comes up. Anything, OK? I'll fly a damn blimp if I have to."

"A blimp?"

"Kidding. But you get the picture, right?"

"I get it. I'll do the best I can. But this is unbelievably short notice on a Friday. It's almost 5 p.m. I can't promise you anything's left. But I'll try Santa Monica Airport too. Maybe they can ferry a bird here. I'll try my best. That's all I can say."

"That's all I ask, Charlie. Thanks. I mean it." Ridge hung up. He gaped at all the bumper-to-bumper cars in both directions on the twelve-lane 110 Freeway and cursed. Then he started thinking about the Cessna fuel-contamination finding. Strangest thing ever. Really strange. No. It was fucking inexplicable.

At 6:30 p.m., Ridge arrived at the apartment. Mister and Pistol met him at the door. Mister, in particular, groused until Ridge emptied a can of Tasty Tuna into his bowl. Pistol was more than satisfied with a few chew-bones. Ridge quickly changed to blue jeans and a black and white Hawaiian shirt. He put on a green flight jacket without insignia, leftover from his Air Force days. Then he rushed to the north balcony to see if the hummingbirds needed food. They were gone. Both tiny birds and the little white eggs. Gone. Only an empty nest and eggshells remained. Ridge searched left, right, all around. Nothing. Gone as quickly as they had arrived. With a pit in his throat, Ridge reasoned, Gone to better things. But damn, I'll miss 'em. Memories only, but after yesterday's call with Peters, maybe that's all I need. They'll be fine. And right now, I gotta focus. Got to get to Terry and Dan. Pronto.

Ridge rushed back inside, grabbed his satchel with the Sig Sauer .357 Magnum and got his 9-millimeter Beretta. Stuffed it and three magazines into the inside-pocket of his flight jacket. Might come in handy. Just then, his cell vibrated. A voicemail. Charlie Dunkle had called, saying: "Eric, found something. Give me a call."

Thank God. But when he tried to call back, there was no signal. That's how it was in L.A. on a Friday evening. Cell towers were overloaded. He decided to try Charlie again when he got to the car. Saying "Adios" to Pistol and Mister, Ridge rushed down to the parking lot. After jumping into the Porsche, he tried Charlie again.

This time it went to voicemail: "Be there in twenty minutes," said Ridge. "See you then."

Traffic was still terrible. Even on surface streets. Ridge brought up the top on his car when dark clouds overhead started to sprinkle. But beforehand, gazing up at the sky, he concluded the rain looked local. Clouds were moving fast to the East. Inland. Good.

It was about 7:30 p.m. and misty when Ridge finally pulled up to the beige metal hanger with the 'Dunkle Aviation' sign out front. He jumped from the car, ran into the rear door of the hangar, and dropped his jaw. Looking through the building and the large main doors out to the runway, Ridge saw Charlie Dunkle, four other men, and…a Huey helicopter. No other bird in sight. And one of the four men huddled around the chopper was none other than Uncle Cho, with his black medical bag in hand.

"Charlie, what's this?" Ridge asked.

"This is Terry's Uncle Cho, his Uncle Sand, and his twin cousins," said Charlie with a grin.

"No, I mean the bird. What's this—a Huey helicopter? Don't ya have anything with wings?"

"That's it," said Charlie. "And, let me tell you, I pulled in some big favors to get ya this on such short notice."

"Jesus. There's nothing else?" said Ridge, hoping against hope that Charlie could find something besides the whirlybird.

"Eric, there's nothing else available. Not tonight."

CHAPTER 66

Ridge had a helicopter rating. But he didn't want to tell Charlie he wasn't current. Ridge hadn't flown a Huey since 'Nam. Army pilots at the firebases had traded him chopper time for a chance to fly his fixed wing aircraft. Oh yeah. It was fun. He did it plenty. But Ridge couldn't take a steady diet of whizzing around *whump-whump-whump* in a bird without wings. It just wasn't natural.

Charlie looked at him. "You've got a chopper rating, right?"

"Oh sure," said Ridge, thinking it time to bend regulations a bit. "Just a little rusty, that's all." Then Ridge studied the band of men around him. As always, Uncle Sand looked tough as nails. Ready to go. The twins were short, solid muscles, all-business. All three were dressed in black pants, and black shirts with outside pockets and epaulets. Their jungle boots, also black, had canvas sides.

"Hi, Mr. Ridge," said Tam. "Uncle Cho filled us in, and our gear is on board. We're ready to rock 'n roll."

Looking in the chopper, Ridge saw two huge duffle bags. "What's with the sacks?"

"Essentials," said Trong. "Terry told Uncle Cho it might get hot in the mountains."

Understanding his point, Ridge turned to Uncle Cho, dressed in a black suit with an open collared white shirt. "Thanks, Uncle Cho," Ridge said smiling, "for getting this altogether on short notice. We'll be headed out soon."

"I'm going," said Uncle Cho.

"No need for that. Terry and the four of us can handle things."

"I'm going," said Uncle Cho.

Looking at Uncle Cho's determined eyes, and not having time to argue, Ridge bit his lip and nodded his head. "OK then. You're goin'. Let's mount up."

As the four Paos climbed into their seats, Charlie asked, "What about a flight plan?"

"No time," said Ridge. "I'm going low—below radar—feet wet across the ocean and up the coast. We'll use GPS to find our destination. Just log us out, OK?"

"You got it. But be careful."

Ridge jumped into the pilot's seat, reminding himself it was like riding a bike. Uncle Sand took the co-pilot's position to his right. Then Ridge checked the back. The Twins were strapped in, facing him. Uncle Cho in the seat across from them had his back to Ridge. But he was belted in, head cocked toward the open side door. Ridge thought he saw a smile at the corner of Uncle Cho's face. Shaking his head, Ridge strapped the checklist to his upper leg and started throwing switches. "Ready to crank," he yelled to Charlie on the ground.

Charlie shouted back, "Clear!"

The blades overhead cranked slowly. Then they caught. The *whump-whump-whump* brought back memories. But with little time to dwell on the past, Ridge lifted off. Then, inside a second, the whole chopper bent forward. And bolted straight at the hanger. Ridge thought he could hear Charlie yell, "Holy Shit!" By tilting left and gently pulling, Ridge got her back on course. To boost Charlie's confidence, he circled and gave Charlie a grin and a big thumbs up as he passed overhead in a left bank. Then they were off, but to what? Ridge had no idea. Using the headsets, he confirmed everybody on board was OK, and said, "Hang on. We're in pursuit."

Climbing to 500 feet, Ridge headed west past Torrance Beach, and took a right. Then he held at 500 feet, and flew feet wet up and around the coast. The dark clouds were well above them. And they seemed to be dissipating. In fact, over the ocean, the night was beautiful. A half-moon shined through cloud openings on the left, and lights of the Beach Cities bounced off cloud bottoms to the right. As white surf broke below their feet, Ridge took a wide swing to the left around LAX Airport. He then pointed like a laser beam at Santa Barbara. The bird made a helluva racket and shook like a mix-master but flew well. Ridge was glad there were enough headsets for everyone, with cushy earmuffs to deaden sound. Keying the intercom button, and using the mic, he asked his crew, "Everything OK?" Seeing a thumbs up from everyone, he added, "Next stop, Terry."

§

As night fell, Terry had more and more trouble seeing what was going on in the Camp. He climbed down closer and saw men running around with night-vision goggles. They reminded him of high-tech two-legged anteaters, with straps over their heads and long optical noses jetting out from eye level. Terry decided it was some type of training exercise, because three men with goggles seemed to be hunting down three others. Then a big black Lincoln Navigator pulled up to the camp. The driver, who looked like the bald guy with Hess earlier in the day, jumped out and ran around to open the right rear door. A short, stocky man in a long black trench coat stepped out, followed by another taller person dressed in black. It was too dark to see anything else—except Baldy escorting both to the Big Tent.

Later, additional lights came on around the tent, and Terry saw Two stretched out on the ground by ropes and four stakes. Then a couple of men lit a fire in front of the Big Tent. As it began to roar, Terry could see better. Two had duct tape across his mouth and looked terrified. Dan—was nowhere in sight. Then Terry's phone began to vibrate. When he answered, Ridge said, "We've lifted off. Headed at you. Should reach the airport inside the hour. How's Dan?"

"Don't see him right now" whispered Terry. "But I don't like what they're doing to the other guy, Two, the security guard we duped back at the judge's house. He's staked out on the ground, by a campfire, near a big tent."

"Doesn't sound good. My plan was to land at Goleta Airport and drive into the mountains. I already reserved a 4-wheel drive with a nav screen. But that'll take too long. Maybe I oughta fly-by first. Could be there in, say forty minutes."

"That's the thing to do," said Terry. "The weather has mostly cleared. I have a large flashlight I grabbed from Dan's car. If things are copasetic, I'll give you a steady beam. If not, look for continuous flashes. The tree canopy is open above my position northwest of the Camp. And by the way, in an emergency, I think there's a camouflaged helicopter pad to the south of the Big Tent. And Eric, a big black SUV just showed up. Profile looks like a Lincoln Navigator, and I saw one just like it leaving the judge's place before I followed Hulk out here. I think it could be the judge."

"OK. Good to know. Call me if problems. If not, I'll fly over from the southeast—about a thousand feet above you. Look for us in thirty-five minutes or so."

"Got it."

Terry hung up, clicked the stopwatch feature on the cheap digital watch worn by Building Inspector Lee, and peered down at the Camp. To get a better view, he crawled up the slope and took cover in a clump of shrub oak. Nothing much happened for over thirty minutes. Then, five men came out of the Big Tent and surrounded Two. The big guy, Hess, bent down next to the wooden stake closest to Two's head. Terry could see the flames of the campfire flicker on the long, shiny blade Hess held. Then, more movement at the Big Tent, and another bald guy emerged pushing Dan in front of him. He shoved Dan to the ground next to Two and Terry watched helplessly as others pounded stakes into the dirt and ran ropes from Dan's wrists and ankles to the wooden pegs. Just then—the distant *whump* of a helicopter. Getting closer. Flashlight in hand, Terry turned and pointed a steady beam to the southeastern sky.

Five seconds later, Terry took sniper fire. The trees around him splintered from bullet strikes as he dove to the ground and yanked the Glock from its holster. As he landed, a cracking sound surprised him. The face of his cellphone, in his left shirt-pocket, had shattered on a rock. When he glanced up again, non-stop fire from left and right below him exploded around him. Bullets whizzed by looking like ropes of light smashing all around, ricocheting off boulders, shattering tree bark and branches, and plowing into the ground. Terry stuck the flashlight in the air with his right hand and signaled continuous flashes. Then he pulled it down, curled both arms around the back of his head and buried his face in the dirt. Within seconds he was struck, like an electric shock, in his right arm. He reached across with his left. His hand came back blood red. Bullets continued crashing left and right, but, dammit, no way he was goin' down without a fight. Gritting his teeth, he stuck his left hand with pistol into the air and started firing rapidly, blindly— toward the bullets from his left.

CHAPTER 67

Flying in from the east, Ridge spotted the campfire first. Then the few low-intensity lights around the camp. Clicking the intercom button, he said, "Camp's ahead. Should be approaching Terry. Keep watch for his flashlight." Just then, continuous flashes of light rose from the ground.

"Flashes—eleven o'clock low," Ridge said into the intercom. "That's Terry. About three-quarters the way up the mountainside. Above the camp." A second later, Ridge saw strings of light, from automatic fire, shooting up into Terry's position. First from the left, then from the right. "Holy Shit, sniper fire from the trees!" Ridge said into the intercom. "And from below! Shit. Shit. Shit."

The area around Terry looked like an exploding fireworks barge. Descending in the dark, Ridge banked left to see better. He clicked the intercom on, "All that shit on the remote side of the mountain, no people to see, no one to hear, nobody to help, nothing. Just trees, rocks, and—"

Before Ridge could finish, he felt thuds and the bird rocked. The chopper's tail jerked up. Regaining control, Ridge pulled around left and saw bright lines of fifty-cal automatic fire screaming up from below. He banked right, and dove. Then he pulled up to his left to avoid additional hits. Just then, the lights went out. He still had control, but bullets had severed electric supply lines. He nosed over to pick up speed, to get away. Once level and far from the firing, he glanced at Uncle Sand in the co-pilot seat next to him.

Sand, hanging on, pointed rearward. In the back, the twins had their flashlights out and focused on their own left hands. Both were holding coiled rope with four fingers. Their left thumbs pointed at the ground, moving up and down, like Romans clamoring for death at the Coliseum.

Ridge shouted to Uncle Sand, "They want to go in?"

"Yes!" shouted Sand. "They know what they're doing."

Looking back at the twins, Ridge saw that both had strapped on shoulder holsters and sheathed knives from their duffle bags. They were still signaling down.

Goddammit! Ridge had seen plenty of chopper assault landings, but he'd never done one. Shit. First time for everything. Here goes. He took the chopper down and turned her around, back toward the camp, using the campfire near the Big Tent as a target. He held course, descended more, and established slow flight at tree-top level. Finally, he hovered near a small clearing one-quarter mile out. The Twins threw their ropes overboard. They slid down, leaping to the dirt from ten feet above ground. Uncle Cho pulled in the ropes. Then he strapped back in his seat and Ridge pulled away, gave Uncle Cho a thumbs up. *Not half bad for a bird without wings.* Then he circled in widening loops around the drop point and followed the twins.

When Tam and Trong hit the ground, they immediately rolled to their shoulders, then to their hips and up to their feet, crouched. They held position cloaked by dense bushes, making sure the area was clear of enemy. Then they zig-zagged through the forest, crouching lower and stooping between thick trunks of trees. As they approached the camp, they used hand signals to communicate. One hundred yards out, Tam and Trong dropped to their stomachs. They crawled, elbows and knees, with pistols ready to fire in their right hands. When they got to the camp, they spotted two bald-headed men, about their own ages, carrying guns and ammunition out of an underground bunker south of the Big Tent. Tam pointed at one, and then himself. Trong moved his head slowly up and down, and flashed thumbs up. Each then approached his victim, sliced his throat, and made sure nothing dropped. They hustled into the bunker. Silent as death. They emerged moments later with two M-16s, extra magazines, and grenades.

§

Once Ridge saw the twins had it under control, he wondered, now what? Being a quick thinker, he turned to Uncle Sand and shouted, "Now what?"

"Circle Terry's position," Uncle Sand yelled. "Shoot the shit outta the bad guys!"

Ridge knew a good idea when he heard one, so he nodded and pointed to the back seat. "Use their rope to tie yourself to the rear seat and blast them from the open side door!" He gave Uncle Sand time to take position, and pulled off target to the southeast. Then he turned around to check Uncle Sand. Not only was he tied in position at the rear of the side door, but Uncle Cho had tied himself to his seat and hung out the forward section of the door. Both had pistols in their hands, taken from the duffle bags.

They were never going to be more ready; Ridge turned the bird and headed northwest toward the camp and Terry. But about three-hundred yards out, the engine started coughing, and the constant *whump-whump-whump* faded from the big blades overhead. Ridge still had control, but not enough to hover over the mountainside where he last saw Terry. Then he remembered the camouflaged helicopter pad Terry mentioned, south of the Big Tent. It was now or never. Recalling his takeoff back at Torrance Airport, Ridge prayed his chopper-landing skills were less rusty. When he turned to signal Uncle Sand that they were going down, Ridge saw that Sand and Uncle Cho had already strapped themselves into their seats. In his head, he said, *This is your Captain speaking. Please remain in your seats for the duration of this flight.* Then, cinching his own belt, Ridge focused on business.

He stayed high and turned to set up a straight-in approach. He aimed at the campfire by the Big Tent, which was less bright, but still visible. Descending as he got closer, Ridge wanted to slow down, but knew if he did, they'd be sitting ducks—so to speak. Then he got lucky. Better lucky than good. Looking east of the campfire he recognized a clearing in the woods where he felt, in his gut, the netting hid the pad. Setting up a high-speed approach and then a sudden hover, Ridge went in for landing. Crashing through the net, the chopper hit on one skid. Then toppled to its right side. The windows blasted inward. The blades shot in all directions, making an ungodly racket. But the seatbelts held. Everything went silent. The dust cleared. Ridge reminded himself: Any landing is OK, as long as you walk away. He unstrapped, and joined the Uncles, who were already climbing out the side door facing the night sky and stars peering through gaping holes in clouds overhead.

§

From his vantage point, Ridge watched the twins race over ground, each pulling a grenade pin and chucking a grenade over his shoulder. The ammunition bunker exploded into a huge inferno. Then with a blistering *whoosh*, the exploding gases mushroomed, blasting the twins in their backsides, and launching them into the air. But like a synchronized swimming team, they were prepared. Each landed on the back of his shoulder, rolled to his feet and, without missing a beat, continued rushing toward Terry's position up the mountainside. With M-16s, locked and loaded, they fell in behind large boulders, and started spraying bullets at snipers in the trees.

At that point, Ridge started to run and immediately went down. He tripped while rushing to the twins. When he got up, he checked his jacket for his Beretta and extra magazines, and said, "Got 'em." Then he realized he'd left his satchel—and his Sig 357—in the chopper after the crash. *Goddammit!* Looking back at the bird, he spotted two bald guys with night-vision goggles strapped to their heads. They were creeping up to the helicopter, like maggots approaching a dead body. Then they turned, saw Ridge, and scrambled his way.

Pulling the Beretta from inside his flight jacket, Ridge snapped off the safety. Without hesitating, he pulled back the slide, chambered a hollow-point and shot from a crouched position. The first few smashed the optical scope at the center of one guy's face. Glass flying, the maggot staggered backwards. Blood blossomed from his goggles. The sonofabitch keeled over backward. Ridge couldn't dwell on it. Shoot or be shot. Kill or be killed. Combat all over again. He turned to the second guy—now only fifty feet away. Ridge emptied the magazine between his heart and head. But the man kept coming. Ridge reached for his knife, ready to go hand-to-hand, just as the attacker crumbled to the ground. Five yards from Ridge's feet.

Ridge rammed home another magazine and shot a bullet into the second maggot's head, just to make sure. Then he swung around and saw Uncle Sand and Uncle Cho, seventy yards away, in a firefight with three goggled attackers. To the other side, closer, a short man in a black trench coat ran behind a bald guy toward a black Lincoln Navigator. Then Ridge spotted a strange boy in a nearby tree watching them like a hawk. Suddenly the boy reared back and hurled what looked like a large bowie knife more than twenty feet. It planted point-first in the back of the bald guy's neck. The short man froze and watched in horror as the back of baldy's head exploded in blood, and he collapsed mid stride. Looking at the lifeless heap, the short man in black seemed to make a decision. He ran around the crumbled guy and, hunched over, rushed toward the Navigator, yanking open the driver's door and scrambling into the vehicle like a cockroach. Meanwhile, the boy in the tree had dropped to the ground and pursued him, jumping onto the rear step, leaping to the roof, grabbing the protruding siderails, and commando crawling forward as the driver smashed the gas pedal and took off like a rocket. Ridge watched in fascination. The boy had a predator stare in his eyes. And, apparently having seen the boy in his mirror, the driver yelled something Ridge couldn't make out over the noise around him. But it sounded strangely like, "Golden Boy! No!"

Next, obviously in abject fear and having no clue where he was or where he was going, the driver raced the Navigator toward a light. Unfortunately, it was attached to a ramp. In seconds, the truck shot up the short incline and came down with a splash, nose-first into a wide shallow pond. Most of the front seat sank below water, even though the rest of the truck stuck up out of the pond.

As the driver clawed at his window, trying to open the door, the boy jumped off the roof, waded through the pond, pulled out another large knife and smashed the window with its butt. Next he grabbed the driver around the neck with his left arm and yanked the man's upper body through the window. Reaching out with his right hand and knife, he slashed the driver from groin to throat. The driver's eyes went wild in disbelief. The boy shouted, "Fuck you, His Eminence!" and pushed the ravaged body back into the truck. Having finished his work, he turned, splashed to the edge of the pond, stepped out, and walked away. North into the woods. Toward the mountains. Never looking back.

CHAPTER 68

Two cracked open his one good eye. He had no idea what was going on except that all hell seemed to have broken loose around him. As the bunker explosion subsided, he saw Hess, flat on the ground near the Big Tent, lift his face from the dirt and glare at One lying next to him with his head covered by both arms. "His Eminence is down! Get up and cut Two loose. Now! Get his ass into the pick-up. I'm not gonna leave that shithead here and let him escape punishment." Then, Hess got up into a crouch and bolted toward his truck.

One belly-crawled toward Two, frantic to follow Hess' orders before something else happened. Two stared up at him with a blank expression while One cut the ropes binding Two's hands. As he turned toward Two's legs, Two reached out and clutched One's head in an arm lock. With a grunt, Two cranked and twisted until One's neck snapped with a distinct crack. He quickly grabbed One's knife and sliced the ropes at his feet. Then he sprang up, knife still in his hand, and raced toward Hess in the truck. With firefights to the east, and sniper shooting to the west, Two knew Hess couldn't hear or see him in pursuit.

Hess yelled out the driver's side window, "One! Where the hell are you?" He twisted in his seat, and not seeing One, slammed his hands on the steering wheel. "Shit, who the fuck needs ya. I'm outta here." But before Hess could stomp on the gas, Two leaped into the truck bed and, driven by pure adrenaline and hate, raced forward on hands and knees to the cab. He pulled himself onto the roof by grabbing the luggage rail over Hess' head as Hess took off like a bullet, spinning tires spewing dirt and mud everywhere. Two, hanging on with his right, freed his left hand and thrust his long arm down like a piston to plant One's blade in Hess' side. As Hess howled and instinctively clutched his side, Two grabbed the steering wheel and yanked as hard as he could. Then he jumped from the swerving truck, rolled, and came up running. The speeding pickup crashed over rocks and through saplings and careened into a ravine where it bounced off boulders, flipped several times, and slammed tail first at the bottom. Two waited—one, two, three heaving heartbeats, until the scent of gas fumes drifted toward him, and within seconds the fuel tanks ignited. Raising an arm to shield his eye, he peeked out as an orange ball of flame and belching smoke engulfed the vehicle.

CHAPTER 69

Uncle Sand got hit. Ridge saw him go down. Now vulnerable, Uncle Cho and Sand were being flanked by the three attackers wearing night-vision goggles. Shit, realized Ridge, they move so goddamn fast with those goggles. The rest of us are just stumblin' around out here.

He then noticed one of the flankers moving top speed in his direction. Ridge hid behind the thickest tree he could find and tried to keep an eye on him. The attacker got within sixty feet and then stormed straight at him. So much for hiding. Ridge glanced down; a red laser beam danced at his feet. He pirouetted and came out on the other side of the tree, blasting the attacker three times in the chest. Only forty feet away, the flanker stopped cold, staggered, and then charged again at Ridge.

"Shit. Bullet-proof vest," mumbled Ridge.

But the real problem was that Ridge had only three bullets left in his pistol. He dove back to the other side of the tree, rolled, and came up crouching, with his 9-millimeter fully extended in two hands. Thinking he was going to die, Ridge carefully squeezed off two shots at the attacker's groin and moved his aim up for a head shot. A bullet whizzed by, ricocheting off a tree to his right. The flanker—still charging—was now fifteen feet away. Ridge set aim on his head and pulled the trigger. The attacker stopped in his tracks. Staring at Ridge through glassy eyes and misty goggles, he crumpled to the ground.

Ridge pulled out his last magazine, rammed it home, and ran full-out toward the Uncles as two goggled attackers closed in on them. With red laser gun sights dancing on both brothers, the shooters were no more than fifteen feet away, walking slowly, deliberately, waiting to take perfect kill shots. Uncle Cho, always protector of his little brother, threw himself on Uncle Sand's prone body, taking the bullets from both guns even as Uncle Sand lifted one arm and started shooting. Ridge fired at the same time. When the smoke cleared, the attackers were laid out facedown over Uncle Cho, who still covered his brother. Ridge kicked both attackers to make sure they were dead, and pulled them off the uncles. Terry's family. Almost like Ridge's family. Sand was hit but still moving, pressing both hands now against what remained of his brother's skull. Ridge dropped to his knees beside him and gently pried the man's hands away, clutching them tight in his own.

Ridge, with tears in his eyes, asked, "Where are you hit?"

"Upper chest—two bullets." Sand choked back a sob. "He shouldn't have come. I told him not to come." He pushed himself to a sitting position and pulled his brother closer, rocking him in his arms. Then, more gunfire—in Terry's direction.

"Stay here," Ridge commanded. "We'll be OK. I'll be back." Ridge ripped the night goggles off one of the dead men and adjusted the damn thing as best he could. He then raced toward the gunfire. It was coming from two snipers, each in different trees. With goggles, Ridge saw the twins throw grenades simultaneously at one tree. They blew it and the sniper to Holy Hell. Ridge, still thirty yards away downhill, saw the second sniper drop from his tree and storm uphill. The twins, without goggles, were in the blind. But Ridge could see the sniper rushing Terry's position, and no gunfire coming from it.

For a sudden second, Ridge's mind flashed to that night, in the aftermath of the bombing, when he carried his faceless buddy in his arms. He screamed "Terry!" Then he charged the hill. With night vision, he moved fast. But so did the goggled sniper. It was a foot race. And the sniper was nearer Terry. Dodging trees and rocks, and running uphill as best he could, Ridge got closer. Closer. But too late.

Before Ridge could raise his weapon, the sniper had already stopped, pointing his rifle down at Terry, and then—a loud, blinding blast. One bullet. To Ridge's amazement, the sniper toppled sideways like a felled tree. When Ridge got to Terry, he was in some sort of foxhole, a large depression in dirt between two huge rocks. He wasn't moving, but next to him, dressed in black, was none other than Sasha Kachingski. Glock in hand. Still smoking. The sniper, sprawled out head-first on his right side, was only two feet from Terry. Ridge quickly shot the sonofabitch in the left temple, just to make sure. Then he pulled off his own goggles and jumped in next to Terry and Sasha.

Terry, bleeding from his right arm and left leg, opened his eyes and smiled up at Ridge. "Welcome to the party, big guy. Ain't much room in here." His voice was thready. "Already got company."

"This is one party I would've gladly missed." Sasha said as she put the Glock back by Terry's side and proceeded to rip the sleeves off her black blouse. She handed one sleeve to Ridge and started to tourniquet Terry's arm while Ridge bent over his leg.

Ridge looked up, cocked his head. It was quiet. No more gunfire. He tied off the tourniquet and sat back on his heels. "What the hell are you doing here?"

"Long story short, my wonderful client, Chesterfield, introduced me to Gimuldin. First couple of dates went OK. So, Gimuldin asked me if I wanted to see his mountain retreat. Picked me up in that big black Navigator with one of those weird-ass bald kids driving. When we got here, well…let's just say it wasn't what I expected. I couldn't believe what was going on, so I opted out. Gimuldin went to take a piss and I headed up the hillside.

"How did you find Terry?"

"With the dark and all the explosions, I got a little lost. Came across your friend here, lying in this foxhole, Glock at his side. I picked it up. Not much later, when that anteater in goggles tried to shoot us, I fired away. Thought he might have a vest, so I aimed at his head. Luckily, the first bullet hit. Unknown to me, your buddy here left me only one shot."

Ridge reached over and turned the sniper's head face up. Besides Ridge's bullet in his left temple, there was a gaping hole in the middle of his forehead. "Sasha, where the hell did you learn to shoot like that."

"My father was Army Ranger. Thought we all needed to know how to handle a firearm."

"Wow. You learned your lessons well," said Ridge. "We owe you big time."

"About that," said Sasha, checking the tightness of the tourniquet that Ridge had tied, "I'm thinking none of this is gonna help my career at Words & Gryme. How about a letter of recommendation?"

"You got it," Ridge and Terry said at the same time.

Just then the bushes around them shook and the twins thundered in, carrying Uncle Sand. "It's over," said Tam. "Everybody's dead or gone, but us. Terry, so sorry. Uncle Cho…"

"What?"

"Didn't make it."

Terry's face turned ashen. "Oh my God." He dropped his head. Then he looked up with watering, wide eyes. "Has anyone seen Dan?"

Ridge scrambled from the foxhole, fitted his goggles again and took off toward the Big Tent. He found Dan. On the ground. Spread out by the dying fire. Tied like a pig for slaughter.

Pulling out his knife, Ridge cut the ropes on Dan's hands and feet, then peeled the tape from his mouth. "You OK, buddy?"

"Yeah, yeah, yeah, I'm alright, but what the hell?" He struggled to sit up, then took Ridge's outstretched hand and got to his feet.

Wobbling a bit, he looked around him, eyes growing wider and wider. "Shit. Looks like a goddamn disaster movie. And my head's splitting. Ears can't stop ringing."

"That's rough," Ridge said smiling. "Real rough. But you'll live. Anyway, that's what you get for laying around while the rest of us worked our asses off."

EPILOGUE

The blue whales were running. Jayne and Ridge had invited Jenny and her new boyfriend, Tom, along on a Sunday whale-watching cruise. It'd been three months since the firefight in the middle of the wilderness and Terry, recovered from his bullet wounds, and Kate, on the mend from her injuries in the car wreck, joined them. The weather was perfect—a crystalline sky with puffy white clouds, mild winds, and calm blue seas. The boat skimmed along at 25 knots until they reached the southwest cliffs of Palos Verdes Peninsula. Using binoculars and looking out to sea, Jayne spotted the first tail.

Ridge pulled within a hundred yards on the windward side, cut the throttles to neutral, and let them drift toward the whales.

"Why cut the throttles?" Tom asked.

"It's the law," said Ridge. "So, humans can't scare, capture, or control the whales."

Tom peered through his own binoculars. "I can't imagine anyone in their right mind harming such beautiful, colossal animals. Can't believe this is my first time whale watching." His enthusiasm was infectious and Jenny glanced over at her mother with a smile.

"Hard to believe we're seeing the largest mammals in the world," Jayne said. "Can you imagine being 100 feet long?"

As the boat drifted further toward the whales, Jenny and Tom grabbed their cameras. Kate used a videocam. Terry, Jayne, and Ridge became the lookouts.

"My God! There's another fluke at two o'clock, about fifty yards out," Jayne shouted, as she watched the whale's tail rise majestically, spread out, and then slip under water.

"Another at eleven o'clock," said Terry.

"Look at that!" Ridge called out from the cockpit. "More off our bow. Rolling." To the west, other whales arched in and out of the water with twenty or thirty seagulls overhead. "Must be lunchtime."

After a breathtaking ten-minute marine show, one of the whales stuck its pectoral fin out of the water. "It looks like he's waving goodbye," Ridge said, pointing. And sure enough, when they got about thirty yards out, all the whales submerged and disappeared.

"That was mind-blowing!" Tom said. "Should we go after them?"

Jenny took his binoculars and scanned the surface around them. "How about we just drift here, have lunch, and hope another pod runs by us on their way south?"

After unanimous consent, they set up lunch on the rear table and, as the visceral excitement of the whale sightings started to wear off and they drifted past the P.V. cliffs toward St. Vincent Lighthouse, conversation turned to other things.

Originally from New Zealand, Tom Road had an accent that made them all smile, even though he'd been in the U.S. for fifteen years. Manager of a computer company that did website designs and other projects, he and Jayne fell naturally into computerese. After ten or fifteen minutes of non-stop jargon, Tom realized Kate, Jenny and Ridge were on the outside looking in, so he changed topics.

"Eric, Jenny tells me you and Terry had quite a bit of excitement in the mountains about three months back. I know you were injured," he said to Terry, "but how'd that all sort out?"

"That's a tough question," Terry broke in.

"By the way, I was really sorry to hear your uncle died," Tom added. "From what Jenny says, it was like a combat zone."

Ridge and Terry looked at each other, a whole silent conversation passing between them. "Thanks, and yeah," Terry said, nodding. "It wasn't what I'd call fun. Not anxious to do it ever again. I spent way too long in the hospital, but Eric finally bailed me and my Uncle Sand out. We're both doing well now." Terry patted his leg. "I'm almost back to normal. And thanks to my Aunt Lani, Uncle Sand's wife, we gave Uncle Cho an amazing send-off."

"It was really an incredible funeral. Never been to anything like it," Jayne said, reaching out to hold Ridge's hand.

"Uncle Sand and I had to attend in wheelchairs," Terry continued, "but…yeah. It was really something. Hundreds of people showed up. Unknown to anyone in the family, Uncle Cho had been providing free medical aid for years to the people of Little Saigon, Thailand Town, and Little Laos here in Southern California. Not only was he appreciated, he was truly loved."

"He made a real difference in the world," Ridge said. "A really positive difference."

"Speaking of making a difference to the world," Terry asked Ridge, "on the flip side, what'd they do with Hess' body at the bottom of the ravine?"

Ridge grimaced. "Not enough body left to do anything with it. They believe it incinerated when his gas tanks blew. Anything left was eaten by coyotes, I imagine. Not much left of his vintage pick-up either. Just the burnt metal of seat frames and blackened truck exterior."

"Good," said Terry. "I'm glad that evil sonofabitch went up in flames."

"Me too," said Kate.

"Dad," Jenny chimed in, "whatever happened to the wrongful death case you had for Judge Millberg's family?"

"The federal investigation into Gimuldin, Hess, and the Raven Society is still underway and who knows how long it'll take. But after the authorities gave Two immunity and he testified before the Grand Jury, they've got plenty to go on. Two's now in the Witness Protection Program, probably somewhere in Arizona. Last time I saw him, he told me why Hess attacked me on the boat in the first place."

"Why?" asked Kate.

"Turns out he saw an article in the *Orange County Register* reporting that Judge Millsberg's son, Justin, said I would be representing the family and investigating his mother's death. According to Two, Hess didn't want anyone looking closely at that case since he'd killed her."

"Oh, no. I hope Justin never hears anything about the *Register* article causing the attack."

"He won't," said Ridge. "But I did tell him and his aunts that Two's testimony nailed Hess, Gimuldin, and other members of the Raven Society for killing Judge Sayor in Phoenix, a Judge Stevens in San Francisco, a Judge Flynn in San Diego, and of course Judge Millsberg. And that, when it came to Judge Millsberg, Tim Sanchez—our intrepid coroner—had been right all along. The physical evidence didn't add up to accidental death or a product-liability case against Chin Motors for causing her death. It was all Hess."

But you still think the car was defective?" asked Jenny.

"Absolutely. Defective because anyone could walk away leaving the engine on with the design of that keyless remote system. In fact, as part of our settlement with Chin Motors, they agreed to advise current owners of the potential problem and to incorporate an audible warning system in next year's vehicles. But no money changed hands in the settlement."

"How did you get paid then?" said Jenny.

"Didn't. Chalk it up to part of our pro bono work for the year."

"Talk about pro bono," said Terry, "what's the bottom line regarding Uncle Cho's case about the Silent Conflict?"

Ridge drew in a breath and shook his head. "Had to dismiss it. Under California law, a lawsuit like his dies if the plaintiff dies."

"Where's the justice in that?" Jayne asked.

"There isn't any," Ridge said. "But we know the Silent Conflict will come up again. It must—because it percolates just below the surface in so many civil law cases. Some other insured defendant, hopefully as brave as Uncle Cho, will get fed up with the insurance industry's control of his case and the legal system's blind eye toward Silent Conflicts, and sue the bastards."

"Here, here!" Tom raised his wine glass in a toast. "Make the bloody bastards pay."

"You bet! Hey, another question," said Terry. "Did Dave Lake ever get in any trouble for using the WebBird to help us investigate Gimuldin."

"No," Ridge said. "His boss, Jack Miles, ran interference. Cleared it all up with the CEO of WingX—an understanding woman you might remember. Sharon Nelson. I've got dinner with Jack and Sharon next week to thank them properly. And you're invited, Terry."

When Jayne heard the name Jack Miles, she stared at Ridge. He gave her a quick nod and wink. Then Kate said, "Hey, what about Dan? Did he get in trouble with his boss, Krug?"

"At first," said Ridge. "But after we all gave our statements— the truth, the whole truth and nothing but the truth— to the FBI, they sent a commendation letter about Dan—the only uniformed officer involved—to Krug. LAPD just loves it when the feds give kudos to locals. So, as far as Krug was concerned, all was forgiven."

"Here, here!" Tom raised his wine glass again. "Sounds like justice to me."

Just then, Jenny jumped up and pointed. "Look, dolphins. Both sides!" Everyone reached for their cameras. One dolphin stood on its tail and did a perfect pirouette. Kate captured it on videocam and shouted, "Better than Dancing with the Stars!"

After the dolphins swam away, Jayne announced it was time for dessert and brought out a cake topped with two dolphins in blue icing. "How's this for appropriate?"

"I hope it's as good as it looks," Ridge said, throwing a kiss to the baker.

After devouring two pieces of cake, Terry asked, "What's the latest on our military aircraft case in Phoenix. The one Judge Sayor threw out just before he was murdered."

"We're on appeal," said Ridge. "But that's one, I'm sure, we're gonna win."

Kate ran her finger through a smudge of icing on her plate and sucked it off her fingertip. "How can you be so sure?"

"Because I've been told by federal prosecutors that Two testified before the Grand Jury that Judge Sayor was being pressured by Gimuldin and the Raven Society. Turns out the Raven Society wanted to prove to certain big-time military contractors that for the right money, it could get those types of cases thrown out of court. But despite what he did in our case, Sayor apparently refused to do the same thing in the other cases, and that's why Hess took him out. The feds are also investigating that big time. But, meanwhile, with Two's testimony, I'm sure the appellate court will reverse Sayor's opinion in our case. It'll go forward."

"So someday we get paid on that case?" asked Kate.

"That's the plan," said Ridge with a smile, "once we earn a settlement or verdict for Wanda James. That way, we can offset all the pro bono work. Maybe even pay for marine fuel for our next whale-watching cruise."

"Talking about paying for things," Terry said, "what about that Huey that landed sideways in the Santa Barbara mountains? What did you and Charlie Dunkle ever do about that?"

"Turned out, it was minimal damage. You can buy a helicopter skid for $500 bucks and used blades for a thousand. Charlie had it fixed for free at Goleta Airport. In fact, while you were in the hospital, Charlie and I flew it back to Torrance together. Good as new. But still, I'm thinking of going easy on helicopter flying from here on out."

"I'm glad to hear it," said Jayne. "Not your best skill set."

Ridge grimaced. "Thanks, darling. But it ranks way above my putting locks on sliding glass doors, right?"

"No kidding!" Jayne said a laugh.

With that vote of confidence, everyone agreed it was time to pack up and get back to the marina. Terry was especially anxious since he had a date with Sasha Kachingski later that night. When he mentioned it, Jayne leaned into Ridge's ear and whispered, "At least, it's not Ava."

Ridge thought of Sasha dug into the mountainside with Terry and how she'd saved him and then tended his wounds. But he also remembered her at the bar after the meeting with Gryme, seemingly trying to compromise him. And the thought of her dating Gimuldin didn't sit well, even though she had no idea what kind of man he was. Still, he whispered back, "In my mind, the jury's still out on Sasha. But yeah, at least she's not Ava."

When they got to the slip, Jenny and Tom headed out to get ready for their own night on the town, Kate left to get back to her kids, and Jayne headed to the apartment to start dinner while Terry and Ridge stayed to close and spray down the boat. They each grabbed an ice cold Pacifico from the fridge to help with the washdown. While they were working, the setting sun turned puffy white clouds above the harbor into pick cotton candy, and white seagulls sailed overhead in a lazy airshow.

It'd been a peaceful, relaxing day and Ridge was feeling particularly fine, ready to go home and spend a worry-free evening with Jayne. And Mister and Pistol, of course. Terry suddenly touched his shoulder.

"Eric." The tone of Terry's voice caught Ridge's attention. "No sudden movements, but there's a guy watching us. Two docks away. Black hooded wetsuit. Tanks and mask. He's huge."

"OK." Ridge casually turned, kneeled down and moved the hose so he could get a look.

Terry bent down next to him. "Is that Mike? The diver who cleans the boat bottoms?"

"Can't be," Ridge said. "He's too big. Besides, Mike never works on Sundays."

Just then, the man launched perfectly off the end of the dock into the water.

Terry, brows drawn together in worry, stared at Ridge. "It couldn't be Hess, could it?"

Ridge hesitated, then shook his head. "Couldn't be. Just… couldn't be."

"You said they never found his body. That it was incinerated, his remains likely eaten by coyotes. But is it possible…?"

"Shit." Ridge shook his head and ran a hand over his face. "Shit. Shit. Shit."

"No kidding."

§

At that moment, the big diver dove deeper and stroked effortlessly, happy as a child in the womb, toward the public dock. So, they had a fun day on the water. Surrounded by friends. By family. We'll see how many more of those they get. But there's plenty of time to take care of 'em, he told himself. What I need now is to find me another judge.

§§

ACKNOWLEDGMENTS

I had to write this book. It kept burning in my mind (as does the next one). But writing a book isn't the same as rewriting it (again, again and again) and getting it traditionally published. That takes a team. And although CONSPIRACY IGNITED is a work of fiction, many if not most of its scenes were inspired by true events, including intense litigations, combat actions, and flying adventures. As such, many people contributed to the foundation of this book, and each touched the story in their own way.

They include my brothers in war, especially USAF Captains Frank Garufy and Dennis Lake, and all of my flying buddies, but particularly the ace Cary Pao ("Kapao"). And kudos to the many fine lawyers I've worked with and against over the decades including stand-out Philip J. Kolczynski (Ka-ching!), and the associates, paralegals and other employees at my law firm, particularly Michelle West, Jeffrey Wigintton and Dan Alba. And a heartfelt thanks to our clients who taught us so much about life, especially how fragile and yet resilient it can be. And a tip of the hat to the litigation experts we've worked with repeatedly over the years including Dr. Anthony Sances, Jr. (biomechanics), Mark Pozzi (fire and forensics) and Robert Anderson (accident reconstruction).

And then there's my military amigos including Charles Payne, and Patrick and Cathy Scott (who helped me plow through rewrites of the first few chapters), my writing professors at NYU and my law professors and the deans at the College of William and Mary. And of course there's also the authors who inspired me through example and advice including Ernest Hemingway, Robert B. Parker, Clive Cussler, Michael Connelly, Robert Crais and fellow William-and-Mary Alum Sarah Collins Honenberger.

Turning to family and lifelong friends, special thanks to Tony ("TK") and Doreen Kruglinski, and Paul ("Pablo") and Melinda Beswick for their advice and encouragement over the years. And then there's my wife June—the cute redhead who sat in front of me in algebra class and became my forever partner, cheerleader, and bedrock through the good, bad and ugly of life. (Note to highschoolers: Be careful where you sit in class.) And along the same lines, thanks to my wonderful daughter Janis (the D.A.) and her New Zealander husband Grae who shared their suggestions and ideas to the betterment of this book. And professional thanks to my website designer Maddee James of xuni.com for always being there and exuding excellence, to my literary agent Dean Krystek, lead agent and managing director at veteran-owned WordLink Literary Agency, for believing in this story, and to the woman- and veteran-owned Amphorae Publishing Group with Lisa Miller (business and marketing manager), Laura Robinson (production manager) and Kristina Makansi (partner and managing editor) for choosing CONSPIRACY IGNITED for publication by its imprint Blank Slate Press. However, I'd be sorely remiss if I didn't double down on thanks to Kristy Makansi, editor-extraordinaire and brilliant cover designer, for fully embracing CONSPIRACY IGNITED and contributing so much to its success.

And last but never least, I must acknowledge my golden retriever, Bosch, always at my side, for every walk, beach run and playtime we had to miss to make this book what it is today.

ABOUT THE AUTHOR

Raymond Paul Johnson attended New York University where he received a regular commission in the USAF through a special U.S. Senate confirmation. He then served as a combat pilot, jet instructor and functional test pilot in the USAF and paramilitary pilot in Laos and Cambodia with the CIA. Ray received the Distinguished Flying Cross, five Air Medals and the Meritorious Service Medal, among other awards. He also earned a Master of Science degree in engineering at the Air Force Institute of Technology and served as DOD Chairperson of the DOD-NASA Space Shuttle Integration Groups. Later, Ray graduated with a law degree from the College of William and Mary and has practiced nationwide as a trial lawyer for over 35 years. He's been chosen as a "Super Lawyer" by *Los Angeles Magazine* every year since 2006. Ray lives in Southern California with his wife, his golden retriever and too many rescue cats to mention.

Printed in the USA
CPSIA information can be obtained
at www.ICGtesting.com
LVHW050438040624
782217LV00019B/136